11/20

TEMPLES
OF
DELIGHT

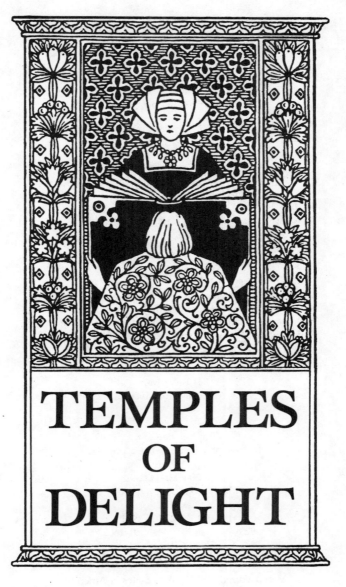

TEMPLES
OF
DELIGHT

Barbara Trapido

GROVE PRESS
New York

Published by Grove Press
A division of Grove Press, Inc.
841 Broadway
New York, New York 10003-4793

Trapido, Barbara.
Temples of delight / Barbara Trapido.
p.   cm.
ISBN 0-8021-1422-9
ISBN 0-8021-3322-3 (pbk.)
I. Title.
PR6070.R342T46   1991
823'.914—dc20   91-16023
CIP

Manufactured in the United States of America

Printed on acid-free paper

Designed by Kathryn Parise

First American Edition 1991

First Evergreen Edition 1993

1 3 5 7 9 10 8 6 4 2

For Mary Simons and Joe Trapido

And for Vina Pulseford

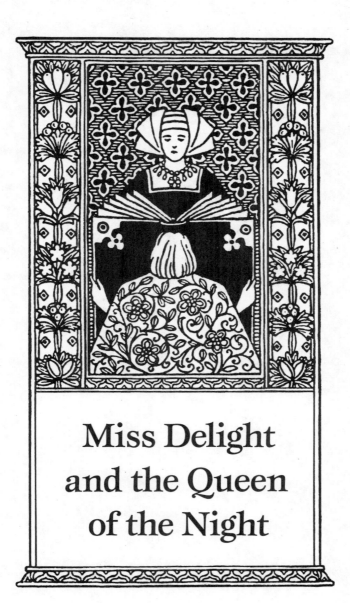

Miss Delight and the Queen of the Night

I

JEM WAS a joyful mystery to Alice. She was something to give thanks for. She had first appeared in the classroom, not at the beginning of term like a normal person, but midterm on a Wednesday. She had appeared, "like a dropped acorn," halfway through the term, halfway through the week, halfway through the Silent Reading Hour. Suddenly there she was in the doorway, almost as tall as the doorway itself. She was wearing an old blazer that screamed its origins from the under-a-pound rack of the Outgrown Uniform Sale and on her feet she wore a pair of down-at-heel, grossly unpolished black pumps. She was carrying her things in a sort of boat-shaped canvas toolbag of considerable size.

"I'm Jem McCrail," she said to Miss Aldridge, in a poised, clear voice that Miss Aldridge took as an affront. "Miss Trotter sent me."

"Ah yes," said Miss Aldridge. "The new gel. But I have you registered here as Veronica Bernadette McCrail."

Jem appeared to ride this hitch with equanimity. "I'm Jem," she said.

Miss Aldridge looked at her from top to toe and lingered pointedly upon the unpolished pumps. "I have no objection to certain legitimate abbreviations of gels' Christian names," she said, "but I fail to see how 'Veronica Bernadette' can possibly shorten to Jem."

"I'm Jem after the 'jem-sengwiches' in P. G. Wodehouse," Jem said.

"I beg your pardon?" Miss Aldridge said.

"You'll find it's in the Lord Emsworth stories," Jem said helpfully.

"His lordship meets an urchin girl in the cowshed. You're probably familiar with the story."

"Perhaps you had better sit down, Veronica Bernadette," Miss Aldridge said, with strong intent to undermine, since she had already determined in this case to start as she meant to go on. "Alice Pilling will take care of you—since her 'better half' is still absenting herself."

Alice reflected on Miss Aldridge's idiom for a moment. She had never thought of herself and Flora as two halves of something before. Certainly not better and worse. And right then she really had every reason to avoid thinking about Flora. To think of her was too dreadful. It made her shudder. The new girl came and sat down in Flora's place.

"During this hour we read in complete silence," Miss Aldridge said, and she bore down upon the new girl with one of the books deemed sufficiently improving for the Silent Reading Hour. Alice observed that Jem had been handed the biography of Oliver Cromwell. She herself had had it until the previous week. "*Complete* silence," Miss Aldridge repeated. "Is that correct, Form Three?"

A half-dozen funereal thirteen-year-olds concurred without enthusiasm. The school was not one that attracted bookish girls on the whole, and there was no one in the third form who appeared positively athirst for a greater understanding of the English Revolution—except perhaps Flora, who was absent. Alice's schoolfellows generally contented themselves with winning all the interschool hockey matches. Most of them left, after taking a gentle course or two in the history of art or religious studies, and went off to mark time in one or another of the preppier secretarial colleges around London. One or two of them made it to cram colleges in Oxford or Cambridge where the Champagne-and-Eights-Week experience was available to them without any of the undergraduate's hard grind. Claire Crouchley's older sister was currently attending a finishing school where she was learning how to emerge gracefully from a Rolls-Royce in a hat.

The fees paid by the girls' parents at Alice's school were a little higher than those at the local Catholic school or at the nearby Day School Trust, but Alice's school boasted not only a boarding establishment and a neo-Georgian clock tower, but an oak-paneled dining hall with refectory tables and a solid air of tradition that had been invented in the 1930s. Once a year, on Founders' Day, the headmistress awarded a monstrous silver shield the size of a firescreen to a girl for

"Excellence in Needlework," while those exhibiting excellence in geography, mathematics or Latin were presented with small plated goblets, rather like eggcups with joke-shop ears.

Jem, Alice noticed, had cast a jaundiced eye over the spine of the Cromwell biography. She waited for Miss Aldridge to proceed down the aisle before coolly extracting from the toolbag a battered paperback entitled *The Leopard*, by one Giuseppe di Lampedusa. This she placed deftly within the covers of the Cromwell biography and soon appeared lost in its pages.

"Naturally," Miss Aldridge said, qualifying benevolently—and her eye lit at once upon Claire Crouchley—"if a gel has a *genuine* question with regard to her reading matter, then I am always available."

It was seldom that a Silent Reading Hour went by, Alice had frequently noted, without Claire Crouchley coming forth with "a genuine question with regard to her reading matter." Pretty, stupid and rich, Claire combined an earnest desire for currying-up with the most minimal conceptual grasp Alice had ever encountered. Still, she could swim extremely well, which made her very popular in the summer months. Alice loathed the swimming pool. It shamed her that she was the only girl in the form who couldn't do a decent front crawl. Thinking up excuses for avoiding the swimming pool was one of the things that brought on her stammer. And that in spite of all the expensive speech therapy sessions with dear Dr. Neumann in Duke Street.

"Please, Miss Aldridge," Claire said at once, "please Miss Aldridge, but what I don't understand in my book is about after the Norman Conquest. I mean, what I want to know is—however did we get back to being *English* again?"

Miss Aldridge, in matters relating to national identity, was always wonderfully reassuring. "We were never really French," she said. "To be sure the kings and nobles who ruled us were French—for a few hundred years—but we soon turned them into good Englishmen."

"But hundreds of years?" Claire said in disbelief, almost as though she, personally, had been required to spend the duration of the Norman Yoke conjugating irregular verbs and munching on snails in garlic butter.

"Excuse me, Miss Aldridge," Jem said, and she looked up from the Lampedusa. "Would you say that during the Roman occupation we all became Italians?"

Miss Aldridge frowned with displeasure. She was close to retirement by then and belonged to a generation of Englishwomen not overkeen on foreigners in general, though Alice thought she had once detected a certain romanticism in Miss Aldridge's attitude toward Bedouin Arabs. Italians were definitely among her least favorite foreigners and tradition had it among some of the girls that she had once had her buttocks pinched while on a package holiday in Sorrento. Alice's imagination had privately elaborated upon this myth, so that she believed Miss Aldridge to have resorted to her armorplated corsetry as a precaution against a sudden airdrop of Italians on Surrey.

"The Ancient Romans were not Italians, Veronica," Miss Aldridge said. "Dear me, no! They were a highly disciplined and very hygienic people."

Behind Claire sat an unfortunate, boy-crazed girl called Lenora Gripe, who dreamed constantly of being a flight attendant but had somehow managed, from the age of nine, to look like a well-worn publican's moll. Alice had always pitied Lenora, not only for her overactive sebaceous glands, but for the way in which Miss Aldridge treated her as though she were the class untouchable. Right then Lenora's tongue was flicking insolently through a salivous ribbon of chewing gum.

"My grandad was demobbed in Italy," she said. "He always used to say, 'Smell Naples and die.' "

"That will do," said Miss Aldridge. "You will go to the cloakroom at once, Lenora, and remove whatever it is that you are eating." The class lapsed once more into dejected silence over its texts.

"She surely doesn't just dole out these appalling books?" Jem whispered suddenly to Alice. "What I mean is, aren't you ever allowed to choose?"

"She doles them out," Alice whispered back. "And most of them are a lot worse than that one. Well, at least yours has got pictures."

"Pictures of a man with warts," Jem said. "What's yours?" Alice had been issued with a collection of gentlemen's essays reprinted from the *Strand* magazine. She was reading a contribution entitled "On Keeping a Diary," in which the writer explained that he consumed his time going to places in order to collect things that he could then write down in his diary.

"Going to places?" Jem said eagerly. "What sort of places?" Somewhat to Alice's surprise, she then stretched her long legs expansively before her and tapped together the toes of the unpolished pumps. " 'Oh, for a beaker full of the warm South'!" she said. "Personally, I'd like to 'smell Naples and live.' Wouldn't you?"

"But he only means going to dinner parties," Alice said. "I mean *dinner* parties . . . "

Alice's father was a successful local building contractor; a kindly self-made man from the north of England who had come south from a small brickyard in a spirit of enterprise. He had largesse to dispense and a pretty, get-ahead wife, Alice's mother, who managed, even with running her own estate agency, to play gracious hostess to all the local pillars of trade. The result was that Alice had witnessed enough middle-aged conviviality around her parents' dining table to have left her unexcited by such occasions. It had also made her a somewhat open-eyed expert on gum recession and tobacco stains.

"Do your parents have dinner parties all the time?" she said.

"Oh, of course," Jem said at once. "All the time."

"New gel!" Miss Aldridge said suddenly, and Alice saw Jem jump a little. "What are you reading?"

In the Lampedusa, as Jem explained to Alice afterwards, Garibaldi had just landed in Sicily, which was very bad news for Fabrizio, prince of Salina.

"I'm reading about Gari— Cromwell," Jem said.

" 'Gary' Cromwell?" said Miss Aldridge, who was not above playing to the gallery at times. " 'Gary' Cromwell?"

"I'm sorry, Miss Aldridge," Jem said, and she went on to display what Alice considered a quite marvelous talent for thinking on her feet. "I meant Oliver Gary Cromwell. 'Gary' from his mother's side, after Gareth, the ancient king of Cornwall."

"Indeed?" said Miss Aldridge suspiciously, while not quite venturing to contradict. "Indeed? And would you kindly favor the class with what you have learned about the Lord Protector from your reading so far?"

"Oh," Jem said, pausing for just a moment. "I—um—I'm afraid I like the Royalists better."

"And why so?" said Miss Aldridge, who sounded affronted. She was a firm Cromwellite, for all that she kept a reproduction of the

Annigoni portrait of Queen Elizabeth II hanging from the form-room wall.

"Because I'm a Catholic, Miss Aldridge," Jem said. "And because the Royalists had nicer clothes." This last was somehow like a red rag to a firmly Protestant bull.

"Nicer clothes?" boomed Miss Aldridge indignantly. "Nicer clothes?"

"Oh yes, Miss Aldridge," Jem said. "Much nicer clothes." She was exuding conviction, Alice thought. Jem's eyes were shining just as though a row of Vandyke portraits had appeared before her, all shimmering with a richness of silks and fine array.

And then, before Miss Aldridge could retort, something happened. Something so wholly unlike anything that had ever happened before that the event bound itself up in Alice's mind inextricably with Jem's coming. It seemed to Alice, from that moment, that Jem possessed quite magical powers of intercession—though whether solely through her own charmed spirit or through the force of her religion, Alice could not know. A stoned black man stepped into the classroom through the open sash window and confronted Miss Aldridge with a dazzling smile.

"Hey, man!" he said, when Miss Aldridge was so obviously not a man but an aging spinster in a Gor-ray plaid skirt and Dr. Scholl's support stockings. "What you wearin' dem fuckin' robes for? You some sorta fuckin' magician?" Miss Aldridge looked up sternly, after an aggrieved glance at the chalk-impregnated tatters of her academic gown, a garment she always wore in deference to the pretentious stuffiness of the Wednesday afternoon "special" assemblies when the marks were read out.

"I must ask you to leave at once!" she said. "I must protest most strongly at your language. There are young ladies present!" The black man glanced round pacifically at the rows of third-formers in grey knee socks.

"Dem pretty scraggy bunch," he said, but he said it more with pity than contempt. "Don' arse me to marry none o' dese womans. No sir!" Then he left, just as he had come, through the window. Stoned blacks, Alice reflected, were a most uncommon thing in Surrey.

"Street theater," Jem said to her brightly into the brief hubbub that followed. "He's probably an unemployed member of the actors' union." Alice had never heard the term *street theater* before. She wondered how Jem could be so knowledgeable. "I hope he's getting an Arts Council grant," Jem said. "He has brought life to dead literature."

To be sure, there was something profoundly dead about all the literature considered suitable for distribution during the Silent Reading Hour. Miss Aldridge kept it locked up in the form-room cupboard, a greyish pile of old hardbacks that had all the appearance of having been got in a job lot from the estate of some deceased wartime schoolmarm. These she distributed, with a punitive delight, once a week at the appointed hour. Fiction was hardly represented at all in the collection and, such as it was, it was pocky and dusty enough to render even the likes of Wilkie Collins stone dead to the girls forever. There were, of course, the worthy biographies. Other than the Oliver Cromwell, which was currently in Jem's possession, there were those of Albert Schweitzer, and of "Little Wolferl" of Salzburg and of the great Dr. Arnold of Rugby. There was a book called *Great World Leaders*, which ran through the whole yellowing ragbag from the Aga Khan and Chiang Kai-shek, to the emperor of Ethiopia and Queen Wilhelmina of the Netherlands. The only qualification for inclusion, Alice considered, was that you had to have been dead for at least ten years.

As Alice watched the stoned black man make his way across the grass toward the gate, she noticed that two butterflies were hovering over the buddleia. It lifted her spirits to see them. It was like dancing inside her head just to have them there and to have Jem in the seat beside her. It was all so delightful and so thoroughly unscheduled, Jem's coming. And it had all happened in a moment. In the twinkling of an eye. Everything had changed. Alice knew at once, on that very first day, that she loved Jem and esteemed her above all others. And that, because of Jem, her whole life—even the Silent Reading Hour—would never be boring again. In a first act of exuberance, she wrote Jem a note and passed it over.

"Dear Jem," said the note. "Are you staying for Prep?"

JEM, IT TURNED OUT, was a boarder. She had no choice but to stay for Prep. Alice had seldom stayed. There were all sorts of things against doing so. There was the intolerable prolonging of the school day after the dismissal bell had gone, and the way in which one was required to line up at teatime amid the jostling, bumping throng for tin plates of bread and margarine. Alice found it distasteful the way that school could seem so much like the army. There was no value for oneself at such times. Only for the great, heaving, sensible corporate mass. School bread reverted to raw doughballs in the mouth. Upon contact with one's saliva, it seemed somehow to unbake itself. Lenora Gripe said that you could roll it into gummy lumps in the palm of your hand and use it to bait fishhooks. At any rate that was what her brothers did. She collected up what was left each day and took it home for their convenience.

Alice's friend Flora Fergusson had always stayed for Prep, right from their days in the junior school. But then Flora's parents had insisted on it. It saved them on food bills if Flora got her "tea" at school, and Flora, being half starved at home through their stinginess, was inured to the spitball bread. Certainly, Alice had never stayed merely for the sake of Flora's companionship as she found herself now doing for Jem's. It was for Jem, and Jem alone, that she joyfully confronted the margarine and doughball bread, wishing to prolong the day's contact.

Jem spent the hour copying up Alice's biology notes under the heading "Flatworms, Nematode Worms and Liver Flukes." She did this,

Alice observed, in a curious, obsolete, ornately looped copperplate hand for which she employed a fountain pen containing brown ink.

"I love your writing," Alice said. "I've never seen brown ink like that."

"It's called Burnt Sienna," Jem said. "I learned the writing from an old copybook I found in the convent stockroom." Jem meant her previous school, which she had evidently left somewhat precipitously. "You had to copy out these discouraging little homilies," she said. " ' 'Tis better to Die than to Lie.' That was the first one. I sometimes wonder if it's true."

"Oh no," said Alice, who was a scrupulously truthful child. "It's much too drastic. It couldn't be."

"Speaking of flatworms and liver flukes," Jem said, "why do you suppose Miss Aldridge is so passionate about Oliver Cromwell?"

Alice searched her mind for all those reasonable, laudable things that had caused the deposition of the king to be a necessary and progressive act. "Well," she said. "Democracy and Parliament. You know."

Jem shook her head. "Fellow feeling in the matter of facial warts," she said.

"But Miss Aldridge hasn't exactly got warts," Alice said in fairness. "They're more moles, really." Jem looked Alice squarely in the eye. "Well," Alice said, capitulating, "I suppose that they are quite warty—for moles, I mean."

"They're warts," Jem said firmly. "And they'll get wartier. You mark my words." Jem had turned aside from the liver fluke and had begun idly to entertain herself with an ornate frontispiece in her science folder. A sort of family tree. The top branch, suitably embellished with calligraphic flourishes, read "Sharon and Trevor Cromwell, 1436." This was followed by several subsidiary branches under which Jem was freely improvising Cromwell spouses and numerous Cromwell progeny.

"But what are you doing?" Alice asked. She noticed that Dawn and Kevin Cromwell had already spawned Gary and Donna. Alice laughed. "Do you think she believed you?" she said. "I mean all that about the ancient king of Cornwall?"

"Don't suppose so," Jem said. "I detected a degree of suspicion. She'll have her nose buried in a Cornish genealogy at this very moment."

"Or in a Cornish pasty," Alice said. It gave them a fit of the giggles. The thought of poor Miss Aldridge rooting in a pasty . . .

"I oughtn't to be made to read books about Cromwell," Jem said suddenly. "It's a violation of my spiritual integrity."

Alice was never altogether sure from then on whether Miss Aldridge's moles did get wartier, or whether she merely imagined it. But one thing was certain. Jem's espousal of the spiritual seemed ever more rich and strange to Alice, whose own family had no use for religion and went to church only at weddings and funerals. Alice's maternal great-grandmother had begun life as an Ulster Protestant and had succeeded in transmitting unreviewed but much-diluted remnants of anti-Catholic bigotry, both to Alice's grandmother and to Alice's mother, but that was absolutely all.

"My father," Jem said one day, "is a devotee of the unrevised eucharistic fast."

"Gosh," said Alice, who had no idea what Jem was talking about.

"He's against ecumenical concessions," Jem said. "And he drives us absolutely miles to mass—to get us away from all that guitars-and-footwashing in the house of God."

"Oh," said Alice, who had never heard the word *ecumenical* before and who had never even been baptized.

"Is your father very religious then?" she asked.

Jem laughed. "He shaves to Gregorian chant," she said. "If you call that religious."

For Alice, until that moment, Catholicism had always seemed a pretty dreary affair, having something to do with barricades on vandalized Belfast housing estates and those horrid little shrines with plaster statuettes of Mary that had been made in molds such as you could get at Hamley's for making Peter Rabbit.

"He's a dear old thing," Jem said indulgently. "He will insist on starving himself from midnight every Saturday and before all holy days of obligation. I expect it's heretical—now that even the pope is into his second bowl of Shreddies by dawn on Sunday morning."

"He does sound terribly strict," Alice said.

"Oh no," Jem said. "He's a romantic, that's all. He's a convert. He converted for my mother. All that nausea amid the stink of incense is like the first bloom of his connubial passion." Alice wasn't at all sure that this wasn't sacrilegious, but she didn't venture to say so. "Afterwards he always carts us off to the French *pâtisserie*," Jem said. "And he buys us great mountains of *brioches* and *pains au chocolat*."

Alice considered this to be quite the pinnacle of glamour. Sunday breakfasts in her own house had always been so thoroughly late, so thoroughly English, so thoroughly secular. A mere rising around ten to Rice Crispies and boiled eggs, while her father read the *Sunday Telegraph* and her mother caught the week's rerun of *The Archers* on Radio 4.

"Well, you are lucky, Jem," she said, "to have such a difficult religion."

ALICE BELIEVED that she knew what all her classmates' fathers did. They owned supermarkets or they made money in Abu Dhabi. They were solicitors, or proprietors of carpet warehouses. They managed high-street banks or they commuted to work in the City.

Everybody knew that Alice's father built and renovated houses, because his name was always on hoardings all over the neighborhood. Sometimes he bought houses and renovated them and sold them again to make money. He picked up others here and there that he modified and let. These began as "improvement properties" and turned into "superior executive units." Sometimes he sold off the executive units when the executives left, in order to liberate money. He used the money then to acquire more ambitious units, to finance speculative building projects and generally to diversify.

Alice was very fond of her father, who was a gentle, unaffected man, still insecure enough about his spelling to have her mother check his invoices. It seemed to her that what he really loved was bricks; that, just as a poet might extol the romance of the empty page, so her father still liked bricks better than buildings. Bricks were his symphonies of mud and straw. Bricks were his arias. That was why he never accompanied her mother to the local Amateur Operatic Society's productions of *Carmen* or *The Merry Wives of Windsor.* He had no need of them. Nor of Gregorian chant.

But Alice found it very difficult to envisage what Jem's father did. She knew all about his rigour with regard to the eucharistic fast. And she knew that Alice Liddell, child friend of Lewis Carroll, had been godmother to one of his mother's great-aunts. Indeed, she had deemed this latter intelligence sufficiently elegant to have honored it with a small untruth. She had allowed Jem to believe that she had been named after Alice in "Wonderland" when in truth she had been named after Alice Springs in Australia. Her mother had been reading *A Town like Alice* in the labor ward before she was born.

"But what exactly does your father do?" Alice finally asked her new friend. It was just after lunch one school day, where Alice had watched Jem twist long skeins of overcooked spaghetti deftly onto a fork instead of chopping it into half-inch maggots along with the general throng.

"Pasta," Jem said, "ought to be *al dente*. As in having 'bite.' My father is a man of letters."

Alice envisaged, uncertainly, a person somewhat in the mold of Bob Cratchit who transcribed business correspondence in longhand with an antique pen. Perhaps he also used brown ink and had looped, copperplate writing.

"Do you mean that he writes letters?" she asked.

"Oh no," Jem said. "Not really. He reads manuscripts. And he scribbles a bit. He busies himself in the summerhouse all day."

"But what's his job?" Alice said.

"Oh," Jem said. "You know. Reading manuscripts. And scribbling a bit in the summerhouse."

Alice duly adjusted her image of Jem's father until she envisaged a person, taller and rather grander than Bob Cratchit, leaning elegantly on a rake in a potting shed with a monocle screwed into his right eye. Behind him, as he scrutinized ancient and powdery fragments of parchment, seedlings quietly germinated against pointed, ecclesiastical windows.

"Frankly, he'd be completely useless at an ordinary sort of job," Jem said. "He's far too otherworldly. But he can tell you all about eighteenth-century gardens, or the history of tatting."

"Tatting?" Alice said.

"It's to do with tying knots," Jem said.

"Sailors tie knots," Alice said. "And scoutmasters. Your father could be a scoutmaster."

"Scoutmasters swear to serve the queen," Jem said grandly. "Catholics are sworn to restore the Catholic Ascendancy. That makes us all potential traitors."

"Gosh," Alice said.

"Anyway," Jem said, "tatting is really more like needlework. It's a sort of crochet."

"Crochet?" Alice said.

"If you were to ask him to mend a bicycle puncture, he couldn't do it," Jem said. "Nor could he tell you who the prime minister is. And he still can't understand why currencies come in baskets. One day he saw a news hoarding that said POUND WEAK and he thought it meant Ezra."

"Ezra?" Alice said.

"Ezra Pound," Jem said. "He's a poet, of course. My father thought that the poet had taken a turn for the worse."

"But if he works in a summerhouse, your father," Alice asked respectfully, "doesn't he suffer a bit from condensation?"

"I expect you're thinking of a greenhouse," Jem said. "A summerhouse is really quite different."

Jem told Alice that her mother came from Normandy but, unlike Claire Crouchley's Normans, Mrs. McCrail had not been anglicized gradually. She had been abruptly dispatched from her home at the age of fifteen to an English convent boarding school. Her father, a stern, widowed farmer, had resorted to this extremity, Jem explained, after finding his daughter prostrated in the bluebell wood under a handsome young chef from the neighboring village.

"Unfortunately," Jem said, "the handsome young chef was wearing an embroidered yellow waistcoat with shiny brass buttons. It meant that he was all too visible to *mon grand-père* as he pressed his sylvan suit."

Alice giggled. "Silver suit?" she said. "You make him sound like the Pearly King."

"Sylvan," Jem said, running the word over her tongue like water to taste its cool grace. "Not silver, Alice. Sylvan, as in 'the change of Philomel, by the barbarous king so rudely forced.' "

"What?" Alice said.

"Sylvan, as in woodland," Jem said. "Have you ever wondered what it's like—being 'rudely forced'? You know. Raped."

"Oh!" Alice said. "Was your mother being raped?"

"I suppose so," Jem said with equanimity. "But it didn't matter, because she was very much in love with the handsome chef. Only then *mon grand-père* came along and thwarted her passion. He marched up like a country roughneck and pried them apart like squabbling puppies." Alice winced as she envisaged the embarrassment of the business. "He promptly ordered the chef off his land *tout de suite*," Jem said. "Yellow waistcoat and all. Then he bundled my mother home with her stockings all spiraled round her knees and her cheeks aflame with lust."

"And then what happened?" Alice asked anxiously.

"Oh," Jem said. "He called in my three uncles from the fields as witnesses to her disheveled state and he thrashed her with his razor strap."

"Oh, but he didn't really?" Alice said.

Jem laughed. " 'Course he did," she said. "Then he made her pray that her poor, dead, sainted mother hadn't been looking down from heaven that afternoon. You know. Casting an eye over her favorite bluebell wood."

"Gosh!" Alice said. She tried to imagine how her own maternal grandfather would have reacted. She was fairly sure that he would have crept away on tiptoes at the first sign of the lovers couched half-clad upon a bank of leaf mold. He would have tried his best not to cough or sneeze.

"Well, you know what the French are like," Jem was saying. "They're all crazy about the Pre-Raphaelites. My grandfather likes to think his dead wife is up there warming the gold bar of heaven for him with her bosom." Alice was too concerned for the plight of Mrs. McCrail to give much thought to the gold bar of heaven.

"So then what happened to her?" Alice asked.

"She died in childbirth," Jem said.

"Your mother?"

"No, of course not," Jem said. "My grandmother. My mother got sent off to the yard to pluck a goose while my grandfather telephoned an English convent boarding school. He had a whiskery old cousin there who taught French and calligraphy. That's how she got to England."

Alice was deeply impressed with the injustice. It sounded to her like *Jane Eyre*, which she had read in the junior school in an abridged edition for Younger Readers.

"Suddenly there she was, poor thing," Jem said. "Stuck in a dorm with hockey fiends and rows of lumpy mattresses. Bit like this place, really." Alice wondered idly if Jem's mother had appeared in the middle of a Wednesday afternoon, dragging a canvas toolbag.

"She'd never so much as seen cauliflower cheese before," Jem said. "Or Bisto. And suddenly there she was, watching *les anglaises* elbowing each other for second helpings of reconstituted custard. She thought she was in hell until she met my father. Have you ever tried to read Dante, Alice?"

Alice sat up at this point with increased excitement. "But she never met your father while she was still at school?" she said incredulously.

"Oh yes," Jem said. "One snowy day before Christmas. She had just led a small party of schoolgirls to the boundary wall to throw snowballs. It was way beyond the playing fields and all strictly *verboten*, because it overlooked a village pub where undergraduates came at weekends. My father and his friends just happened to pull up while the girls were all peering over the wall. Most of the girls were such ninnies, of course, they were already nearly wetting themselves because they were breaking the school rules, but my mother was delighted. She's always liked men a lot better than women and these ones were all wrapped in jolly college scarves and stamping and laughing. In fact they were the first English people she'd ever seen looking happy."

Alice hadn't got round to thinking much about men as yet. It seemed to her only girls like Lenora Gripe were interested in men. But when they came filtered through Jem's transforming power, men did sound rather jolly. She suddenly envisaged that things might be rather different if a clutch of brightly scarved undergraduates were to tumble out of a car just beyond the wall of the playing field. She imagined them singing, like Mario Lanza in *The Student Prince*, of which operetta her mother possessed a treasured recording.

"My mother picked out my father at once," Jem said, "because he was the tallest and by far the best looking. She threw a snowball at him, which hit him right between the eyes and knocked his glasses off. She was very accurate, you see, because she'd grown up shooting hares."

"And then?" Alice asked.

"Well," Jem said. "The other girls were so unnerved by her success that they all ran away in panic. Meanwhile my mother just waited and watched my father pick up his glasses and pack a snowball very slowly and deliberately. He'd heard all the giggling behind the wall, you see, so he marched up meaning to ram it down some horrid little schoolgirl's gabardine. But there was only my mother, straining to lean her chin on the wall. She's five foot two in her shoes, you see. She's about the same size as you. She's sort of pretty and fair and blue eyed, like you, with the same little pointed chin." Alice glowed with the compliment. Not that she was vain, or even dressy. In fact she quite disliked the way her mother tried to coax her into boutiques. But a compliment from Jem was rather different. "I must get my height from my father," Jem said. "Unless it's from the growth hormones they put in the school soyamince. Anyway, then my mother began to explain to him why she'd done it."

Jem assumed an enviably convincing French accent. " 'Pardon, monsieur,' she said, 'but I 'ave threw hat you *la boule de neige* for that you are, of all your friend, *le plus beau*.' " Alice felt a tingle of joy pass over the surface of her skin.

"Well," Jem said. "As you can imagine, my pater thought she was an absolute knockout. He dropped the snowball immediately and kissed his fingers to her. *'Mademoiselle,'* he said, in his very best French— which isn't too bad, really—*'le mur est assez haut, mais le pub ici est très agréable. Vous êtes forte à l'escalade?'* "

"What's *'escalade'*?" Alice asked.

"It means 'climbing,' " Jem said.

"Oh, but she never climbed over the wall!" Alice said in disbelief. "Oh Jem! Did she really? How romantic!"

"Well, she was a bit taken with him," Jem confided. "After all, he was the only person, other than the whiskery cousin, who had spoken French to her in three months. Anyway, it was a Saturday and the others had all run away. Nobody was going to miss her until teatime."

"And I'll bet the pub food was a lot better than the school tea," Alice observed with feeling.

"Well, yes," Jem said. "Food can be quite sexy, can't it? And so was the company. After that she kept leaping over the wall every Saturday for the next six months. By the time the whiskery cousin found out and told *mon grand-père* . . . well, all I can say is it was much too late for the razor strap."

"You don't mean she was—?"

"Pregnant," Jem said amiably. "Oh yes. With my oldest sister. It didn't really matter, because my father took instruction and they got married."

Alice balked a bit at the thought of him taking instruction. "I don't see why he needed any instruction if he'd already got her pregnant," she said.

"Instruction in Catholicism," Jem said. "He became a catechumen. He was the only son of a manse in Aberdeenshire, you see."

"But wasn't your mother a bit scared to go home?" Alice asked. "I mean what with your grandfather being such a fiend?"

"Oh no," Jem said casually. "My father took along a crate of best Highland whiskey. My grandfather and my uncles all drank him under the table on the eve of the wedding. They sang bawdy French songs till cockcrow and then the maid found them next morning, asleep in their shoes on the parlor floor, surrounded by umpteen empty bottles of Laphroaig." Jem paused. "After the wedding my grandfather took out the razor strap," she said, "and he gave it to my father as a present." Alice was appalled.

"But he surely didn't mean your father to—to use it, did he?"

Jem laughed. "Oh, I'm sure he did," she said. "But my father couldn't possibly. Even slug pellets make him feel like Goebbels. He has my sisters and me collect up all the garden snails in buckets and chuck them over the wall of the Protestant graveyard."

"Oh, he doesn't!" Alice said in delight.

"He says each snail will get us off about point zero two seconds in purgatory," Jem said. The two girls began to move indoors upon hearing the school bell. " 'Course, they're probably not really married," Jem said casually. "Not in the eyes of Mother Church. Well— when you think of all that whiskey within hours of the nuptial mass."

"You are lucky, Jem," Alice said, "to have such interesting parents!"

JEM HAD COME to Alice's school because the convent school had expelled her. This blessed severance was one for which Alice became unendingly grateful. It had occurred, Jem said, because of an orange. Not William of Orange. Just a common, or garden, orange.

"Sister Teresa was taking our form for a singing lesson in the hall," Jem said, "when she inadvertently sat down on an orange."

"Why was there an orange in the hall?" Alice asked.

"Search me," Jem said. "But she considered it not in keeping with her vocation to have orange juice on her habit, so she demanded to know who had put it there. She kept waving her baton about in a frenzy and uttering the direst threats, but nobody owned up."

"I'm not surprised," said Alice.

"Well, it's a funny thing that," Jem said, "but Catholic girls will usually own up to absolutely everything. Especially to things they haven't done."

"Oh go on," Alice said. "Who'd be so daft as all that?"

"Our Lord," Jem said severely, "took upon himself all the sins of the world."

"Oh, but that's different!" Alice said. "Surely, Jem, that's quite different?"

"Well of course it's different," Jem said. "But it does make for a sort of precedent, doesn't it? That's for people who like to wrap their masochism in messianic disguises."

"What's 'masochism'?" Alice said.

"Anyway," Jem said, "the fact is that Sister Teresa went berserk." She took on the persona of the poor, demented nun. " 'If I, a woman consecrated to God, can sit on an orange,' " Jem mimicked wonderfully, " 'you all shall sit on an orange'!"

"Oh she didn't!" Alice cried in delight. "Oh, she never did!"

"Poor woman," Jem said. "She'd never really had her marbles about her person. Not since she'd been deeply disappointed in love."

"But how do you know?" Alice said.

"In her youth," Jem said, ignoring the question, "Sister Teresa had been loved by a merchant seaman. He had golden curls and wide blue eyes. But alas, while he was away at sea, her mother hid all his letters. Then she told poor Sister Tee that he'd been drowned in the Persian Gulf. So she shaved her head forthwith and espoused the Lord."

Alice was momentarily cast down by the poignant, monastic vignette. "That's dreadful!" she said. "What sort of a mother would do a thing like that?"

"Gullibility," Jem said sternly, "is the sin of stupidity. Look at Othello. One peek at his wife's noserag in the wrong hands and he thinks she's been sleeping around. Anyway, the orange tapped reservoirs of dottiness in poor Sister Tee. She made us all line up from the shortest to the tallest and sit on the stupid thing. Well, I'm pretty tall, you see, so I was last. The orange had rather passed its best by the time I came along."

"And?"

"I refused to sit on it," Jem said.

"And?"

"Well, she had a fit."

"So?"

"What I mean is, she had a fit," Jem said. "You know. A proper epileptic fit. All frothing and twitching. She was 'as one possessed by an hundred demons.' "

"Golly!" Alice said.

"Well, after that, Sister Superior telephoned my parents," Jem said. "She got through to Daddy in the summerhouse."

"Has he got a phone in the summerhouse?" Alice asked.

" 'Course he has," Jem said. "A cordless telephone. You know. Anyway, he came up at once, but unfortunately he refused to be horrified. I'm afraid he faced the whole incident with rather inappropriate levity."

"With what?" Alice said.

"He burst out laughing," Jem said. "And just when Sister Superior was in her fullest flow on the Imitation of Christ. She'd put the orange in front of him on a silver platter, you see. And there it was, all sort of ravaged and oozy. Next thing I knew was we were both out, bag and baggage. Banished from paradise for ever and for aye."

"It doesn't sound too much like paradise," Alice said doubtfully, but the gravity of the sentence impressed her nonetheless. Jem shook it off bravely.

"Daddy took me to a restaurant," Jem said. "We ate fillet steak in *béarnaise* sauce and all he said was, 'Well, Jemsie, I suppose those villainous Protestants will have to educate you from now on. Heaven help me, they're even more expensive.' "

"And your mother?" Alice said. "What did she say?"

"Oh, not much," Jem said vaguely. "She's too much the demon Gaulish child-whacker to bother with verbiage at such moments."

 ALICE ALWAYS KNEW that she owed her education to Jem. Until the coming of Jem there had simply been those books that you wanted to read and those books that you got made to read. It was this very dichotomy at the heart of things that had caused Miss Trotter to introduce the Silent Reading Hour in the first place. The headmistress had uncovered a regrettable fondness among her girls for Agatha Christie and Sue Barton. She had even whispered hoarsely in the assembly hall that "certain gels" had been observed reading what she called "comic papers and Christmas annuals."

Claire Crouchley's desk had always been well supplied with "comic papers and Christmas annuals" in the form of *Bunty* and *Diane*. She had been in the habit of lending these out to her classmates in the library periods, but after the head's purification program, she was obliged to stow them in her schoolbag and lend them out only in the breaks. It was from watching Jem read Claire's girls' papers that Alice had acquired her first taste for literary analysis.

Jem, Alice observed, read these works with great enjoyment, but there was something in the manner of her doing so that gave her the air of an anthropologist embarking upon a new field study.

"It's interesting," Jem would say, flicking through the cheap, absorbent pages. "There's always a ballerina being struck down by paralyzing illness. That's until some pioneering young doctor appears—all of three pages later—with his bag full of surgical tricks and his head full of wedding bells."

"Yes," Alice said, "that's right."

"The ballerina alternates with a gymnast," Jem said, "who is forever being foiled by a half-crazed rival in league with a foreigner. The foreigner always gets a foothold in the school through the Modern Languages Department—or through the Ancillary Services."

"Anne what?" Alice asked.

"The villains always scream Red Menace," Jem said. "Or else they're proles."

"There's a demon dinner lady in this one I'm reading," Alice said.

"Oh yes, I've read that one," Jem said. "She's plotting against the new self-service dinner alternative. The editorial board is obviously trying to relocate 'Gothic Horror' in the comprehensive school. Wouldn't you say it was inconsistent with the genre—Breeze-Block Gothic?"

Alice loved the way Jem talked, even when she couldn't understand half of what Jem said. It was infectious the way Jem grooved on words.

It was because Jem possessed so much of what Alice thought of as "culture"—and because she had crossed it in equal measure with street wisdom—that Alice was able to discover all sorts of previously unsampled joys. Jem, within the week, had devised a foolproof system for maneuvering herself and Alice invisibly on and off the school premises in the lunch hour—an accomplishment that resulted in the girls spending many blissful, liberated hours window-shopping in the town center, or idling pleasantly in coffee bars. And then, for a period of two successive Wednesdays, Jem demonstrated for Alice with what delightful ease one could absent oneself from the "special" afternoon assemblies. One simply marked a little time in the sixth-form toilets before heading out for the soundproofed cubicles off the music room.

"If you stand on the lavatory seat until you hear the first hymn," Jem advised, "then the prefects can't spot your feet under the door. Anyway, when it comes to malingerers, they're always much too busy scouring the third-form washrooms. They never think to police their own cabbage patch. They believe all crime takes place in the ghetto."

In the music room, Jem treated Alice to a recording of *The Magic Flute*. She extracted it from the unlocked cupboard behind the pianos where Mrs. Fergusson kept all the hardware for "music appreciation." It went without saying that Jem's course in music appreciation held attractions far beyond that offered either by Mrs. Fergusson, or in the assembly hall where Miss Trotter always found musical composition to be pregnant with moral instruction. ("Well," she would say brightly, of the Trumpet Voluntary, or the *Saint Matthew Passion*, or the *Four Seasons*, "that inspiring piece of music serves to remind us all of the brisk yet disciplined manner in which we carry out our tasks here in the Upper School. Dismiss in single file, gels!")

The Magic Flute was her father's favorite opera, Jem said.

"And mine too," she said. "So you must tell me that it's the most marvelous thing you ever did hear."

Alice found that it was. Something about being with Jem made one able to see things through her eyes. There was a curious, insidious, ritualistic power in the soul of the thing which Alice at first tried to resist. And it needled her that the story was so idiotic and inconsistent. It didn't seem to make any sense.

"It makes sense in the way that a dream makes sense," Jem said. "You don't expect a dream to be 'consistent,' do you? But you know that it's very deeply to do with the nature of your being."

And who was Sarastro? Alice was troubled that the opera should be raising up this dubious, patriarchal child abductor and dressing him in the garb of the high priest. What was his claim upon the Temple of Wisdom and why did such marvelous, sonorous male choruses sing homage to him when he passed in his chariot drawn by lions? He had stolen the daughter of the Queen of the Night. And why did Prince Tamino change sides? And why didn't Pamina spit in Sarastro's eye and insist that he let her go? Alice's objections made Jem laugh.

"Sarastro can make lions appear in the wilderness," she said. "Sarastro can produce food and wine from the forest floor. He's got the talisman. Do you expect him to behave as if he were running the Citizens Advice Bureau?"

But why, again—if this *was* the Temple of Wisdom and not some bogus male hangout—why, then, was it blighted by a fevered black sex maniac intent upon raping Pamina? Anyway, wasn't it racist to have a black man forever creeping in and out through Pamina's windows and seething about his own "ugliness"? The stoned black man hadn't been ugly when he had climbed in through the classroom windows. Nor had he been intent upon rape. He hadn't even thought the girls pretty. Pamina *is* very pretty, but Monostatos thinks she's pretty just *because* she's white. What rubbish! Wouldn't a man like that undermine the whole validity of the Temple?

"The Temple will weather the failings of its inmates," Jem said. "The Temple *is* the failings of its inmates. But then everything is transformed in the furnace of inspiration. There are sages standing in God's holy fire."

"What?" Alice said, but her attention was diverted, suddenly, because right there, near the end of the opera, Papageno and his girlfriend were quite definitely stammering. They were singing a duet. "Pa-pa-pa-pa. Pa-pa-pa-pa. Pa-pa-gena. Pa-pa-geno."

"They're stammering," Alice said. "Jem, they're stammering." She was startled by the realization that she had not stammered in Jem's company. Not once. The stammer just wasn't there.

In Jem's presence, of course, truanting was not a necessary expedient for the evocation of magic. Lessons themselves became an enchantment in her company, their tedium transformed "in the furnace of inspiration." Take needlework, for example, where Jem succeeded in creating such delirious burlesque in the ironing alcove out of Miss Cummings's idiotic insistence upon "allowing for growth."

"I reckon these shorts are big enough for both of us," Jem said, and she flicked out Alice's half-made shorts invitingly. "Here you are, Alice. You have the left leg and I'll have the right."

"She'll see us," Alice said.

"Oh come on. She can't see round corners," Jem said.

"It's her glasses," Alice said. "They help her to see round everywhere."

"Only God and a periscope can see round corners," Jem said.

"And Sarastro," Alice said. Jem smiled at her. In an instant they had zipped themselves into the shorts, and there they stood, like Siamese twins, tight as pincushions and helpless with silent laughter.

Of course Jem had been quite right as usual. Miss Cummings had been completely blind to their antics and would have remained so had not Miss Trotter happened to pass the window at that moment. She no sooner spotted them than she took a deep breath, changed color, and surged forward into the needlework room, carrying her bosom before her.

"Remove the shorts at once!" she boomed, and she navigated the aisle with remarkable speed, given her stately bulk. The two girls found that they could not remove the shorts. Alice picked ineffectually at the zip, which had jammed on stray threads from the unfinished placket.

"Remove them immediately!" Miss Trotter commanded. The seams, though strained, refused to budge. This was hardly surprising, Alice reflected silently, since Miss Cummings had always insisted upon a run-and-fell seam of unrivaled finesse and durability.

"Please, Miss Trotter, we can't," she said humbly.

"The fact is," Jem said in that fatal voice with its unwittingly insubordinate clarity, "the fact is that Alice Pilling and I have become completely inseparable."

Miss Trotter's nostrils flared. "Report to my office at once!" she said.

The girls found that to comply with Miss Trotter's instruction was no mean feat in the circumstances. They shuffled and hopped their way along the length of the corridor in a condition of glorious hilarity. In later years, when she remembered that gauntlet of absurdity, Alice could frankly not remember ever again having felt so completely, so girlishly happy. Even after Miss Trotter had snatched up the scissors from her desk tray and had unseamed the girls from waistband to gusset, the heady feeling had not left her. "The fact is," Jem had said, "that Alice Pilling and I have become completely inseparable." Oh, the bliss of it! To have Jem and to be so completely inseparable!

That was the first time Alice had ever been given a detention, and her mother had required an explanation.

"If you ask me," said Mrs. Pilling, once Alice had portrayed for her the essence of the prank, "this 'Jem' McCrail of yours sounds like a thoroughly bad influence." But Mrs. Pilling had already decided to defuse the power of the enemy by incorporation. "Perhaps you would like to ask her home," she said.

JEM SPENT her first weekend away from school at Alice's house. It was an event to which Alice looked forward with intense pleasure. Her mother, though she had by this time become an active and thriving business-woman, still found time to watch over the event with that protective interest crossed with managerial engineering that characterized all her doings with regard to her only child. Mrs. Pilling packed a brace of pork pies, a homemade carrot cake and a large bottle of ginger beer into a saddlebag. She suggested to Alice that the girls make use of the fine summer weather to cycle along the riverbank for a picnic. To this purpose she had called upon Alice's father to overhaul the spare lady's bicycle, which normally hung unused upon a bracket fixed to the garage wall. He was engaged upon this task on the front lawn when Alice's friend made her entrance.

Jem came in time for lunch, looking radiant in her civvies. Her brown curls were buoyant around her temples and she wore a man's gabardine raincoat, which spoke eloquently to Alice of alternative chic. Her large, broad feet were, as usual, clad in the old black pumps. At the gate she embraced Alice and kissed her on both cheeks, for she was wont to employ most un-English modes of salutation. Then she strode across the grass to where Mr. Pilling was busy cleaning the bicycle chain. She held out her hand to him like a self-possessed adult.

"Mr. Pilling?" she said, her voice falling like golden rain, "Jem McCrail."

Alice's father, taken unawares, paused to wipe his hands hastily on one of his cleaning rags. "Messy things, bicycles," he said, and he displayed both hands by way of apology. But Jem was inexplicably delighted. She seized his right hand and shook it.

"Oh, but this is wonderful!" she said. "I must say that I think you're wonderful. I've never seen anyone do anything like this before."

"Jem's father can't fix bikes," Alice said, by way of explanation. "He can't even mend a puncture."

Mr. Pilling chuckled pleasantly. To him the notion of a man unfamiliar with the workings of a cogwheel and an inner tube was so beyond credibility that he considered Alice's remarks to be in the nature of jest.

"What do we have our daughters for, eh?" he said. "If not so they can slander us in public?"

"No, really," Alice said. "He can't. Can he, Jem? Jem's father can't even tell you who the prime minister is. But he knows all about eighteenth-century gardens."

"Oh aye," said Harry Pilling.

"And all about tatting," Alice said.

Mr. Pilling had by now replaced the chain and had tightened it. "Come again, flower?" he said.

"Tatting," Alice said. "It's a kind of crochet work." Mr. Pilling promptly dropped his small screwdriver onto the grass. Jem returned it to him with a dazzling smile. "Once Jem's father saw a news hoarding that said POUND WEAK," Alice said eagerly. "He thought it meant Ezra was poorly."

"Ezra?" said her father, without looking up. "Are you talking to me in riddles today, my pet?" He was holding the back wheel of the bicycle aloft and was test-turning the pedals with his foot. The action had activated the gear ratchet, which was responding with a satisfying, rhythmic whirr-click.

"Ezra Pound is a poet," Alice said. "Jem's father reads him in the summerhouse."

"Oh aye," her father said absently, but he was not really listening to her. Neither, it seemed, was Jem. She was staring at the gear ratchet with a fascination that Alice found perplexing.

"But it's so beautiful!" Jem said. "Mr. Pilling, it's so lovely."

Alice's father raised an eyebrow, suspecting her of affectation. "It's a bicycle, bonny lass," he said. "Five gears, two wheels and four brake blocks'." Then he offered Jem the handlebars. She took them as if she were being offered the golden bough. "There you go, girls," he said. "Enjoy your picnic now."

"Oh *thank* you, Mr. Pilling," Jem said. "We will!"

Alice and Jem, having gorged themselves on carrot cake, lay side by side on the riverbank with the saddlebag between them. They were blinking upwards into the dappled light, which came to them filtered through a row of feathery trees.

"Who's Flora?" Jem said.

"A friend," Alice said. "Her father died three weeks ago." She sounded more than a little uneasy. Flora had been away from school ever since the funeral. Flora, who had never been absent in her whole school life before. Flora, who had regularly reaped praises in the assembly hall for her inspiring attendance record.

"Do you like her?" Jem said. Alice was thrown by the question. She had never consciously considered Flora in these terms before. Flora was a fact of life. A friend of very long standing rather than of passionate attachment. Not like Jem.

"Yes," Alice said. "Of course I do."

"Do you like her more than me?" Jem said.

"No," Alice said. "Of course I don't."

"Do you like us both the same?" Jem said.

"No," Alice said. "I like you better." Jem let go a contented sigh and stretched her arms expansively.

"Oh voom, oh vam," she said happily. "Oh me and my. What do you think of 'Oh,' then, Alice? The great, poetical 'O'? Quote me a line beginning with 'O.' "

" 'Oh, to be in England now that April's there,' " Alice said. Jem sat up, eager to play along.

" 'O! what a fall was there, my countrymen,' " she said.

" 'O God, our help in ages past,' " Alice said.

" 'O chestnut tree, great-rooted blossomer,' " Jem said.

" 'Oh, sunflower! Weary of time,' " Alice said. Jem laughed. She stood up, shaking bits of grass from her hair.

"That's not 'Oh.' That's 'Ah,' " she said. "Funny how different they are." She paused, then quoted almost roughly, " 'But ah, but O thou terrible, why wouldst thou rude on me thy wring-world right foot rock?' "

Alice felt herself jolted by the curious, abrasive rhythm of the lines. "What's that?" she said.

"Hopkins on God," Jem said, making a small, ironic bow. "Father Gerard Hopkins, S.J."

"What's 'S.J.'?" Alice said.

"Subtle Jesuit," Jem said. "Isn't it lovely here? Can I please come again?"

Mrs. Pilling passed her daughter's friend a bowl of whipped cream across the dining table. "And are your sisters married?" she asked.

Jem took up the cream spoon. It was like a miniature soup ladle. The cream fell in a generous plop onto the summit of her chocolate mousse. Largesse impelled her to give of herself with an equivalent generosity.

"Not yet, Mrs. Pilling," she said. "I'm afraid that Patch cohabits with a heathen in a state of sin. And Maddie—" She paused and gouged decisively into the dark riches within her bowl. "Well, Maddie, for the moment, has an active but accident-prone love life." Mr. and Mrs. Pilling glanced quickly at each other and then back again at their daughter's new friend. "Maddie has a penchant for suicide cases," Jem said.

"Suicide cases?" Mrs. Pilling said. "You don't mean to say that her young men kill themselves?"

Jem smiled. "They fail," she said. "But only just, Mrs. Pilling. Maddie works in the accident unit, you see. She's a medical student."

"What a difficult environment," Mrs. Pilling said politely, "for a young girl."

"Oh, not for Maddie," Jem said. "As far as she's concerned, the place is an ideal dating agency. I do think that, in her case, job satisfaction has begun to addle the brain." She settled expansively to her theme, offering chapter and verse. "Take last Sunday," she said. "There was Daddy, happily driving us back from mass when we passed a crashed-out Fiat. Maddie absolutely insisted that he stop so that she could collect spare parts. Well naturally, Daddy thought she meant the gearbox and the hubcaps, but not so Maddie. She meant the liver and the kidneys of whoever was expiring in the wreckage." Alice's parents gave no answer to this at all. "Maddie leans toward the macabre," Jem said, perhaps a little extraneously. "Take last hols, for example. She secreted one of her resurrected melancholics in her bedroom for the night. Well, didn't the poor creature of course start slitting his wrists in the small hours—with my sister's Swiss army knife."

"B'ye," said Alice's father. "Whatever next?"

"Well," Jem said. "Tourniquets and things. There he was, poor man. Groaning his last and decanting absolutely quarts of blood all over Mummy's new wallpaper. She's just done up Maddie's bedroom, you see. She's used that quilted tapestry stuff which the French like stapling to their walls."

"Jem's mother comes from Normandy," Alice said.

"Oh aye," said Alice's father.

"Unfortunately, it was most terribly expensive," Jem said. "The wallpaper I mean. Mummy had had it sent specially—from a shop in the place des Victoires."

"Eat up, Alice," Mrs. Pilling said.

"Anyway," Jem said. "I'm glad to say that Maddie has given him up for *un autre*. A musician this time. He keeps on trying to hang himself with a cello string and a block of ice."

"Oh aye," Mr. Pilling said again. "And what does he do with the block of ice then?" Jem paused to endow Alice's father with her most enchanting smile. He coughed a little shyly into his pudding.

"He stands on it and he waits for it to melt," she said. "With the cello string round his throat. Maddie, of course, keeps having to treat him for chilblains." She paused to make further inroads into her chocolate mousse. "Marvelous pudding, Mrs. Pilling," she said. "Is it rum I can taste? Or is it curaçao?" Mrs. Pilling composed herself for speech, but Jem went on. "I have to say that Patch has been wallpapering too," she said. "But rather more modestly. Patch has stuck brown wrapping paper to her walls. It's wonderfully cheap and it has such an elegant pinstripe. Patch is an art student, you see."

Patch was Jem's favorite sister. Jem made that very clear to Alice as they sat up eating toffees in bed that night. She lived in London, Jem said, with her boyfriend and her baby son Teddy. Patch was not married to her boyfriend, Jem explained, because he was Jewish and, unlike Mr. McCrail, he had been unwilling to "take instruction." He was what Jem called "a proper Jew." He had a prayer shawl and a yarmulke, she said.

"What's a yarmulke?" Alice said.

"You know," Jem said. "It's one of those skullcap things that Jews wear. He has to wear his all the time, even in bed. He keeps it on with a hair slide. Gosh, aren't your parents lovely?"

"You don't mean he's got those horrid sort of hairy corkscrew bits by his ears?" Alice said anxiously. She had seen such people at Heathrow Airport on her way to her parents' holiday house in Spain and she had found them unattractive. She did so terribly want Patch's man to be attractive.

"Oh no," Jem said. "He's very clean-shaven. He's like a tennis coach. Only he does read the Scriptures rather a lot. And he does have this terribly Orthodox family way back in darkest Manchester. They run a gentleman's outfitters which they have to keep closed all of Saturday."

"Why?" Alice said.

"Because it's the Sabbath of course," Jem said.

"But what does Patch do about the baby?" Alice asked. "I mean, is he Catholic or is he Jewish?"

"Oh, he's both," Jem said at once. "But that's not a problem at all. Teddy's been circumcised and baptized—like Jesus."

The talmudic scholar had frequently expressed an eagerness to marry Patch, Jem said, but he would not marry her in the Catholic church. "She wouldn't at all mind marrying a Jew," Jem said. "Just so long as she could have her wedding in the Catholic church. Then she wouldn't be forever doing penance for her carnal sins. After all, even the first pope had a Jewish mother-in-law."

Alice laughed. "But how can the pope have a mother-in-law?" she said. "You'd have to be married to have a mother-in-law."

"He was," Jem said. "The first pope was married. It says so in Saint Mark."

"Did they have popes in Saint Mark?" Alice said.

"The first pope was Saint Peter," Jem said. "It says in Saint Mark that his mother-in-law was sick. What Patch says is, trust a Jew to have a sick mother-in-law."

Alice turned her attention from Saint Peter to the lovers, willing Jem
further to beguile her with narrative. "How did they meet?" she said.

"Oh, they met while Patch was out sketching in the Victoria and
Albert Museum with the art school," Jem said. She reached her hand
into the bag of toffees. "They fell in love immediately. Patch thought he
looked exactly like Modigliani, and so he does."

One of the joys of Jem's family, Alice reflected, was that they all fell
in love at first sight. They had no sooner met than they "changed
eyes." They felt the instant pang of Cupid's fiery, poisoned dart. A
dizzying speed had so far characterized all their courtships. They
were like people in storybooks.

"To tell you the truth, it was all most terribly embarrassing for
Patch," Jem was saying, "because Modigliani came up behind her just
as she was sketching Michelangelo's David. She was right in the
middle of drawing the curls around David's beautiful, foliated penis."

Alice found that the word *penis* caused the hair follicles on her
forearms to contract with shock. She couldn't remember having heard
anyone utter it before. It was a word one tried not to dwell on in
biology textbooks.

"I don't know if you've ever really scrutinized David's penis," Jem
said, "but he looks as though he's just had his pubic hair styled by
Vidal Sassoon."

Alice couldn't remember ever having looked at David's penis. She
would probably have predicted that it was broken off, like nearly all
the male appendages on old statues. In general, leafing through art
books could leave one with the disturbing impression that male parts
were not only bizarre to the point of being unbelievable, but they were
quite immoderately hazard-prone.

"Of course, quite the worst of it," Jem continued, "is that David has
a foreskin. It hadn't occurred to Patch as at all incongruous before, but
once there was this gorgeous talmudic scholar breathing into the nape
of her neck—well, it made her blush."

"Oh golly!" Alice said. "Oh cringe!"

"Anyway," Jem said. "Modigliani just stood there and smirked his
dimpled smirk. He said, all *sotto voce* into her ear, 'Who is this very
fine man, can you tell me?' Well, Patch said shyly that it was David,
from the Bible. 'You mean the same David who won King Saul's
beautiful daughter with the gift of an hundred Philistine foreskins?'

he said. Naturally, Patch's neck went absolutely scarlet. She dropped her pencil with a clatter. Modigliani picked it up and gave it back to her. A pencil is very significant at such moments."

Alice downed the last of her toffee. "A pencil?" she said.

"Oh definitely," Jem said. " 'Pencil,' 'penis.' It's obviously the same word. Did you know that David had auburn hair? It says so in the Bible."

"You are lucky, Jem," Alice said. "To be so brainy."

During the hour that Jem was at mass, Alice put her clothes on and went down the road to Flora's house. She had not seen Flora since the funeral, where Flora had avoided her eye. She reached the threshold of Flora's front garden and paused. The draggy, unlined curtains still hung drawn at the lofty windows and the crop of dandelions, ever present on the unkempt lawn, was rather more profuse. Alice walked down the path with her heart in her mouth. She entered the porch and rang. There was a faint scuffle from within and then silence. Nobody came to admit her. After a while she retreated, shaking slightly, to the road.

"Hello," Jem said, appearing suddenly at her elbow. "You should have come with me. The priest was lovely. He had auburn hair. Like David." Alice blinked away a tear. "Who lives there?" Jem said.

"Flora," Alice said. She added quickly, "But tell me some more about Patch. Is her boyfriend an artist?"

"Oh no," Jem said. "He's an accountant." Jem had never as yet disappointed her, but Alice found this disappointing. And just when she most needed buoying up. She did so want the best for Patch and she could not help thinking that being an accountant was not very different from buying and selling executive units. She wondered, was accountancy romantic? Saul was an accountant in the City, Jem said, with a plate-glass office and two secretaries. That was his name. Saul Gluckman.

"Oh, she wouldn't want an art student," Jem said confidently. "Oh no. One can get pretty sick of all those unwashed, pansified junkies in the art school. Saul is such a divinely fastidious man and art students all smell of clay. They have printer's ink under their fingernails. No. Saul is not only as beautiful as an angel, he's also a little bit rich. That's fun for Patch, you'd have to admit." Put like that, Alice conceded that, yes, perhaps accountancy could have its attractions.

"Patch is not a manager," Jem said. "She was crying out for a man with managerial skills. Now she and Saul have gone into business together—well, in their spare time, that is."

"What do they sell?" Alice asked.

"Gnomes," Jem said.

"Oh, not gnomes!" Alice wailed, but Jem overrode her anguish.

"They're very good gnomes," she said. "Not those crass red plaster things you get in gardening shops."

"Still . . . ," Alice said. "I mean, gnomes—"

" 'Quality Gnomes of Knightsbridge,' " Jem said. "That's what they're called. Patch designs and makes all the gnomes individually, out of high-glazed bone china. Then she sells them for absolutely pots of money. Saul keeps the books and sends in lists of figures to the taxman, which gets her huge deductions."

"But nobody buys gnomes," Alice said. She knew that her own mother, who was one of life's great consumers, would sooner have owned a lilac shag-pile lavatory seat cover than consider lowering the tone of her garden with a gnome.

"Oh, heaps of people," Jem said. "Just so long as they're expensive enough, people think it's wildly avant-garde to have a gnome or two in the garden. Especially if he's winking or flashing."

The visit to Flora's had left Alice prickly. "Gnomes don't flash," she said. "I admit they wink."

"They flash," Jem said. "They always have those bulging paunches with their fly buttons about to burst off. I would say that gnomes were definitely bacchanalian." Patch, Jem said, had just been commissioned by a descendant of Kaiser Wilhelm's to conjure a whole gaggle of gnomes to inhabit the recesses of the conservatory. "So, you see," she said, "Patch is doing gnomes By Appointment to Foreign Royalty." Alice had no immediate answer to this. "Gnomes are alternative," Jem said. "They have a sort of 'inglenook' chic." Alice laughed. Her mind shed Flora. Jem was wonderful. And one of the greatest things about her was the way she turned all your cherished assumptions upside down.

"Jem?" she said, because there was something puzzling her about Patch and the talmudic scholar. "If Patch is always going to confession—and then she must go straight back home and—and . . ." She meant that Patch would be forever seeking absolution for the same frequently recurring sin of the flesh.

"Oh," Jem said casually. "But only Protestants care about such trivial little sins. People like Oliver Cromwell and Miss Aldridge. Catholics don't get that fussed about a bit of fornication."

"Don't they?" Alice said.

"Jews mind terribly, of course," Jem said. "You're supposed to be taken outside the city walls and stoned to death." Alice blinked at her. Jem laughed. "Just as well that Manchester hasn't got walls," she said.

Alice was eager for her parents to admire and love Jem just as she did—and yet they were inexplicably short on rapture. What was worse, Alice had overheard them after the visit discussing Jem behind her back.

"And the state of the girl's shoes!" she heard her mother remark. "Don't tell me that you failed to notice them, Harry. One can only wonder what sort of home the child comes from."

Alice heard the crackle as her father lowered his newspaper. Then she heard him utter a short, patronizing laugh.

"And the chat that girl has in her!" he said. "Talks the hind legs off a donkey." A donkey? Jem's inspired and ever more captivating discourse? How dared they! Alice felt the first painful thrust of a wedge threatening to divide her from her parents.

"But, Harry, *such* talk!" Mrs. Pilling said. "The impertinence! The personal remarks. 'Rum in the chocolate mousse, Mrs. Pilling? Or is it curaçao?' I'd like to give that girl curaçao!"

"Cheer up, Valerie," said Alice's father. "It won't last. Our Alice won't stand for all that faldeelah for long."

Mrs. Pilling had failed to mention here that she felt disquiet over the disappearance of a five-pound note from her handbag that Sunday afternoon. She had also failed to mention the absence of a silver bracelet Harry had bought her in Spain. Was it possible that she could have lost them? The money *and* the bracelet? And really, one did not want to provoke anything. Not now. Not with all the upset poor little Alice had had over Mr. Fergusson's dying.

"What about Flora?" Mr. Pilling said. "She not come back to school yet?"

ALICE COULD HARDLY remember a time without Flora. They had been at nursery school together. Flora was then a small, dark-haired girl, smaller even than Alice, with prominent teeth and shabby clothes. She had spent all her time at the painting easel while other children hustled for tricycles or jammed plastic bricks into the playdough. She had endlessly painted houses. There had been something exceptional about Flora's paintings, even then. The houses were not frontally presented, but contrived from a variety of angles with an unerring grasp of perspective. They were also quite remarkable for their meticulous attention to detail. If a line of washing hung between two trees in one of Flora's paintings, then the laundry represented there—down to each perfect scallop of lace on each perfect pair of knickers—bore testimony to an infant mind of relentless and perhaps obsessional application. The sun that shone down upon Flora's houses was never that facile, childish orb that wears a smile and trails its rays like a spider's legs. It was a faceless and intricate meshwork of glowing light rays, complex and unwelcoming.

Alice, who did not care for the rough-and-tumble of the nursery school, had nonetheless not immediately gravitated toward this other quiet, thoughtful child, perhaps because there was something austere about Flora; an emotional constraint that made her less than seductive. In fact Alice could not remember having spoken to Flora before the night, almost two years later, when the infant class had rehearsed its Christmas play.

On that occasion, Flora had been cast in the star part. Flora, who had little clout in the infant group's pecking order, was to play the Christmas Fairy. Alice, meanwhile, had been cast as a currant in the Christmas pudding. As an unassuming child with no expectations of stardom, Alice had weathered the casting disclosures with perfect equanimity, but her mother's disappointment had been sufficient to provoke Mrs. Pilling to intercede privately with the drama teacher. Miss Hemsworth had bowed to parental pressure only to the extent of offering to promote Alice one notch in the hierarchy of vine fruits and to recast her as a raisin.

"But such a pretty little blond girl," Mrs. Pilling said. "Surely—?"

"Unfortunately she stammers," Miss Hemsworth said firmly. "We couldn't possibly give Alice a speaking part."

On the night of the dress rehearsal, Alice sat dutifully zipped into her flaccid sphere of brown satin. She looked every inch an outsize brown raisin with wrinkled, stockinette knees. Meanwhile, before her eyes, Flora was metamorphosing. Alice had not been aware before that night that Flora possessed an ability for metamorphosis, but the drama teacher had somehow perceived it through all Flora's pallor and shabby clothes. She stood in a garment of white tulle and had just placed a glittering tiara on her sleek, dark head, when Alice, much affected by Flora's sudden magic and wishing somehow to be drawn up into it, reached out to her with a question.

"What are you g-getting-g-ging-ging. Getting for Christmas, F-lf-lf-?" she said. "Flora?"

Flora stroked her wand. "My big present is going to be a hot-water bottle," she said confidently. "So that I won't feel cold in bed."

Alice was both astonished and embarrassed. She did not dare, after that, to inquire what Flora thought her smaller presents might be, especially as she knew that her own parents were giving her a toy grocery shop for her "big present" that year.

Alice, as the only child of indulgent and comfortably-off parents, had always been liberally endowed with material goods. The Pillings had observed their little daughter falling in love with the grocery shop during an autumnal visit to Hamley's, and they had ordered one for her at once. They always took her to Hamley's after her visits to Dr. Neumann, though Alice had never demanded it. She enjoyed herself so much at Dr. Neumann's that she never felt the need of presents afterwards. To go there was like a visit to a storybook grandfather. First Dr. Neumann would conspire with her to send her parents off so that he and she could play really silly little games together all on their own. She always laughed so much with him because he had such a stack of funny little rhymes that he made her repeat and say out loud. And he always forgot them and muddled them up, so that she would have to correct him and say them properly. "Do forgive me, Alice," he would say. "But I am such a forgetful and foolish old man." It was the greatest fun to help him out and remind him how they went.

"I think your f-fairy dress," Alice said, "it's all l-l-l. It's all f-floaty and nice."

Mrs. Pilling came backstage just then to help with zips and tights. She noticed the little fairy girl in conversation with her daughter and promptly invited her to tea. Since Alice was an only child, Mrs. Pilling was constantly alert to the need for compensating her with worldly goods and a well-contrived social life. She was an effective agent for her daughter, who in later years recognized it as no accident that her mother had become a successful estate agent. Agenting was a natural inclination with Mrs. Pilling. She liked to see her clients well provisioned.

Flora came just after Christmas—a time when Mrs. Pilling was even better equipped than usual to place before her daughter's guest a spread of great variety and delight. Afterwards she supervised the little girls as they made pink and white coconut ice at the cooker. Then they had taken it upstairs and eaten it, squatting on the floor of the toy grocery shop in Alice's pink and white bedroom. The toy grocery shop was the size of a Wendy house and had a striped canvas awning over a real display window, while inside its shelves bulged seductively with toy provender. Out in front it had a freestanding barrow with brightly colored imitation fruits that smelt like the real thing, if "scratched-and-sniffed."

Flora had been much impressed by the amenities that afternoon and Mrs. Pilling had delighted in hosting her. Such a thin, pale, graceful child and so easily pleased! Mrs. Pilling positively itched to purchase little frocks for Flora and to fix a brace to her protruding front teeth. She began at once referring to Flora as Alice's "little friend" and she soon instituted a regular visiting day.

As time went by, the grocery shop made way for a teenage dolls' house and the girls graduated to playing with two straw-blond Sindy dolls, which Alice's mother kept adequately supplied with luxury consumer durables. The dolls owned everything from a miniature, functioning hair dryer and a plastic Jacuzzi bath to a gypsy caravan and a riding stable full of plastic horses. Alice's father had made the Sindy dolls a dream home at his workbench in the garage. The dream home boasted a fitted, mahogany kitchen and a stone-clad fireplace.

Thus liberally equipped with props, Alice and Flora occasionally took to enacting for the Sindy dolls a fully operatic double wedding. The ceremony leaned heavily on one they had seen in an old fifties movie on the television one Saturday, and featured identical slipper-satin wedding gowns as pink and white as coconut ice. Gradually, as the props waned and the girls grew, the wedding became their own. Flora and Alice would curl up on Alice's bed to envisage themselves as those lovely pink and white brides. Carrying ivory prayer books and lily of the valley, they would float down the aisle before a throng of ringletted bridesmaids dressed in clouds of flounced organdy. A barrel-chested Welsh baritone, like a cousin of Richard Burton's, would sing "I'll walk with God" from the pulpit.

Only the bridegrooms remained a little shadowy. While they had played weddings with Sindy dolls the girls had used a boy soldier doll in battle dress who had deputized for both, but it was hard to imagine bridegrooms for themselves. They were really not much interested in husbands. Far more so in their children. Alice decided to have lots and lots of children and all of them with lovely names like Amanda-Jane and Arabella and Dominic and Ganymede. Her children would wear velvet knickerbockers and Kate Greenaway frocks and would go to boarding school in a Swiss chalet along with Flora's children, where they would all be the best of friends.

"But too many children will be expensive," Flora said. "I'm having two and mine aren't called such silly names as yours. Mine are called Andrew and Janet."

"All right," said Alice, who was by nature accommodating. "Those are nice names, Flora." Sometimes the girls drew pictures of their children. Only then the sad thing was that Alice's children never looked the way she knew they really looked. That was because she was no good at drawing. The poor little things stood, face forward like mug shots, their hands perpetually in their pockets and seeming as if they were afflicted with water on the brain. She felt as if she were letting them down. Flora's two children looked so nice when she drew them, because Flora could draw so capably. They had properly jointed limbs and hands poised to pluck apples or to catch beach balls.

"I w-w-wish you w-would-would draw them for me, Flora," Alice said, but Flora would not.

"If I drew them, then they would be my children," she said. Alice accepted this, since it was asserted with such sureness. She was ill-equipped to appreciate that Flora had not much give-and-take. In all their games it was Alice who reached out, Flora who vetoed. Curious, when, from the outside, it was so apparent that Alice was the donor and Flora the recipient; the little matchgirl at the gate. There was always a kind of holding back with Flora. Unstated, unformulated, but subtly manifest in her behavior was the expectation that, while Alice was possessed of the golden spoon, she herself held the key to the future.

FLORA'S FATHER was a miser. He was an educated and scholarly man of the drier and dustier sort, in command of a decent professional income, but it distressed him to part with money. In spite of this affliction—or paradoxically, because of it—the family lived in a large, neo-Georgian house in what Alice's mother, since the advent of her career as a house agent, had taken to calling "a heritage-style period property in a sought-after prime locality."

Mr. Fergusson had married late in life and was already set in his ways. He was a silver-haired ascetic, handsome in a pale, cadaverous way, and already close to fifty. Flora's mother was a shy young music student with a small, pointed face and a graceful, gliding carriage bearing witness to many years at the exercise bar in ballet classes. Upon her marriage, Mrs. Fergusson, being otherworldly and much in awe of her husband, had immediately allowed herself to be plucked from the music school and absorbed into his abstemious, bookish, bachelor life in an ill-appointed tenement house off the Fulham Road.

There, for the next three years, she shared a greasy old gas cooker on an upstairs landing with three cantankerous, aged residents from the floor below and carried washing-up water in a plastic bucket from the bathroom two floors down. Having done this right through her pregnancy, the young Mrs. Fergusson's carriage had gradually become less graceful and the doctor had been obliged to prescribe elastic support bandages and finally surgery for severe varicose veins.

Since there was no refrigerator in the apartment—Mr. Fergusson having declared such an appliance an unnecessary luxury in a temperate climate—Mrs. Fergusson had been required to shop daily for their admittedly frugal requirements. When the baby came, she dragged both the shopping and the pram up the three flights of stairs each morning—a feat made necessary by her elderly neighbors, who refused her permission to leave the baby's carriage in the hall. She ran this gauntlet under the vigilance of their stony eyes each morning, and observed them with a faint heart as they scrutinized the stairway for any resulting scuff marks. Mr. Fergusson, naturally, remained aloof from such trivial domestic difficulties, which was perhaps just as well, since he would very likely have declared in favor of the elderlies.

The demands of her domestic duties left Mrs. Fergusson little time for her music, though she had been considered one of the more promising students at the music school. Her Scarlatti scores languished, leprous with neglect, in a damp gas cupboard from which they emerged only with the move to the prime locality four years later. There had been "no money" for a piano and no room for one either, since all available space in the apartment had been taken up either by the sleeping area, which was cordoned off by a sagging cretonne drape, or by the dining area, which was occupied by a paint-stained plywood table and matching chrome-legged chairs. A curious, bench-like settle, covered in scarred green rexine, ran the length of one wall and looked as if it had been discarded from one of British Rail's more modestly appointed waiting rooms. So the house was devoid of music. It went without saying that the elderlies, who regularly banged on the ceiling with broom handles at the sound of a footfall on the floorboards, would have considered Scarlatti sufficient grounds to petition for the Fergussons' eviction.

The arrival of the baby had made things additionally difficult for Mrs. Fergusson, who had never been welcomed in a house full of hard-eyed geriatrics. Her husband, with his sober habits and prematurely ossified mind, had always been regarded as "a proper gentleman"—an honorary old-age pensioner almost—but Mrs. Fergusson's youth, for all that she was timorous and biddable, jarred against the house tradition and her baby was considered an outrage.

Flora's mother had at first studied assiduously to ingratiate herself with the tenants through excessive acts of servitude. She had polished the cracked linoleum on the landings, shined up the brass door handles and scraped decades of carbonized filth from the cooker until a submerged pattern of blue and white mottling had appeared from the oven walls to reward her. The tenants, however, had either considered her efforts an impertinent assault upon the house lifestyle, or they had allowed her labors to pass unnoticed and unacknowledged. Invariably, within the week they had left porridge pots to boil over on the newly scrubbed hobs and had greased up the splash back with layers of congealed mutton fat.

From then on Mrs. Fergusson had striven instead to become acceptable through invisibility. She had assumed, for the rest of her days, a kind of greyish camouflage that worked its way deep into her being. Exiled from the music school and denied the train fare to visit her parents, she had become effectively orphaned in the clutches of her husband—a predicament she resolved by assimilating Mr. Fergusson's attitudes with all the immoderate zeal of a sycophant.

Thus it was that the woman Alice knew throughout Flora's childhood was mean-minded, dyspeptic and grudging. She held her mouth permanently drawn into a tight, disgruntled little knot like an anal sphincter. For Alice she possessed an aura of shredded suet and Milk of Magnesia. Alice had watched her sometimes as she stood at her kitchen table, rolling gluey balls of mashed potato for the evening meal on a grey, floured board, or contriving dumplings like outsize lumps in school tapioca pudding. Alice, whose own household leaned toward hedonism in matters of food, was thoroughly puzzled by the sight of Flora's mother conserving used tea bags in old jam jars and grumbling about her lodgers' profligate use of hot water. Mrs. Fergusson grumbled about everything, it seemed to Alice—except her husband. She grumbled that Flora went through light bulbs too quickly and grew out of her netball socks. She grumbled about tuppenny price rises on washing soda and gravy browning.

The Fergussons' move from the tenement house had come about when Flora was three. At that time Mr. Fergusson had been thrown into a quandary by the offer of a job as curator of a metropolitan museum housing major manuscript collections. Since the act of parting with money had always pained him even more than the acquisition of it had given him satisfaction (and since he was well aware that a significant increase in his salary would result in an increased tax liability), the prospect of a larger yield to the Inland Revenue caused him many a sleepless night.

In due course, Flora's father resolved his dilemma by accepting the job and at the same time preparing to invest the entirety of his fiscal hoardings, plus a large proportion of his new income, in the purchase of a house so far above his means that his tax relief on the purchase would be considerable and the monthly outlay such as to justify a continued regime of the most rigorous domestic economy. His plan was by no means to have his family enjoy the comfort of less confined quarters, but to fill the house with lodgers, whose rent would be paid in cash and would consequently go undeclared into his coffers.

Without consulting his wife, Mr. Fergusson resolved not only upon the purchase of the heritage-style period property, but also upon inducing his own widowed mother to sell up her small semidetached house in Bournemouth, so that she might add her takings to the project in return for taking up residence within her son's household. This scheme had several benefits, as he perceived them. It meant that his mother's property was sold before death duties could rise to haunt him, and it made available a resident, unpaid childminder who would liberate his wife for some suitably lowly form of employment. This last would allow Mr. Fergusson to conserve even more of his own money without giving his wife too great a taste for the emancipating power of earned income. Furthermore, his mother would bring along with her sufficient furnishings and effects to render the purchase of additional household items unnecessary.

So it was that the young Mrs. Fergusson moved into her elegant, five-bedroomed house, with her husband, her child, her mother-in-law and a handful of cold, gloomy lodgers who wore their overcoats indoors from October right through March. She existed cheek by jowl with neighbors who owned two cars apiece and who manicured velvet lawns over summer weekends, after invigorating bouts of tennis. Against the tinkle of their Scotch tumbling over ice cubes, and the aroma of their charcoal-grilled al fresco lunches, Mrs. Fergusson let down the hems of such threadbare curtains as she could claw from her mother-in-law's collection and reassembled the cretonne drapes to hang, patched and joined, at the drawing room windows. Even after assiduous pressing, the fade lines of old hems showed up stubbornly against the panes and all the curtains refused to reach the sills, leaving unsightly inch-deep gaps. Thus it was that the house, over the years, took on the look of a shelter for battered wives and became a focus for agitation among the more zealous members of the residents' association.

The Fergusson family never experienced the joys of its gas-fired central heating system, since both Mr. Fergusson and his mother believed the achievement of warmth to be morally justifiable only after the hauling of coal sacks. Flora's father sanctioned the activation of the hot-water system for an hour once a week, on Sunday evenings, for purposes of bathing, while for washing dishes Mrs. Fergusson stood over the cooker in her well-appointed new kitchen, heating water in a tin whistling kettle of the sort made for boy scouts to hang over campfires.

Predictably, Mrs. Fergusson the elder did not materialize as an unqualified asset, though she had indeed added to the furnishings. She had brought with her four grubby old half-moon rugs, which were placed at the hearthstones of the Fergussons' Adam-style fireplaces, and she had contributed an assemblage of clumsy, wartime "suites" in walnut veneer. These equipped two of the bedrooms and helped to supplement the green rexine settle in the drawing room, while at the same time bestowing an air of forties Oxo-commercial coziness that married ill with the architectural pretensions of the Fergussons' elm-floored investment property.

The old woman ensured that the aura of geriatric vigilance that had permeated the tenement house followed Flora's mother to the suburbs. Mrs. Fergusson the elder, always eager to see slights to her person and her possessions, was wont ceaselessly to remind her daughter-in-law and her grandchild from whence the household valuables had come. She was much inclined—as Alice discovered to her terror— to pounce out from corners with triumphant accusations of rough handling. Flora had apparently become serenely accustomed to her grandmother's mean-minded rebukes, which accompanied her daily efforts to rake out ash from the grates.

"I'll thank you not to tread muck into that hearthrug, Flora!" the old woman would shriek vengefully. "You'll kindly remember where it came from!" But Alice as a small child was once reduced to tears by the old woman's wrath. She had provoked it by touching one of the potbellied Hummel figurines that stood about cluttering the mantelshelves.

Flora's grandmother had already been partially incontinent when she moved in and she had come accompanied by an ill-tempered lapdog with a similar affliction and with patches of untreated mange. Furthermore, she came with an old gramophone and a pile of Bing Crosby records that she played alternately with the Coldstream Guards doing a miscellany of Allied war tunes.

Mrs. Fergusson duly gained employment as a part-time piano teacher in the junior department of what became Alice's and Flora's school. Since she was without formal qualifications, her salary was satisfactorily low, while her position came with the fringe benefit of a free place for Flora until the child became eligible to compete for the twelve-to-sixteen scholarship.

When Mrs. Fergusson was not engaged upon her teaching duties, she continued as before to buy half-price broken biscuits from Woolworth's and to glean free, dropped vegetables from the leavings of the weekly market stalls. She made oatmeal porridge for breakfast each morning, and for lunch over weekends and school holidays she contrived a greenish, oil-globule soup out of bacon rinds and cabbage water. This potage, liberally seasoned with the kind of pulverized white pepper that Alice's mother reserved for throwing into burglars' eyes, had always disconcerted Alice almost as much as the heavy, moral virtue that Flora's parents made of one's ability to swallow gristle. Flora had become a great favorite with all the school dinner ladies, because her youthful training had ensured that she could bolt lumps of gristle the size of walnuts without gagging. Alice found it a disturbing accomplishment in her friend. She did not like to look at Flora across the table during school dinner, because swallowing gristle always made Flora lose her calm, dignified look and momentarily take on the aspect of a farmyard turkey.

There were things that Alice couldn't begin to understand about her friend. How could a person like Flora gulp green oil-globule soup? How could the Flora who could draw like an angel and play the *Well-tempered Klavier* in the assembly hall be the same Flora who nonchalantly forked up rubbery obscenities of beef cartilage and gulped them in a film of school gravy? What, in short, made Flora tick? At twelve she had duly qualified for the twelve-to-sixteen scholarship. Yet, though her artwork and her music were excellent, Flora had never seemed to be especially bright. However did she do it?

It made Alice uneasy sometimes, imagining what became of Flora when she wasn't there to look at her. Did she exist on an endless treadmill of theorems and conjugations? And why? Did her parents tie her to her desk each night? Or were her scholarly performances yet another feature of her ruthless singleness of purpose?

AFTER MR. FERGUSSON'S DEATH, both Flora and her mother absented themselves from school premises for very nearly a month. While this was quite long enough to provoke the odd murmur in the school staff room, Alice herself never ventured to question the family's claim to extended grief. Especially since the Fergussons' loss had come about as a direct result of interference on the part of Mrs. Pilling.

Alice had been helping her mother fill two trolleys with groceries in the local supermarket one Friday afternoon when they noticed Mrs. Fergusson at the other end of the aisle. Mrs. Fergusson had stopped rummaging in a basket of cut-price tins, and was looking up with an expression of modified elation.

"Brian," she said to her husband, who stood about two yards in front of her. "Brian, what about this for tomorrow night?" Alice saw that she was grasping a ham-shaped tin of cured pork shoulder. It was an item, dense with sodium phosphate and gelatine, such as her own mother disdained to purchase except for inclusion in her annual charity hampers for the old-folks' home at Christmas.

"Dear oh dear," said Mrs. Pilling in low tones to her daughter. "Would you look at the poor woman, Alice? Is there anything lifts her spirits like a bargain?" She shook her head with pitying condescension. "I don't know," she said. "Really I don't. Fourpence off ox tripe. Tuppence off shredded suet. Poor old Flora."

"Mum?" Alice said. "What do people do with shredded suet?"

"Oh well," said her mother. "They make puddings. But it's very out

· 51 ·

of fashion. That's unless you want to give your husband a heart attack."

"Won't Mr. Fergusson have a heart attack?" Alice said. Her mother gave her an affectionate squeeze and a small, wry smile.

"I doubt it, lovey," she said. "Mr. Fergusson'll go on forever—just for the pleasure of making that poor woman miserable." She tossed a stack of Indonesian condiments into her basket and winked. "That was naughty of me, Alice," she said. "Wasn't it?"

When the Fergussons came level, Mrs. Fergusson was still grasping the ham-shaped tin. She looked rather guilty, Alice thought, as if caught out in the pursuit of prohibited luxuries. She glanced at the tin and then addressed Mrs. Pilling woman to woman.

"Our wedding anniversary tomorrow . . . ," she said, "something a little bit special . . ." Her smile showed prematurely receding gums.

Mrs. Pilling could bear it no longer. "Your wedding anniversary?" she said. "Tomorrow? Millie, you will put back that ridiculous tin this instant because Harry and I are taking you out to dinner!"

"Oh no," said Mrs. Fergusson weakly. "Oh no. Thank you, Valerie, but we couldn't."

"Nonsense!" said Mrs. Pilling. "This will be my treat and I won't take no for an answer. We'll have a nice table for six at The Fisherman's Grotto and the girls shall come along too. What do you say, Alice? You and Flora?"

"Oh yes please," Alice said, thinking how generous her mother always was and how pretty her teeth were when she smiled. "Oh yes, if Flora's coming."

"Of course she's coming," Mrs. Pilling said. "Flora is practically one of the family."

Mrs. Fergusson was casting about awkwardly. "Oh, but we couldn't," she said. "No, no. Really we couldn't. Brian would get indigestion, just thinking about the expense—"

"The expense will be all mine, Millie," Mrs. Pilling said, with just a touch of put-down. "And I can assure you that I'll not get indigestion over it."

Mr. Fergusson was suddenly at her side and smiling his handsome, pallid smile at Alice's mother. "What nonsense you talk, Millie," he said, his sharp tone just a little bit embarrassing, Alice thought, in company like that. "Thank you, Valerie. We will accept with pleasure." Alice had noticed in the past that he possessed a manner bordering on old-fashioned gallantry with her mother, even though he behaved like a stingy old tyrant with his own poor rag-and-patch woman. Was that because her mother had an indigo eyelash tint and had her hair rinsed "champagne blond"?

"But, dear," wheedled Mrs. Fergusson miserably. "There's Mother. You know she won't be left with anyone, even if we could afford a sitter. She'd have one of her turns at the very idea."

"Left?" said Mr. Fergusson. "Left?" Like a bird, Alice thought, pick-picking at a worm in a flowerbed. "Who said Mother would be left?"

"But Brian, dear," Mrs. Fergusson crooned abjectly. "Valerie did say six. 'A table for six.' Now six would mean three Pillings, if Alice comes, plus you and me and Flora—but perhaps Flora wouldn't mind . . ." Mrs. Pilling accepted that they had beaten her.

"My arithmetic!" she said, feigning error. "So sorry. A table for seven, to be sure." Alice wondered at the time how her mother meant to square the event with her father, who was fond of society in general, but he did like to choose his own and the elderly person in question was hardly one of his favorites. "A table for seven," her mother repeated, and her voice seemed slightly to lack conviction. "Until tomorrow then. Harry and I will call for you at eight."

The evening began every bit as badly as could have been expected, as Alice watched the elder Mrs. Fergusson, reeking of Woodbines and stale urine, climb ungraciously into her father's new estate car.

"And why ever they did away with the old running boards," she said, "I myself will never know. Grappling hooks is what I shall need to get myself into this monstrosity!"

She was wearing a peculiarly nasty old anorak, Alice observed. It was spilling out bits of its quilting through several cigarette burn holes along the forearms and she wore it over a pair of evil-smelling emerald green flares that were encrusted with mud around the bottoms of their twenty-four-inch trouser legs.

Neither was the restaurant particularly suitable, given that it was the choice of Alice's mother, who inclined toward culinary novelty and was therefore bound to favor a place like The Fisherman's Grotto—a newish establishment, which preeningly laid bare for its diners the workings of its open-plan kitchen and chose to underline the fresh-ness of its cuisine by scorning a printed menu in favor of reciting waiters. These made virtuoso monologues of the day's somewhat fussed-up provender. It materialized as a technique suitable only for frequent diners-out like Alice's parents and did not go down at all well with the uninitiated or with the hard of hearing. As for Alice and Flora, they were left feeling like failures at Listening Comprehension.

The Pillings' waiter, who could not but perceive these difficulties, was nonetheless thoroughly proficient in recitation and loath to play down his facility. He produced his catalog with lightning speed, glanced disdainfully at the lesser clientele, and began all over again. The old woman extracted a waxy-looking ear trumpet from her hand-bag and clapped it to her left ear.

"Is there a decent Scotch broth in the house?" she quizzed unpleas-antly, once the waiter was halfway through his soliloquy. Unhappily, there was not.

"But the fish soup," said Mrs. Pilling coaxingly. "That sounds nice. Try it, Mrs. Fergusson. Try the bully-bess."

The food took a great while to come, since the restaurant, for all its pretentious trappings, was manned by two affected young women in lycra footless tights who had the look of ballet-school dropouts run to ample haunch. In the interim the girls drank Coke, which filled their stomachs with air bubbles and took away their appetites. Their mothers sipped modestly at sparkling white wine. Mr. Fergusson and Flora's grandmother were in the meantime revealing a wholly unex-pected enthusiasm for neat Scotch whiskey, which they called to have replenished with remarkable frequency.

When it finally appeared, the food could hardly have been more unsuitable. Flora, who could bolt gristle without batting an eyelid, now flatly refused to eat her trout because it came with grilled eyes, while her father, who had ordered a plateful of mussels in sycophantic emulation of Alice's mother, appeared by then to be too drunk to lift his fork. Alice suddenly noticed, to her very great surprise, that Mr. Fergusson had given over his attention to fondling her mother's knee. The old woman, meanwhile, having slurped her way loudly through less than half a plateful of *bouillabaisse*, had abandoned the activity in favor of lighting Woodbines, which she stubbed out into her mussel shells.

In the midst of this, Alice was both touched and embarrassed to observe her father manfully making a stab at conversation. Possibly in order to rescue his wife by attempting to divert Flora's father from lechery, Mr. Pilling had fixed upon a topic that was closest to his heart and was directing his discourse relentlessly at Mr. Fergusson.

"Bricks!" he was saying. " 'Course there's a lot more to getting the little blighters from A to B than you might think, Mr. Fergusson. And when I remember the yard's deliveries in the old days! Way back now, Mr. Fergusson. 'Delivered' is hardly the word. Avalanche, more like it! Tipper lorries belching 'em out in clouds of filthy red dust! Oh dear, oh dear! And all those hours spent sorting out the broken ones. And nowadays, eh? Look at 'em nowadays, Mr. Fergusson! There they come, clean as a whistle. Plastic-wrapped. 'Course it's all metric packs nowadays. All centimeters these days." He sighed as he contemplated the radical nature of the advance. "Never a broken brick in sight, Mr. Fergusson. Not these days. No fuss. No mess. My lads wouldn't know a broken brick from I don't know what. It can make you think, Mr. Fergusson. Progress, eh?"

Alice thought that Flora's father wasn't even trying to look as if he were listening. Anyway, bricks wouldn't ever make Mr. Fergusson think. He was much too weedy. He spent all day with old manuscripts. It crossed Alice's mind suddenly that Flora's father looked like a butter bean. He was as washed out and concave as a butter bean, only not so starchy. He was like one of those butter beans that one grew on saturated cotton wool in junior school. The kind that went wrinkled and shed its thick white skin. Only Mr. Fergusson was saturated in whiskey. He was looking white and wrinkly as if he were about to shed his skin. Snakes also shed their skin. Mr. Fergusson was being quite horrible and slithery, the way he was sucking up to her mother. Perhaps he was more like a snake? And he hadn't even touched his mussels. They were all going to waste.

Alice saw her mother edge her thigh away from him with an effort at good humor and direct Mr. Fergusson's attention to his food. Her mother was looking lovely, Alice thought, in her elegant trousers and ivory silk shirt. She wore two gold bracelets on her wrist and she had gold earrings and shiny eye makeup. Alice felt no compulsion to emulate her mother in this respect, but she did feel proud of her; proud that her mother had so much drive and glamour; that she had the resources at the end of the day to take so much trouble and give pleasure with her appearance.

"Come on, Brian, eat up," she said. "Your beautiful shellfish. Look. Your mussels are all getting cold."

When Alice went to the ladies' room, she had been preceded by Flora and her mother. It perhaps explained why they had not seen her enter and cross to one of the loos.

"Don't be ridiculous, Flora," Mrs. Fergusson was saying. "You know very well he can't abide the woman. Vulgar little body that she is—and poor Mr. P. hardly capable of signing his name—"

"I want to go home," Flora said. Alice was frozen wretchedly behind the door of the loo.

"We can't go now," said Mrs. Fergusson. "Besides, your father likes a nice pudding."

When Alice returned to the table, it was just in time to see that Mr. Fergusson had begun to eat. He had evidently made a greedy rush upon his plate, because the mussels were almost all gone. At the same time, the old woman rose from her seat. She pursued a giddy course between the tables toward the ladies' room, but unfortunately the voluminous trouser hems defeated her. The emerald green flares, having slipped an inch or two, had become twin booby traps. Alice watched in horror as Flora's grandmother began to walk up the insides of her trouser legs. Then, before anyone could stop her, the old woman fell, groaning and cursing, in a drunken heap on the floor.

Mrs. Fergusson witnessed the fall from the other end of the restaurant. She leaped to the rescue along with Alice's father. Between them, and with some difficulty, they returned the elderly person to her seat. She was protesting loudly in rather embarrassing language and there was a compromising damp stain down one leg of the green flares. But the worst of it was that her upper dentures were missing. Flora retreated to her seat and sat, wooden with humiliation, making efforts toward invisibility. Yet, even in drink, the old woman's sharp instinct for nastiness rose to the fore.

"Flora!" she shrieked through shrunken lips, "I'll thank you to pick up my teeth, child, and not sit there gawping like a bilious goldfish!" The child began to rise, but Mrs. Pilling firmly stopped her.

"Stay right there, my darling," she said. "I'll see what I can do." Alice's mother approached the balletic proprietors, who helped her scan the floor. The teeth were duly uncovered and returned by one of the reciting waiters, who bore them icily toward the Pillings' table in the center of a starched white napkin. The teeth lay leering ghoulishly, tobacco brown, against their backdrop of boil-white linen.

"The sense of occasion has got to Mother, I'm afraid," said Mrs. Fergusson, twisting her fingers wretchedly in the placket of her blouse. But Alice's father, being a straight man, had had enough of hypocrisy.

"The old trout's pissed as a stoat!" he said. "For pity's sake, Valerie, get yourself and the children into the car, eh? Let's have the bill and get the hell out of here double bloody quick, if you'll excuse my French."

Alas, too late. As Mr. Pilling summoned the waiter, the old woman leaned ominously sideways toward a potted palm.

"Oh my sainted aunt!" said Alice's mother, and she hid her eyes behind one carefully manicured hand. "She's going to be sick, Harry. Do something, please!"

Mr. Pilling passed over his napkin, but the spillage was unfortunately not such as could be contained within its capacity. The old woman sat, beyond shame or restraint, belching forth audible rivulets of vomit that ran over her blouse front and down into the folds of the emerald flares. Flora's mother, who had risen to her feet, scraped and mopped in silent mortification. The balletic twosome advanced stonily, bearing a roll of paper kitchen towel and a large green plastic refuse bag.

Mrs. Pilling ushered Alice and Flora to the coatstand, where she donned her small silver fox fur while the two girls buttoned their gabardines. Alice saw her mother make a special point of taking Flora's hand.

"I'm sorry about the dessert trolley, girls," she said. "But never you mind, my darlings. We'll make a nice batch of chocolate brownies in the morning. What do you say to that?"

It was at that moment that Alice turned and looked back at the table. Her father was busy settling the bill and issuing the largest tip of his life. Mrs. Fergusson was making unsuccessful efforts to remove the impenitent old woman from her seat. But what really engaged her attention was Mr. Fergusson. She wondered if anyone else had noticed that he had begun to look very strange—or was it only the shadows and the candlelight? Could his face really have been changing its shape? Could Mr. Fergusson really have been shedding his skin? It seemed altogether consistent with the bizarre quality of the night. Flora's father had been so different from his usual self all evening and now his physiognomy was changing. His skin was a mess of violent, swollen lumps and his eyes, which had almost disappeared, seemed fixed at some point beyond the salt grinder. Alice tried not to stare at him, but she could not stop. Then Mrs. Pilling saw Alice's expression and she followed her daughter's gaze.

"Harry!" she cried out in agitation and distress. "Call a doctor! Call an ambulance! Oh for pity's sake, somebody, do something!"

When Alice at last began to confide the rudiments of this morbid occasion to her new friend, Jem showed every sign of taking it with the most "inappropriate levity."

"I expect he died from catching sight of the bill," she said. "Or else poor Mrs. Thingummy managed to slip ground glass into his *moulès*. Never mind, Alice. From what you've said about him, Flora is probably off lighting bonfires and dancing in the street."

"Oh, for heaven's sake," Alice said. "Don't."

"At least your mother was saved from 'a fate worse than death,' " Jem said brightly. "Imagine if she'd had him in the car all the way home. Or she might have been 'rudely forced' in the car park while your father was dishing out tips." She reclined expansively on the grass of the school playing field. " 'Jug, Jug,' " she said. " 'Twit twit twit.' " That's T. S. Eliot on the subject of violation."

Alice winced. "It was the mussels, Jem," she said. "He was allergic to shellfish. He only ordered them because he—because my mother—" She stopped. "But she didn't know. None of us knew. He'd never eaten them before."

"Three score years and never eaten a mussel," Jem said. "Ah me! And to think my parents eat them all the time. They're aphrodisiac, you know." She paused, waiting for Alice to recover her humor, but Alice remained as she was, staring down wretchedly into the grass of the playing field. "Serves him right for being so creepmouse about his eating habits. Forget about him, Alice. He sounds worse than creepmouse. He sounds like a slug. A 'creepslug.' " She glanced at Alice, who still did not respond. "Alas, the poor sot," she said. "The lecherous ignoramus. And to think of his soul dispatched 'unhouseled' to meet his Maker."

"Oh, but he wasn't an ignoramus," Alice said quickly. "He couldn't have been. He'd been to Cambridge and everything. Jem, he could even read Anglo-Saxon."

"He was ignorant in matters crustacean," Jem said firmly. "And that's unforgivable. Especially for a creepslug. A 'Giant Mollusc.' What did you do with him, by the way? Chuck him over the wall of the Protestant graveyard?" Alice made no response.

"Do you know?" Jem said, straining for her attention. "One of Maddie's boyfriends has made an academic study of snails. It's uncompleted, unfortunately." Alice said nothing. "It's uncompleted," Jem said, "because he doesn't have enough evidence. He keeps going off to the ends of the earth to check on exotic specimens, but then he always finds the French have got there first and they've eaten them all with garlic butter." Alice still said nothing. "He's a strange sort of man," Jem said. "He's not quite suicidal, but he emulates the Passion of Our Lord."

"What?" Alice said.

"He bears the stigmata," Jem said. "He has a wound in the side of his chest. It oozes blood in Holy Week."

"Oh yuk!" Alice said.

"He got septicemia last Good Friday," Jem said. "From all his relatives. They kept plunging their hands in it. That's how Maddie met him. In the Casualty." Alice did not respond. She was trying not to think of Mr. Fergusson as a Giant Mollusc, but she could not stop his funeral from flashing upon her inward eye. She heard the oration in the Chapel of Rest and she saw his coffin, so brash and new, being carried through the ugly modern graves with their granite tombstones and their nasty glass orbs of everlasting plastic flowers gathering condensation and mold. She saw her mother throwing earth and flowers into the pit. And Flora, stunned, avoiding her eye. Flora flanked by her two joyless female custodians in dowdy clothes. Suddenly, as her mind indulged a moment's surreal license, she envisaged Mr. Fergusson, airborne and in his clothes, a Giant Mollusc in his dark suit, as if catapulted through the air and over the wall of the cemetery. She wondered, would he land in the undergrowth or on the motorway, but there was no real landscape beyond the edges of her mind. He was leering horribly and especially at her.

"Still," Jem was saying, "at least he's Catholic."

"No, he isn't," Alice said. "He wasn't."

" 'Course he is," Jem said. "Protestants don't bleed in Holy Week." Alice looked at her rather absently.

"I've written some stories," Jem said. "You can read them if you like."

"Stories?" Alice said with interest and she shook off the Giant Mollusc. "What do you mean 'stories'?"

Jem shrugged modestly. "School stories," she said. "And a novel. The novel is a more sustained work of greater maturity."

Alice looked at her with amazement. "What?" she said.

"A sustained work of greater maturity," Jem said.

"You don't mean it's got chapters and everything?" she said.

"Oh, they've all got chapters," Jem said casually. "I've got them all under my bed in a box. I could get one for you right away."

"But the dorms are out of bounds until home time," Alice said. She had no sooner said it than she knew that it was not so. Not for Jem. Jem could open doors into the mountainside. Jem was already on her feet.

"Alice," she said cautiously, "I've never actually shown what I write to anyone else before."

Alice felt so profoundly honored that she almost wept. To have first access to Jem's most precious and private self! Access in advance of Patch, or Maddie, or the talmudic scholar. Access in advance even of the man of letters!

"Oh Jem—," she said, but words failed her. "Oh Jem—"

 ALICE MADE A START that afternoon during religious studies. Miss Paton, as luck would have it, was disposed to discuss "sudden bereavement."

"Slugdeath and the Giant Mollusc," Jem whispered to Alice at once, but Alice felt, nonetheless, that she needed escape from the topic. And what better escape than to bury oneself in the first of Jem's inviting stories?

Alice had used to enjoy religious studies in the junior school when Miss Brooks had always told them stories out of the Bible. Since she had received no religious education, either at home or in church, these stories occasionally engaged Alice with all the furious emotive power of fairy tale and myth, filling her with terror. Most dramatic among them, she remembered, were the sacrifice of Isaac, the boyhood of Samuel, and the Angel of the Annunciation. These three stories could make her hair stand on end.

Just to think of Abraham and Isaac! It was like Hansel and Gretel. Your parents could lure you into the woods and suddenly they were wearing different faces. Mr. Wolfman and Mrs. Witch Lady. Here is my murderer's knife. Here is my poisoned cake. Of course your parents wouldn't really, would they? Only sometimes in dreams. People could turn round and they weren't your parents. They had the wrong faces. And nothing was but what was not.

Then Samuel. Only to imagine it! Not only did your mother hand you over to some appalling, black-clad priest, just as if you were a harvest cabbage, or a pot of quince jam, but then the priest made you go to bed all by yourself in the temple every night. And then, on top of it all, you woke up because the voice of God was booming your name in all that terrifying, supernatural darkness. And the priest didn't tell you to tuck in with him for the rest of the night the way your mother would have done. No. He sent you back to your own dark room to wait for the voice to come again.

Last of all, there was the angel. No mere voice, but a real presence. Corporeal. Moving through locked doors. Alice had not been tutored in prayer, but if three things occasionally induced attempts at it, then these were those three things. Abraham and Isaac, the boyhood of Samuel and the Angel of the Annunciation. She prayed that God would find no special reason to single her out, either directly or by messenger. She petitioned against the glinting knife and the disembodied voice in the awful dark, and the angel of God in his white clothes. Alice had thought angels were women until the coming of that angel. Afterwards, she knew that angels were male. They had names like Michael and Gabriel.

The knife and the voice of God would on balance be less unthinkable than the angel. The feathered deputy, strong as iron for all his poncy dress. Moving inexorably through the fastened casement. Oh the horror of it! Please God—if there is a God—save me from the iron angel in his exquisite robes of silk.

These powerful and dream-haunting narratives did not pursue Alice into the Upper School religious studies class. The lessons there were dominated by moral education for responsibility. Miss Paton, who now led "discussion" from the floor, concentrated on social and family topics. This meant that the class was disposed, once a week, to pool its ignorance and bigotry on such matters as abortion, homelessness, alcohol abuse and bereavement.

"A sudden death in the family," said Miss Paton. "I would like you all to think about it, Form Three. How would you go about giving comfort to a bereaved friend?"

Jem's first story was called *The Divine Miss Davidene Delight*. It was handwritten in a series of lined exercise books stamped "Convent of the Ascension," which Jem had filched, in batches, from the stock cupboard of her previous school. Alice was drawn into the narrative with immediate and grateful pleasure, since Jem had wasted little time on the scenery and had plunged right into the story.

"I've seen her!" Jem had written, *"I have actually, truly seen her!" Diana's sapphire blue eyes half closed themselves in rapture as she spoke. "The divine Miss Delight is back from Lausanne and—would you believe it, Minerva my dearest—she is wearing the most glorious, the most exquisite new tailor-modish rig-out!" Minerva the Unmoved remained most formidably unmoved.*

"The woman is a walking clothes rail," she observed, hoping to dampen her friend's ardor, for she considered this passion of Diana's for the class mistress to be silly and most unseemly. *"How unsuitably and immoderately Miss Delight indulges in the purchase of unnecessary hats and shoes!"* she said.

"My sister cried buckets when her pony died," Claire said. "He had cancer."

"Our goldfish died yesterday," Lenora said. "My brother fed him sawdust."

"The most comforting thing one could do," Jem said, "would be to supplicate for the remission of the dead person's sin." For a moment Miss Paton stopped and stared at her. So did all of the girls. "Well," Jem said, a little defensively, because she felt the eyes of the class upon her, "surely? If the 'bereavement' was all that 'sudden,' then the dead person is very likely to have died in a state of unabsolved sin. It would be a comfort for his relatives to know that one was trying to save him from the everlasting bonfire."

"How dare you?" Miss Paton said. "A member of this class has recently suffered the tragic loss of a parent." Alice determinedly read on.

It was teatime at the Moated Grange School for Young Ladies, went Jem's text. *And the two "young ladies" in question were waiting in the bun queue to be served by the benevolent Christabel Lockwood. Christabel was the current bun monitor of the lower fifth.*

"Psst," Alice whispered, and she nudged Jem discreetly. "Don't you spell *current* with an *a*?"

"Only if it's *currant* as in Christmas pudding," Jem said. "What I mean there is 'of the moment.' "

"But not if it says, 'Christabel was the currant bun monitor—' "

"She wasn't the 'currant bun monitor,' for heavens' sake," Jem said. "She was the bun monitor for that week."

"Oh I see," Alice said. "Sorry, Jem. It's terribly good so far."

"It's not a work of great maturity," said Jem, who had written the story when she was ten years old, "but it's formative, I suppose." Alice read on.

"But Min," persisted the rapturous Diana. "Miss Delight is wearing the most perfect sea green silk. So altogether and utterly smart. And on her shoes, such exquisite rosettes."

"Alice," said Miss Paton kindly. "I had hoped that you, of all people, might add to our discussion."

"Yes, Miss Paton," Alice said, looking up. She thought wistfully how elegant it might have been to have had a class mistress clothed in tailor-modish sea green silk. Miss Paton was dressed from throat to hem in discouraging polyester Prussian blue. Alice involuntarily scanned her feet for signs of exquisite rosettes.

"Well now," said Miss Paton. "You could help us here, Alice, I'm sure. How would you go about giving comfort to a bereaved friend?"

Alice thought about Flora's averted eyes at the funeral and about the faint shuffle of feet behind Flora's front door. "P-p-p," she said. "I-I w-would-would l-l-l." She stopped and took a breath. Jem's story was lying in her lap. "I would give my f-friend a good book," she said. "To read. And t-t-t." She stopped. Miss Paton waited for a moment. Lenora Gripe began to snigger.

"To take her mind off her grief," Miss Paton said. "And give her strength? A thoughtful answer, Alice. Well done." She looked around the room to locate the source of sniggering. " 'A good book,' " she quoted sternly in the direction of Lenora Gripe, " 'is the precious life-blood of a master spirit.' Can anybody tell me which of our great writers said that?"

"Shakespeare?" Claire volunteered hopefully.

"No," said Miss Paton. "Not quite Shakespeare."

"Milton," Jem said. Miss Paton, being loath to encourage preco-ciousness, ignored her.

"Please, Miss Paton," Claire said. "Not Shakespeare. I meant Mil-ton. Wasn't it Milton, Miss Paton?"

"ALICE," JEM SAID, "would you keep all my stories for me?"

"Well, of course I'll keep them," Alice said. She was both surprised and honored by the request. "But, Jem, are you sure?" Jem was holding a pile of eight exercise books at the time. The girls had met at the far end of the playing field—a thing they had taken to doing half an hour before the morning's first bell.

"I don't mean just these," Jem said. "I mean all of them. I don't quite like to leave the whole box under my bed. Some idiot is bound to ferret them out and flash them round the dormitory." She paused, a bit hesitant. "I suppose you must have noticed that they all think I'm a bit peculiar."

"They're all stupid, that's why," Alice said. It didn't occur to her how dramatically, with the utterance, she was separating herself from the coziness of that dominant consenting world to which she had always, more or less, belonged. "Of course I'll keep them for you," she said. "But they're so good, Jem. Shouldn't you keep them at home? Shouldn't your father keep them for you? They're 'manuscripts,' aren't they? He could keep them for you in the summerhouse."

Jem took longer than usual to make reply. "Frankly," she said, eventually, "my father is a teeny bit of a fire hazard. He's rather absentminded, you see."

"What do you mean, 'a fire hazard'?" Alice asked.

"Well," Jem said. "Not only does he smoke like a chimney, but he's quite likely to use the odd manuscript for kindling."

"Oh never!" Alice said. "Oh no, he wouldn't do that!"

"Only on the chilliest of winter mornings," Jem said, amending the accusation with a sanguine laugh. "And then only when the anthracite's run out. He's got a little Russian stove in there. It gets greedy for food twice a day."

Alice gulped. "You must give them to me today," she said. "You must give me the whole box. I'll take them this afternoon. I'll phone my mother to fetch me in the car. Jem, I'll take care of those stories for you for as long as ever you need."

"Thank you, Alice," Jem said. "I know you will. You will always be my dearest friend." She turned quickly and flicked through the topmost of the exercise books before emotion became an embarrassment. Then she handed the batch to Alice.

The books constituted the first two thirds of her "novel." It was called *My Last Duchess.* Alice opened the first of the books and skimmed the first page.

Gabriella Alessandra Gallo, she read, *looked out from her bedroom window on to the Cuillin Hills. They loomed, black, enclosing, beyond the blacker waters of the loch. She was almost nine years old. Gabriella was young, but not so young that she could not remember those other hills which had risen from that other water which had filled the Golfo da Gaeta.*

"I will never forget you, Papa dearest," she said. "I know that I will find you again."

It was at this point Alice registered that Flora had come back to school. She was approaching across the playing field in the company of Claire Crouchley. Claire had taken on an air of guardianship and was walking slightly ahead.

"Hello, you two!" Claire called out. "I knew that we'd find you here. I know you always come here. I've been wondering what you do."

"Hello F-flora," Alice said. "Th-this is Jem." She put the books down beside her on the grass.

Alice, who had harbored an uneasy notion of coexisting with Jem and Flora, recognized within those next few seconds that this was not a possibility. Flora was holding back, saying nothing, but something right then about the choreography of the group made it apparent that Flora was pointedly lining up with Claire.

"Hello, Flora," Jem said. Flora ignored her. She was watching Claire, who had bent suddenly to swoop on the topmost of the exercise books.

"What are all these?" she said. " 'Convent of the Ascension'?"

"It's my old school," Jem said. "It's nothing." She made a move to retrieve the book but Claire stepped back, holding it tauntingly behind her.

"Oh come on, Claire," Alice said. "They're only books. Give them back. They're Jem's." Claire opened one of them and began, stumblingly, to read out loud.

"*Umm-bert-oh, her husband, the Duke, the Demon Padd-ronn*—padd-ronn?—*was dead*. Blimey!"

" 'Pah-drone-eh,' " Jem said. "It means the big smell at the top."

"Pah yourself," Claire said wittily. "We haven't all swallowed a dictionary. Anyway, what is it?"

"It's a story," Jem said. "Alice is reading it."

"All that's one story?" Claire said.

"It's a longish story," Jem said. "Alice is reading it, that's all."

"But those are exercise books," Claire said suspiciously. "You don't get stories like that in exercise books. And anyway it's all in your writing."

"Give me a break," Jem said. "It's in my writing because I wrote it." She took advantage of Claire's puzzlement to take back the book. Then she gathered up the others and handed them quickly to Alice. Claire's mouth was fixed half open. It was beyond her experience, Alice guessed, to grasp that people actually wrote "proper" stories. Novels appeared as if by virgin birth on the shelves of W. H. Smith alongside the comic papers and Christmas annuals.

"Say, Jem," Claire said. "If you're letting Alice read it then you've got to let me and Flora read it too." She paused, waiting for a response. Jem gave her none. "If I told Miss Aldridge you were here you'd be in trouble," she said. "And I've seen both of you bunking assembly." This was true. If Claire told Miss Aldridge, they would be in trouble.

"All right," Jem said. "I don't mind if you read it. So long as Alice can read it first. She's only just started it. She can give you a bit of it tomorrow."

Alice took Jem's box of stories home that night. She read *My Last Duchess* to the end of the first third. Though its period was twentieth century, the story was an ambitious and somewhat camped-up combination of bittersweet Highland romance and higher Renaissance intrigue. Its heroine, the beautiful Gabriella, was the offspring of a daring cross-cultural union between an impoverished Highland chieftain's daughter and a young, well-born Italian medical man. The story, which opened on the Isle of Skye, at once flashed back to recreate Gabriella's early life in a harsh rural idyll, set east of Naples, where her father had nobly elected to tend the discarded, ailing poor.

The story then described how the good doctor made his dutiful rounds by mule, performing emergency eye surgery, or tracheotomies, on the floors of peasant hovels. His patients, too poor to pay him in money, brought him gifts of new-laid eggs and jars of olive oil. Dr. Gallo had met his wife on the Isle of Skye during a tour of the Western Isles he had made as a medical student. He had undertaken it, being a devotee of travel literature, after having read Samuel Johnson's account of his travels in those islands.

Jem's text portrayed vividly not only the landscape of southern Italy, but the doctor's growing up; how, as a boy, he had sat for hours in the summerhouse together with his English tutor, reading Captain Marryat and Sir Walter Scott and the stories of the Mabinogion.

Next day, Alice dutifully brought in the first four exercise books and handed them over to Claire. Claire read them with scant attention, in the breaks and in the library period, sitting in a huddle with Flora, who was conspicuously uninterested in the project. But over the next three days, Jem's novel became the readiest vehicle for underlining Flora's severance from Alice. While Alice and Flora themselves hung back, the battle was waged between Jem and Claire, with *My Last Duchess* as the weapon.

"But why do they live in Naples when they're Scottish?" Claire said. "I mean, why don't they live in Scotland?"

"Because Gabriella's father's Italian," Jem said, "that's why. You'll have noticed that he's called Dr. Gionata Gallo and not Dr. Hamish McCleod."

"Bit thick, isn't it?" Claire said. "A Highland chief's daughter marrying a greasy Eyetie?'

"He's not a 'greasy Eyetie,' you ignorant bigot," Jem said. "He's from an old Neapolitan family. It's her mother's family that has no money.

Do you know anything about the Western Isles? Or about the history of Scotland?" Claire gawped, gracelessly. Jem seemed to feel quite bruised. "Just because Dr. Gallo chooses to treat the poor," she said, "and not hang about like his colleagues, growing fat on treating the rich, that doesn't make him a prole." Claire retreated into the text with Flora, but she was soon back again, this time faking great splutters of mirth. She had got to the place where a peasant woman had given the doctor a demijohn of home-pressed olive oil.

"Oil?" Claire said. "Can you imagine anyone paying the doctor in oil!"

"The first pressing of the olive," Jem said grandly, "is not a gift to be scorned."

Claire spluttered some more. "And I love this," she said. " 'Virgin' oil. Bit daft, isn't it?"

"Why don't you stop reading it?" Jem said. "And give me a break?"

"Oh no," Claire said. "Do let's carry on, Flora."

That night Alice read on. The story turned on the disappearance of Gabriella's father who, having enemies among the local men of property, had been suddenly framed on a drugs charge. A stash had been planted in his garden, under his olive trees. The doctor was arrested and thrown into a van. His wife and daughter never saw him again. The connubial idyll was abruptly shattered and the poor widow, broken by years of fruitless inquiries, eventually returned to the Highlands with her child, where her health and her mind gave way.

Alice wept over the vivid and moving depiction of Gabriella's broken mother, with her delicate, faded Celtic looks and her increasingly tenuous grip on reality. But Gabriella herself grew strong in beauty and wisdom. At seventeen she entered the medical school at Aberdeen, where she fell in love with Angus, a fellow student. Life, however, was not simple for Gabriella, who was tormented by memories of her father's disappearance and—liberated, finally, by her invalid mother's death—ready to continue the search for him.

In order to fund these inquiries, Gabriella took on a modeling job. Jem had accomplished all this delightfully. The convivial bustle of student life and the fine, brave, handsome Highlander who jumped off the pages in his climbing boots were all there to savor and relish.

So were the subsequent descriptions of Gabriella's glamorous model-ing life, as her job swept her off on sudden flights to Morocco and Bermuda and Milan. And then the pitiful climax, as it became impos-sible for Gabriella to continue with her studies. She made her terrible choice in favor of earning money to fund her quest and dedicating her life to finding her father. The decision resulted in a heartbreaking severance with the Highland medical student. Angus, like Miss Al-dridge, could not get on with foreigners. Nor with Gabriella's new world of high fashion and fast flights. He was a man's man; a straight man; a man for the heather and the saddle and the salmon pool. Angus retired, bruised, to his Highland solitude and his textbooks, vowing never to marry.

Alice brought in the exercise books with a heavy heart next morning. She handed them over to Claire. Even Claire was mercifully silent that day and returned the batch to Jem without a word.

Gabriella, meanwhile, Alice discovered that evening, was as lonely in heart and as frustrated in her quest as she was successful in her career. Putting Angus determinedly behind her, she eventually made a love-less marriage with the dazzling Umberto, an aristocratic Neapolitan who carted her off to produce a son and heir for his *palazzo*—his other two wives having both died childless in mysterious circumstances. Jem had succeeded in creating around Umberto an extraordinary aura of decadent and encrusted grandeur, of powerful sexual magnetism and menacing, Italianate intrigue. Umberto was, of course, the very prince of the drug ring. The Demon Padrone himself, anxious to nobble Gabriella in her attempts to discover her father and at the same time to ensure his posterity by the espousal of a young and fecund wife.

Jem had contrived the denouement so artfully, with such an eye for pulling out the stops, that Alice slept with her bedside lamp on all through that night for fear of waking to find that the Demon Padrone was standing over her bed. Just before she fell asleep, Alice read that Gabriella had made a chilling discovery. Childless and berated for it by her impatient and ruthless husband, Gabriella walked secretly one evening in the ancient, forbidden burial ground where the family's hunting dogs had been entombed. While doing so, she found that the earth had thrown up the skeleton of a human hand among a smattering of canine bones—a hand upon which her father's ring was still encircling the bone. Hiding the precious relic in the cleavage of her evening gown, Gabriella swiftly left the graveyard and hastened, next, to bury the object in a stone plant pot on her balcony, under a brilliant cyclamen.

"She *plants* it?" Claire said. "She plants the hand?"

"It's not unprecedented actually," Jem said, "to obscure parts of the dead in plant pots. It happens in 'Isabella; or, The Pot of Basil.' "

"Who's Basil?" Claire said. "Is that her father's name, by any chance?"

"Basil is a plant," Jem said. "The man whose remains were in the pot was called Claudio."

"So was that her father's name then?" Claire said. "Clordio?"

" 'Cloud-i-o,' " Jem said. "As in cumulonimbus. Gabriella's father was called Gionata, you may remember."

"Oh, excuse me," Claire said sarcastically. "Anyway, why's she so sneaky about being at the doggies' graves?"

"Women aren't allowed into the burial ground," Jem said. "It has to do with the cult of Diana."

"Crumbs," Claire said. "Who's Diana when she's at home?"

"The goddess," Jem said. " 'Queen and huntress, chaste and fair.' She's rather inclined to be jealous."

"But I thought Italians were Catholics," Claire said. "I didn't know Catholics had a goddess."

"Of course they have a goddess," Flora said. It was almost the first whole sentence Alice had heard her utter in days. Jem looked up and blinked at her.

"I beg your pardon?" she said.

"I think you heard me," Flora said. She paused for a moment, poised, impressive, like a hanging judge about to pass sentence. "Just one query," she said. "I assume she never gets back to her medical school? Your 'heroine'? In other words, she's a dropout. Why bother writing a book about a dropout?" Jem stared at her. So did Alice and Claire. They were all of them aware that in the question lay a declaration of cold war.

The war was won by Flora. Jem dropped out. That is, while Alice never believed that Jem had "dropped out," all the others believed it. True, Jem had dropped unexpectedly, cruelly, out of Alice's life, leaving no address. She had departed at sixteen, just as suddenly as she had come. Since she was not in general popular among the girls, most of the class had little difficulty in dismissing her departure as petulance when she had failed to get the Upper School scholarship.

"She was always a bad sport," Claire said. Jem had, in truth, got the highest mark in the scholarship examination, but Miss Trotter, since the result had been "so close," as she said, had felt entitled to use her discretion in making the award to Flora. She had called in both girls to her office and had explained the matter very frankly. All of her staff had agreed, she said, that of the two Flora was the more "steady." Flora was the more direct. Flora was the more likely to bring honor to the school in all her future achievements. Jem surprised Alice by leaving that same afternoon. She appeared from the dormitories after lunch, no longer in school uniform, and was once again dragging the canvas toolbag.

"But wait!" Alice said. "Jem, wait for me!" To accompany Jem off the premises and all the way to the railway station meant absenting herself from geography, but Jem had taught her how to manage these things with something like aplomb.

"Please don't go," she said, but Jem only smiled. A small wistful smile such as Alice had not seen on her friend before. "Look—I know it's unfair about the scholarship," Alice said, talking fast, "but at least your family aren't such misers as Flora's. I mean, they'd go on paying your fees, you see. Not like the Fergussons. I reckon that's why Miss Trotter did it, don't you? Please, Jem. Don't go."

Jem looked for a moment as though she meant to speak but in the end she said nothing. Then the girls went through the barrier and on to the platform.

"I'll write to you," Jem said as the train pulled in.

"But what about your stories?" Alice said, remembering suddenly, and clutching at straws. "You can't go yet, Jem. I've got all your stories!"

"Hang on to them," Jem said, and she touched Alice's arm before boarding the train. "I'll be back."

"Soon?" Alice said. "Will you be back soon?" Then the guard blew his whistle. "But I don't even know your address!" Alice cried, over the first rumblings of the wheels.

"I'll write to you," Jem said again. "Alice, you will always be my dearest friend."

"What?" Alice called, because she couldn't catch the words and Jem was getting further away.

"I'll never forget you," Jem called out, but the sound of her voice was drowned in a roar of gathering speed.

 MRS. PILLING hated to see Alice moping in her room over a box of old exercise books. She opened the curtains and let the sunlight in.

"At your age you should be out enjoying yourself," she said. "Come on, lovey. You'll get over it. You'll make new friends." In her heart Mrs. Pilling felt enormous relief at the passing of Jem McCrail, but it made her angry that Alice had been treated so badly. "If the wretched girl can't write to you," she said, "or even pick up the telephone, then she doesn't deserve your friendship."

After Directory Inquiries had proved itself quite unequal to the business of uncovering either Saul Gluckman or Patch McCrail, Alice pinned all her hopes on Quality Gnomes of Knightsbridge, but here too, it seemed, the system fell short of full efficiency. As to Jem's father, Gordon McCrail, and his French wife, Minette, while Alice knew all about their wallpaper and their personal habits, she did not know about their domicile. Alice, though she had always longed for it, had somehow never got round to meeting Jem's parents throughout the two years of their friendship. There were always so many persons to be attended to in the household when the school holidays came along. Authors breezed into the McCrail ménage, clutching manuscripts completed in tax havens abroad. Or Catholic aunts in great numbers appeared from Normandy, clutching baskets of pungent cheeses wrapped in straw. Jem had had the most wonderful stories about all of them.

"Why not call on Flora?" Mrs. Pilling suggested hopefully. "The two of you were always such very good friends."

Alice took to visiting the library and poring over books. She read her way, with difficulty at first, through all the books to which Jem, over the years, had thrown out such casual and easy reference. She read *The Leopard* by Giuseppe di Lampedusa. She read *Hamlet*. She read Keats. She read T. S. Eliot. She read the Gospel According to Saint Mark. She read John Donne and Hopkins. She read Samuel Johnson on his travels in the Western Isles. Most of all she read the libretto of *The Magic Flute*. She read it over and over, in English at first, trying to catch at its mysterious truths. Then she opted for an out-of-school course in German.

Mrs. Pilling, who had never intended that her daughter should become a bluestocking bent over grammar books, bought her a fake "fun fur" with corded pink toggles and shiny boots and a personal stereo and some tickets for *The Rocky Horror Show*. Alice left the fun fur untouched in the box and filled the personal stereo with cassettes of *The Magic Flute*.

"Alice, the girl was a thief, I must tell you," Mrs. Pilling said one day. "You're old enough to know the truth now. I'm sorry but it's a fact." And she reported to her daughter the disappearance of the five-pound note and the silver bracelet.

"I don't believe you," Alice said fiercely. "You always disliked her."

"Darling—," said her mother. Alice put her fingers in her ears.

"Stop it, I'm not listening," Alice said. "If you say that again, I will hate you forever." It caused a widening of that distance between mother and daughter that had begun with Jem's weekend out.

Not that Jem had intended the Pillings to dislike her. Far from it. Jem had repeatedly and sincerely told Alice how much she liked and admired Alice's parents.

"Your father's a love," she assured her friend. "I think he's completely marvelous." And Jem had genuinely adored Alice's mother. It had given her pleasure to loiter in the carpeted offices and to caress the streamlined desk lamps. She had gorged with enthusiasm on Mrs. Pilling's cooking and had always been hungry for more.

"Your mother, Alice!" Jem had said one day, with dizzy admiration. She had been witnessing Mrs. Pilling's performance on the office telephone. "Crumbs, your mother! I reckon she could sell a pebble-dashed prefab in the flight path for Heathrow Airport."

Well, yes, but Alice knew by then that Jem's mother would never call a *vol-au-vent* a "volley-vong," the way her own mother did. In fact she would have no truck with such a thing at all. Thanks to Jem's vivid evocation of her own mother's cuisine, Alice knew that "marmite" was not really a name that had come into being along with an English yeast extract, but rather a heavy clay pot in which Minette McCrail prepared the *cassoulet*. It was through Minette McCrail's cooking, simple and perfect—the occasional preserved goose, the *charcuterie*, the wholesome country terrines—that Alice began inwardly to find dissatisfaction with her own mother's catering, whose star turns for the local aldermen she came to perceive as artful shortcuts to rather showy and novel effects.

Competent, indefatigable and generous, Mrs. Pilling had been the acknowledged star of the local businessmen's buffet for over a decade. Her freezer was always kept stocked with bumper bags of cocktail bits and a large Black Forest cake. Mrs. Pilling excelled at the club sandwich. She gleaned recipes unceasingly from every magazine and cereal packet, which she pasted onto alphabetically ordered cataloging cards and kept in a pristine kitchen file box.

As a small child Alice had always enjoyed helping her mother paste up recipes. It had taught her to be organized and neat and purposeful. It was an activity she associated with learning to read. Because of it she knew her alphabet and she had noticed quite early on how nice the recipes sounded, because they all had alliterative titles. This had given her a cozy feeling about figures of speech, which she had carried over into the English class at school. But it had not taught her the kinds of things that had made Jem so dazzling in class. If Jem were ever required to call upon examples of alliteration, her mind would conjure Felix Randal the Farrier in a moment, complete with his "great grey drayhorse" and his "bright and battering sandal." The "rough, rude sea" would surface at once, and the furrow would follow free in the wake of the flying foam. Alice's thoughts, meanwhile, would flutter prosaically toward the kitchen file box with its "Tasty Tuna Starter," its "Tahini Temptation," and its "Kiwi Cocktail Quickie."

Alice began to notice that her mother's recipes came and went like padded shoulders and double-breasted coats. She judged this faddishness a lesser thing than the apparently classical timelessness of Mrs. McCrail's terrines. Alice took stock and realized that her mother's "Prawn and Parmesan" quiche had given way of late to

"Lobster and Lymeswold." She observed the demise of her favorite "Damson Delight," which had been upstaged by a pudding experience entitled "Star Fruit Stunner." Alice grieved for the contented hours that she and her mother had spent together as she had gained know-how in the art of presenting canapés. She had so enjoyed, as a little girl, learning to arrange these on shallow oval dishes with an eye to color and radial effect. "Presentation is everything," her mother had advised, and she had made small, expert adjustments here and there to Alice's childish arrangements. Now that Mrs. Pilling managed a thriving estate agency she had acquired another maxim. "Locality is everything."

"Food," Jem had said, "is sometimes very sexy." Mrs. McCrail, Alice knew, bought beef fillets whole from the butcher's and sliced them herself into inch-thick rounds with her time-worn Sabatier knives. She stood at the Aga in a bloodstained butcher's apron, spatula in hand, and worked rough magic in a gridded cast-iron pan, while her family and guests consumed the simplest endive salad at the kitchen table. Her backless, wedge-heeled sandals—worn, Jem said, to give her height—would clack on the floor as she worked.

"Beefstek for me is een-out!" she would pronounce commandingly, and she would slap onto each plate an aromatic slab, singed without and bleeding within, coated in a dense gravel of pounded black pepper. It was all, Jem had assured her, analogous with the act of sex. Alice wondered now what messages one could decipher from canapés.

Jem had always presented her parents by implication as sexual operatives. This had had a curious effect upon Alice's burgeoning fantasies. It meant that not only had Gordon McCrail become a sort of proxy father figure, guardian and guide, but he had also become her most powerful masculine heartthrob. Like Sarastro, he was never dimmed by the taking on of flesh and blood. His power was never clouded by actuality. Gordon McCrail would always be the tallest and most comely of that clutch of scarved undergrads, leaping from a small red sports car; Gordon McCrail, only son of the manse in Aberdeenshire, so gracefully paying court in French over the convent wall; Gordon—dared she think of him as Gordon?—nurturing his daughters on that seductive combination of high culture and delicate irony. Oh, the charm of a man like that! A man of letters! Alice tried not to feel let down by the fact that her own parents had met in 1960 at the Young Conservatives Ball.

With Jem's departure, Alice found herself occasionally having conversations with Mr. McCrail inside her head. When her own life bored or depressed her, she would come with relief upon Gordon McCrail making long-distance calls from his telephone in the summerhouse to American publishing houses, or shaving to Gregorian chant. This had happened for the first time after Mrs. Pilling had taken Alice to a local Amateur Operatic Society's performance of *Carmen*. Alice's mother had subsequently bought a recording of the opera's "greatest hits" and had filled the house for a fortnight with the sounds of singing gypsies. Alice had found the gypsies hard on the ear after Jem's illicit reeducation course in the music room.

"*Carmen* is a potboiler," she remembered Jem saying once. "Even Bizet knew it. Gordon is very amusing when he's quoting foreign composers. It's because he can't say his *r*'s. 'If the people want wubbish, give 'em wubbish.' That's what Bizet said."

Curiously, Jem had never mentioned this endearing speech impediment before. She had also suddenly begun to call him Gordon.

Alice once found herself waking from a dream, some months after Jem had gone. A dream in which she had come upon Gordon washing his car in a great sweep of drive that led to a stone country house. She knew at once that the house was Jem's house. Alice was in a crisp summer frock, pastel green in hue. Her hair was newly bobbed to the jawline and it gleamed like silk in the sunlight from recent washing. Mr. McCrail wore a fetching pair of braces over a striped shirt and looked just like Jem, she thought, though he was very obviously a man. His clothes looked dashingly Simpsons of Piccadilly. Over his shirt he wore an apron printed all over with black and white typeface that said TIMES COOK OF THE YEAR.

"I bowwowed it fwom my wife," he said, employing his deficient *r*'s. "It's far too big for her, I'm afwaid." He was washing his car to *The Magic Flute*, which was emanating from a cassette machine behind him and, since his glasses had steamed up from the hot water, he had taken them off to look at her. Alice wore no petticoat under her cotton frock and the sun was shining through it. His eyes followed the length of her brown summer legs through the fabric.

"My wife is vewy much your height," he said. "You have the same pwetty eyes, my dear."

In the dream, Alice was perfectly clear that Minette McCrail was a rival. She knew that, stripped of her butcher's apron and wedge-heeled sandals, Mrs. McCrail lay sluiced and pinkly couched upon tumbled satin in the bedroom upstairs, playfully rump upwards, like the king's mistress in the Boucher painting that Jem had once shown her. Alice had thought at the time that the king's mistress had looked like an advertisement for Johnson's Baby Powder. She talked aloud, then, in her sleep.

"What's that, my lovey?" Mrs. Pilling said. She was fervently solic-itous for Alice's well-being and often these days came to look at her as she slept.

"Johnson's Baby Powder," Alice said irritably in sleep.

"That's right, my lovey," Mrs. Pilling said. She pulled up Alice's quilt and gave her a wistful pat. It was so difficult to know what was best for Alice these days, now that the offer of new toys and chocolate brownies no longer met her needs. Perhaps the girl needed a boy-friend? A nice, tall schoolboy to pick up the phone and ask her to the pictures.

But in the dream Mr. McCrail was wiping his glasses on his shirt-tails. He was smiling irresistibly into Alice's eyes. "Ever seen *The Magic Flute,* young Alice?" he said. From somewhere behind him came the sound of Tamino's singing. Tamino was singing his love for a woman whom he had not found. All he had was the knowledge that her image purified his heart.

Miss Trotter arranged a meeting with Alice's parents at the lower-sixth parent evening. It was in the same week that Alice had discovered the stammering judge in *The Marriage of Figaro.* She wrote a letter to Mozart about it in her head.

Dear Mozart.
    Did you have a speech defect? It would make me very happy to know this because letters sometimes scramble themselves on my

tongue. I ask you this because of your stammering judge and because of the Pa-Pa-Papageno song. I know that you sometimes used to write your name backwards. Trazom. I know this from a book I once read called *Little Wolferl of Salzburg*.

Yours sincerely,
Alice

"My staff, as you know, were delighted with Alice's exam results last summer," Miss Trotter said. "Her progress ever since has been quite outstanding."

"She's been working much too hard, I think, since the McCrail girl left," said Mrs. Pilling. "And it worries me, Miss Trotter, that her stammer has got so much worse."

"Ah yes," said Miss Trotter. "The McCrail girl. We never quite knew what we were up against there, though I must admit she came to us with a most ambiguous report from her convent school in South London." Mrs. Pilling made some inquiries. In response Miss Trotter consented to seek out Jem McCrail's file.

"Veronica's fees were paid to us by standing order," she said. "They were paid through an Italian bank with arrangements to terminate when the girl turned sixteen. I confess that this, rather mercifully, gave us the way out."

"Italian bank?" Mrs. Pilling said. "Good heavens."

"I do have an address for the girl's mother," Miss Trotter said, reluctantly. "But I would strongly advise at this stage against having Alice make contact. We would all, I think, like Alice to have as few distractions as possible." She ran her finger along the line of an index card. "Ah, here we are," she said. "If you're quite sure that you really want it." Mrs. Pilling hesitated for just long enough to allow Miss Trotter to continue. She replaced the card and shut the file. "Mrs. Pilling," Miss Trotter said, "my staff and I believe that Alice should try for Oxford."

The Prince and the Highland Brain Surgeon

II

ALICE HEARD NOTHING from Jem for nearly four years. She understood only in retrospect how much of that time was spent in grieving. It was a grief that seldom surfaced, a kind of internal bleeding. Jem had taught her to read a lot, which, though gratifying in itself, had brought distance. Distance from her family; distance from almost all her peers. Nonetheless, Alice had experienced a cautious reconciliation with Flora; a truce bounded by two unstated conditions. Neither Flora's father nor Jem McCrail was ever mentioned between them.

Time had not been kind to Flora since her father's death. The three Fergusson women, left behind in possession of a significant accumulation of wealth and a very large, eminently marketable house in a most salubrious locality, showed no signs of easing up. Not a bit of it. The two Mrs. Fergussons dedicated themselves still further to the pursuit of the deceased man's frugality and watched each other the more zealously for every smallest lapse. A drop of milk over the margin, a scrape of margarine in excess of strictest need: these things would bring down the one upon the other with triumphant reprimand. And both of them watched Flora.

As time went by, a series of small strokes somewhat reduced the mobility and the mental faculties of the elder Mrs. Fergusson, and doubled the incontinence and the stench, but they did little to curtail her poisoned vigilance.

Flora's grandmother, who at first had remained adamant that no one other than her daughter-in-law be responsible for her personal hygiene, had come gradually, through increasing mental confusion and tetchiness, to permit no interference at all. Flora's mother, in consequence, had been obliged to desist from dragging heavy, soiled bed linen from the old woman's room to knead by hand in the bath-tub. She left the old person untouched.

District nurses, who came and went in their smart blue uniforms, were similarly obliged to leave their parcels of disposable sheets and incontinence pads stockpiling in the Fergussons' porch. Nonethe-less, they always paused to fill in the record card, which they had pinned to the back of the weather door. OBJECT OF VISIT, the record card stated (and it provided a little blank box). "To bathe the patient," the nurses filled in, after unclipping their roller pens from the breast pockets of their uniforms. They always specified the date and the hour with conscientious precision. RESULT OF VISIT, the record card stated (and it provided another little blank box). "Bath refused," wrote the nurses. Then they added their signatures, and sped off gratefully in their cars.

Alice's mother had understandably not ventured to intervene again, though she fretted in private over Flora's pallor and dowdiness, and over her unreformed front teeth, almost as much as she worried in private over Alice.

"Flora will spend her time blowing dust off piles of old papers," Mrs. Pilling said to her husband. "She'll end up in a museum, just like her father." She bit her freshly glossed lower lip. "And if we're not careful, Harry," she said, "our Alice will go the same way. She spends the whole day reading. What a pity if she ended up having to wear glasses." Her parents placated themselves by contemplating the very likely appearance of a nice young man—one of these days.

Just as the girls had entered their second term in the upper sixth, something rather glamorous happened to Flora, which was an-nounced in the Wednesday assembly. She won a scholarship, awarded by the French government, to the Ecole du Louvre in Paris. The assembled schoolgirls clapped and cheered, and Mrs. Fergusson, who for eleven years had played the piano to accompany the hymns, faltered for the very first time.

That Wednesday, Alice saw Flora once again metamorphose. The exchange with her mother was brief and devastating. Flora, in general so dutiful, so accepting of austere parental decree, bloomed, took on color, grew tall and spoke.

"I'm going, Mother," she said, and Alice saw clearly—as she had seen only once before on the occasion of the infant Christmas play— that Flora was compellingly beautiful. "Neither you, nor my grand- mother nor hell itself will stop me."

"You'll starve, my girl," her mother said, and she drew up her mouth in that mean, pinched little gesture, born of all those decades of repressing Scarlatti in the gas cupboard. "It'll be no use me saying I told you so."

Flora uttered one brief, ruthless laugh, her voice terrifying, once more the hanging judge.

"Fortunately I'm very well prepared for that," she said. "Because you've starved me all of my life."

As far as Alice observed it, Flora simply stopped speaking to her mother after that. With unswerving and awesome resolution she sat out the remainder of the school year in almost total silence at home. She gulped the last of the oil-globule soup with her mind fixed on the cross-Channel ferry and the call of her future beyond Calais.

"But you can't n-n-not speak-speak to her, can you?" Alice ventured one day. Flora shrugged. Unlike Jem, Flora had never readily painted the features of her domestic life for Alice. The texture of personal interaction was not a strong interest with her. "I-I mean live in the same house and n-not speak?" Alice persisted. "You can't."

"Why not?" Flora said.

"W-well," Alice said. "W-what about mealtimes? W-when you're s-sitting at the s-same table?" Flora looked at her a little curiously.

"What's the problem?" Flora said. "I really don't see that there's a problem. I don't need her. I don't need her anymore." Alice had wanted to convey that one necessarily bent a little; was sometimes falsely kind. One gave and took; was pliable. One accommodated. But not so Flora. She had never courted popularity. This, in the end, had made her a highly unsuitable companion for Claire Crouchley.

When finally June was over, Flora laundered and mended her clothes and packed them into a small tin trunk. Alice's mother, who hesitated to ply any Fergusson with largesse in the form of food, did not feed Flora a leave-taking supper or take the girls out to tea. She bought the child a pair of fine kid gloves and a grossly expensive leather portfolio for toting about works of art. The Pillings drove Flora to Victoria Station, where Alice and her mother took turns with a Kleenex to dab at the moisture that afflicted their eyes.

"Paris, eh?" said Mr. Pilling, and was after that quite stuck for words. He shook Flora's hand. Mrs. Pilling kissed her.

"Take care of yourself, lovey," she said.

"I will," Flora said. Her eyes were not afflicted with moisture. She had them fixed on the future.

"Goodbye, Flora," Alice said. She wanted to volunteer that she would come and visit Flora and wondered why she felt herself constrained. "I—" she said. "F-flora, maybe w-we. We. Well—' But Flora gave her no help.

"Goodbye, Alice," she said.

"Goodbye," Alice said again. Flora never came home in the vacations and Alice did not see her again until the day she got Jem's letter. That was two years on.

Alice's place at Oxford distanced her still further from her parents and did little to modify her stammer, but for Miss Trotter and her staff her achievement was judged as one to have upstaged Flora's. It was Alice's place at Oxford, not Flora's Parisian scholarship, that had warranted the granting of a half-holiday.

"Hip-hip," called Miss Trotter from the podium, and she raised her right arm like Caesar.

"Hurrah!" roared the school in unison.

The application to Oxford had been stage-managed from beginning to end by Miss Trotter, who had herself been "up," as she put it, shortly after the war. Her Oxford vintage, combined with the fact that almost none of her girls ever aspired to university at all, meant that her information was considerably out of date. The Pillings' information, on the other hand, was wholly nonexistent.

Miss Trotter had proceeded confidently upon two firmly held convictions. The first was that her own women's college had remained a pinnacle of scholarly distinction, and the second was that the universities—"even, alas, our two oldest and most distinguished universities"—were currently dominated by a fifth column of younger, left-wing dons, who would misguidedly give preference to applicants from inner-city schools.

Thus it was that Alice found herself ensconced in a single-sex women's college favoring solid, hardworking and predominantly un-distinguished young women from fee-paying girls' boarding schools. She was signed up, somewhat against her inclination, as a student of classics.

"I w-would p-p-p. Prefer English literature," Alice said, but Miss Trotter had blithely overridden her.

"Why so, Alice?" she said. "Your Latin results have always been very pleasing. Very pleasing indeed."

Alice searched for reasons. They were all to do with those magic doors into the mountainside that Jem had opened for her. And she could not begin to think of Jem now. Not before Miss Trotter. Not without weeping.

"I-I think I am a bit tired of Jul-l-l-yus-s-s Caesar," she said. ("Yulyo Chesaray," as she remembered Jem calling him, merely in order to annoy Mrs. Waters in the fourth-form history class.) "I am n-not very interested in th-throwing bridges ac-c-c-c. Ac-cross the Rhine."

Miss Trotter had considered this an eccentric objection, easily over-ruled. Since the state schools no longer supported classics depart-ments, she calculated, Alice would find herself less invidiously faced with competition from "the wrong sort of gel" in this field. In her mind's eye she envisaged a consignment of applicants, all dropping their aitches and chewing gum in the Examination Schools.

Alice's first impression, as a result, was that to be at university was rather like being permanently committed to the Prep room. Having scotched, within the first few days, the airy, secret hope that Jem would somehow, marvelously, be there, the rising star of Balliol—a hope that had caused her to take with her the cardboard box full of exercise books labeled "Convent of the Ascension"—Alice watched with a degree of detachment as her fellow students giggled over an aging fellow's exposed bra strap in the dining hall, or hid their pud-ding plates under the tables in order to wheedle seconds from the college servants. Alice, who had no stomach for participating in these antics, was quickly labeled as haughty. She retreated once more into reading, and into conscientious essay writing and translations for tutors who were, in dress and style, not wholly unlike Miss Aldridge. Nowhere, it appeared, was there a pedagogue to be found whose shoes, like those of Miss Davidene Delight, could boast of exquisite rosettes.

Alice encountered Roland Dent while on a solitary walk along the river. He collided with her while traversing the river frontage on a bicycle. Roland was wearing a navy blue tracksuit and yelling instructions through a megaphone to a group of schoolboy oarsmen in a boat.

"So frightfully sorry," said Roland Dent and, having resurrected her, promptly asked her to tea. He had a big, engaging public-school voice of the more traditional sort; the sort calculated to cause mild derision among people like Alice's parents.

"The Rodent's found a hag," said the party in the boat and, so it seemed, he had. Roland Dent was twenty-six. He was the son of an army chaplain. Having failed the eye test, which had kept him from becoming a professional soldier, he had borne the consequent frustration with fortitude and had become, instead, a successful and popular schoolmaster in a reputable boys' private school. The role, as it turned out, suited him admirably, providing ample scope for his judicious and robust flair for leadership. He was excellent value for his employers, since he taught mathematics competently, had no difficulties with crowd control and exhibited a rare enthusiasm for helping out with games.

Roland was optimistic and easygoing. Having soon found that his mildly substandard eyes were really perfectly adequate for the purpose of flinging chalk, he now fought the good fight from the classroom with laudable equanimity.

"W-w-w-w," Alice said. "Th-th-th. I—" She stopped, took a deep breath and started again. "Thank you," she said. "Excuse me. I but I used to h-have quite-quite a bad stammer." Roland Dent was charmed. His unflagging energies quickly both camouflaged and intensified Alice's somewhat muted sense of self, and his agreeable, blameless male egotism meant that he simply did not notice. He noticed only her lovely serenity and her silences, and he fell for her pretty blue eyes.

Roland began to call on her with scrupulous regularity. On Tuesday afternoons he would appear on foot direct from the sports field, still dressed in his navy blue tracksuit and usually with a whistle still hanging around his neck. On Friday evenings and Saturdays he would come, sometimes in his much-cherished mid-fifties Citroën DS, sometimes on a bicycle, but always vigorously sluiced, shaved and handsome.

While his major enthusiasms were for team games, military survival techniques, and old motor cars, Roland was nonetheless sufficiently largehearted to be attentive and courteous to women, who were so obviously necessary for the satisfaction of bodily lusts and the provision of stable family lives. It was the least one could do, after all, to treat the dear things properly. They were also marvelously well adapted for producing tea at cricket fixtures, for turning out to do one proud in pretty frocks at prizegiving and for serving as occasional tennis partners.

Alice did not play tennis, but his affection for her, which expressed itself as a delicately patronizing and proprietorial tenderness, was nonetheless completely genuine and deepened quickly into love. He was charmed by her slightness of stature, by her quiet thoughtfulness and by her fragility. The stammer did not bother him and neither did her fear of water or her inability to drive. He assumed, in his sanguine way, that all these things would right themselves under the effect of his benign and forthright government, just as it always was with his apprehensive new first-formers. He believed, in his nice, unassuming way, that Alice was brighter than he was, but this did not ruffle his self-esteem. The only thing that ruffled him a little was Alice's curious reticence when it came to sex.

Given that Roland's sexual energies were in no way unequal to his considerable energies for field and water sports, he proved himself quite remarkably patient and gentlemanly in the face of Alice's reluctance. It galled him a little from time to time that, after three months with Alice, he had still engaged in nothing with her beyond what he would have considered routine as a schoolboy with his partner on the night of the sixth-form dance. But he was confident of her in the long run and convinced she was worth the wait. His intentions toward her were entirely honorable and it did not take him long to resolve within himself that Alice was the woman he was going to marry. She

was a sweet, quiet, lovely little thing with a jolly decent brain. Roland
was justly confident that he would become a housemaster quite soon
and probably, in the long run, a head. He was completely confident
that he could make Alice an adequate and supportive husband.

When Alice, at the end of her third term, decided to move from her
college room into digs, Roland Dent was more than ready to sanction
the arrangement and to take on all the major humping of books and
trunks—though he did pause a little quizzically over the box of Jem's
convent exercise books.

" 'Convent of the Ascension'?" he said jovially, before shipping them
out to his Citroën. "This a skeleton in your cupboard, my poppet?
Been concealing an idolatrous past?"

"I d-don't think so," Alice said earnestly. She was often rather slow to
pick up on the style of his jokes; a thing that he invariably found
endearing. Right then it made him laugh.

"I can't see that it's f-f-f-funny for a person to be a C-thacoholic."
Alice said. Roland put down the books and kissed her.

"My adorable funny-face," he said. "Dear me. I detect that you have
leanings."

"The convent exercise books," he said. "Don't look so worried,
sweetie. I'm teasing you. I never knew about the convent school,
that's all."

"Oh," Alice said. "No. They belonged to my best friend. She was
C-catholic."

" 'Was'?" Roland said with levity. "She isn't dead, I trust?"

"I don't know," Alice said bleakly. She had intermittently wondered
if Jem had perhaps died on that train. Could the train have crashed
and she not been told? She struggled without success against the fall of
tears. Roland was appalled.

"Oh, sweetie," he said, and he drew her neat blond head protectively toward him until it lay against the zip of the navy blue tracksuit.
"Oh good Lord, my darling."

That was the first time that Roland had called her "my darling."
She had sat in his car after that, with her things piled all around
them, and had poured out what sounded to him like an oddly intense and lingering schoolgirl crush on a brainy little RC who,

having unscrupulously won her friendship through blatant insubordination and constant flouting of school rules, had then abandoned her and never bothered to write. Alice's distress angered him. Bloody Romans, he thought. They could be so bloody devious. He wasn't a person not to live and let live, but, there, it had to be said: the moment you befriended one of them, you ran the risk, so to speak, of having another of them plant a bloody bomb in your barracks and that was a fact.

"Roland," Alice said. "Do you think you could help me to find her?" Roland hesitated, just a moment.

"Is it really necessary?" he said. Alice did not answer him. "Oh good Lord!" he said. "Of course I'll help you, sweetie. If the thought of a little girlie nostalgia can make you dry your eyes." He paused. "She'll probably bore you rigid, my darling, and she'll almost certainly disappoint you." Roland kissed her. "It is also just possible," he added lightly, "that said Catholic schoolgirl has gone off and taken the vow of silence. Listen, old thing. If we find this little package has shaved her head and is scrubbing floors in a nunnery with a toothbrush, or whatever—that's when we'll call it a day."

Alice said nothing. She contemplated the convent as a serious possibility.

"I mean, they do come on a bit like the Moonies occasionally," Roland said. "The old RCs. Nothing against them, you understand me, but they're awfully good at the three-line whip."

"I really loved her, Roland," Alice said.

"Oh, poppet," he said. "Don't be an idiot. Don't debase the terminology." He meant that "love" was what existed between a man and a woman; between himself and her. He switched on his engine and smiled at her with all his love. "Ever read these silly bloody women who write away to the magazines?" he said. " 'Dear Marj Proops, My heart belongs to the games mistress. Please put me on to Lesbian Line.' All that. The sisters were always wildly keen on it, I remember. Used to keep them in hoots for hours."

"What?" Alice said.

"Agony aunties," he said. "No?" He put the palm of his hand protectively to her face. "What a superior creature you are. Always reading the Old Worthies." Alice didn't really feel equipped to answer him. "Do you think me a fascist?" he said.

Alice shook her head. "I think you're very kind," she said.

Roland was, for the moment, satisfied. "You mustn't think that I don't understand," he said. "I mean about schoolgirl friendships. I've had the sisters to keep me informed." He lapsed, after a knowing sigh, into a lighthearted parody that succeeded in making Alice laugh against her better judgment, but his tone reminded her so vividly of Claire Crouchley. " 'You're not my *best* friend, Mavis,' " he said. " 'You're only my second-best friend. Gertie is my *absolutely-absolutely* best friend. That's ever since the middle of last week.' " He was much gratified to see her smile.

"That's better," he said. "My adorable silly. I'm madly proud of you, as you must know." Roland placed his arm around her shoulders. "And you are coming home with me? To meet the parents? 'Course you are," he said.

Alice dispatched a letter to Miss Trotter before the following weekend. Then she left in the car with Roland to visit his parents in Hampshire. The idea daunted her a little, and only partly because Roland's father was a clergyman. On this score she had misgivings that Roland's father might suddenly demand of her, the uninitiate, that she chant the Athanasian Creed.

"R-roland," she said, with some hesitancy, en route. "I've never even been christened." Roland merely laughed, as he did about all her little deviations from what he considered to be the norm.

"Oh, jolly good," he said. "Yet another candidate for 'to Such as are of Riper Years.' I shall of course inform my father at once."

"N-no—" Alice said.

"And would you like him to assemble the regiment?" he said. "Around the font, I mean."

Why was he always teasing her? she wondered. And so often about things that were real concerns of hers. And why did his jokes so often disconcert her, when they were always so benignly meant? "Don't look so alarmed, my poppet," he said. "The parents don't live in the Middle Ages, you know."

 But it did seem to Alice that Roland's parents lived in some sort of a time warp, charming as it was. They were called Father and Mother. That was what Roland called them. They called each other Peter and Heather. Alice thought that they were like an affectionate, middle-class couple before the First World War, managing sensibly on limited means. Heather Dent bottled fruit in glass preserving jars with a rubber rim and a clamp. In the evenings, to Alice's astonishment, she mended socks. She sat in a wing armchair beside an Edwardian fireplace with a darning mushroom and a basket filled with plaited skeins of wool.

Peter Dent kept bees. He worked each morning at an old pedestal desk in a room full of books, with a threadbare Turkey carpet on a dark, oak-stained floor; a room that, for all that he seemed to her otherwise wholly without pretension, he referred to as his "library." Roland's mother, wearing a straw hat like Virginia Woolf and sitting in the garden at a battered cricket table, observed to Alice, as she poured the afternoon tea, that the russet apples had been very abundant the previous year. She had brought out the teacups and saucers on a tray with an embroidered cloth. The Dent household possessed no such thing as a mug, except for the one that was kept in the bathroom to accommodate Father's shaving brush. It depicted the coronation of His Majesty King Edward the Seventh.

"Darling," said Mother to Roland over tea, "will you ride tomorrow if it's fine?"

Peter Dent was relentlessly agreeable, both to Alice and to his family, in a manner just short of heartiness. When he invited Roland to drink his home-brewed beer, the two of them drank it out of pint-sized tankards while the ladies drank his elderflower champagne. And when Father gripped Roland by the shoulder and said was he "winning the battle," it took Alice some time to realize that he was asking Roland about his schoolmastering job.

At mealtimes, Father sat in a chair that matched all the others, only his was very much larger and it came with arms. He carved roast English lamb and gave great quantities to Alice, whom he had seated at his elbow.

"Build you up there, shall we?" he said, affably ho-ho. "My word, Roland, but she's not very large, now is she? This delightful young woman of yours."

Alice felt a little put down. Her size ought surely not to signify? And was she all that delightful? Well, at least she didn't go round saying, 'But Father, what big feet you have. And, goodness-me-ho-ho, your girth is just slightly on the increase. Let us take him off the home brew, shall we, Roland?"

"This is really f-f-f-f. I'm afraid this is more than I can eat," Alice said. "May I give it to R-roland?"

Father graciously ignored the stammer and talked at her in a mellow, reassuring voice full of easy humor and anecdote. Put in mind of courtship—no doubt by the sight of his son's proprietorial manner with Alice—he was disposed to retail for her entertainment how he had met his wife. It made a good story and he told it well, but it left Alice feeling uncomfortable. Father, it seemed, had fixed his heart upon a person whom he described as "a pretty but excessively pious young lady" who had been Heather Dent's best friend in youth. He had pursued her through zealous but self-serving attendance at Holy Communion over a period of some twelve months.

"But the girl was so unshakably stonehearted," he said, "that my attendance at Communion became protracted into habit." Alice envisaged Father kneeling at the altar rail beside the pretty but excessively pious young lady and passing eager smiles to her over the transubstantiated host. She found it a little bit startling. He was so very much like Roland: so jovial and kind; so politely understated in any outward show of spirituality at all. Peter Dent glanced appreciatively at his wife. Then he returned to Alice.

"Finally she put me on to Heather," he said. "Who was, of course, far prettier—only nowhere near so pious."

"Oh, Peter," said Roland's mother sweetly, and she did indeed look far prettier than almost anyone. They were a handsome family, Alice could appreciate that. Father was a fine-looking man and so was Roland. The sisters, who were not there, were displayed handsomely, in various stages of childhood, in the photographs upon the piano. Father bent again to Alice.

"Heather's friend became a nun," he said. "Perhaps driven to it by the unwelcome tenacity of my attentions." Alice was not quite sure whether she was meant to laugh at this or not. Her smile wavered uncertainly and ceased. She thought, momentarily, about Jem scrubbing floors in a nunnery with a toothbrush.

"She must have become a C-thathacil-l-l-lic," she said, and she blushed a bit. "A Catholic," she repeated.

Peter Dent laughed and filled her glass for the third time with his homemade burgundy. "Oh, good Lord no," he said. "She didn't go quite as far as all that."

Roland smiled at Alice. "Careful, there, Father," he said. "I do believe that Alice has 'leanings.' "

Father promptly imposed more lamb upon her and pulled a humorous face.

"Oh, Roly," said Mother indulgently. "Don't be such a tease."

"And where," said Father to Alice, "did you meet this reprehensible young man?" But there was nothing reprehensible about Roland. Alice sat up very straight while she was at Father's dining table. Little Miss Deportment. Just in case of unexpected sallies.

"I was w-walking by the river," she said.

"I flattened her," Roland said cheerfully. "I ran into her on my bicycle."

"Oh Roly," said Mother again, but rather vaguely, as though it gave her no real surprise that young men should barge about knocking women over on riverbanks.

Alice was wholly charmed by Mother, but haunted by her too, and not only because her best friend had got her to a nunnery. There was something about her so curiously other, which Alice found both seductive and alarming. She was so handsome and graceful and pliant, as though she sucked her serenity from some opiate nectar. She behaved like a woman in a Renoir painting, caught contentedly in the frame. As though she existed as an obliging emanation of her husband's gentler and more feminine thoughts; as though she might cease to exist if Father stopped willing her into being—which of course he never would. Good Lord no! He was far too much of a gentleman where women were concerned. Or did Mother feel, as Alice felt with Roland, that there were whole areas of her self that Father did not see? Or had those parts of her simply died over the years from underexposure? Did she, Alice, behave like that with Roland? Perhaps she did. And was this really all there was of Heather Dent? This person who had spent her life gliding through a company of men. Men, like Roland, who liked drill and radar and mapping and rope and rivers and armored cars. Men who liked to think of throwing bridges over the Rhine. Men who liked dressing up in khaki and sitting around long tables and talking about "the enemy"—just as if they were all in a film with Sir John Mills? It made Alice afraid. It made her retreat even more from Roland's very evident passion and honorable regard.

She was very quiet most of the time in Roland's parents' house. And Roland, being Roland, merely became the more solicitous for her happiness.

"The parents giving you a hard time by any chance?" he said. "They think you're terrific, by the way."

Alice shook her head. "I think your parents are lovely," she said. "And so are you, Roland." But when he bent to kiss her, she stepped backwards. "Roland? Why do you think you like me? I mean what is it about me, do you think?"

"Oh, good Lord, because I do!" he said impatiently. "Because you're the dearest, nicest, prettiest little thing and whyever shouldn't I 'like' you?"

"But why?" Alice said. Roland sighed.

"Dearest poppet," he said. "I dote on you. You know perfectly well that I dote on you. Or must I always be telling you?"

"N-no," Alice said. "No. I only thought—" Roland embraced her. He looked at her carefully.

"You are really fond of me, aren't you?" he said. "I mean really fond of me?" Alice nodded. Yes, she was really fond of Roland. All the more so for that curiously delicate word he had chosen for the purpose of encompassing her reticent emotions.

"Well then," he said. "That settles it. You think too much, you know. I really ought to make you play tennis."

And that was the weekend. The house so full of jolly male laughter and kindness and teasing. It was like having Roland in stereo, bombarding one with benign misunderstanding; with benign and courteous refusal ever to acknowledge that one might not be quite what one seemed. Being there underlined for Alice a conviction that she was somehow cheating Roland. And she wished so sincerely to be honest. 'Tis better to Die than to Lie. If ever she endeavored to indicate as much, Roland invariably laughed at her and temporarily steamrollered her anxieties out of existence. Or he repackaged them all as evidence of her endearing feminine charm.

ROLAND, though he could not seriously approve of Alice's new landlord, was prepared to regard him for the time being as just another of life's enjoyable jokes. Privately, he had sanctioned her move from college because he believed that it would license more extended and unsupervised house calls than had been possible in that institution, and lend strength to his intention to make his presence felt in Alice's bed.

Alice herself was delighted with her digs and very fond of the landlord. She was also rather proud of the speed with which she had found them. The undergraduate grapevine had contended that one began one's search for a room by knocking on doors at the salubrious north end of the Woodstock Road and then gradually worked one's way, in the face of rejection, southward and westward toward the houses cheek by jowl with industrial effluence and railway fallout that lined the Oxford Canal. Alice began with the Oxford Canal and found herself a room within the hour—an attic room that was large, well lit, and mercifully underfurnished with junk-shop seconds.

The attic was reached via three flights of stairs that were permanently obstructed by Lego bricks, crumpled laundry, old newspapers and unwashed coffee mugs, but, once inside, the room was definitely nice. Alice was especially fond of her desk, which was of the lift-up school-classroom sort and had a hole in the top for an inkwell. It was copiously incised with schoolboy graffiti and said "Jeffreys is a dunderhead" across the front.

"It's a throw-out from somebody's Prep room," Alice said to Roland. She enjoyed the idea of working at it. She was enjoying the work enormously. In spite of her earlier misgivings, she was finding the course extremely rewarding and had steeped herself in Roman elegy, even in the face of Roland's wry smiles. She enjoyed learning Greek and embraced Homer, especially, as enormously *simpático*.

"Jeffreys . . ." Roland said. "Jeffreys . . . There is a Jeffreys in the third form. Son of, for an absolute cert. He's a dunderhead too. In my experience, Alice, the apple never falls far from the tree." Roland had already inspected the accumulation of dust on the stairtreads of the landlord's house and had deduced to his satisfaction that in such an establishment a young woman's private life would be a matter of careless disregard.

Alice, meanwhile, felt that her new domicile was broadening to her experience in other ways. She had put away her clothes in the drawers of a somewhat rickety old chest that were lined with pages from the *London Review of Books*. Then she had stowed the cardboard box full of Jem's stories in the alcove alongside the chimney breast.

The room was in the house of one Dr. David Morgan and his Californian wife, Maya. While Maya was almost invisible, through dedication to her typewriter, David certainly was not. It was he who had received her in the hall on the afternoon of her first inquiry. He had come to the door with his bespectacled, harassed look and with a saucepan full of scorched greenish vegetables in his hand. There was an assertive backdrop of child protest emanating from the nearby downstairs loo.

"Come in," David said, and he looked round, without real expectation, for a landing pad for his saucepan.

"There's no paper!" screamed the child. "David! There isn't any *paper!*"

"Coming, William," David called mildly, and gave the saucepan to Alice. It contained an encrusted lava of half-carbonized spinach and split peas. "Excuse me," he said, and he looked around once again in the faint hope of finding a roll of toilet paper among the medley that cluttered the staircase.

"*There's no paper!*" screamed the child persistently. David sifted through a pile of old newspapers, testing them, Alice thought, for quality.

"Excuse me," he said again.

"DAVID!" screamed the child, like a demented tyrant. "I said there's NO PAPER!!" David smiled absently at Alice.

"Well, how fortunate," he said, apparently to the air in general, "that we subscribe, in this establishment, to the *Times Higher Educational Supplement.*"

Alice drew a small packet of tissues from her handbag and passed them over at once. "You might w-want these," she said. David looked at her in wonder.

"A woman who keeps Kleenex about her person," he said. "You're not from America, are you?"

"No," Alice said. "I c-come from Surrey."

"'Course, Maya's from America," he said, inexplicably. "But she exists in reaction to such things. Stick the pan in the sink for me, would you?"

"DAVID!!" screamed the child, like Rumplestiltskin about to go through the floor. *"THERE'S NO PAPER!!"*

"Excuse me," David said once more, and he moved off toward the lavatory.

In the kitchen every surface was a little bit sticky with a compound of cooking fat and dust. Leaning towers of books rose above strewn crockery, dropped underclothing and yesterday's food. Alice scraped the carbonized pulses into the dustbin. Then she added the saucepan to the sink, which had the look of a miniature scrapyard. On the radio somebody was halfway through a talk on Jackson Pollock and the Cold War. When David came in, he asked her to sit down.

"I'm sorry," he said. "You'll have to tell me your name."

"I'm Alice," she said.

"Forgive me," David said. "I suppose I know you. You'll be one of my tutees."

"N-no," Alice said. "I c-c-came b-b-b—" She stopped and breathed deeply and started again. "Can I be your lodger, please?" she said.

David laughed. "Whyever not?" he replied. He removed a pile of clothing from the chair opposite hers. Then he sat down and spoke philosophically. "Our previous lodger has just shipped out and left us an astronomical phone bill. You don't look to me like a person who would run up phone bills."

"No," Alice said, but she felt immediately that his benevolence required insurance against exploitation. "You sh-sh—. You oughtn't to trust people," she said. "You should p-put a lock on the phone."

David smiled. "You have a stammer," he said, as though this were a matter of considerable academic interest. "Like your creator. All his sisters, too. Did you know that? All the Dodgsons stammered."

"No," Alice said. She wondered how it was that Jem had never told her that Lewis Carroll stammered. And all his sisters, too. "Actually," she said candidly, "I'm not called after that Alice at all. I'm called after Alice Springs in Australia." David laughed with pleasure and shook her hand.

"Now then," he said. "I've destroyed the children's supper. Do you possess any talent, Alice, for recycling carbonized spinach?"

"Oh gosh," Alice said. "I th-threw it away. I'm sorry. Have you got a lot of children to feed?"

"Only three," he said. "A four-year-old and two in junior school. I also have a somewhat itinerant teenage stepdaughter. Why does it feel like thirty-five? I make heavy weather of it, I suppose."

"Do you l-look after them on your own?" Alice said.

"Oh no. But Maya is really very busy right now. She's trying to finish something."

They took stock of the fridge's contents. Its gasket was somewhat malfunctioning, which had caused a build-up of stalactites in the freezer box.

"The f-fish f-fing-ingers are all in prison," she said.

"Oh well," he said. "They've been in there quite a while. The kids have all been vegetarians since we took them to the Rare Breeds farm. Only trouble is they don't very much like vegetables."

"Do they live on treacle?" Alice said. "Like the sisters at the bottom of the well?" David laughed.

"My stepdaughter is a vegetarian too," he said, a little warningly. "That's in a manner of speaking. She's rather fond of grass. And the odd magic mushroom. Let me not mislead you into thinking that this is a well-ordered and problem-free environment."

"But I like it here," Alice said. "I really do." She made her mother's

Tahini Temptation and a bowl of Damson Delight with a plastic tub of plums that had gone past their best at the back of the fridge.

"Are you a being from earth?" said David. "Or what manner of being are you?"

Maya and David Morgan's house, both inside and out, was so stridently unimproved that it emboldened Alice with a curious, perverse pleasure. A small element of subversive relish that Roland, all unwittingly, had always helped to suppress in her, but that she had experienced in such large, heady measure all those years ago with Jem. Somehow, in a small way, it brought her alive as Roland never did. When he sensed it—which was seldom, because his presence naturally modified it—it made him just as irritable as his beautiful manners permitted. He was never directly irritable with Alice, but rather at its source. His irritation took the form of jovial, ideological sniping against David and Maya Morgan.

"Typical bloody Labour voters," Roland once observed, as he passed over the Morgans' threshold. "Tell them a bloody mile off from the umpteen unwashed milk bottles."

It ruffled Alice a little when he carried on like this. To be sure David Morgan voted Labour, but Maya, being an alien, couldn't even vote. And, to be sure, the Morgans did seem to have a remarkable number of uncollected milk bottles on the doorstep. In addition, groundsel and plastic dustbin bags adorned the pathway to the front door and, at the back, the garden sprouted a single but flourishing crop of abandoned cardboard boxes. The garden was approached along a damp, concreted side passage that existed as an obstacle course of disused children's bicycles, broken garden tools, rotting dining chairs, and—inexplicably—a large roll of well-rusted chicken wire.

But Alice was always protective of David Morgan against such knee-jerk sallies. She had liked him and respected him from the first. He was simply a busy, kind, harassed and evidently penniless academic of exactly the sort about whom Miss Trotter had been so ridiculously anxious. His causes were always scrupulously egalitarian, his integrity unimpeachable, and two of his three young children were at the local state junior school.

David's front windows, which faithfully reflected his egalitarian inclinations, appeared to exist not so much for the admission of sunlight as to serve as community notice boards for the propagation of information. Notices large and small gave a wealth of detail concerning Woodcraft Folk jumble sales, meetings campaigning for the preservation of local nursery schools and for the protection of union rights. They appealed for unilateral disarmament and declared themselves to be against apartheid, against compulsory redundancies, against acid rain and against tyrannical state encroachment upon local government and public services. Many of them had already passed the "sell by" date, but this was not policy on David's part. It was neglect. He was busy and overcommitted to his students and his children and he clearly found domestic organization extremely difficult. And Maya, being airy-fairy and preoccupied, really didn't help him much at all.

Unlike Roland, David found the art of living rather complicated. But, as far as Alice could see, this had very little to do with his voting habits.

"M-my grandma always votes Labour," she said. "She thinks my father's a t-t-traitor because he votes Conservative. But her milk bottles alw-ways sh-shine like crystal." Roland laughed good-humoredly. It seemed to him automatically amusing that his Alice should have a northern grandmother. He kissed her and patronized her with his genial and relentless loyalty.

"If she's your 'grandma,' my poppet," he said, "then I'm absolutely sure she's as charming and decent a little body as ever walked the earth. Anyway, everyone votes Labour up north, Alice. What else can poor Grandma do? She resides in the Soviet Socialist Republic of Chester-le-Street. It's a one-party state up there."

"Not in Chester-le-Street," Alice said. "She lives in a mining village near Hetton-le-Hole." Roland laughed again, as if it made no difference. He had never been to either.

"Sweetie," he said tenderly. "You get the dearest little hint of Geordie in your voice every time you say the word 'grandma.' "

"Anyway," Alice said. "David's too b-busy to keep his house clean. He's working f-for everybody's house. He cares about everybody's family." Roland raised an eyebrow. " 'In my Father's house are ma-many m-mansions,' " Alice said stoutly.

"Oh, I say!" Roland said, and his laughter became more robust.

"We're having recourse to the Good Book now—in defense of our favorite heathen filthpacket?" Alice had noticed before that if ever she referred to the Bible, Roland behaved as though she were somehow, endearingly, amusingly, poaching on his area of expertise. He reacted much as though she had begun to quote him batting averages.

"Any word as yet on the little chum?" he said.

"Not yet," Alice said, because Miss Trotter had not yet answered her letter. Perhaps she never would.

AMONG DAVID MORGAN'S COLLECTION of eclectic posters was one, smaller and less obtrusive than the rest, that became a particular weapon in Roland's jovial armory. IF YOU CAN READ THIS, it said, THANK A TEACHER.

"And if you can't bloody read it," said Roland—deliberately within the hearing of Maya Morgan, whom he considered a tiresomely limp, outdated sort of flower person—"try sacking the teacher instead." He was provokingly airing his contempt for the local state junior school, the one attended by the elder two of the three little Morgan children. Admittedly, he did not know at that stage that the children could not read. And, admittedly again, Alice thought, Roland had a case. Alice, who had twice, recently, gone to collect the children from school, had observed through the classroom door that the children sat talking and jostling at tables that were arranged as if the classroom were a café. They called out and ran about during work time and made paper airplanes of the worksheets. It was all a very far cry from the Silent Reading Hour and it gave Alice a grudging new respect for Miss Aldridge and *Great World Leaders*.

But Maya ought not to be the butt of Roland's snipes, Alice thought. Maya was an innocuous woman, pacific and somewhat overearnest. She wasn't even "political." She wore salmon corduroy trousers and a blouse with macramé on the boobs. She spent her time typing at a heavy old Remington in a cubbyhole that must once have been the coalshed. It pained Alice to think that, had the Morgans not needed her rent money, Maya could have housed her Remington in the attic bedroom instead, and typed at the nice little desk. And, unlike David, who was entertained by Roland, Maya was so readily shockable. It seemed unfair that Roland should enjoy picking on her. She so invariably responded to him with an anxious, bruised sensitivity. But Roland thought her intolerably holier-than-thou and sallied forth uncontrite.

"Education is not about the three R's, Roland," Maya explained to him at once. "We can read, can't we, and look at all of us. Do we stand up well under scrutiny?"

"Well, there's nothing wrong with *me*," Roland said.

"The woman is an absolute bloody spineless wimp," Roland said to Alice in private. "And what does she do, neglecting her kids all day and cowering in that ghastly Black Hole of Calcutta? She writing her memoirs, or something?"

Alice did not know. She didn't terribly like to enter the cubbyhole because, pinned to the wall, Maya had a blown-up, poster-size photograph of herself in childbirth. It had been taken by her previous husband, and the person emerging from her alarmingly extended pubes was Iona, David's fourteen-year-old stepdaughter. Iona, who had in common with Roland Dent that she detested and despised her mother, had drawn moustaches on the poster with a thick black marking pen—both on herself and on her mother. And she had given herself horns and a vicious-looking pitchfork, which was piercing her mother's gargantuan parts with its prongs. Iona was extraordinary, and somewhat alarming, Alice thought.

"She's writing a novel," Iona told Alice. "Only it gets longer and more fucking boring by the day."

"Have you read it?" Alice said.

" 'Course I haven't read it," Iona said. "Fuck. Why should I, when it's such a pile of shit?" Iona, who was a bright and able child, was committed to the redundant rump of the local secondary school where she sat among obstructive bruisers who played football with their schoolbags during lessons. She had seemingly contrived this position through resolute underachievement and in order to annoy her mother. She could be wildly funny about her classmates and about what the curriculum considered suitable for the "less able child," particularly to Roland, who—much to her mother's chagrin and to Alice's surprise—got on with Iona like a house on fire.

Iona's mother had been abandoned by her American husband and had brought her child to England at the age of seven, an angry, destructive, bright little girl who had sunk her teeth into the flesh of her new classmates, had repeatedly flooded the junior school toilets and had frequently played truant. Now, seven years later, and with a tolerant and understanding stepfather who had even gone to the lengths of adopting her, Iona continued to play truant. She also chain-smoked, painted over the windows of her bedroom with matt-black emulsion paint, stayed out all night without picking up the phone and hung out over weekends with drunken, neofascist public-school boys in black winkle-picker shoes.

Iona's dress was a curious hybrid of puff-sleeved milkmaid blouses worn with a studded biker's jacket, filthy scarlet cheerleader's skirt and high-heeled black suede ankle boots. These last she had swathed in metal chains and she wore them, invariably, over derelict black fishnet tights with enormous holes held together here and there with lumps of Blu-Tack. Iona dyed her hair black. She wore black lipstick and black nail varnish on the stumps of severely bitten fingernails and she always wore six earrings—three pendant human skulls modeled in lead, a crucifix and a pair of smallish meat hooks. On Saturday nights Iona sometimes crimped her hair with a sort of hand-held waffle iron, which she plugged into the wall. She would coat the hair in styling mousse before clamping it between the jaws of the waffle iron. The effect on the hair was Tom-and-Jerry electrified zigzag, while on the waffle iron it was a Chinese lacquer of old hairspray and styling mousse textured with unattractive layers of caramelized hair.

Yet Roland, unlike Alice, seemed wholly untroubled by Iona. Or was it, as Alice suspected, that Iona looked to Roland like walking ammunition against her mother?

"Spunky little thing," he remarked, after Iona had passed him on the stairs looking like a well-rumpled extra on the set of a Dracula movie. "Now come on, Alice, don't be a prude. Weren't you ever a 'teenager,' my poppet?" It came to Alice, with some surprise, that she still was a "teenager," in fact. "My adorable, old-fashioned girl,"

Roland said. "Just because you've been sensibly brought up. I'm quite sure your mother never spent her time slouching in an unreconstituted coalhole."

"No," Alice said, and she thought of her mother, with her intercom and her BMW and her opalescent fingernails. "No, she didn't, I suppose." She hadn't talked to him much about her parents.

Alice, before she began to teach Thomas and Sophie Morgan to read, guardedly petitioned Roland for know-how.

"How do you teach people to read?" she said.

"I don't," Roland said. "My boys all come to me having passed the Common Entrance Examination."

"Yes, but how do you do it?" Alice said. Roland surprised her then by casually letting drop that he had done a stint of teaching practice in a secondary school in Hackney where he had evidently taught illiterates with a high degree of success. He was not at all given to considering this achievement remarkable, nor to analyzing quite how he had done it. Not until Alice so insistently began to press him.

"Much the same as teaching anything else, that's all," he said. "Nine-tenths positive thinking and twelve-tenths crowd control. You can't teach anything if your class is hanging from the wall bars. Oh, I don't know, Alice. Just the usual carrot and stick."

"Sorry?" Alice said.

"House points when they get it right and whack them when they shirk," Roland said. "Just above the ankle and it seldom leaves a mark."

"Are you s-saying you h-hit them?" Alice said.

Roland laughed. "Only when it was absolutely necessary," he said. "Come on, Alice. Snot-nosed rabble? No bloody discipline, you understand. Someone had to do it."

"And h-house points?" Alice said. "In H-hackney?"

"Speaking metaphorically, of course," Roland said. "Gold stars, silver stars, boiled sweets, any old tripe. First you invent the currency and then you ration it like blazes. Never pays to play the soup kitchen with a bunch of kids, you know. Why are you interrogating me like this?"

"Well—," Alice said. "I'm only asking." And Roland smiled, knowingly.

"Do I take it that the poor little Morgan tribe can't read?" he said. "Well, well, well."

"Only Thomas and Sophie," Alice replied. "William is too young."

Roland kissed her. "Frankly, I shouldn't bother if I were you," he said. "I mean, if the kids' own parents don't think them worth the price of a decent prep school." There were times when Roland, for all his evident humanity, was capable of utterances like this.

"They don't have any m-money," Alice said. "And they don't believe in p-privilege. David wants the same f-for everybody's children."

"How frightfully perverted," Roland said promptly. "You'd expect the chap would at least try and root for his own kids." Nonetheless, Roland appeared next day with a set of aged Beacon Readers and a box of homemade word cards in bold lowercase.

"No special magic, sweetie," he said. "If you're serious about all this. Ten minutes every day and go rather miserly on the house points. Tell me: what are these infants forbidden—or do they have *carte blanche*?"

"White sugar and red food coloring," Alice said. "Maya doesn't allow them in the house."

"Right," Roland said, with a rare dollop of malice. "I believe that what meets the case here is cherry-flavored lollipops. And another thing, my poppet. Blow their noses before you begin."

"What for?" Alice said.

"Induces murderous intent," he said. "Proximity to minors wiping snot all over their shirtcuffs."

Alice, in the event, used Smarties and perfumed erasers and little plastic space toys, which were currently endowed with prestige. She was anything but miserly with the treats and handed them out very readily. Indeed, Sophie and Thomas would do nothing until they had made a smash-and-grab raid on her treasure store. But she heard them every day and by the end of the term they could read.

David was in his kitchen when Sophie read to him, stumblingly, from *The Magic Iron Pot*.

" 'The-pot-said—"I skip, I skip—I-skip-to-the-rich-man's-house-and-bring-back-what-ever-you-need," ' " Sophie read. David was burning his fingers on a casserole at the time. The casserole, like everything David cooked, came a sort of army camouflage green. He dropped it on the floor where it lay like seaweed at low tide.

"Ouch!" he said. "Good God. Sophie! Are you telling me you can read?" And he smiled with pleasure through his steamed-up lenses.

"And me," Thomas said.

"I'm better," Sophie said.

"Shurrup bum-head," Thomas said. "We both done it the same with Alice."

"The woman is a marvel," David said. "Well done, small-fry." And he went to call Maya from the coalshed.

"The children can read," he said. "Listen."

Thomas took the book and began to read. " 'As-soon-as-it-was-filled-it-said—"I skip-I skip"—it-skipped-away-and-went-from-the-rich-wo-man's-kitchen-to-the-poor-wo-man's-kitchen,' " Thomas incanted.

"A suitable tale of socialist redress," Roland said, just to needle Maya. She appeared not to hear him. Neither did she appear at all surprised or impressed.

"Learning readiness," she said. She was addressing David as he shoveled his dinner from the floor. "Everyone finds his own pace."

"Poppycock," Roland said. "Alice has taught your kids to read, Maya. She's been wiping their snotty little noses and sticking them in a book day after day."

"It's true," David said. "Alice taught them."

Maya looked rather vaguely at Alice. Then she looked at David. "Alice stammers," she said. "I wonder why?" She eyed the remnants of strewn supper with indifference and returned fairly promptly to the coalshed.

The unexpected result of Alice's allotting daily time to the younger children's reading was Iona's evident jealousy. She, who had hitherto affected to regard Alice as little more than Roland's sidekick, now took to lingering in Alice's room and finding excuses to stay. Alice, who could not hear the little ones with Iona so loomingly present, sought to divert her on one of these occasions with the loan of *The Divine Miss Davidene Delight.* Iona opened one of the books at random and screamed with laughter.

" 'But she has the most heavenly new hat, Minerva, to match those sea green eyes. And yet quite serviceable too, I think. You would not consider it an extravagance.' "

It was only when Roland appeared that she was prevailed upon to leave. "But listen to this, Roland," Iona said, dawdling insistently and mincing through Jem's prose.

"Diana flung herself in a reverie upon the ancient oaken bench alongside the bun queue—"

"Bun queue?" Roland said absently. Iona struck a Sarah Bernhardt pose for him in the doorway. It was lost on him because he had sat down to consult the sports pages of his daily newspaper.

" 'She has signed her name in my autograph book. Only imagine, Minerva. The divine Miss Delight agreed to sign! And she has done so in green Indian ink. It is as green as the ocean. Ah, Minerva dearest, the sea will be my element.' "

Roland was focused on the county cricket scores. "On your way then, Minerva dearest," he said.

Iona looked at Alice. "Only if I can have some more of these," she said.

"If you like," Alice said. She lent Iona the first six exercise books containing My Last Duchess.

"Thanks," Iona said, and she carried them off to her matt-black bedroom to pore over them in private.

In the case of My Last Duchess, the effect upon Iona was really rather extraordinary. Within the week she had bought herself a typewriter, considerably more antique than that of her mother and funded on the back of Maya's stolen cashcard. She baldly informed Roland of this as he was overhauling it for her at Alice's desk. Iona was sprawled indolently beside him on the floor, smoking and piling up her cigarette ends in the damp dregs of a coffee mug. The typewriter appealed to Roland, who was fond of fine old mechanisms. He accorded it all the respect he showed for his pretty old Citroën DS. It was puzzling to Alice that he took considerably more interest in the typewriter than he had ever taken in Thomas and Sophie's progress, though they were bright little children and had romped ahead with remarkable speed to The King of the Golden River.

"Rather a pity that it's lost its *H*," he said with respect.

"Sod the fucking *H*!" Iona said vehemently. "Christ, Roland! How do you get to be so fucking anal? If you didn't have a fucking size eight cricket bat shoved permanently up your arse, I reckon you'd be a really okay bloke."

"Could be that you mean a long Harrow, Iona," Roland said agreeably, without looking up from his renovations.

"What?" Iona said.

"After a size six you get a short Harrow and a long Harrow," Roland said.

"Fuck!" Iona said. "Cricket bats. Who gives a fuck? And I don't give a fuck about the *H* on that thing either. Just make it go. I mean who needs *H*? Old Wurzel Gummidge downstairs in the rathole's got *H* and where the fuck has it ever got her?"

Roland's cough was the best he could manage in the circumstances to convey a semblance of polite neutrality. He fitted a sheet of paper carefully into the roller and wound it on.

"We'll keep the language in check a bit, shall we?" he said, but only half seriously, and he tapped at the space bar until the bell rang, making a nice little "ting." "We have two ladies in our midst." He meant Alice and Sophie. Alice yearned right then not to be one of the ladies, but it seemed that there was little she could do about it. The manner that Roland exhibited with Iona—a manner halfway between reform school instructor and messmate—was one she envied, even though she was not aware that, had he only made use of it with her, it could have brought out her own dormant liveliness. Roland so depended upon her stillness.

"Ladies?" Iona said. "Where? Do you mean virgins, Roland?"

Roland worked on in a stiff, schoolmasterish silence, as if he hadn't heard. He tapped out "the quick brown fox," first in lowercase and then in uppercase. After that he typed out all the numbers and the signs. Then he shut the case and stood up, lifting the typewriter carefully from below.

"Done," he said, quite pleasantly. "Now be off with you, my smelly one. Sophie and Thomas as well. Leave me in peace with my girlfriend."

Roland often told Iona she was smelly. Alice found it offensive, the more so because it was true, but Iona did not seem to mind at all.

Roland would wisecrack with her about coal-tar soap and brands of deodorant. He would offer to fix her up with a camel driver for a husband. He would inquire whether she was maturing a small batch of Camembert in one of the armpits of the leather biker's jacket. She would merely hazard in return that his jockstrap came sterilized Optical White, or she would volunteer to drink Jackson's Orange Pekoe from his groin guard.

Roland handed her the typewriter. "Hold it from below now, Iona," he said. "Don't trust to the case, all right? That's a very fine machine you've got there."

"Christ!" Iona said. " 'Fine machine.' You crazy bloody wanker. I'll buy you a Mister Coffee for your birthday."

Roland bent down and picked up the coffee mug full of cigarette ends. He planted it on top of the typewriter. Then he held open the door, his affability unaffected. "Plotting the great novel then, are we?" he said. "Aiming to steal our mother's thunder?"

"Fuck!" Iona said with feeling. She dropped her last cigarette end in the doorway and extinguished it by grinding it into Alice's carpet. "Hardly need to write a fucking novel then, do I? I can hop off round next door's 'n' get myself fucked by old Koplinski. That'd 'steal her thunder.' Night, Roland." And she left.

Paul Koplinski produced an afternoon soap opera for housewives' television. He lived in the house that adjoined the Morgans', but his house, unlike the Morgans', was in a constant state of improvement. Builders worked round the clock to open up rooms, glaze walls, insert joists, remove chimney breasts, reposition sections of staircase and turn the garden from Victorian semi into a composite of Hansel and Gretel and the Hanging Gardens of Babylon. Flowerbeds were either raised up or cast down, mezzanine floors appeared overnight, a small clapboard weather porch now extruded from the facade, and the kitchen was gradually fixing its ambience halfway between Catalonia and Tuscany. Paul Koplinski was English, in spite of his name, and came from the Midlands. He wore mirror lenses and tried hard to appear transatlantic, but his battery of whining, down-market English phrases sabotaged his aspiration. "Pop in for a coffay then," he said. "D'you fancy popping in for a coffay, then?"

Paul Koplinski, Alice had observed the only time she had popped in for a coffee, was big in the business of "us" and "them." Since he maintained a builder's skip semipermanently at the front of his house, it had seemed to her that his major hobby was lying in wait to catch the populace in the act of illegal dumping. Yet the skip came to consciousness every morning with a satisfactory new crop of usurping old mattresses, broken furniture and household rubbish. Only the Morgans, as their side passage bore impressive witness, were sufficiently scrupulous never to poach on Paul Koplinski's expensively rented skip space.

"My builders are pushed for space and honestlay!" he whined at Alice as usual. He wrenched first at an old gas fire, and then at a section of rain-soaked, rubber-backed Axminster carpet and cast them into the road. "Look at that! They've been dumping on me again!"

"I'm s-sorry," Alice said. That was when Paul Koplinski had asked her to pop in for a coffee and had tried to get lechy. He lived on his own and grumbled about his alimony payments. He was pretty well off, really, Alice thought, but he wanted to be a person who had gold records fixed to his walls. Instead he constructed storylines which morons then wrote up. He had tried to interest Maya in writing up storylines for his soap opera, but she was too dedicated to rewriting her novel—a dreary affair, Paul blabbed, full of battered women and housing problems. Still, she slept with him more readily each time it got rejected. This last he had not told Alice. That was why Alice at once dismissed Iona's imputation as a destructive adolescent lie. As for Roland, he addressed the matter not at all. It was of no interest to him to contemplate Maya Morgan between the sheets, her husband's or anyone else's. As for poor old Iona—one would need to be a peculiarly bent sort of pedophile to get within touching distance. Roland wanted Alice between his sheets. Sweet, pretty, fragile Alice who stammered over his name and provoked in him great climaxes of tenderness.

WHEN THE LETTER CAME, eventually, from Miss Trotter's new secretary, it had been sent second class to Alice's college and lodged there in the wrong pigeonhole. The address it provided was somewhere in London East. 149 Belbury Close.

"Council estate," said Roland, all too briskly. "Still game are we, my poppet?"

"Yes, of course," Alice said.

"Jolly good," said Roland. He said it as though he were awarding her a Venturer's badge in the Brownies. It was arranged that he would drive down with her that Saturday afternoon and on the way back, rather at his insistence, they would stay overnight in Surrey. That way he could meet his girlfriend's parents.

The experience was quite the worst that Alice could remember. Worse than the day that Flora's father had swelled up before her eyes and shed his skin. The place Miss Trotter's records had provided materialized not as one of a neat row of little council houses that Alice had begun cautiously to envisage, but as a nightmarish, windowless extrusion of vandalized concrete, partly boarded up and sparsely occupied by incoherent and half-drugged squatters.

"Sh-she n-n-n—," Alice said. "R-roland, she never lived here. Th-this is s-some mistake."

"Turning back then, are we?" Roland said.

"No," Alice said. Roland, though he was anything but happy to leave his beautiful old Citroën unattended, got out and accompanied her through the filth of dog turds, empty syringes and abandoned plastic carrier bags that lay strewn along the concrete waste.

There was nobody in 149 Belbury Close, though through the ruptured plywood of the front door Alice could see that, in the middle of
the otherwise empty floor, lay a pile of empty vodka bottles and the
demented remains of a heap of miscellaneous furniture to which
someone—perhaps to keep warm—had at some time applied a
match. The retreat along the narrow, open corridor that led to the
staircase afflicted Alice with paralyzing vertigo.

"Close your eyes and give me your hand," Roland said firmly. That
was what she did. Once across the concrete waste, she registered, a
moment before Roland, that the Citroën had been stripped of its wing
mirrors. Neither of them spoke for fully ten minutes in the car.

"I'm sorry, Roland," Alice said.

"I think," Roland replied, a little stiffly, "I really think, Alice, that
the less we say about this venture, the better we both shall like it."

"Yes," Alice said. "But I'm still s-sorry." She knew that for Roland to
lose his wing mirrors bore no comparison with her own horribly raw
and bleeding grief for Jem McCrail, but the experience had left her
humbled. If any power in the relationship had ever been hers, that
was the case no longer. Roland had supported her through this hideous and ill-advised quest. Roland was kind and sensible. Roland was
more than she deserved. She belonged to him. Her voice, when it
came, was small and supplicant.

"Can we say n-n-n-n. Not tell my parents?" she said. "Please,
Roland."

" 'Course," Roland said. "Nothing at all, my darling."

It did not help that, in the midst of Alice's repressed grief and confusion, Mr. and Mrs. Pilling were evidently incapable of warming to
Roland. Though he made laudable efforts, in the wake of Alice's un-
helpful silences, to make himself agreeable, the Pillings were disconcerted by his style. They misunderstood his humor and were affronted
by his accent, which they took, quite without justification, as a put-
down to themselves. His manners struck them as lordly and—since
schoolmasters featured for them among the poorer and lowlier catego-
ries of humanity—they were roused to silent indignation by the ease
with which authority sat on him. Most of all they were alarmed by his
proprietorial air with their daughter. No, thought Mrs. Pilling, Alice

could not possibly want such a toff. No, of course not. Especially not a toff who was in truth no more than a lackey in a boys' school.

Roland was not the nice young man whom the Pillings had had in mind. He embodied and made specific for Alice's parents all the unformulated misgiving they had experienced in watching Alice leave them for Oxford. Furthermore, since Alice was so much more muted even than usual, it seemed to them perfectly obvious that Roland was not good for her. Over "drinks" Alice spoke hardly at all. Even when questioned directly she sometimes did not notice. Roland, in acting to protect her, talked valiantly in her stead with all the good humor he could muster. He did this, though Mrs. Pilling distracted him with refreshment that he found both unpalatable and quite shockingly extravagant.

Roland observed that Alice's mother drank an alcoholic liquid that came the color of glacé cherries. In the context, he resigned himself to drinking whiskey, thinking that to ask for beer might be construed as inappropriate. She offered him a platter of dubious green pulp on crackers. The pulp contained lumps of black olive, which was not a thing he cared for. Though his ears might well have been deceiving him, he thought she had called it some sort of mole. Pureed Surrey mole? Surely not! Roland ate rather a lot of it, in order that his negative feelings toward it should not become too apparent. And how on earth was it that his sweet, rather plainly dressed Alice should have a mother like this, with those artificial streaks in her hair and decked out in gold jewelry just for a Saturday night at home? Evidently he was wrong about the apple and the tree. Or else Alice was a miracle.

"And what about your new room, my lovey?" Mrs. Pilling said. "Tell us all about it, Alice." Alice, sunk in wretchedness, answered not at all. She appeared not even to hear. Roland had never seen her like that. She was like a deaf mute. As he watched her sit and play with her fingernail, his heart went out to her. Cover for the darling girl, he thought. Keep the parents off her back. In doing so he reached without thinking for a form of innocuous but class-bound humor that came to him very easily.

"The poor dear girl," he said, "is billeted in the most frightful tip."
He spoke just as he might have done to amuse his own dear mother.
"Alice has fallen among filthy Marxists," he continued. " 'Filthy' being
the operative word. It's my belief that she'll get back to find the
Department of Health and Public Safety has placed a cordon around
the premises."

The Pillings were both offended. Roland sensed too late that his
public was not with him and found that his hosts were staring at him
with hostility and distaste.

Roland was far too polite to dream of voicing criticism to Alice of her
parents. He was also far too ready to think the best of them. They
were thoroughly decent types, the Pillings, resourceful and straight.
Bit short on humor, to be sure, but then the old boy came from up
north. And—God Almighty—had the poor dears really thought he
was suggesting that their darling daughter was wallowing in filth?
How absurd! But seriously, Roland thought, hats off to the poor old
things. Given that they were hardly educated people to say the least,
they had really done Alice proud—even if they did seem to watch her
far too much, as though she were an item on the television. How
frightful to be an only child, he thought, and be burdened with all
that overbearing concern. No wonder the poor kid stammered. And
all that flashy money. That was a teeny bit embarrassing; teeny bit
omnipresent, so to speak. He had not realized that building contractors could manage to get that rich.

Roland, like his parents, was careful with money and fairly modest
in his needs. It never crossed his mind that the Pillings simply enjoyed spending their money. He decided, charitably, that their con-
spicuous expenditure denoted a pitiable state of insecurity. The poor
things, he thought, with their millionaire sofas and gadgetry and
their swimming pool and their house on the Costa del something-or-
other. If only one could reassure them that it simply wasn't necessary
to go in for such obvious display.

Roland's alimentary tract was groaning as he reflected on Mrs.
Pilling's food. Whatever had it all been for? The poultry so messed
about with pine nuts and red wine. And following so hard upon the
pureed mole. Oh help! And then there were two kinds of pudding—

the "Passion-Fruit" whatever and "Mango Brûlée." (Had she really called it "Mango Brûlée"?) I mean whatever had happened to caramel custard, if one was wanting to be a bit splashy? Or raspberry fool? His own mother managed so splendidly with the greengages and red currants that grew in the kitchen garden.

After the meal was over, Roland searched the visitor's bathroom cabinet in vain for indigestion tablets. Then he went for a walk instead. He was delighted when Alice met him on the way back, though she had done so mainly to avoid her mother's talk.

"My darling, my baby!" Mrs. Pilling had said. "You're not serious about this man!"

They turned and walked on in silence for more than half an hour. A silence that Roland loved and relished. What a marvelous girl Alice was! All the more so, now that he could appreciate her background. Here was Alice, the last person on earth to hanker after fancy furniture and hair tints and expensive tropical fruits. He stopped and kissed her. Alice was rather wooden.

"You're thinking about your friend," he said. "I'm sorry, dearest poppet. I'm afraid I failed you."

"No," Alice said. "Please. You tried."

Roland's stomach suddenly protested audibly in the darkness. "Do excuse me, I've eaten far too well." Alice said nothing. She knew that Roland liked boarding-school food. "Tell me, Alice," he said, with scrupulous politeness. "That greenish puree—"

"Guacamole?" Alice said. "It's avocado and tomatoes."

"Ah," Roland said. "Ah yes. Ah yes, of course. I see."

Once Alice had returned from her disturbing trip to 149 Belbury Close, she saw, with some relief, that Iona had replaced *My Last Duchess* in the box beside the chimney breast. She picked up the books now and read them from beginning to end. Doing so confirmed for her that the story was really quite remarkable. It was, just as Jem had said, "a more sustained work of greater maturity." It was quite different from all the other stories.

When she got to the part about the human hand in the hunting dogs' burial ground, the time had advanced well into the small hours. She remembered Claire's confusion over the Catholic goddess and

Flora's well-aimed, poisoned dart. "Of course they have a goddess." Even Jem had been lost for words. What a mystery Flora was. As much so in her own way as Jem. Yet Jem's warmth could touch Alice, even now. And Flora? Was Flora capable of warmth? Alice wondered. Or had her father's perennial thou-shalt-not made its way to the core of her being? Did all those years of companionship over the Sindy dolls' dream home and the pink and white brides mean nothing to her? Was there a coldness within Flora that no hot-water bottle could cherish? Alice struggled to suppress her thoughts on Flora. She focused again on the goddess. *Did* Catholics have a goddess? They had a Queen of Heaven. A peasant girl who had assumed the throne after carrying the heavens within her womb. How curiously radical Jem's religion was, with its insistent raising of the humble and meek. She wondered now, in passing, why it had no appeal for her charming, egalitarian landlord. But then David didn't want thrones at all, not for anyone, regardless of gender. And had Jem, like the Queen of Heaven, been humbly born? She had always seemed so much more like the Queen of the Night. And how did 149 Belbury Close square with the man of letters? And above all, where was Jem? Where?

Alice returned to the text. She read on right to the end. Jem's novel reached a final climax as the demon Umberto, having caught his wife red-handed in cahoots with the aged gardener, had flung her into the Ferrari and driven her at speed along the Amalfi coast with intent to fake an accident and pitch Gabriella over a cliff. He was fortuitously aborted in this design by a sudden cascade of falling sheet metal from the roof of a small white van that had appeared, as if from nowhere, to impede his perilous way forward. Umberto was dramatically decapitated. The car, veering to the seaward side, had its fall broken by rocks. Gabriella, as she recovered from unconsciousness, became aware that the man wrenching open the twisted passenger door had begun to address her in an Aberdeenshire accent.

"Angus!" Gabriella said. "Oh my own dear Angus." Before Umberto had flung her into the Ferrari, Gabriella had managed to leave a few vital messages upon the Highlander's answering machine. Angus, who had by now become an eminent brain surgeon, had also recently inherited a red sandstone castle, which rose majestically from a cliff-top over the North Sea. Alice put down the book. She heard Jem's voice across the years, countering Claire Crouchley's barracking jibes.

"Well," Jem had said. "Since a severed head is more than even a Highland brain surgeon can fix, off they go, back to the lochs and the purple heather. What's to stop them?"

"But how is it Gabriella has a baby?" Claire had said. "I thought she couldn't have any children."

But that, of course, was poor Umberto! The Demon Padrone was infertile. Gabriella's baby, a beautiful dark-eyed girl, had been conceived, out of wedlock, on the journey back from Amalfi. The act had been committed in the sleeping car of the Flying Scotsman. Alice now wondered whether Angus had produced from his rucksack a bottle of Laphroaig. And had he "taken instruction"?

 ROLAND HAD MET Dr. Gubbins at a schoolmasters' conference shortly after he had met Alice. Then, a good while later, he had run into him at Twickenham. Dr. Gubbins, the headmaster of a boys' public school in the north of England, had, on both occasions, been very much impressed with Roland. He had prolonged the contact beyond the rugby match by proposing that Roland accompany him to a restaurant, to which Roland had readily agreed. For Dr. Gubbins the occasion had provided an extended opportunity to size up Roland for a job. He had a shrewd eye for what he was after, and it seemed to him that Roland, for all he was still very young, was of the sort that these days was becoming rarer than gold. He paused in the act of forking up Scottish salmon.

"Are you married?" he asked. It was, frankly, necessary to know this sort of thing. One did not wish to place a chap in a position of academic and pastoral responsibility, only to find him landed with quite the wrong sort of spouse. Anything was possible these days. Young women cavorting with the upper sixth in states of half undress and what-have-you.

"No, sir," Roland said, but his smile gave away his pleasure as he thought of Alice back in Oxford, with her neat blond head and her thoughtful expression, bent over her work. He saw her well-ordered pens and reference books beside her on that funny little desk at the top of the Morgans' house. "Jeffreys is a dunderhead." Oh, dearest Alice! What a bright, adorable girl she was. Absolutely one in a million. It delighted him to think that one day, quite soon, he would be parking his size twelve shoes at the end of her bed as a matter of simple and gratifying routine. Alice would be marvelous once she had got over her shyness. How could she possibly not be? He had never dreamed of pressuring her; not really pressuring her. And her modesty, for all that he found it difficult at times, was a part of what he had come to esteem about her so highly. He would marry Alice and she would be wonderful. Nothing could possibly be a problem. His own parents were very fond of her, and her parents—well, they would come round to the idea. They were decent sorts, after all. Little bit nouveau, but fundamentally full of thoroughness and good sense. He envisaged that his father would marry them. He wondered tenderly whether Alice would stumble over her marriage vows. "I, Alice Amelia, take thee thee, R-roland Al-Alla-ll-Alexander, to be my lawful w-wedded husband."

"No, I'm not married," Roland said, glowing slightly as he spoke. "That is to say, not yet." Dr. Gubbins looked up at him acutely. "My girlfriend has eight terms ahead of her," he continued. "I wouldn't want marriage to get in her way."

"Ah, she's with you at Oxford," mused the doctor with approval. Everything about Roland appeared to meet with his approval. "Jolly good," he said. "PPE?"

"Classics," said Roland.

"Ah yes indeed," said the doctor with enthusiasm, thanking God that it wasn't sociology. Or French. He was keen to have his senior staff meet Roland. And also Mrs. Gubbins.

"These little chess players of yours," he said. "Care to bring them up in the spring? Few of the front-runners, what do you say? Bring the little woman with you."

Roland drove to Yorkshire in the Citroën DS. It was a pleasure to drive in his beautiful old car through the moors and dales. It comfortably accommodated the four little boys who constituted the pick of his first-form chess players, plus himself and Alice. Alice had been puzzled by the invitation to herself and a little reluctant to come. She had her first set of exams that term and would have preferred to stay at home with her ancient texts. And she was furthermore not much at ease with the prospect of three nights in a boys' public school, but

Roland had jollied her out of misgivings. He knew very well that the occasion would have less to do with his chess players and more to do with himself; that effectively he was being interviewed and so indeed was Alice. But he had not told her that for fear of alarming her.

"Oh come on, sweetie. It's 'The North,' isn't it? I thought you had people up there?"

"B-but a headmaster," Alice said.

"Well, you've survived a clergyman, haven't you?" Roland said. "Come for my sake, poppet. Let me show off your prettiness a bit." Alice winced just slightly. "I would like your company," he said.

Roland enjoyed the trip enormously. He was in no way aware that to Alice he was not showing up to best advantage. First, he was gently, complacently bigoted about the north of England; bigoted and genially patronizing. He considered it the repository of people—good, plain, simple sorts—who had not had quite the vision or the enterprise to make something of themselves. Of course once upon a time there had been George Stephenson and the traction engine and so on, but that, unfortunately, was history. "The North," in these present times, was full of people who expended their energies on growing leeks, on breeding pigeons, on eating faggots with mushy peas, and also on voting Labour. Admittedly, Yorkshire had, in the past, been capable of producing the odd decent cricketer. Credit where credit was due. But even this was now history.

Dr. Gubbins's school, of course, would be quite another matter. An elite southern implant, set in beautiful, rural North Yorkshire, with an intake of bright, enterprising boys who spoke Standard English, had all performed creditably in the Common Entrance Examination and were now benefiting from the marvelous open countryside and the bracing, cleaner air. The servants would be natives, of course. One might have some difficulty understanding them at first, but that could be overcome. Once one was attuned to the lingo.

Alice went north every year after Christmas; well north of Dr. Gubbins's part of North Yorkshire. She and her parents visited her grandmother, who still lived in the terraced cottage in a mining village where her father had grown up. There was an old iron range in the living room over which Alice's grandmother hung her washing and in which she baked her bread. She adored her son and was proud of him, and of his glamorous, get-ahead wife and his dear little daughter, her favorite grandchild. She was pained by Harry's voting habits, admittedly, but she courteously never referred to them. She called Alice "pet," and "a little old-fashioned 'un," and took her to meet old Mrs. Benn and old Mrs. Ball, whose fifty-year-old daughter Margaret did beautiful crochet work and minded her invalid father-in-law whose leg had been crushed in a pit accident midway between the wars when he was no more than a lad of sixteen. Alice's grandma said "B'ye!" when anything surprised or excited her. Her voice cracked with vigorous laughter and she still did her laundry by hand or in what she called "the boiler." Much as her son and her daughter-in-law had tried to foist technology upon her, she had displayed no interest at all in having her own machine, nor even in the idea of the launderette, which she resolutely referred to as "the washhouse."

In the car on the way up to Yorkshire, Roland's boys affected silly Yorkshire accents and made jokes about bingo halls. They pointed out arthritic old yokels from the car windows and said "ee by gum" if ever they saw one of them wearing a cloth cap. In between, they talked incessantly in their jarring little posh voices, dropping anecdotes with regard to their parents' importance and telling knock-knock jokes in French.

"Frappe-frappe."

"Qui est-ce?"

"C'est Monsieur le Docteur."

"Sir? What do you call a man with a spade in his head, sir?"

"Sir? And then, you see, my grandfather was actually asked to rule the island, sir. But unfortunately he was far too busy."

The boys were called Whitecross, Pyecroft, Burnley and Craggs. They did not appear to have any first names. Roland was fond of his clever little boys and rather proud of them. He was also sufficiently sanguine to tolerate Alice's relative constraint with them, attributing it, as he did, to her inexperience with exuberant male children. He seemed untroubled by their prattle. Only once, when Whitecross had talked almost literally nonstop for fully fifteen minutes, Roland had said firmly, midanecdote: "Put a sock in it, will you, Whitecross?" And Whitecross had actually stopped. The silence pulsed expectantly for something like thirty seconds and then, into its tautness, Burnley sang the Orlando Gibbons *Magnificat*.

Burnley sang with astonishing purity. He had entered Roland's first form from a highly repressive and much esteemed choir school where his clear, unwavering soprano voice—soprano for not very much longer—had been rigorously and accurately trained. It did not enter Burnley's mind as he sang how radical was his text, nor how startlingly written from below, but he enunciated beautifully. "He hath scattered the proud in the ee-maj-in-ay-see-on of their hearts," sang Burnley, who five minutes before had been miming the yokels in the Hovis advertisements.

For Alice, Roland's trite little burgeoning toffs, who laughed at the likes of her grandmother's friends, simply gave her a new and profounder respect for David Morgan, who had so resolutely kept his children in the state schools. They might not teach very much, he said, but they taught people how to live with each other. She could see that—given ten years—if you were to put Roland's pupils in a workingman's club, they would never merge and blend; never talk merely as one man to another. They would store up hatred and envy and they would very likely emerge with a workingman's knee in the groin. Roland, admittedly, was different. Roland talked courteously to almost everybody. He was full of kindness and he never bragged. Never. Moreover, Roland was not rich. Yet even he, merely by opening his mouth, had had the capacity to make Alice's wealthy and successful parents feel put down. And why was he so obtuse about privilege and snobbery and bigotry? It was a kind of appalling innocence he had. An incurable, complacent blind spot. Right now it made Alice extremely queasy.

The trip was also a new and daunting opportunity to watch Roland wearing his schoolmaster's hat unrelievedly for hours and hours on end. Until the trip such opportunities had been brief and fairly intermittent; a few minutes here and there, if ever she had called for him at his school, which was almost never. Now it was interminable and most of it stuck in a car.

Alice found herself not very comfortable with Roland's crowd control, highly effective as it was. Given how gentle and patient and courteous he invariably was with her, his manner with the children surprised and shocked her with its rigorously Spartan style. Roland was unambiguously disciplinarian in a comfortably pragmatic sort of way. He was uncomplicated and untroubled by the inequalities of command and he perceived a great convenience in the expedient of short rope. Since this was tempered by his energy and competence, his basic kindness and his obvious commitment, his boys all evidently adored him. But to Alice, right then, it was distasteful. Roland had become a dictator with four small subjects in a row in the back of his car. The cues by which he either laughed with them or censured them, or hemmed them in with protocol, were ones that she could not read.

And being out of the schoolroom was making things a little harder for the children. Alice could appreciate that. The situation implied a degree of informality that left the boundaries of license and prohibition somewhat blurred. In the circumstances, Roland's judgments seemed to her really most curious at times. He had allowed Whitecross, for example, to make a belittling reference to "girls."

"Here," Roland said, passing the Ordnance Survey map unceremoniously over his shoulder. "Pyecroft, give us the route. 8753. Just beyond the station. Got it?"

"Yes sir," said the boy. "But wouldn't Miss Pilling like to navigate, sir? She's sitting beside you, sir."

"Don't be thick, Pyecroft," said Whitecross. "Miss Pilling's a girl!" Half-suppressed mirth and gigglings emanated from the back in response to this idiotic remark, yet Roland said absolutely nothing. This was because he too thought it was funny, Alice realized. When she looked at him he was experiencing a certain difficulty in trying not to smile. And what was so funny, when she had got an A for her O-level geography, while Roland's snotty little first-formers were still four years away from taking it?

On the other hand, when Pyecroft had been a little bit outspoken about one of the other masters, then Roland had made a great palaver about it and had practically held a summary execution—even though he had told her afterwards that what the child had said was true.

"Sir?" said Craggs. "Can me and Burnley have extra time on our Symmetry, when we get back, sir?"

"No," Roland said. "Tuesday is the deadline."

"But sir, that's not fair, sir," said Burnley. "Mr. Braithwaite's given Pyecroft till Thursday, sir. Because of him being in the chess team, sir." Roland ignored him.

"Sir?" Craggs said candidly. "Why are you always so strict, sir?"

"Because," Roland said, baldly stating the truth, "that way life is a lot simpler for me, and rather more difficult for you. You're at school,

Craggs, not watching *Sesame Street*. I don't exist to stand on my head for you, do I?"

"No sir," said Craggs.

"Least you're not all weedy and sarcastic, sir," Whitecross said. "You're not always picking on people."

"Not like Mr. Braithwaite," Pyecroft said with feeling. Alice understood that he was speaking, however audibly, to Whitecross and not to Roland. "*And* he's got these hairs growing out of his nose," Pyecroft elaborated. "*And* he pongs like anything when he leans over your algebra."

Roland, in response to this injudicious gripe, seemed suddenly to exude an aura of ominous, court-martialing silence. He stopped the car while the four boys held their breath, and contrived an effective pause before going into action. Then he turned upon the already quailing Pyecroft a fixed, withering stare of quite intimidating censure. Pyecroft, Alice thought, was really the most bearable of the four boys. He was smallish and rather nice to look at, and—granted that he talked like all the others—he had, on the whole, exercised a greater degree of reticence.

"Are you asking to get beaten, Pyecroft?" Roland said. The child could not look at him. He looked down into his lap and he began to sweat. The tips of his ears had turned an embarrassing luminous pink.

". . . sir," he said, almost inaudibly.

"Look at me," Roland said determinedly, giving him no place to hide. "Get your head up, boy." The child raised his head and fixed his eyes with enormous difficulty in the region of Roland's left shoulder. "That's better," Roland said. "Speak up now, Pyecroft. Don't mumble."

"Yes sir," said the child. "I-I mean, no sir."

"No sir what?" Roland said. Oh, God in heaven, Alice thought. It made her cringe inside. She had never thought aggressively about Roland, but right then, when her eyes fixed on the ice ax in his cubbyhole, which he had bought that very morning on the way up in preparation for a trip to Snowdonia, she felt a momentary itch to lodge it in his skull, just to break the tension. Couldn't he see that the child could hardly speak?

"I'm waiting, Pyecroft," Roland said.

"No sir I don't want to get beaten sir," said the child.

"Good," Roland said. "Then I think we understand each other. You in the eleven for next Thursday?"

"Yes sir," said the child.

"I shall arrange to have you replaced," Roland said. "Mr. Leeming will be advised about it just as soon as we get back." A muscle in the child's face twitched, then stopped. He looked as if sentenced to death. He half opened his mouth in timorous horror and froze.

"Do you have anything to say?" Roland said.

"No sir," said the child.

"Good," Roland said. "Then we'll go on." He turned slowly and started the engine. Heavy silence. Alice resented it. In the back, the child was obviously struggling not to cry. The air in the car was toxic. All of them—she and all four children—had been poisoned by the fallout, and for what? So that Roland could close ranks with some disgusting old fart with smelly breath.

Soon afterwards they stopped to stretch their legs and to refresh themselves at a roadside café. Everybody was talking again, except for Alice, though Pyecroft had lost his jauntiness. Roland sat with Alice, drinking tea. The children were at the other end of the room, buying Cokes at the counter and sticky things to eat. Suddenly Whitecross was at Roland's elbow.

"Sir?" he said. "I'm sorry to disturb you, sir."

"What is it?" Roland said.

"Sir?" said Whitecross. "You know Pyecroft, sir?"

"Yes," Roland said. "I know Pyecroft."

"Well—," said Whitecross. "He's upset, sir."

"I know," Roland said nicely. "Of course he is." He said it wholly without guilt, as though Pyecroft's state of mind had no bearing on himself as the means of provoking it.

"Please sir. He wants to know, sir—couldn't you just beat him and then let him play in the match, sir?"

Roland looked curiously at Whitecross. "You his messenger, are you?" he said.

"Well sir, he's sort of a bit shy, sir," Whitecross said.

Roland smiled at him. "Yes, I know that," he said. "But he does know how to speak, Whitecross."

"Yes sir," Whitecross said. "See he's just got this new bat, sir."

"Oh really?" Roland said with genuine interest. "And what sort of new bat has Pyecroft got?"

"It's a Gray-Nicholls Scoop, sir," said Whitecross.

Roland looked impressed. "That's a very nice bat," he said. "Mind, he's turning out a very nice little batsman is Pyecroft. Very stylish. He deserves it."

"Yes sir," Whitecross said. "See, his father's just bought it for him, sir. He's spent all week knocking it in, sir."

Roland nodded. "I'm sure he's taking good care of it," he said.

Whitecross paused before resolving upon a new tack. "It's been a bit like the porter's scene in *Macbeth,* sir," he said. "Pyecroft and his new bat." Roland looked at him curiously. " '*Frappe-frappe-frappe,*' sir," Whitecross said, valiantly attempting to woo Roland with entertainment on behalf of his friend. " 'Here's a frapping, indeed!' "

Roland laughed. If this goes on much longer, Alice thought, I will quite literally die cringing. Right here in the café, in front of Roland and the children.

"So you see, sir," Whitecross said. "About Pyecroft's bat, sir—well—he's been sleeping with it beside his bed every night, sir."

Roland put a hand on the child's shoulder. "Whitecross," he said kindly, "he can't play. I won't let him. Now you know that and so does he. All right?" Then he took his hand back again.

"Yes sir," Whitecross said.

"Tell him his bat'll keep till the week after next," Roland said.

"Yes sir," Whitecross said. He hovered for a moment. Roland began to drink his tea.

"Whitecross," he said after a while. "If you hang about here any longer, I might begin charging you rent."

"Yes sir," Whitecross said. Then he left.

Roland looked out of the window. "Such beautiful country," he said.

Alice said nothing for a bit. "I feel sorry for him," she blurted out abruptly.

Roland smiled at her. "He's a nice kid," he said. "That goes for both of them. Thick as thieves since the first day of term. Shouldn't wonder if it doesn't last them all of their lives." You're not my best friend, Mavis, Alice thought resentfully. You're only my second-best friend. Gertie is my absolutely-absolutely best friend. Ever since last week.

Alice did not think that Pyecroft was an especially nice kid. But she still felt sorry for him.

"I feel sorry for him," she said again. Roland smiled at her again. It did not cross his mind at that moment that Alice was throwing him some kind of challenge, because Alice was not confrontational. Nor that she was expressing any serious unease about him. He was never very analytical about his role as a teacher. He was highly effective, that was all. And what had he done? He had let little Pyecroft know that he would not license rudeness about another member of staff. He had been quite emphatic, it was true, but there was no sense in pussy-footing around just because a child was a little bit shy. That way he would only get more shy. And if one didn't make these things clear in the first form one only stored up trouble for later on. In any case, there was never very much point in laying down the law ineffectually. Not if you expected to be obeyed. He had barred the child from participating in precisely one cricket fixture and that was it. Hardly the end of the world. Of course the boy was a bit crestfallen and would probably cry himself to sleep that night. That was life. Rough with the smooth and all that. As for Whitecross—well, he had the gift of the gab. This was not surprising, given that his father was one of the country's more flamboyant queen's counsels. He had been thoroughly delightful and entertaining, as he very often was—just so long as you didn't give him his head too much—and his performance over the new Gray-Nicholls was really most accomplished and amusing. But perhaps all this talk about discipline and cricket bats and algebra and so on—it was hardly the darling girl's day-to-day milieu.

"I'm sorry about the ever-present jackboot, sweetie," Roland said gracefully. "Rather unavoidable in present company. Little bit tedious for you, I'm sure."

Alice shook her head. It wasn't a little bit tedious, she thought. It was a little bit repellent. She wasn't quite sure why. She didn't feel superior to Roland. Quite the reverse, in fact. And she conceded that if she were in charge of Roland's boys, they would probably be running riot all over the café. They would probably not know one end of the Gray-Nicholls Scoop from the other and they would probably not have their Symmetry completed for Tuesday. And Burnley would probably not sing anything like as accurately or sit anything like as ramrod still in the choir stalls every Sunday, waiting for his cue in the *Nunc Dimittis.* But they would probably all get by. There was something so terribly strange, so terribly disturbing to her about it all. Made worse, somehow, because she was so certain that Roland was not sadistic, as doubtless some of the masters were. It was his very straightness that she found deterring. What point was there in drilling children as if you were grooming an officer class for the next war? Yes sir; no sir; three bags full sir. David's children were much more fun to be with. They talked crazy nonsense that made you laugh. They talked back to you as if you were just another person and not as if you were Monty of El Alamein. If you had said to Thomas, "Are you asking to get beaten, Morgan?" he would have pulled funny faces and made farty noises and said, "Have you got a pea for a brain, Jug-head?"—or something to that effect.

"He's a smashing kid, is little Pyecroft," Roland said. "Bright as a button. And, frankly, he's absolutely right about old Braithwaite. Hopeless bloody package. Should have been drowned at birth." He took off his glasses while he spoke and wiped them idly on a napkin. Then he put them on again. "Incessantly bloody sarcastic," he said. "And victimizing."

"V-victimizing?" Alice said, wishing to air her own sarcasm just a little, but Roland seemed to miss it.

"Ineffectual too," he said. "Except in making even boys like Pyecroft take against maths. He's my head of department. Ah well." Roland had never mentioned to her before that his head of department was a trial. He was much too courteous to impose his grumbles on her, or to bore her in any way with shop. "Poppet," he said, with a gentle, nice solicitude, because he thought she had the look of being wrung out, "are you very tired? We've not much further now." Alice shook her head.

"R-roland," she said, apparently from nowhere. "I've got O-level geography." Roland smiled at her. Dear, adorable Alice! Just very occasionally her discourse took on something of the surrealistic dottiness of David Morgan's children's. Something jumped out at you from nowhere. It amused him. It could be rather charming in a girl—the sudden, idiotic non sequitur.

"Oh jolly good," he said, and he laughed.

"I've got an A," she said. Roland's eyes twinkled. It always entertained him if an adult person so naively, transparently, paraded achievement. It was so absolutely "not done," but then Alice paraded so seldom and she was still so very young. Alice was not yet twenty. How lucky they were, to have found each other so early in their lives.

"Clever girlie, aren't you?" he said appreciatively. He related her remarks to nothing that had foregone. "Seriously, sweetie, I've never imagined you got into Oxford on very much less." Roland always behaved as though "getting into Oxford" automatically denoted superior intellect. Roland had gone from his public school to a university in the Midlands. He had never thought of himself as "academic." More as a "practical" person. She dismissed the issue as not worth pursuing.

Roland looked at the map. While he did so, Alice glanced across the café toward the counter. Whitecross, to the amusement of the others, was trying his hand at satire with the servingwoman. Craggs and Burnley were falling about and even Pyecroft was smiling. Whitecross was inquiring exuberantly after "Yorkshire parkin" in his best "ee by gum" voice. He was trying hard not to laugh as he spoke. After a while she turned and looked at Roland. He was still studying the map.

"One of them's putting on a silly voice," she said. She didn't like to say "Whitecross." No doubt if she had known his name, and if she were ever to have used it to the child, he would have been deeply affronted, as if she'd thought he was a girl. "Roland," she said. "I think that you should make him stop it."

Roland looked up. He cast an eye casually over the quartet of happy little boys at the other end of the room and noticed, to his satisfaction, that Pyecroft had cheered up.

"What's that?" he said.

"Your boys. They were asking for Yorkshire parkin in silly voices," Alice said. "You should make them stop it."

Roland laughed. "Oh, good Lord, sweetie," he said. "Give them a break. They're children. Let them have a bit of fun."

"But it's not f-funny," Alice said. Roland smiled at her a little flirtatiously. He loved the way she looked. Her straight shoulders, her square-cut pale hair, that adorably prim, earnest demeanor she had. He longed to kiss her there and then and would have done if only his pupils had not been in the room. And that morning, when they had stopped in one of those touristy little villages, he had doubled back into an antique shop and had bought her the prettiest little ring. He had made the purchase with extraordinary rapidity, but he knew the moment he saw it that the ring was absolutely perfect for her. Such a delicate, quiet little silver ring with a cluster of small blue stones the color of cornflowers. Roland was cautious in the management of his money, but he knew how to spend it where it mattered. Nothing mattered more to him than that Alice should wear this beautiful little ring as a statement of his esteem and love and unending loyalty; of his intent to honor her with his body and to endow her with his goods. He had written out a check, without balking, for nearly four hundred pounds.

"But it isn't f-funny," Alice said. "Roland, it's much worse th-th-worse th—. Well, I think it's highly offensive."

"You get quite dour once you've crossed the Derwent," Roland said, balancing affection and levity. "My word, poppet, but you do."

"I don't," Alice said, sounding quite dour. Roland smiled. An instinct rose in him to tease her just a little, because, really, between those innocent, wide-spaced eyes, like a new kitten's, which underlined her adorable seriousness, and, more recently, the effect of old Morgan's rather heavy socialist blather, she needed now and again to be coaxed into lightness. He looked up at Whitecross and called to him, beckoning him to approach.

"Whitecross, come here a moment, will you?" he said. The child approached with alacrity.

"Sir?" he said.

"Find any of that 'parkin' of yours, then, did you?"

The boy was all jauntiness in return. "Oh yes, sir!" he said emphatically. "Bit yummy, sir. Trouble is, Burnley's just scoffing it all, sir. He's sort of like a Hoover, sir. It's because he's got to be castrated next week, sir. Mr. Farnley's booked him in at the vet's, you see—it's to keep him in the choir, sir. And now he's scoffing all the parkin because he's emotionally disturbed, sir. Could you get him a psychiatrist, do you think, sir?" Roland laughed. "*And* he's got foot-and-mouth," Whitecross said. "So he's contaminating it all with his disgusting slobber. Just look at him, sir. And we've gone and used up all our money, worse luck, sir. We can't even buy any more of it."

Roland laughed again. He drew a pound from his trouser pocket and handed it to Whitecross. "Buy it on me," he said. "And don't make a nuisance of yourselves with the shopgirl." The "shopgirl," Alice observed, was significantly older than Roland. She was probably somebody's mother.

"No sir," Whitecross said. "Gosh, thank you, sir. Would you and Miss Pilling like some of it, sir?"

"Not for me, thank you," Roland said. "Save a small bite for Miss Pilling, would you? She feels very strongly about parkin."

"Yes, of course sir," Whitecross said. He moved off, hailing his chums across the length of the café and waving his pound in the air. He enacted a small, unsolicited burlesque as he did so, expressly for Roland's entertainment, price one pound. He did it in the "ee by gum" voice, which was really fairly accomplished as the genre went. Whitecross was the cockiest of the four little smart-arses and clearly held great sway among his peers.

"Burnley?!" he cried out. "Ee Sow-face!' Hast never scoffed all t' parkin there, lad?! Ee-aye, an' 'ere's t' gaffer's missus 'ud fancy a bite of it an' all! Oh aye! She's that keen on't Yorkshire parkin, is t' gaffer's missus, as t' gaffer says she can't rightly get enough of it." This final quip—touched as it was with a kind of innocent double entendre— emerged three-quarters drowned, as Whitecross and all his compatriots showed dangerous signs of choking to death on laughter. Roland looked at Alice.

"You're blushing just the teeniest bit," he said tenderly. Alice said nothing. They were ganging up on her, she thought. And it had to do with the fact that they could all pee standing up. If you couldn't pee standing up it seemed that it canceled out your O-level geography. Roland was infinitely, delicately charmed by the sudden high color in her cheeks. "How pretty you are, my Alice," he said. "Do I deserve anything half so fine as you?"

"Roland," Alice said. "Sup-p-p. I th-th-th." Roland's smile was like a small devoted kiss.

"Come now," he said. "Stop. Breathe deeply and try again." Alice stopped and breathed deeply and tried again.

"I think I had better go back to Dr. Neumann," she said. "That's if he's still alive."

And they all got back into the car. After that Burnley sang an extraordinary devotional song about Saint Nicholas, who had apparently leapt direct from his mother's womb to the font. And then, with his first breath, without the ghost of a stammer, had cried out the praises of God.

 ALICE DETESTED old Gubbins. He stank of pipe tobacco and he leaned over her just like Pyecroft's Mr. Braithwaite, with his seriously brown, stained teeth. The chaplain talked clichés in the chapel that night and got Roland to read one of the lessons. And when Roland came back to her and stood beside her in the pew, she thought that he sang "All my Hope on God is Founded" sort of as though God were his commanding officer. And she knew suddenly, very clearly, that she did not love him. Well, "love" him, yes. He was an absolute dear. She would always love him. But not ever have him make love to her. Not love him like that. Let's not debase the terminology. She did not want his body. There was something about the open, decent muscularity of everything that he stood for that made her retreat from it. She would always be retreating from it. The day had proved to her that that would never change, much as she had somehow expected and hoped that it would. Because nobody could have been worthier and nicer than Roland. Dear, kind, patient Roland. Competent, cheerful, handsome Roland, who would have constructed an emergency survival shelter for her in the tundra if ever that had become necessary; Roland, who could get every schoolboy to hang adoringly on his coat sleeve, simply by issuing grid references. Dear Roland, who had wanted so much to be a soldier—just about as much as he now looked forward to being Alice's loyal and decent husband.

Dr. and Mrs. Gubbins were besotted with Roland and pleased by his choice of woman. They made genteel innuendoes over dinner in the dining hall where the food was unspeakable and where Dr. Gubbins said grace in a sort of posh-voiced Latin that sounded exactly like Miss Trotter's—rather as if they were both ventriloquist's dummies in those nostalgically revived recordings of Uncle Mac on *Children's Hour*. Alice always made Latin sound as much like Italian as possible. It was a futile gesture; a small candle that she kept alight for Jem. "The Ancient Romans were not Italians, Veronica! Dear me, no! They were a highly disciplined and very hygienic people."

Roland was highly disciplined and very hygienic. And he was definitely not Italian. Good Lord no! Alice had never seen Roland unshaven. One probably could have drunk Jackson's Orange Pekoe from his groin guard as the unwashed Iona Morgan had saucily volunteered. Alice shuddered and she faltered in the hymn. That night she and Roland would sleep in adjoining bedrooms. What if the wall had a sliding panel? What if old Gubbins was seriously kinked and had fixed up two-way mirrors behind the reproduction of Gainsborough's *Blue Boy* that hung over the fireplace?

"Sorry, God," Alice said, inside her head. "I have really given you very little attention all of my life. And here I am in church singing a hymn to you and what I am really thinking about is Roland's groin. Inside Roland's well-pressed trousers lies a sort of Giant Mollusc. And I don't want it. I really would rather not think about it, if you could help me to that. I really and truly cannot contemplate the prospect of Roland's crotch with anything like equanimity. Is there something seriously the matter with me? It must surely be that I do not want anybody's crotch, if I do not want Roland's. The only men I have ever sighed for are John Donne, one-time Dean of Saint Paul's, and the Reverend Gerard Hopkins, S.J. And then, of course, most curious of all, there is Sarastro, Grand Master of the Brotherhood. Two of these are dead and the third never existed. Never will." But how can I be saying these things? Alice thought. And to God of all people! And I a guest in his house! And what is this that I'm saying? I the secular one that has never leapt up to the font? Am I saying that I hanker after wacky, religious men? Because one of these poses in his winding sheet and beseeches God to ravish him and batter his heart. The second swings like a hallucinated yo-yo. God oozes for him, and flashes, and rips him open with the lion's claw. Sometimes God comes to him like Darth Vader in charge of the electroshock clinic. As for Sarastro—what is he? A religious poseur in the Temple of Wisdom? An abductor? A manipulator? A sort of decadent, alternative pope? Or what is he? Can one take him straight? One might bloody well have to, since he has the power and the magic. Sarastro can make devouring lions appear in the forest and he can set tables there too, like holy altars of food. Wine issues from the ground for him, like the ooze of oil, crushed. Then, of course, there are Messrs. Gordon McCrail and Saul Gluckman— champions respectively of the Latin mass and the Talmud. But maybe I only care for these two because they were filtered to me through Jem. I savor the taste of Jem's word-magic more than Roland's mouth on my mouth. These things Alice did not venture to address to God directly.

"The way I am is not the way that you meant us to be, dear God— Sir," she resumed, and she felt herself, like Pyecroft, trying not to cry. "You meant us to go forth and multiply and Roland would be excellent for that. He is designed to make a very satisfactory mate. He is healthy and loyal and indefatigable and kind and lovely to look at. Roland is a 'verray, parfit gentil knyght.' Any woman with half a brain would jump at him. Look. I'm sorry. If I could be as easy and straight and normal and generally satisfactory as Roland, well, I would be. Really I would. But I couldn't be in a million years. My most venial sin must lie in seeming so. Because Roland will not believe that I am not all these things and I, in my weediness and inexperience, have led him on. Can I say in mitigation that Roland has never seriously listened to a word I say? I know it's true that I stammer and that I've stammered rather badly for most of this year." And then a light entered Alice's mind. "I stammer worst when I'm with Roland," she said. "Roland is the problem. What a terrible pity. What a charming man. Please God. Seriously. I cannot remove my undies for Roland Alexander Dent; for a person who says, 'Pyecroft is turning out a nice little batsman.' I can't. Oh, please God, spare me for eternity from confrontation with Roland's crotch."

Alice stopped and reflected upon her own appalling impertinence, because wouldn't God be rooting for Roland? He surely had every reason to. Roland seemed to proceed on that assumption, anyway. It was part of what made him so equable and nice. All his hope on God was founded, even though he was far too polite and far too understated ever to make that overt. (And even though bloody God had given him the wrong sort of eyes to be a soldier with. "Sod you, God.

Couldn't you have let him cheat on the eye test and have an armored vehicle and a snakebite kit?")

But Roland's God wasn't like that, so she might as well be saving her breath. If Roland's God had decided in his wisdom not to let you play on Thursday, there was no twisting his arm to have it otherwise. And Roland's God would never ooze or flash. Good Lord no! Nor would Roland ever get himself up in a winding sheet and beseech his God to ravish him. Good Lord no! God sat comfortably at the head of Roland's mess table articulating the grace in a public-school accent like Uncle Mac's. Alice was in no doubt at all, suddenly, that Roland's God would always pee standing up.

From three places down, Alice could hear that Burnley's voice was rising. It was rising perpendicular, like the pillars of the nave, and hanging pendant, beautiful, in the groins of the fanning vaults.

Mrs. Gubbins was dowdy beyond belief. She looked like a hippopotamus in clothes, Alice thought. And she marched Alice round her vegetable garden next morning where she talked about lettuces having "hearts" in a curious, deep, transvestite voice. Then she observed—within the hearing of one of the skivvies, Alice was sure—that the "local people," while they were "honest as the day," were just a wee bit short on grey matter.

Alice thought that the school, with its crenellated battlements and its ivy and its arrow slits in the tower, was like her own old school only writ so much grander and more deeply pretentious. The weekend was full of playing fields and chess and chapel and boys in blazers and Roland in his element and the senior boys sizing up her legs.

Then, finally, on the Sunday afternoon, Roland took her out in the car, saying happily how tremendously good it was to be alone with her in such superb countryside and wasn't it a delight, after Oxfordshire, to be winding through such dales. Roland was resting on his laurels. Dr. Gubbins had, as he had anticipated, offered him a job, not only as head of maths, but, within a term of taking up that appointment, as one of his housemasters as well. It would mean he could be shot of old Braithwaite by Michaelmas and do what he was good at without the additional grind of having to cover for a fool.

At the same time, as soon as Alice had written her finals, he could offer her that truly charming little stone house, with sheep on a green hillside visible from the upstairs sitting-room window and stone flags on the kitchen floor. The kitchen had a range and an old painted dresser that ran the whole length of one wall. Upstairs were the four pretty bedrooms, already becomingly papered with trellis patterns and small flowers. The house was within the school complex and from its rooms one could hear the hourly chime of the school clock in the tower. It did not daunt Roland that the house had no central heating. He was happy to undertake the lighting up of the old Russian stove each morning, and, for the rest, one would encourage one's family to take brisk walks and put on sensible clothing. All the bedrooms had their lovely old fireplaces intact, with tiles and lead-blacked hearth-stones and, well, if anyone were ill (and it was extremely unlikely ever to be himself) one would not hesitate to make up a fire for them in the grate.

Roland savored the prospect as he drove. He would not want to stay in the north forever, naturally, but what a perfect place to start one's married life and raise a young family. Apple trees abounded in the garden for one's children to climb. There was a swing, and a stone wall, beyond which lay open fields and grazing land.

He gave thought, considerately, to the environment from Alice's point of view. There were an awful lot of males about, to be sure, but his mother might be in a position to advise her on that. She had managed a happy and stable married life within a similar situation. Would it make his little Alice feel out of countenance? he wondered. She was a bit constrained with boys. But he would give her so much of his love and attention. Really. She would not feel bereft. She was not a great one for the gaggle anyway, if her college was anything to go by. Still, she ought to have the company of women from time to time. Not a gruesome old bat like Mrs. Gubbins, of course. Alice needed a girlfriend. Or failing that, a daughter.

Much as Roland relished the prospect of fathering male children, he hoped, for Alice's sake, that his first child would be a girl. He turned his thoughts for a moment to that ghastly cock-up over the myste-rious, vanishing RC. His heart still bled for Alice whenever he thought about that day. That this wretched child should have beguiled her with lies and claimed her heart and then abandoned her in that peremptory way. Quite extraordinary, really. People didn't behave like that. He had some intention of approaching the headmistress himself, once he could do so unambiguously in his role as Alice's fiancé, and see if something could be unraveled. Not that he wanted this dubious creature in his house, but to have it settled would be to let the matter rest. And Alice deserved to know.

Right then, Roland was conscious of a debt of gratitude to Alice. Granted, he was terribly good at his job, and his little boys had shown up extremely well, but darling Alice, who had not wanted to come with him in the first place, had really done him proud. She was so exquisitely pretty in that unfussed, sensible way. So polite and quiet; so attentive and respectful to her hosts. Her conversation—always circumspect and a little bit restrained by the stammer—had been intelligent, diplomatic and well informed. Sometimes, in the past, when they were on their own, she had said some rather curious things. Funny little troubled eccentric things, but, really, only because she wanted coaxing out of them. Yes, Alice had been absolutely splendid these last two days. Alice had come up trumps. Dr. Gubbins had clearly been delighted by her—as well he bloody should be! Even the old battle-ax had been quite enchanted. Roland smiled. That could well materialize as too much of a good thing of course, but the Gubbinses were due to retire quite soon. Mrs. Gubbins would not be haunting Alice for long.

Roland recalled with amusement the affable severity with which this awesome person had marched Alice off around the vegetable garden, stamping across the hall in those seven-league brogues and sounding every inch like the Red Queen on the warpath. He would have to protect his darling wife from the overzealous interest of this daunting, pedagogical matron—just for a year or two. Keep the girl busy, that was the trick. Find her a nice little part-time job until the babies came along. This would not be a problem—not now that he had taught her how to drive. He was confident, also, that within the year he would have taught her how to swim properly. Funny that she didn't like water.

"Sweetie," Roland said, and he drew the car to a halt at the verge. "Your turn to take the wheel, I think."

 ALICE HAD VERY RECENTLY begun to enjoy driving the car. For a good while after Roland had started to teach her it had remained one of those things, like swimming twenty-five meters, that she believed only other people accomplished. But suddenly it had felt quite different. Being able to drive was enormously gratifying. It was like a passport to adulthood. Or it would have been, had not her parents immediately announced their intention of buying her a brand-new car for her birthday. Alice had not suggested it or even hinted at it. And it was compromising too, because Roland, she knew, thought it indefensible for her to have a brand-new car when he was available to look over any number of decent secondhand cars for her and to guide her choice with care, but there it was. She could not let them down. They would sweep her into whatever was the adult equivalent of Hamley's toy shop and wait to see which one of the shiny little new cars could make their baby's eyes shine brightest. To watch her would make their own eyes shine bright.

And that afternoon Alice could not enjoy the driving. She could not enjoy anything at all really, because brewing on the horizon was an inescapable confrontation.

Roland had noticed her new competence with satisfaction. Only that week, he had stopped feeling always on duty, like an instructor, while Alice drove his car. Teaching her had not been easy, but he had begun at last to sit back like a passenger and relax. Right then, he had folded up the Ordnance Survey map and had put it in the cubbyhole alongside his shining new ice ax.

"You're driving well, Alice," he said. "Have you got a date yet for your test?" Alice shook her head.

"You've been incrbed-beb-beb— incredibly k-k-k-," Alice said. "You've been very kind, Roland. It's been v-vv-very h-h-h." She stopped and tried again. "Your car," she said. "I hope I haven't abused it." Roland gestured graciously. He was eager to pass on good news.

"Dr. Gubbins offered me a job as head of department this morning," he said. "His head of maths is retiring at the end of the summer." He paused. "And one of the housemasters is moving on. He means to have me take that over after Christmas." He paused and smiled at her, trying to look modest. "I think that congratulations are in order," he said. "Don't you?"

"Oh yes," Alice said. "Oh y-yes. But-but you'll miss W-whitescroff and Pyecross-scroft."

Roland gestured yes-no. "I shall miss *you*, my dearest poppet," he said. "So now you see that all the driving lessons have been mere selfishness on my part. I mean to have you up and down rather often over the next two years." He paused and sighed. "Seven eight-week terms. That's quite a long haul, admittedly, but we shall have every minute of the vacations together. I do promise you that." He smiled at her with intent to give solace. "Will you like to live up here with me, my sweetie—in this beautiful, empty country?" Alice could not formulate a reply before he said, "And 'Grandma' might appreciate having you so close."

Alice briefly clenched and unclenched her hands. All weekend he had been so surrounded by Gubbinses and housemasters and the chaplain and the schoolboys that there had been no opportunity to speak, and anyway it would not have been fair. And now that the moment had really come, it was going to be so difficult. It was always difficult to talk seriously with Roland.

"But this is-isn-n-isn't the Social-l-lis Plerublic of Chelester-s-s-s-s— Street," she said.

Roland laughed. "Not quite," he said. "But it is very much closer. You're tongue-tied today, my poppet. Are you feeling tired?"

"R-roland—," Alice said. "Th-thw-th-th—"

"First things first," Roland said. "You relax. Talk later. I've bought you a present. It's very small, but it signifies something very momentous for me." He spoke with a kind of innuendo that brought ice to

Alice's throat. Was this, she speculated, Roland's delicate way of saying that he had bought a packet of condoms and that he meant to use them on her?

"I've bought you the prettiest little ring," he said. "I shall give it to you shortly." Alice felt so powerfully reproached that she could not respond at all, but Roland did not require it. "Before I give it to you," he said, "There is something that I mean to do first."

"W-what?" Alice said.

"Make love to you," he said. Alice turned and looked at him. She opened her mouth. Before words had formulated themselves, Roland spoke again. "Eyes on the road, my sweetie," he said. "The terrain is just a wee bit unpredictable around here. Rather dominated by the course of the Tees, as you'll have noticed." Alice turned her eyes quickly back to the road.

"W-we can't," she said. "W-we m-mu-b-b-b." She damned her affliction more so at that moment and more vehemently than at any other time in her life. "Not with old G-Bugg-ug-ug-ug-gub—" Roland laughed. He was in a mood so glowing with good feeling that it bordered on skittishness.

"Do try not to call him 'old bugger' to his face," he said. "And calm yourself, sweetie. I really do not mean that we should perform the act under his nose. There's a nice little area of dense mixed woodland coming up to our left in a half a mile or so, and that is where you will pull up."

It was suddenly perfectly clear to Alice that Roland had planned the route they had taken with intent. He had studied the map and had arranged that they should approach the area of dense mixed woodland with an hour to kill before they would need to head back for the chess finals and old Gubbins presenting the cup. It undoubtedly explained the presence of Roland's Eurohike compressed foam exercise mat, which lay, compactly rolled, upon the backseat of the car. How thoughtful he was, as ever, to be insuring against her discomfort from pine needles and sharp twigs. He would take her delicately in this pleasant pastoral setting, after which he would affiance her with his pretty little ring and then they would return to receive the Gubbinses' congratulations. Whitecross would rally the foursome to the expression of respectful witticisms and her life would be sealed for ever. *Mann und Weib und Weib und Mann.*

"N-no!" she said.

"Oh but yes," Roland said firmly. "Absolutely, definitely yes, my poppet. I have been idiotically patient and you have been idiotically shy. It has all been completely silly and unnecessary and as from right now it is going to stop." He was beginning to talk to her just slightly in his Whitescruff-and-Pyecrust voice. "I hope that I make myself perfectly clear," he said.

"Yss," Alice said. She wondered, would he ask her to speak up and not to mumble?

"Good," Roland said. She drove on for a half a minute in quaking silence. Mrs. McCrail flashed absurdly across her mind, along with the bluebell wood and the chef and the yellow waistcoat and the torn stockings in spirals around Mrs. McCrail's legs and the four strong men in the parlor and the razor strap. Are you asking to get beaten, Pykestaff?

"I c-can't," she said. "S-somebody will see us."

"Absolutely nobody is going to see us," Roland said. A tone of indulgent certainty was coloring stage one of his crowd-control voice. "It's completely, divinely empty up here. And at all events, my sweetie, nobody is going to see very much of you. I shall 'cover' you, as they put it so delicately in the horse trade. And if any passing Yorkshireman should happen to catch an eyeful of my buttocks bobbing in the undergrowth, well, he's bloody welcome, is all I can say. I shall be far too busy to care."

Shock waves passed through Alice's brain, sabotaging all possibility of speech. She saw the letters in her head, all churned into a can of Alphabetti-Spaghetti. The best she could do would be to spoon them out at random.

"R—," she said, and her tongue jammed; a cramped muscle against her hard palate. Roland waited for her to proceed. Then he accepted that she could not. Having made his point so forcefully, he felt very tenderly toward her. The poor darling girl. But really. One could not pussyfoot around forever, and who could tell? It might even do wonders for the stammer. She'd been so curiously sheltered all her life. So puzzling, when one considered how pretty she was. Had nobody noticed that, back in darkest Surrey? What had been the matter with everybody? Had all the males been blind? How else was it that she hadn't gone through any of the usual teenage induction processes; the groping in darkened, smoke-filled rooms with the record player pulsing out heavy rock and somebody's vomit on the stairs? She was like a princess locked in a tower. And right now, he had to say it, her face was an absolute picture. He couldn't help wanting to tease her.

"Chin up, my sweetie," he said. "This isn't a funeral, you know." Then he reached out to her, moving a little closer; making to put his arm around her shoulders.

For some months afterwards, Alice could remember almost nothing of what had happened. She remembered only the face of Mr. Fergusson as he had swelled and swelled and haunted her dreams. Dreams that shut off always as he was about to burst his skin. All the letters in the spaghetti can had suddenly ranked themselves in rows.

"Don't you dare touch me or I'll kill you!" Alice screamed. As she spoke, she pushed down on the accelerator pedal and swung the wheel violently to the right in an impulse to avoid Roland and the area of dense, mixed woodland, both of which were looming to her left. They had come upon the little bridge so suddenly, and there, equally suddenly, was the small white van, but the terrain, as Roland had rightly observed, was a wee bit unpredictable. Alice, having swung at the wheel, then braked. The Citroën skated sideways through the parapet. It juddered through a section of masonry and fell heavily into the water at an angle of north-northeast.

Roland was really rather splendid in the circumstances. Given that the look of hysteria and distaste on Alice's face as she screamed at him not to touch her was enough to paralyze him for a moment and render ineffectual all his well-assimilated survival strategies. Given that it was enough, finally, to force the truth upon his sanguine consciousness, so that he knew, quite suddenly, quite certainly, that Alice did not love him and that, rather than have him make love to her, she was hurling his beautiful old car into the river at great risk to both their lives.

The first thing he did was wrench her toward him to the passenger side of the vehicle. Nonetheless, the fall knocked her unconscious.

The Citroën began to sink fast and the doors and windows were jammed. Roland worked very quickly and with laudable presence of mind. He thanked his stars for the Snowdonia trip, without which he would not have purchased the ice ax. And without the ice ax they might quite conceivably both have drowned.

Once he had got her to the surface, Roland laid Alice on the riverbank and turned her carefully facedown onto her side. He tilted up her chin and checked the pulse in her neck. He suspected, after brief examination, that she had fractured some of her ribs. His forearms had begun to run with blood from numerous superficial lacerations acquired through contact with the window frame. When he turned for help toward the bridge and the road, it was with enormous relief that he saw the driver of the small white van. The man, who was young, probably younger than Roland, was peering from the ruptured parapet with an expression of wonder and disbelief.

 WHEN ALICE WOKE in the hospital bed, she had been dreaming of Whitecross and Pyecroft. There had been some sort of explosion and Pyecroft was crying. Waking was like rising from the bottom of the sea. There was a pressure on her ears and steel bands seemed to bind her chest.

"I feel sorry for him," she said. Her speech was slurred and unintelligible. There was a nurse with her, who was fussing with something attached to her arm.

"There now, pet," she said. "There now," She had a voice a bit like Grandma's. Alice had broken a collarbone and three of her ribs were cracked. The pain in her chest was like intense bruising.

"Where's Roland?" she said.

Roland, having been treated for shock and minor lacerations, had telephoned Mrs. Gubbins from the hospital. The chess tournament was over by then and so was evensong. The boys were in the dining hall having their supper. He would stay to get a report on Alice's condition, he told her. Then he would return as soon as possible to the school. Mrs. Gubbins was all concern. She would drive over immediately, she said, and wait to run him back.

"You're very kind," he said. Then the nurse called him to Alice.

That was the most grueling encounter of Roland's life thus far. He knew also that ahead of him, at the school, lay the gauntlet of kindly well-wishers, and that there was no prospect of being properly alone until he had delivered himself of the four small boys, whom he would have to convey southward by train. He understood, deeply and certainly, that Alice did not love him and that she would not marry him. The Citroën was a watery wreck along with all his hopes and in the Citroën was his jacket, which he had torn off in the wake of the fall. In the pocket of the jacket was the pretty silver ring with the little blue stones like cornflowers.

His meeting with Alice was brief and, on his part, constrained by a stiff propriety. Roland was not much given to raking at sores, which seemed to him both unmanly and a pointless waste of words. He made no reference to the part he had played in her rescue and, in his hurt, which he shielded under distant politeness, he considered neither how drugged Alice was, nor how confused about what had actually happened. He stopped short at the foot of her bed and considered her smile inappropriate.

"How are you?" he said briskly, clearing his throat.

"I'm fine," she said, rather stupidly. She took in very little other than that he was wearing an unfamiliar shirt. "Your shirt has checks on it," she said.

"Yes," Roland said indifferently.

"Will your car be all right?" she said. "I think we crashed."

Roland winced briefly, controlling irritation. "We're alive," he said curtly. "I daresay that's more important." Alice smiled at him again, rather dreamily, overcome with drowsiness.

"I dreamed about Pyecroft," she said. "I think he was crying." Roland brushed this aside as whimsical irrelevance. It injured him that she showed herself suddenly so thoroughly deficient in taste.

"I must be off now, Alice," he said. Alice tried to raise her hand but failed. The limb would not move for her.

"Don't go," she said.

"I shall leave by train in the morning," he said. "I telephoned your people about an hour ago. They'll be here by noon tomorrow."

"Thank you," Alice said. She blinked at him, not really minding that she did not know what he was talking about. She was occupied with the unfamiliar, weaving plaid of his shirt. Did the thin white vertical stripe go under the broad horizontal stripe, or over? She could not determine it. "Don't go," she said again.

"I'm afraid I have been pestering you," he said. "It won't ever happen again." He stepped forward and reached out coldly, formally, to shake her hand. She tried again to raise her arm but failed. Roland withdrew toward the door. "Well," he said. "All the best to you. Goodbye, Alice."

"I'm so tired," Alice said, and she blinked at him again. "Are you so tired as well?" Roland made no reply. His mouth curled tensely as he turned and walked quickly out of the room. "I'm so tired," Alice said again, but this time she said it to the ceiling. Then she fell asleep.

Dr. Gubbins poured brandy for Roland and called him "my poor dear chap."

"And the better half?" he mused kindly. "Three cracked ribs, eh? A broken collarbone? Dear-dear-dear, oh dear."

"May I trouble you for the loan of a train timetable, sir?" Roland said. Dr. Gubbins looked quite flustered.

"Now look here, my dear fellow," he said. "You're not at all recovered. Absolutely no sense in leaving us in a hurry. Pitch camp here for a day or two. Only wants me to get your headmaster on the blower." He pulled up a chair and sat down. "Your boys will make do splendidly and I'm quite sure your dear intended will be in no hurry at all to see you go."

Roland was not accustomed to dissembling. He knew that to announce the dissolution of his hopes with Alice would not look terribly good. It would suggest that the motor accident had been in some way attendant upon emotional crisis, which of course it had. But there was nothing else for it. And the way he felt right then, perhaps he did not want the job there anyway.

"Sir," he said. "I must tell you that Alice is no longer my 'intended.' All that—well it came unstuck this afternoon."

Dr. Gubbins looked most distinctly out of countenance. He juggled a bit with his brandy goblet and put it down. Then he picked it up again.

"Well bless my soul," he said. "I'm very surprised to hear this. Very surprised." He got up and went to the window. "If the young lady has changed her mind," he said, "it may well be that she will change it back again. Excellent young fellow like you."

Roland stared fixedly into the amber liquid in his glass. "No," he said. "It seems that I have all along not properly understood her feelings." He could not have been expected to appreciate that Alice had not understood them either.

Pyecroft had won the chess tournament. He had been presented with a small silver goblet, like an eggcup with joke-shop ears. He was holding it under the bedclothes after lights-out. He knew that his father would be pleased about it and it was something he could write about in his next letter to make up for what had happened about Thursday's cricket match. Also he was pleased because Mr. Dent would be proud of him. He had lain awake in the strange, cold dormitory, hoping that Sir would've come in and spoken to him about it, but he hadn't. Pyecroft started to cry. He had been away at school for a term and a half and he wanted to go home. He wanted to be with his mother and his little sister Ellie. His mother had used to collect him from his day school in the car and drive him home and give him tea and help him with his prep and he'd always got "Excellent Work." She'd sometimes watched afternoon television with him and called him "Georgie," but at school he hated people to know that he was called Georgie, because then they'd call him "Georgie-Porgie Pudding and Piecrust" and tease him and say he kissed girls, which he never did. He wanted to go home and not be at school anymore, but then he wouldn't ever see Whitecross and Whitecross was his best friend and had come to his house over Christmas. When the school clock struck midnight he lost count. He thought he had counted thirteen. Then he fell asleep. That was more than could be said for Roland, who heard the clock strike three.

Mrs. Gubbins drove them to the railway station in time for the mid-morning train. Roland thanked her and shook her hand and settled the children in their seats around a table in a nonsmoker. His manner was more peremptory than usual as he handed out sheets of squared paper and set them an exercise on coordinates. Whitecross, who opened his mouth to protest, looked at Roland and closed it again. Roland looked at his watch.

"All right," he said. "Make a start. I'll be back to check it in thirty minutes." Then he took himself to the buffet car and drank a cup of black coffee. Once he had drunk it, he sat and stared expressionless into the landscape.

"Sir," Whitecross said. "Excuse me, sir." He was standing in the doorway of the buffet car with a small electronic chess set in his hand. Roland looked up irritably.

"What do you want?" he said. Whitecross cast about, improvising, hoping to snatch at something he could want.

"We were all wondering, sir," he said. "Will you be coming on the trip to Snowdonia, sir?"

"Yes of course," Roland said. "What are you doing here? Why aren't you busy doing your prep?"

"Well sir, it only took us about twenty minutes," he said. Roland looked at his watch. He had been staring out of the window for over an hour.

"Good Lord," he said. "I'm sorry, Whitecross. I suppose that I have been rather unpleasant."

"Just a bit, sir," Whitecross said. "Play you at chess if you like, sir." Roland sighed and made the effort.

"All right. Sit down," he said.

"Black to suit your mood, sir?" Whitecross said, and he turned the black pieces to Roland's side of the table.

"Don't push it, Whitecross," Roland said. "Nice little chess set you have here."

"It's Pyecroft's," said the child. "His father sent it to him."

"Pyecroft's father sounds like thoroughly good news," Roland said.

"Oh yes sir," said the child. "And he says he'll take us both hang gliding. That's when we're a little bit older."

"Your move," Roland said.

"Yes sir," said the child. "Sir, d'you know my sister?"

"Move, Whitecross," Roland said. "How the blazes should I know your sister?"

"Yes you do, sir," Whitecross said. "She came to *Ruddigore*, sir. I introduced you, remember? She's got an MGB roadster, sir."

"Oh yes," Roland said. "I remember." Whitecross moved one of his pawns.

"She thinks you're smashing, sir," he said. "In fact she made me introduce her." He paused for effect. Roland said nothing. He moved one of his pawns. "She's very pretty, sir," Whitecross said. "And she's always had heaps of boyfriends."

"She talk as much as you do, Whitecross?" Roland said.

"No sir," said the child.

"Good," Roland said. "Your move, Whitecross. Get on with it, will you?"

 HARRY AND VALERIE PILLING arrived the following day. They had taken the express train to Darlington and had rented a car from there. They were at their daughter's bedside shortly after midday. Roland's communication of the previous evening had been delivered to them with the same stiff restraint as he had shown in his leave-taking with Alice. It had not crossed their minds to consider whether he had been injured or badly shaken; nor whether anything had passed between him and their daughter to have caused in him such a coolness. They had been very much affronted by it and by other things as well. That he should have involved their baby in a motor car accident by allowing her to drive without a license; that he should, on top of this, have made clear his unabashed intention to abandon her in hospital and travel south next day with a party of schoolboys—but what else would one have expected? Roland was a cold fish. A schoolmaster who put on airs. He was never their sort of person. Never the man for little Alice.

It was a great relief to them to find that their daughter was sitting up in bed and playing rummy with such a nice young man. He was the driver of the small white van. They kissed her and praised her for her bravery and shook her visitor warmly by the hand.

"Aye, she's champion," Matthew said, in his engaging Bobby Shafto accent, so much stronger than Alice's father's. "She's been that plucky—haven't you now, my pet?" The Pillings did not read this as impertinence. They read it as northern friendliness. For Harry Pilling, in particular, his bond with Matthew Riley was immediate and warm.

Their backgrounds were not at all dissimilar. Besides—though he was decently modest about it—it seemed that the boy had saved dear Alice's life.

Matthew Riley had grown up in a mining village not twenty miles from Grandma's home. His father, way back, had been a rural Irish immigrant who had trained pit ponies until the mines had ceased to use them. Then he had been kept on as a gardener until the pit closed down in the sixties. Matthew was born that year, a latecomer in the family. His father was fifty when he was born; an aging man with nothing much to do. He grew marrows in the back garden and kept—in a drawer along with his tobacco pouch—a handful of dog-eared holy cards from his rural Irish past. In one of these, the Blessed Virgin Mary was depicted being assumed into heaven with her feet on pink-tipped clouds. Her eyeballs were turning upwards in a manner Matthew had seen only once, on a man who had collapsed on the bus with an epileptic seizure.

Such tacky little icons had no meaning at all for Matthew, nor for any of his sisters, though at each of their births a priest had come along and urged them toward the font. It was all a part of what he despised about his father. Matthew was a bright, engaging child who, as the youngest in the family and the only male, had commanded a fair chunk of his mother's attention. By this time all but one of Mrs. Riley's daughters were married and she had nurtured Matthew in his progress through the junior school and had seen him off to the secondary school with the highest hopes for him in her heart. He had not disappointed her. She had kept him at school until his eighteenth year, after which he had gone on to take a degree in maths and physics at the University of Newcastle-upon-Tyne.

Nonetheless, the year in which Alice met Matthew had not been a good one for him. It had been a year of setbacks. Matthew was an ambitious young man, who had determined early in life to direct himself in a manner as unlike his father as possible. To this purpose he had solicited the advice of his lecturers as to the possibility of going on to graduate work, either in London or in America. He had filled out various application forms and had been interviewed in London by a well-disposed academic, prepared to act as his supervisor. Everyone, including Matthew, assumed that his exam results would be high enough for him to get a grant.

Old Mr. Riley timed his dying for maximum inconvenience. He went into his death routine on the morning of Matthew's first examination paper and lingered until the fourth and fifth. It was an ugly death, during which Matthew's life was full of ambulance drivers and crying women and holy cards and the priest. It was full of green bile and wheezing and hollow-eyed ghouls in the men's surgical ward of the hospital to which Alice was now consigned. More surprising to him, the fact that his feelings for his father were profoundly negative produced in him turbulent and highly distracting emotions. In short, he fudged his examination scripts and emerged with a lower second, which did for his chances of a grant. He had been marking time since the funeral, rethinking his prospects and working, meanwhile, as a van driver for a firm of china manufacturers for whom he delivered to a range of wholesalers. That was not exactly what he was doing when he encountered Alice and Roland on the bridge, but his boss, who was fond of him, had occasionally allowed him the use of the van at weekends. He had not been injured at all in the confrontation. His van had not even been touched. He had simply braked and watched in astonishment, as the girl in the Citroën had inexplicably swung the car into the river.

When Alice was tired and needed to rest, it was Matthew who ushered her parents to the hospital canteen. It was Matthew who fetched them cups of tea and arranged their lodgings and ran their errands. In doing so he rode easily over the barriers of age, unfamiliarity and circumstance.

Over the ensuing three days, the Pillings' gratitude toward Matthew Riley grew and flowered. They cared little for the old Citroën on the riverbed, nor for the circumstances by which their daughter had got it there, but their hearts went out to the golden boy who had managed to get Alice out. The details hardly concerned them. They concentrated on the fact that Matthew Riley had stuck around while Roland had indefensibly retreated and that Matthew had fortuitously been on the bridge. They knew by his own engagingly modest account that Matthew had shattered the window glass of Roland's motor car with a hammer that he happened to have had in his van. They were reassured by his approachable style and much affected, on the evening of the third day, by his story of his dying father and the fudged examination scripts. Clearly what the boy needed was a start in life. What Matthew needed was a patron and a nice little job down south.

"Double your wages for a start, my lad," said Harry Pilling. "Be doing myself a favor."

Harry Pilling's idea was that Matthew Riley would live rent-free in one of the executive units, which he would decorate to his employer's specifications in his own time. He would exchange the little white van for a grey one with his new employer's name on it, and would work by and large in the area of landscape gardening. Mr. Pilling had no doubt that Matthew was a handy lad and canny upstairs into the bargain. If, after a month, his work was pleasing, he said—and there was little doubt in his mind that it would be—Harry Pilling would keep him on part-time throughout the duration of his graduate studies, which would be funded through an interest-free personal loan.

If Harry Pilling had had any intention at that stage to make Matthew both his right-hand man and his son-in-law, he was not in any way aware of it, but thus it was that Matthew Riley became the hired man. He worked hard and he prospered and he pleased his employer exceedingly. He resumed his plans immediately to pursue his studies in London and, in the bedroom of the "unit" that he had helped to decorate and refurbish, he installed his maths and physics textbooks along with all his other reading matter—his three paperback adult adventure stories, his brace of joke books, his half-dozen old Giles cartoon collections and his most recent twelve-month run of the *Beano*. In the living room he kept his computer magazines.

Matthew was a simple man, unspoiled by his higher education. Though his degree in mathematics was as good as Roland's, for all that Roland had not contended with a dying parent during his finals, he did not come across as a posh-voiced pedagogue with manners to provoke feelings of inadequacy in self-made building contractors. Matthew in workman's overalls did not stand out inconveniently as a target in the class war. Matthew was the perfect chameleon. He smiled easily and doffed his cap and made exactly the right sort of jokes. He said "no worries," and "champion-champion," and made himself indispensable. The Pillings were naturally delighted with him in every possible way.

For one thing, he was so good for little Alice, who had been so much shaken and disturbed by the accident that (naturally) she had been required, on doctor's orders, to take out the summer term of her second year and spend it, dosed on little white pills, recovering at home. All through May and half of June, while Matthew toiled and whistled and made patios and laid turf, Alice remained largely recumbent and listless in the pink and white bedroom with the Sindy dolls' dream home still evident in the corner; lovingly and relentlessly cared for by the parents who had so nearly lost her.

Roland, meanwhile, when he returned from North Yorkshire, undertook, within the week, to call upon David Morgan. There were belongings of his to be collected from the attic and it seemed to him, in any case, that the visit was a necessary courtesy. When Roland rang the doorbell, David gratefully interrupted his reading of the bedtime story and went downstairs, pursued by the voices of his protesting children. He admitted Roland to his kitchen and gave account of his own somewhat dramatic recent events. It seemed, then, that all was change.

"Maya," David said, "has left me." It had all of it happened so quickly, so unexpectedly. Maya had encountered Iona in Paul Koplinski's bed. There had followed an enormous showdown, after which Iona had moved in next door with her leather jacket, her waffle iron, her typewriter and the manuscript of what she was pleased to call her "novel." Maya had promptly followed suit and had moved in with her macramé blouse, her salmon corduroy trousers and the ancient Remington. Paul Koplinski had then fled into Worcestershire, while Iona had escaped to her father in California, taking with her a completed typescript distinguished by the absence of all its aitches.

Maya, in a state of inconsolable distress, had gone off the very next morning on the eight-fifteen to Malvern in the hopes of tracking down Paul Koplinski. She had first given audience to David during which, amid grief and self-torture, she had suddenly set fire to her novel, in the face of David's loyal but futile attempts to stop her. The children, throughout this anguished confrontation, remained, mercifully, asleep.

Roland listened in subdued silence. By the time David was through with his telling, the children had long since stopped yelling for him to come back and finish their story. The two men then walked briskly to the corner off-license and brought back some cans of beer.

"Alice has left me too," Roland said, and he then told his own story. He had otherwise told it to nobody, and it seemed odd to him, as he heard himself tell it, that he had chosen to unload on David. But David was a good, kind listener and in many ways deeply understanding. Besides, so many things divided them that it was not, after all, like unloading over anyone who mattered. Only that, by the time they had shaken each other by the hand and had gone to bed, David and Roland had both recognized how very much they liked each other. That was something, at least, to have come out of all that bruising.

Roland spent the night there in David Morgan's house. It was late, and he no longer had a motor car. Because he could not bear to, he did not sleep in Alice's bed. Neither did he sleep in Iona's bed, for fear of taking on the smell of sweat and leather. He slept, uncomfortably, on a pile of sofa cushions on the Morgans' living-room floor—a couch from which he was woken by four-year-old William hell-bent on conversation.

"I can make my willie go stiff when I fiddle with it," said the child.

"Oh, jolly good," Roland said.

"I 'speck my daddy's willie's much more bigger'n yours," said the child.

"Possibly," said Roland, who had no particular stomach for the competition. He needed to find a razor before he could take himself to work.

Alice got better very slowly. She was hazy about the accident and seemed more numbed than disturbed by the nature of Roland's departure. She missed his friendship and she missed David and Thomas and Sophie. And she missed some of her books. But she missed nothing more than mildly and concentrating was difficult. It was all as though these things had happened in another incarnation. She could not quite see them through the fog and she was incapable of much emotion. Her emotions, it seemed, had been anesthetized. The effect of this was greatly to enhance her prettiness. Her face was undisturbed by any extremes of anxiety, unhappiness or pleasure. She slept a lot and rested. She played cards with Matthew Riley, who visited her most afternoons and let her win. He chatted easily and he occasionally made her smile, but only slightly.

She told him once about Flora and the pink and white brides and the bridegroom doll that the brides had had to share. It was no particular surprise to Alice when Matthew promptly kissed her, because nothing mattered deeply anymore, though it was diverting when he called her his "pet lamb" and his "rosebud" and his "bonny lass." It was not even that much of a surprise to wake up one day and find that Matthew's hand was inside her blouse. There was something so homely about Matthew Riley that it did not seem in any way momentous. He had none of Roland's rather inhibiting good manners, nor his imposing presence, nor any of that brisk, commandeering style. Besides, she had cared very deeply for Roland, though not, sadly, in the appropriate way. She had cared about him too deeply, perhaps, to enact with him something so intimate without conviction or commitment.

Alice was rosy and sleepy, and the day was warm, and nothing mattered very much anymore. And had not Matthew saved her from drowning in the Tees?

"Let's have your little drawers off, rosebud," Matthew Riley said. The only thought that troubled Alice occurred to her once the act was over.

"But what if I'm pregnant?" she said. Matthew was back in his Levis by then, though his chest and his feet were still bare. He smiled at her rather engagingly.

"No worries, flower petal," he said. "I'll make an honest woman of you yet." When he laughed and leaned over her and kissed her and spoke again, it was with every semblance of send-up. "How to make friends and influence people," he said. "Marry the boss's daughter. That's just for a start." It made Alice smile. He had so evidently uttered it in jest.

IN THE EVENT, Matthew was rather advanced in his views on marriage. He believed in extended living-together relationships as a responsible prelude to commitment. Nonetheless, Alice's parents were delighted with the development. They saw no reason at all why "sensible young people these days" should not live together out of matrimony. In truth they found it reassuring to be in possession of a daughter whose behavior was at last manifesting itself as firmly of the present. They would have been much more troubled had Matthew begun to manifest signs of sacramental commitment. Had he, for instance, exhibited a sudden Irish-Catholic reversion and sent Alice off to take instruction. But Matthew was resolutely secular, and his gods, like theirs, were all material.

Harry Pilling, on his daughter's behalf, embarked upon a nest-building program without any delay. Mr. Pilling, largely with his own hands, refurbished one of the more ambitious units, adding molded features to the ceilings and installing expensive track lighting and dimmer switches. He put his fatherly love into every premeditated nook. He carved out a balustraded sleeping gallery and picked out a luxury range in what he called "door furniture" for all the knobs and locks.

Mrs. Pilling chose the rest of the furniture. The keynote here—since Alice was an old-fashioned little thing—was mellow cottage pine and cane. The table linen and bed linen were all coordinated with care, as were the cutlery and the china. In short, Harry and Valerie Pilling built their daughter a dream home as fine as that of the Sindy dolls, in which she could mercifully give up thinking about Homer and *The Year of Salamis* and the Temples of Reason and Wisdom. Alice was now so much better that she could make a festoon blind for the sitting-room window and embark upon a system of index cards as a means of collecting recipes.

"But, you funny little love," her mother said, "mine are all on hard disk these days. Why don't we transcribe yours?"

Indeed Alice was so much better by July that her mother renewed her driving lessons and signed her up for a word-processing course, which she attended twice a week. Mrs. Pilling had also given her daughter a small stopgap job in the agency as a way of lending interest to her day. It was not long before Alice could take a driving test and she was usefully employed within the brightly lit offices where Jem had once so admired the functional cabinets and the spongy, wall-to-wall carpeting.

And Matthew, who all through the term had been attending a weekly seminar in London prior to his date of registration in the autumn, was already, prematurely, at work on the beginnings of his Ph.D. dissertation.

By August the Pillings were off to their holiday house in Spain. Building operations came to their annual standstill and the young people, due to join their elders for two weeks in early September, were left to keep an eye out at the agency, which was being capably managed by Mrs. Pilling's two highly competent assistants.

"Goodbye, my darlings, and do take care," said Mrs. Pilling, and she embraced Matt and Alice and blew kisses to them from the car.

And then two things happened. The first, which caused her first and only quarrel with Matthew, was that Alice, one day, all on the spur of the moment, bought two expensive tickets for *The Magic Flute*. The second was that Flora's grandmother set fire to the superior, heritage-style investment property. She lit up a Woodbine in the fuel cupboard one morning, and she trapped both herself and her daughter-in-law.

The house was not much damaged, since the blaze, though ferocious, was contained within the single-storied kitchen wing at the back, but both women were done for almost immediately. A lighted match applied to a cigarette had made swift common cause with a gas leak. The bodies were barely recognizable.

Since almost nobody knew the Fergusson women, who had kept so very much to themselves, Alice had been required to come forward, at the request of the local police. They needed her to help trace living relatives and—since the deaths had not been by natural cause—to be of use in the matter of identification and inquest.

Flora, it seemed, had no telephone number and, though Alice could remember the name of Flora's art school, Flora proved rather difficult to trace. Either she or Matthew, Alice suggested, ought really to get on an airplane and find her. Matthew seemed the more at liberty, since Police Constable Curruthers had said he would have need of Alice at the coroner's court over the following days. And Matthew, though he knew not much French and had never been abroad before, was jauntier than Alice and less daunted in the face of the unknown. In short, he was very much game to try and confident that he would find her.

After Matthew had gone, P.C. Curruthers asked all sorts of questions and he thanked Alice politely for bearing up so well. He offered himself to drive her to the coroner's court next day, which was attached to the local police station. The coroner's court had benches and a podium, and it had some minor rooms leading off it. P.C. Curruthers shepherded her into one of these and gave her a cup of tea. Then he got up and left the room for a minute.

When he returned he was carrying two large, bright green plastic garbage bags, just like the one that, years before in The Fisherman's Grotto, had held the old woman's vomit.

"At this point I sometimes have to warn my ladies to pull themselves together," said P.C. Curruthers rather sternly. He had no cause to warn Alice, however, who handled the identification with laudable togetherness. The green plastic bags had luggage labels with names on them tied to the tops with string. P.C. Curruthers opened the string and asked her to look inside them. Inside were bits of charred clothing welded together with skin and hair.

"That was her anorak," Alice said, who marveled that, here and there, stray dog hairs from the incontinent canine were still visible on the fabric. "She wore it once when we went out to dinner together," Alice said. Then she turned to the second plastic bag. The younger Mrs. Fergusson was easier. Most of the bits were rather less charred.

"Those are her shoes," Alice said. "She always wore them in the music room."

"Well done," said P.C. Curruthers. "You've been very helpful, Miss Pilling. Thank you." He tied up the two plastic bags again with the labels and the string. "Would you care for another cup of tea?" he said.

It was not Matthew's fault that he fell in love with Flora, nor Flora's that she fell in love with Matthew. They had no sooner met than they changed eyes. They felt the instant pang of Cupid's fiery, poisoned dart. They were like people in a storybook.

And Flora had once again metamorphosed. She had become the Christmas fairy. Flora was glittering. She was beautiful. The braces that Fabrice and Thierry had had fixed to her protruding teeth had done their job very well and, when she smiled, each node on their fine metal tracks shone like a tiny jewel. And then her context was extremely advantageous. The window was shuttered, and the chair she sat in, like a burnished throne, glowed on the marble. It glowed also against the ivory, and the lacquered wood.

Fabrice and Thierry, the two adoring, elegant young men who flanked her like gilded cupidons, were her neighbors in the grey Parisian apartment house where she had her studio in the seventh *arrondissement*. They were tour guides to the Far East and had just that day come back. When they were in Paris they lived together harmoniously in the apartment, which was like an enchanted cave; a robber's den. Matthew, who had climbed the four flights of three-hundred-year-old stairs, had followed the sound of their muffled laughter and had entered through the open door.

The three of them stopped and stared at him. Each had a glass in hand and Thierry, in addition, held a bottle of *sirop de cassis*.

"Who are you?" Flora said.

"I'm Matthew Riley," Matthew said, the Geordie accent sounding with incongruous charm in the enchanter's cave, and he put down his shoulder bag with its British Airways label. "I'm looking for Flora

Fergusson." Fabrice and Thierry looked at each other over Flora's head and smiled.

"*Ça va mal!*" Thierry said. "*Mauvaises nouvelles!*" The two of them tinkled with laughter.

"*Le roi, sire, est mort,*" Fabrice said. "*Vive la reine!*" And they laughed again and clinked their glasses over Flora's head. Matthew looked anxiously for a moment from left to right, like a knight in the bower of the *belle dame sans merci.*

"I'm not a burglar or anything," he said. "I've come from Alice."

The room was filled with ebony and ivory. All the chairs had feet and claws. Strange masks winked at Matthew from the walls. Filigree screens had made a labyrinth of the floor as he approached. Behind the throne where Flora sat stood a large, floor-standing dragon with a golden ball in its mouth. Beyond it, suspended before the shuttered window, hung a miniature conservatory full of bonsai trees.

Flora stood up and glided toward him. She offered him her hand.

"I'm Flora Fergusson," she said.

"*Notre princesse en exil,*" Thierry said. "*Destinée à hériter le royaume.*"

"Your mother and grandmother are dead," Matthew said. Flora stood, poised, emotionless, like a person possessed of the future. "They died in a fire," he said.

Flora and Matthew did not return that night. They spent the time in Flora's studio, which, unlike Fabrice and Thierry's place, was wholly unadorned. The walls were whitewashed like a Puritan church and the window ledge held a row of jam jars with a collection of brushes and pencils. Flora's clothes hung on two coat hangers behind the door, and the portfolio, given to her as a present by Mrs. Pilling years before, leaned against one wall. There was a small, rough trestle table and in one corner, alongside a glazed sink and a gas ring, was an old ticking mattress on the floor. Matthew, upon entering, had stared around the room in wonder. Then he took her in his arms and kissed her. Flora did not resist.

"I don't know what's the matter with me," he said. "I'm supposed to be marrying Alice." They returned to England late the following afternoon. That was the afternoon of the day on which Alice had identified the bodies.

WHEN ALICE GOT HOME from the coroner's court she set to work at once. It was not very convenient to have Flora come that night when they had tickets for the opera, but Alice was neither affronted nor surprised that Matt had not considered it. He had no interest in *The Magic Flute* and had made it perfectly clear that the ticket was wasted on him. Now she too would have to forgo it, because Flora was once again bereaved. Under normal circumstances, Flora would have loved to attend the opera, and Matthew would have been delighted to hand over his ticket. But could one possibly propose such a thing to a person whose relatives' charred remnants were currently residing in emerald plastic bags in the coroner's refrigerator? No. Surely not! They would eat an early supper and take time to welcome Flora nicely. There was no help for it. That was what duty required of them.

To this purpose, though the day was young, Alice placed a vase of cut flowers on the guest-room bedside table. She drew one of her fitted rose pink sheets over the mattress and slipped the duvet and the pillows into their coordinating rose pink floral covers. She left a pair of folded rose pink bath towels on the bedcover and she checked the cupboard for coat hangers. Then she placed a selection of reading matter—soothing, judiciously chosen—upon the bedside table next to the flowers. She adjusted the bedside lamp and the dimmer switch. After that she turned to her cooking.

Alice consulted her recipe cards and pulled ingredients from her new fridge-freezer. She prepared small wood pigeons for roasting in a *bain-marie* of red burgundy, having first stuffed the cavity with pine nuts and raisins, just as her mother had shown her. She made a cranberry sorbet, which she froze in the shells of three hollow oranges. Once she had made dainty matchsticks of her vegetables, she sat down and drank a cup of coffee. Then she turned to count vol-au-vent cases. She prepared a filling for them, of asparagus and herbs and double cream, to be spooned in and warmed up later. Finally, because the day was long, she turned her attention, prematurely, to the art of laying her table.

She arranged the place settings with care, making pretty starched crowns of the three plum-colored napkins and organizing her cutlery on the matching plum-colored cloth. Her plates and her candlesticks were all a pleasing, shiny white with a single decorative outer rim the color of blackberry fool. Alice stood back and plumped the sofa cushions and tidied Matt's computer magazines. She swallowed one of her little white pills. The clock said half past twelve.

Mrs. Pilling's assistant created a diversion, calling by with such of the day's business post as required attention. She also brought two letters addressed personally to Alice. Having delivered them, she left at once. Alice began with her own two letters. One came from David Morgan. The other, which sat fatly in the envelope, had been addressed in flamboyant copperplate and written in brown ink. Burnt Sienna. It was a letter that Alice, over the past four years, had given up hoping for.

Jem had written from a Catholic hospital in Hampshire. The letter, which covered sheets and sheets, contained a five-pound note and had a magazine extract stapled to its final page. The letter went as follows:

Dear Alice,
    I hope this letter finds you happy and well, as you surely deserve to be so. In truth, I hope that it finds you at all. I hope also—(so much hoping, dear friend, and all in the first three lines!)—that you will believe me when I say that I always meant to write to you. Always, but never quite *yet*. Not *yet*. Not until I could give good account of myself; not until I had accomplished something worthy of

bringing before you. What a dismal show-off I always was and now I have missed my chance with you.

I write to you now, having nothing to boast of and nothing to display except my continued affection for you and my remorse at having treated you so badly. I write to you, I confess it, only because my dear friend here—(my other and more recent "dearest friend")—has urged me so insistently to do so. At the risk of sounding tediously melodramatic, he has urged me to do so while my hand can still hold the pen. He is Father Michael Mullholland and he is helping me, very assiduously, with the business of dying.

Dear sweet Alice, I am dying. Try not to let this cheaply emotive reality distress you too unduly, since it is in truth a very workaday affair and nothing quite like the bombshell that it sounds to the uninitiated. At the moment, it is not even more than tolerably painful. Nonetheless, having made such a monumental shipwreck of my life, I am applying myself conscientiously to getting the dying part of it right.

The dear adorable man I refer to has just this morning been haranguing me on your behalf against my "talent for excess." This as I take up my pen. He says that I must write to you a "straight" letter, without all this emotional string-pulling, and that I must not bounce so theatrically between flaunting and sackcloth. Alas these are the twin sides of my deficient psychopathology. And I have tried to counter by pointing out to him that death itself is a kind of excess, is it not? Especially at my age. But still, he is my constant solace and while I cannot hope to be his, I have finally this morning extracted from him an admission that I entertain him more than any other case of terminal decrepitude that he has encountered along the way. I am more than a little in love with him, of course, but this is merely routine and nothing very much to worry about, since all Catholic women must fall in love with priests the way that other women must fall in love with psychotherapists. And how can it signify, now that I am seriously on the blink?

Here then, told to you "straight," is my story: I have no family and I never had. But then by now you will have worked out for yourself that Gordon and Minette and the whiskery cousin, etc., were all no more than so much eyewash. I always read voraciously and I discovered with you, my darling friend (and only friend, since I was always wildly unpopular with my peers, not to mention my elders), a kind of talent for social ventriloquism. My disadvantageous background probably explains in part why I adored your parents so much and why they always viewed me with such alarm. I believe they saw me as some aspirant cuckoo in the nest which they had so carefully made for you. In order to steal some of your enviable magic, I once nicked a five-pound note from your mother's purse and a bracelet from her jewel box. I herewith return to her the five-pound note but, if I may, I would like to keep the bracelet because it is all that I have in the way of a keepsake from your household and she would not deny it to me now. I have it on my wrist and, in a few weeks' time, when I undergo some minor surgery from which I will certainly not recover, I intend to lobby even then to wear it into the operating theater.

As to my parentage. I was got upon a pretty Celtic peasant by an Italian medic who had read Samuel Johnson, though, unlike Gabriella Gallo, my mother was never a chieftain's daughter and—again unlike Gabriella—I never found any trace of my father's bones. He has always been immensely careful to cover his tracks, clever man, though he did provide me with an expensive education until the year I turned sixteen. That was the year Miss Trotter gave the scholarship to Flora. She explained to me that—in spite of my somewhat freakishly high IQ—Flora was a "steadier" proposition than I—and it is only since talking with Father Mullholland that I have begun to concede the truth of this without too much poisoning bitterness.

Flora, I think, was my first major reason for neglecting to write to you, my friend. I could hardly think of you without pain. And, having used all my wiles to wrest you from that girl, I found that calling you to mind only tormented me with the thought that Flora had probably got you back again. The other was simply that my material circumstances were such that I felt compromised and snobbish and ashamed. My mother, you see, had long since ceased to be an apple-cheeked Celtic peasant and had become (that other predictable stereotype) an urban Celtic drunk. She was, as they say in Scotland, heavily given to bevying. In short, having been sent packing and having in my mind the resolution to do my A-levels at the local comprehensive school, I couldn't, in the event, cope with the business of living at home with my mother. I promptly gave up school, raised some money—not quite as elegantly as Gabriella I'm afraid, but then I wasn't quite as elegantly slim. I worked as a cocktail waitress in a club for slightly bent businessmen. (Don't laugh, dear friend. All it took, quite frankly, was decent tits and a willingness to flirt and bleach one's hair. And once 'twas discovered I had the equivalent of three and a half brains compared with the rest of the work force, I got to fiddle the roulette.)

Then I went to Italy. I "smelled Naples," dearest Alice, and I "lived." I bummed around and found little jobs and in short had a rather exquisite time, though I never once encountered the Demon Padrone. (Did you?) Only think if we could have done it all together.

After I left, my mother quite simply continued the process of drinking herself to death. She had got to that point, even before I ignominiously took flight, where she was no longer actually recognizable as the core of the person she once had been. I can say, without exercising any talent for excess—nor even any talent for bitterness—that she would have sold me boots an' all to the glue factory to fund her next half-jack of vodka.

But ah, but o! dear Alice. Italy is the most marvelous, the most wonderful place. And oh that poor Miss Aldridge with her warts and corsets to be so sadly blind! And then—damn and blast it, Alice—I got so very ill. Having (of course) no medical insurance and no leg to stand on, and being (of course) illegally employed, I came back to England about six weeks ago—five months pregnant. (Again, perhaps, "of course"—for my life is rather embarrassingly like a cheap novel.) I believe the father of my child to be a wholly untraceable Roman bike mechanic; the consequence of a one-night stand, but even now, I can't, quite honestly, be sure. I came upon him in the dusk on the Appian Way where he was tinkering with his back wheel, and something, I suspect, about his activity and his sweetness reminded me of that first time I ever met your father, who was mending a push-bike for me on the front lawn. Worse and worse, as you see. The murk within is thick as witches' broth.

Anyway, to be as brief as possible, dear Alice, I am sick and here I am. The invisible worm. I do not think I will take up my bed and walk, though Father Mullholland assures me that it happens quite often in these parts. One of the few things I ever told you which was true was that I was a Catholic, as indeed I still am, though I hope a slightly better one for this last difficult month than I ever was till now. My baby is almost certainly viable, according to the medicine men who troop in to touch me up three times a day, and that has rather ruled out chemotherapy in my case. I have never even begun to consider it. The great bore of this is that it means I cannot live, but there it is. Not the great bore, sweet Alice. No. Why don't I speak the truth to you? The great heartache. The great grey greasy grief. 'Tis better to Die, after all, than to Lie, and so I tell you, Alice, the appalling, throat-lumping grief of not seeing one's dear own baby— that is possibly all I could want to live for and it is the reason why I can't. Yet the neatness of it pleases me. I believe that in my flesh I shall see God. Pray for me, dear Alice—if you can possibly see your way to such an expedient—and come sometime to see my charming priest, who will put you in touch with my baby. I do so want my baby to know you. You knew me, you see, before all this rot and putrefaction. I send you my love and my sincerest good wishes.

Veronica Bernadette McCrail (Alias Jem)

P.S. I forgot to tell you I was expelled from the convent school for stealing. I repeatedly stole from the stockroom cupboard and the library in spite of constant warnings. I also stole money.

P.P.S. You will notice that I have appended to this letter a prepublication puff for one "Aoin le Fey." She is about to be launched, as you see, by an American publishing house called "Angeletti." I clipped it from a newspaper which somebody's transatlantic visitor had left here in the lobby. It seems—or am I hallucinating?—that she has plagiarized my novel. Is't not moderately diverting, dear friend? Are you acquainted with this Woeful Lunatick, or who in the world is this person? (Doubtless another Celtic drunk if her name is aught to go by.) I include it for your amusement only and please do not think that I mind. I have no further use for such stuff, as you will surely understand. I can hardly take it with me and my guess is that *My Last Duchess* will not keep Miss le Fey in bagels and lox for very long at all.

Love again,
Veronica

Once her weeping had abated, Alice got up and paced the floor. She was overcome with shivering, though the day was warm, and her teeth were knocking together so that she could hear them like a manic drumbeat. To read the letter over and over had taken more than an hour. And infiltrating ever more strongly into her horror and sadness and longing were uglier, more sullying emotions of rejection and doubt and resentment. Jem lay dying. She hadn't even said what of. Some form of cancer, presumably, given the reference to chemotherapy. Before that happened, she would undergo surgery, she said, from which she would not survive. Surgery to extract the child? She besought Alice to visit the child through her go-between; her "more recent dearest friend," the "adorable" priest with whom she was half in "love." Nowhere in the letter was there the faintest suggestion that

Jem actually wanted to see her. Why not? Instead, she had devoted whole paragraphs to praising some killjoy priest who was lecturing her on "excess" and was colluding with her to give up her life. Was Jem no longer interested in renewing acquaintance with the living? Was the priest's advantage that his stock-in-trade was suffering and death? Or was Jem—dared one think it—manipulating her? Playing her against a rival? Had Jem always done that? Played her against Patch and Maddie and Minette and the man of letters? No! But was the whole thing—again, dared one think it—a bundle of macabre fabrication? The infected stigmata writ large?

Then there was the extraordinary business of the plagiarized manuscript, about which she affected not to care. If she did not care, why had she appended the cutting? Was it an accusation? Alice was invaded with guilt that all these months gone by she had left the cardboard box of convent exercise books in the attic of the Morgans' house. God in heaven, she had actually handed *My Last Duchess* to Iona Morgan on a plate!

Alice went determinedly to the telephone. She first called National Directory Inquiries and she then called International. The first call confirmed for her that the Catholic hospital existed. The second call yielded up the number of a New York publishing house in the name of Giovanni B. Angeletti. Then she sat down and tried to read David's letter, the first she had had from him. In normal circumstances it would have been a lovely surprise.

David wished her well and said he was in hopes of having her return to her room next term. He had been playing squash with Roland, he said, and had recently experienced a satisfactory leap forward with his research. Everything at home was delightful, since Maya, who had left him in the spring, he said, had changed her mind and come back. She had come back with a haircut and a part-time job and pretty clothes and she seemed like a woman reborn. Everything was going very nicely there, not least because Iona had left them and gone to America. Maya, who had previously destroyed her novel, had moved with her typewriter into Iona's room, had scraped the matt-black paint off the windows and had started again from scratch. This time something wholly new and the writing was giving her great joy. Iona, who was staying with her father in California, was herself having some success with literary endeavors, he said, but he would tell all when she came back. He was clearly concerned for Iona, who, it seemed, had had some sort of sexual imbroglio with the villainous Paul Koplinski. But David's major emotion was quite evidently relief. Maya was employing a twice-weekly cleaning woman and William was, at last, in nursery school. They were all off the next day to the Peak District for a family holiday, he said. Now that Maya had her cashcard to herself, they could afford such pleasant things. Thomas and Sophie had progressed from *The King of the Golden River* to *Treasure Island* and *The Secret Garden*, he said, and both of them sent her their love. Roland, too, had said to convey his good wishes, though he thought it sensible not to write himself.

The letter, in the circumstances, caused some muted stirrings in Alice's consciousness, like troubled twitchings in a dream. She understood that somewhere there was a subtext involving Roland and David and a desk with a row of books. The desk said "Jeffreys is a dunderhead" across it. But right now the major thrust of the nightmare had all to do with Jem. Perhaps it always had?

Alice got up and rang New York. The call gave access to the answering machine of Giovanni B. Angeletti. First it played her some Marvin Gaye. Then it spoke to her in transatlantic tones that she found offensively confrontational.

"There is nobody here wishes to speak with you right now," said the voice of Giovanni B. Angeletti. "If your message is urgent and you cannot write, you have one minute after the bleep. Make it good."

Alice made it good. She was too angry to notice quite how good. Or that the stammer had departed like chaff before the wind.

"My name is Alice Pilling," she said. Then she gave her telephone number. She paused briefly, but only to grind her teeth. "You have a novel in your possession," she said. "*My Last Duchess*. You think you are going to publish it, but you will do so over my dead body. Iona Morgan, alias Aoin le Fey, has plagiarized it lock, stock and barrel from its author, who is Jem McCrail. You will phone me back within the hour, Mr. Angeletti, or I will speak to you only through the courts." And she sent the phone crashing onto its cradle.

When the telephone rang twenty minutes later, she knew it would almost certainly be Angeletti, but it was not.

"Tell-me-you-love-it. Tell-me-you-love-it, tell-me-you-love-it," said the heavy breather, in a state of evident arousal. "Suck me off now,

Princess Piglet," he said. Alice put the phone down and checked the progress of her cranberry sorbet. The telephone rang again.

"You're squealing for it, Piglet," said the heavy breather this time. "Higher now baby-love. Harder now. Harder." Alice put the phone down and gave the asparagus and cream a stir. Then the telephone rang again. It was not Angeletti. It was the heavy breather.

"You're coming," said the heavy breather in a condition of rhythmic convulsion. "You're coming now baby-love; you're coming; you're coming." Alice dropped the receiver and left it to dangle on its flex. She tried hard not to cry. The day had been a difficult one.

"Pull yourself together," she said firmly, speaking low. At this point I sometimes have to warn my ladies to pull themselves together. Alice felt profoundly violated and sick with fear. She wasn't "coming." She never had. She had no idea about what it could feel like. There was possibly something the matter with her and the heavy breather had sussed it. He had picked her out from the multitude in the phone book. He would find her out and expose her. And would Matthew and Flora, oh please God, return before there came the heavy tramp of his ominous boots on the gravel! Jem was dying, or pretending to die, while some barbarous, ill-mannered publisher was busy stealing her novel. The morning had been full of green plastic bags and particles of human skin. She ought, she thought, to get up and bathe and put on prettier clothes. She was wearing a navy skirt and lace-ups and a rather spoilsport, missish white blouse. But she could not take her clothes off. Not now when the heavy breather might appear like the Commendatore. Tramp, tramp, tramp, tramp.

She got up and tidied Matthew's computer magazines again and put Scarlatti at the ready on the CD player. Then she sat down, to stare fixedly at the front door, waiting for Matthew and Flora.

 MATTHEW AND FLORA came early. The trains had favored them on the route from Heathrow. They had not planned upon making disclosures to Alice so abruptly, but there it was. They did. Matthew's ardor for his Parisian enchantress was difficult to conceal and, for Flora, disclosure meant, understandably, the grim satisfaction of fifteen years' redress. Fifteen years of feeling herself at the receiving end of the Pillings' generosity; a little matchgirl, tempted by the comfort and luxury of a suburban playroom in the house of a wealthy and ignorant building contractor, and of his wife who couldn't pronounce *bouillabaisse*. She burned with love for her own father—handsome, scholarly, punitive and austere—brought low by her gregarious patrons in an orgy of *nouvelle cuisine*. And guilt, of course, caused Flora to overreact with Alice. Guilt because Alice, all through their childhood, had been so open, so blameless, so affectionate, so endowed with innocent blue eyes. The eyes were staring at her right now. Flora fixed her mind firmly on the McCrail girl, who had come to Alice in the wake of her father's death, thereby rendering ineffectual all the force of her own gesture toward rejection.

"Matthew is in love with me," Flora said. "So we'll stay here until the funeral if that's all right, but I would like to make it clear that afterwards he's coming back with me." Alice stood and blinked, her back against the pretty dining table, which she had so recently dressed in its plum-colored cloth. Behind her the tall candles rose, pastel pink. In one hand she held her glass of white wine and, in the other, an oval plate with vol-au-vents, which she had been in the act of offering to Flora.

Matthew looked awkwardly at his feet throughout, but Flora sat beside him, ramrod straight on the two-seater cane sofa, which was padded with a buttoned floral print. She looked Alice straight in the eye.

"I wouldn't normally indulge myself like this," she said. "I don't think I'm a self-indulgent person. But you and your family—you owe me rather a lot. And all I'm taking in compensation is Matt."

"U-owe you alla-alla-alla." Alice stopped and breathed deeply and started again. "I don't unders-stand you," she said.

"You and your family," Flora said, forming icicles with her cold venom. "When I think about how the three of you took me up in my infancy and bought me and fed me poisoned gifts. Oh, all through my childhood, Alice Pilling! Your family bought me—with coconut ice and visits to the pantomime and a Sindy doll house. A witch's house all made of poisoned candy."

"But I th-th," Alice said. "Flora. I-I—you—I believed that you wanted to come."

Flora's lip curled impressively. "Oh, I wanted to come all right," she said. "I wanted to come all right. It was all too much to resist. And then, one fine day, came the biggest poisoned gift of all. Dinner in a restaurant during which you killed my father. To be followed, if you remember, by the offer of chocolate brownies."

"But it wasn't her f-fault," Alice said. "My m-mother. Sh-she didn't kn-n-n. Please. Anyway, n-not-not me. F-f-f."

Flora was provoked to cold clarity by the evidence of Alice's stammer. "Your mother," Flora said. "And of course your father." The sins of the fathers, her demeanor spoke eloquently, were to be visited on the children and the children's children too. Flora had returned to pronounce the fairy's curse.

"Flora," Alice said. "You shouldn't-sh-shouldn't say th-th. Your mother is dead. We sh-sh. You—'

"My mother?" Flora said. "My mother? Listen, Alice. I don't give that for my mother. Or for my grandmother. Not for either of them. Not if they'd been seven years burning themselves to extinction. Your family killed my father. I loved and revered that man."

"R-really?" Alice said "D-did you really?" And it occurred to her with shock that Flora *had* loved him. Of course! She had loved him intensely. Had become a star of self-denial for him; had learned to swallow gristle for him; to perform in tests for him. Of course! Why had she not realized that before? Mr. Fergusson, the twisted swine, had had more than his just share of all-male magnetism. How else could one have accounted for Mrs. Fergusson's obscene compliance? And he had been very handsome, as she remembered, in that grimly ascetic way.

"I—," she said, and stopped. "I'm deeply sorry, Flora."

"You left me at the mercy of those abject crones," Flora said. "And in return I'm taking Matt." Alice looked down at the vol-au-vents, because Flora's gaze was disconcerting her. Then she looked up at Matthew. She thought how becoming he was in his boyish way. She wondered why she didn't really mind. Flora's hatred, yes. But not Matt's defection. Not too terribly. But her parents—they would be saddened by it. Her father had lent Matt fat sums of money and loved him as his very own son. And right then Flora's righteous vengeance was turning her stomach all to rope.

"I th-think th-th-th—" She paused and started again. "Would you l-l-like two tickets for the opera t-tonight?" she said. "They're to s-see *The M-Magic Flute*."

Flora laughed unkindly. "The last of the poisoned gifts," she said. "Thank you, Alice. We'll take them with pleasure."

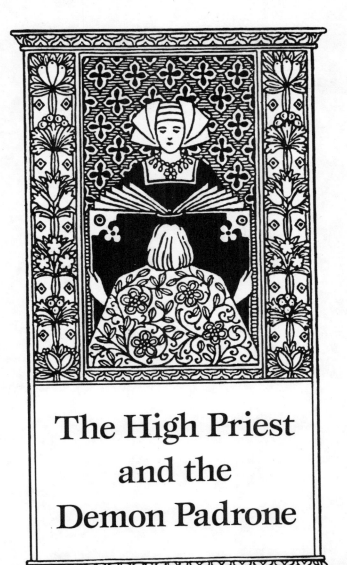

The High Priest
and the
Demon Padrone

III

WHEN THE KNOCKING CAME, it was suitably loud and resonant. Alice got up from the supper table and went to answer the door. It was not the Commendatore. It was Giovanni B. Angeletti. He was wearing a black felt hat and a voluminous black gabardine coat that fell unbuttoned from his shoulders. Under it he wore evening dress.

"Mizz Pilling?" he said. "Giovanni Angeletti." He removed the hat to reveal lank, receding black hair. The handshake was brief and purposeful, with the touch of a steel clamp. It was apparent to Alice that his whole being was bristling with barely contained animosity. "I got a little message to call you," he said. "But there's something the matter with your phone." Alice blanched and raised a hand to her mouth. She remembered, with deep embarrassment, that the telephone receiver was still dangling from its flex.

"Oh, but I'm terribly sorry," she said. "Please. You haven't come all the way from New York?" Angeletti waved the question aside with ill-disguised impatience. He was tall and powerfully built and she saw now, by the light of the hall, that his eyes, which were hooded and predatory, came an unlovely greenish mud brown. There was also something in the cast of his jaw that induced irrational aversion in her; something reminiscent of the public executioner in a children's television cartoon that she had always watched with Flora.

"I got in to London this morning," he said. Then he added, as if for children and idiots, "I have my messages conveyed to my hotel."

"Yes," Alice said. "Yes of course."

In the living room, where the table had been decked in its pink and white best, she introduced him to Matthew and Flora.

"Mr. Angeletti," she said, "is a publisher from New York." She turned with hospitable effort to the public executioner. "Will you join us for supper?" she said. "Excuse me. It *is* rather early, but M-Matthew and Flora have tickets for the opera."

Angeletti cast an eye over the table. "No thank you," he said. "The time is short, Mizz Pilling, and, frankly, pigeons remind me of bird shit." Matthew, being still uneasy in the wake of Flora's righteous wrath, laughed rather too loudly in response, Alice thought. He observed, in broader Northumbrian than usual, that the association would have come from "growing up in New York."

"I was raised in San Francisco," Angeletti said. Then he returned his attention to Alice. "Mizz Pilling, you called up my office with an allegation the *Duchess* is plagiarized."

"Oh it's plagiarized all right," Alice said.

"Now that's a pretty radical allegation," Angeletti said. "May I suggest that we waste no more time in social pleasantries. You have a manuscript?"

"Yes," Alice said. "I've got a manuscript."

"Good," said Angeletti. "You show me your manuscript and I guess we can resolve the matter at once."

Alice turned to Flora for support. "You'll confirm this for me, Flora," she said. "That story of Jem's. You'll remember it. It was called *My Last Duchess.*"

"Isn't that Robert Browning?" Flora said unhelpfully.

"Oh please!" Alice said. "Of course it's Robert Browning. Jem was reading it on the playing f-field that f-first day you came back." Flora smoothed her sleeve.

"Do me a favor and count me out," she said. "I don't know what's going on here, but it all begins to sound predictably baroque. Actually I remember very little to do with Jem—other than that she always told lies."

"Flora," Alice said. "Jem's story has been stolen. She-she needs us. She needs both of us."

"I owe Jem nothing," Flora said. "But perhaps you do." Alice winced. While she grappled to take on board her own failings toward her dearest friend, it seemed to her that Flora owed Jem a lot. Flora had robbed Jem of her scholarship. And now she was going to sit back and watch Angeletti steal Jem's novel. Flora continued to stroke her sleeve with infuriating serenity. She was sitting, composed and upright, Alice thought, like a teacher's pet in a deportment class. "She'll have had you on about the novel," Flora said. "Frankly, Jem's mendacity stood out a mile—that's for anyone less gullible than you."

Gullibility, Alice thought ruefully, is the sin of stupidity. Jem had told her that. She was acutely aware that Flora was not only reducing her credibility by the second, but was doing so with malicious intent. It distressed her that Flora could wish to do this to her.

"Mizz Pilling," Angeletti said. "The manuscript."

"The manuscript," Alice said, summoning courage, "is in a cardboard box in Oxford." As he clenched his teeth and swallowed, she saw the Adam's apple in Angeletti's throat rise and fall, prominent, like a frog in the belly of a snake. Then he looked at his watch.

"Grab your wrap," he said. "I have a cab waiting outside."

"A *cab*?" Alice said. "But you can't take a cab to Oxford. That's just silly."

Angeletti turned his hooded eyes on her as evenly as he could. "I have twenty thousand copies of that little book waiting for distribution in a warehouse," he said. "That's excluding book club deals, et cetera. Have you any idea what I stand to lose in the event that you should turn out to be right?"

"No," Alice said, "I haven't."

"You would oblige me, Mizz Pilling," he said, "if you would desist from practicing thrift on my behalf and jump into that cab. Just you leave me to pick up the tab."

Alice got her jacket. As she left she turned momentarily to Matthew and Flora, who had already usurped her space. Flora, unlike Matthew, was doing so with the air of being the Lord's anointed.

"Matt," she said, "the tickets are by the phone."

"Well, if you're sure you don't mind—," Matthew said.

"Thank you, Alice," Flora said. "You're very kind."

The taxi driver was reading a paperback with two large rats on the cover. The rats' eyes had been picked out in gold bas-relief. He stowed the book resignedly in the glove compartment when Angeletti and Alice got in.

"Where to, squire?" he said.

"Oxford," Angeletti said.

There was a cellular telephone on the seat beside them in the back, which Angeletti, she deduced, had brought with him. For over an hour in the cab, he said almost nothing to her at all. He evidently felt no compulsion toward the softening effect of small talk. He made a few unintelligible but litigious-sounding telephone calls from the cellular telephone. That was all. Intermittently, he chewed on ingots of Juicy Fruit or he smoked disgusting cigars.

One of the telephone calls made reference to the New York City Police Department and one of them was to a hospital. Another was to a person called something like "Aaron Schmutzburger." All the calls had to do with "Mary-Lou" and somebody called "MacMahon." Except for one. This arranged for the last-minute sale of a ticket to the English National Opera. Alice did not seriously begin to follow any of the calls. She had had the most terrible day. She was thinking about Matthew and Flora, and about the coroner's court and the heavy breather. And about Jem's unbearable dying and the convent exercise books containing *My Last Duchess*. With regard to these last she searched her memory repeatedly and fervently.

Iona had definitely returned them all to her and Alice had put them back in the alcove cupboard beside the attic fireplace. She hoped to God that they were still there. All that furious typing—that would have been Iona transcribing the thing. She would surely not have entered in and stolen the books back again after Alice had left for North Yorkshire? By the sounds of it she had been far too busy moving into Paul Koplinski's bed. And then in shipping herself off to America. On balance, the likelihood was that the books would still be there. Iona was far too sloppy to cover her tracks really well. And, in any case, she would have executed the plagiarism not with any serious intent to defraud; merely as a way of being outrageous; to jump the gun and needle her mother and cock two fingers at Alice. Otherwise, why hadn't she tried to write her own story? Had she stolen it rather as Jem had stolen the bracelet and the five-pound note? If Angeletti had been an easier sort of person, one more ready to see merit in "social pleasantries," it might have been possible to convey these things, but he was not. He appeared resolutely indisposed toward any interaction with her. Besides, he was preoccupied with a cordless telephone and his cigars were making her feel sick.

Nonetheless, in the gaps between the phone calls, Alice struggled to talk at Angeletti as coherently as she could. She wished to set the scene with regard to herself and Jem and Flora and Iona and Maya and Maya's novel in the coalhole and the convent exercise books and the typewriter bought with the stolen cashcard.

When they got to David Morgan's house, Angeletti told the driver to wait. Since the house was deserted, Alice deduced that the family was still on holiday. She led Angeletti down the obstructed side passage where, as luck would have it, he became immediately entangled in the Morgans' roll of rusted chicken wire.

"What the hell!" he said edgily. Alice, after a protracted effort, succeeded in liberating him, though not before a small right-angular rent had appeared in the back of the gabardine coat. Then, having broken in through the lavatory window and let Angeletti into the kitchen, she excused herself and made her way up the three flights of stairs.

It stirred her with a strange and powerful emotion to be back in her old room. It induced a flow of gratitude that Maya and David had left it all so faithfully untouched—as if the room were waiting for her to reenter and take up the threads of her life. Her A_4 pad, with the half-completed essay, lay open on the desk and her Greek-English dictionary, also open, lay facedown on the pad.

But the convent exercise books were not there. Nor were they in what had been Iona's room, nor in David and Maya's bedroom. They were not to be found in the coalhole, though Alice braved the blown-up photograph of Maya giving birth. She looked through every drawer and shelf. The exercise books were nowhere. Alice accepted this disheartening reality only after sifting determinedly through the Morgans' semipermanent piles of litter on the stair treads and all the mantelshelves.

Back in the kitchen, Angeletti was smoking a cigar. He was once again talking on his telephone. She waited politely for him to stop.

"It's not there," Alice said. "The books aren't there. I think we ought to look next door." Angeletti glanced pointedly at his watch, but he got up all the same, and followed her out through the door and down the side passage of Koplinski's similarly unoccupied house. Alice sensed that he was doing so with the air of one unreasonably indulging a deluded nonentity at a time highly inconvenient to himself.

"We'll have to pick the window," she said, and she climbed precariously onto the stone sill of Koplinski's mezzanine floor.

"Mizz Pilling?" Angeletti said unhelpfully. "May I ask, do you know what you are doing? I have no wish to be apprehended in conspiracy with an infamous cat burglar."

"If you have a p-plastic credit card," Alice said, between her teeth, "I wish that you would p-pass it over." Angeletti produced from a breast pocket an extensive ribbon of credit cards from which Alice pointedly chose the gold American Express.

The daylight had begun to recede by the time they had broken and entered, and Paul Koplinski's builders appeared to have repositioned all the staircase light switches. As a result Angeletti discovered almost too late that he was walking from the first-floor landing into a void created by one of Koplinski's more devastating structural modifications. Alice pulled him back in the nick of time.

"Look out," she said, and she found the switch, though it was hanging backless from the wall, pending fixture. "He's made a double-volume sitting room down there."

"Pardon me?" Angeletti said.

"He's taken out the ceiling," Alice said. Angeletti sat down on the staircase.

"You go right ahead, Mizz Pilling," he said. "You do what you must. Bear in mind I give you thirty minutes. I have important personal business to attend to in the morning and your cabdrivers don't come cheap."

"Yes, all right," Alice said. "I'll be quick."

"I feel bound to point out," he added gratuitously, "that for you to move another step in this habitation without first checking on your medical coverage is probably inadvisable."

"Yes," Alice said. She began in the attic and worked her way back to the ground floor. The cardboard box was nowhere. After thirty minutes of scrupulous but fruitless searching, she confronted Angeletti.

"It's not here," she said. "I think it's very possible that Iona Morgan destroyed it—or she's taken it with her to America." Angeletti fixed his penetrating gaze upon her as she spoke. "In which case," she said, struggling to arrest the spasm in her lower lip, "I haven't got a manuscript, I'm afraid. You'll have to believe me, that's all."

"You're saying there was only one copy?" he said. Alice's irritation became intense.

"Well, yes," she said. "Of course. It was handwritten in school exercise books, after all—by a thirteen-year-old schoolgirl. I told you all that on the way here."

"I guess I wasn't listening to you," Angeletti said. "I had other things on my mind."

"Well thanks for nothing," Alice said, and she wiped away the unobtrusive beginnings of tears.

"Handwritten in school exercise books?" Angeletti said. "Mizz Pilling, I'm sorry for your evident distress. Now look. As I see it, it's like this. Your friend once wrote a story. A while back now, I guess. It happens to share a title with a book currently on my list. So what? It's not unprecedented. A title is there for the taking. In this case it's Robert Browning's, as your friend already observed."

"Flora," Alice said with feeling, "is not my friend." Angeletti got up. She was aware that she had finally lost all shred of credibility for him.

"Let's get out of here," he said. "Come on. This is becoming ridiculous." She followed him hangdog to the front door. In the porch he glanced again at his watch. He offered her a shepherding arm and proceeded down the front steps with an air of gracious and politic appeasement. "No hard feelings," he said. "Though I won't pretend this little fiasco has not cost me my seat at the opera this evening. C'est la vie. I guess I'll be heading back now. Can I have the driver drop you off, Mizz Pilling?"

"No thank you," Alice said curtly, feeling her own temperature rise as his seemed to fall.

"You're sure?" Angeletti said. "Look, it's no problem." He paused to lift her spirits with an ill-timed pleasantry. "It's too bad those pigeons'll be cold by now," he said. "I'm sorry I pulled you away from your dinner like that."

It was at this moment that Alice was diverted from indignation by the sight of Koplinski's skip. It was bulging with fallout from the newly banished floor and ceiling.

"I know what," she said. "Koplinski's dumped it!"

"What's that?" said Angeletti.

"Over there," Alice said. "He'll have dumped the cardboard box with all Jem's stories and then he'll have dumped all that other stuff on top of it, don't you see?"

Angeletti looked as if turned to stone. "Are we talking about the dumpster?" he said. The color was draining from his face.

"Well yes," Alice said. "That skip over there. I mean, after somebody's shipped out to America and you're glad to see the back of them, mightn't you dump their stuff?"

Angeletti stood staring in disbelief at Koplinski's immoderate mountain of Victorian lath and plaster.

"I'd like to believe you're joking," he said. But Alice had already approached the skip and she immediately started to delve.

With her first incursion into that weighty latticework of old beams and slats of wattle she ripped her right thumbnail to the quick, but she carried on regardless. The mountain was topped with heavy old floor joists, meshed together with batons and rusty four-inch nails. With each heave the meshwork rocked briefly leftward and reestablished itself very much as before. Blood gushed from the palm of Alice's right hand where a splinter had wedged itself into her flesh. With the pain it came to her with sudden force how outrageously—how unprofessionally—Angeletti had behaved toward her. First he had stolen Jem's novel and then he had effectively frog-marched her from her own front door. Ever since he had tyrannized over her, either with bossiness or with petulance. Or he had patronized her from the dizzy heights of his own provoking sense of self-importance.

"Since you've behaved all evening like the Grand Inquisitor," she said, "I expect you to help me now. Oh yes! For three hours and more I've watched you write me off as a liar and a madwoman. And you? And you?!" She sucked at the blood and dust that ran from her palm, remembering with what easy, girlish confidence she had once promised Jem to look after those stories for as long as ever Jem needed her. The appalling memory brought a surge of remorse that lent strength to the confrontation.

"I've got something to tell you!" she said. " 'Mister' Angeletti! Because my friend who wrote that story is right now lying on her deathbed. She has no family to defend her. Only me. She is about to die in childbirth while you try and publish a stolen novel. Well, you'll do that over my dead body."

Angeletti blinked at her skeptically. "Women do not schedule themselves in advance to die in childbirth, Mizz Pilling," he said. "You will have to do better than that."

"And I wonder what you would know about it?" Alice said. "From your very vast personal experience? I wonder how many of the women you know have just happened to die in childbirth?" Angeletti fixed her intensely with a moment's pure loathing.

"It could be that my mother died in childbirth," he said. "I find your manner both presumptuous and hectoring, Mizz Pilling."

Alice, meanwhile, had wrenched again at the resolute joists and slats. The action had yielded the same impotent result.

"Oh yeah?" she said. "*Me* 'presumptuous and hectoring'? Ha! And I'm really not at all surprised about your 'mother' dying in childbirth. It'll have been from catching sight of you. Now Jem McCrail—" She paused as misery began to overwhelm her. "Jem McCrail is dying. She's pregnant and she won't have chemotherapy because she wants to save the baby." Her voice rose in volume as the blood dripped from her hands and, remarkably, the words kept on coming. "My dearest friend is dying," Alice said. "And, God knows, this isn't much that I'm doing for her now, and, God knows, it's late, but I'm going to do it. All anyone ever did for Jem was steal from her and steal again. Flora stole her scholarship and everyone stole her talent. But you, Mr. Angeletti—only you—could possibly be gross enough to steal from her her unborn baby."

Angeletti, she noticed, had begun to look unexpectedly subdued. It drove her to further heights of confrontation. "So why don't you put your conviction where your mouth is?" she said. "Since you won't believe a word that I say, why don't you help me to get this junk off here and prove yourself so right? Go on. Because if you don't, then you're not only a bully and a thief, Mr. Angeletti. You're a ninny into the bargain."

Angeletti cast an eye a little dubiously over his clothes. "I'm not exactly dressed for heavy work," he said, conceding with difficulty. "But if you're quite serious about this, Mizz Pilling, I'd be more than happy to hire you some workmen in the morning. Right now I think it's apparent that we should talk." Alice snorted with contempt. With all her remaining strength she heaved vengefully at the meshwork of aged joists, which showered Angeletti's clothes with plaster dust and smuts. Some of it went down his neck.

" 'Talk'?!" she said. "As if I hadn't had my fill of listening to you talk from the moment I got you on the answering machine." Angeletti stood silent, tensing his executioner's jaw. The action lent to his physiognomy a kind of menacing presence that would normally have caused her to quail. But Alice was blinking down into the skip. For a moment she stopped in her tracks. Her brain had taken a photograph that had just that second made its print upon her consciousness. That moment when the wood had moved, she had seen—or had she?—for the merest particle of a second, a dusty section of black fishnet tights and the broken jaw of the waffle iron. Underneath these items she had seen about four square centimeters of manila, printed with the letters 'sion.' Ascension.

"Please," she said hoarsely, hardly daring to believe it. "Mr. Angeletti, please. I'm sorry if I was rude to you, but I think I may have found it." Angeletti, when she looked at him, was staring at her fixedly. "Please," she said. "Help me."

Angeletti took off his coat. He moved to place it on Paul Koplinski's wall. Then he took off his dinner jacket. After that he removed his cuff links. He put them into his trouser pockets and rolled up the sleeves of his beautiful silk shirt.

"Oh hurry up," Alice said. "Oh please." Angeletti was removing his black silk tie. He approached the skip rather grimly.

"Stand back," he said. Alice stood back. She watched as he leaned his right arm into the skip and heaved the knot of joists to the ground in one huge, marvelous, creaking arc. Alice saw the woodwork rise and crash in a filthy cloud of disintegrating plaster.

"Gosh!" she said. "How did you do that?"

"I work out," Angeletti said. "With weights." He was fastidiously trying to dust the filth from off his hands.

"Gosh!" Alice said again, because there, like a benediction under the black fishnet tights and the waffle iron, lay the cardboard box with the pile of convent exercise books.

"There you are!" Alice said. "There it is." Angeletti exhumed the cardboard box and carried it solemnly to the streetlamp. He sat down on the curbstone and began at once to read quietly to himself.

"Well?" Alice said anxiously, and she approached him to read the book over his shoulder. "Well?" He said nothing. He kept on reading.

"Do you know what?" she said. "I've just remembered something. I'll bet your 'Mizz' le Fey's typescript is missing all its aitches." Angeletti said nothing. He kept on reading.

"Well, surely you believe me now?" she said. When Angeletti did not reply, Alice took Jem's letter from her pocket where it had lain now for something like nine hours. She unfolded it and handed it to him. "Wouldn't you say—I mean making allowances for illness and growing up—wouldn't you say that was the same person's handwriting? You see, nobody in England writes like that anymore. She learned it from an old copybook." Angeletti looked at it.

"May I read the letter?" he said.

"Please do," Alice said. "You will find that it's a bit strange." She watched him closely as he read the letter carefully once through. Finally he folded it and returned it to her.

"Well?" Alice said. Angeletti looked as though he were struggling to rise above the heavy drama of its contents.

"I'd have to admit it lends a degree of credence to your assertions," Angeletti said.

" 'Degree of credence'?" Alice said. "What else can you possibly want?"

"Mizz Pilling, forgive me," he said. "It may be that I owe you a big apology. I would like to hold my horses on that until I speak with the writer of that letter."

"Jem?" Alice said. "You mean us to go and see Jem? Well, that's what I've wanted to do all evening. It's only you has kept on stopping me."

"When did you get the letter?" Angeletti said.

"Today," Alice said. "This afternoon."

"What's the date on it?" he said. Alice, in her feverish haste to read the letter, had not stopped to register its date. She passed it over to Angeletti. He unfolded it and checked it.

"August seventh," he said. "Okay. I suggest we wait until the morning. It's gotten kind of late to visit a hospital for the dying."

"Yes," Alice said. "So what do we do now?"

"Let's go," Angeletti said. "If it's no problem for you, I'd like to head out and check into a nearby hotel. That way I can undertake any necessary business as early as possible." He unrolled his shirtsleeves as he spoke. Then he lifted the box of books, which he began to carry toward the car. "Get my clothes there, will you?" he said.

Before she got back into the taxi, Alice cast an eye over the impressive pyramid of debris that Angeletti had so dramatically deposited in the gutter outside Koplinski's house. She felt suddenly sufficiently skittish to want to write Paul Koplinski a note.

"Can I borrow a pencil?" she said. She fixed the note firmly to the apex of the remaining debris in the skip. "Dear Mr. Koplinski," it said. "Don't worry about all this mess. I wasn't dumping on you. Truly. I was only taking out. Thanks a million. Alice."

"Where to, squire?" said the driver. He had made significant inroads into the rat book, which he shelved, once more, in the glove compartment.

"Southampton," Angeletti said.

"Come again?" said the driver. First they stopped briefly at a wooden prefab alongside the railway station where Alice and the cabbie ate hamburgers and chips. Angeletti, having inquired without hope after hot fudge sauce, ate two scoops of vanilla ice cream on a bath bun and washed it down with Cherry Coke.

"If that's your idea of a good wholesome supper," Alice said, "it's hardly any wonder that you wouldn't eat my pigeons." Angeletti, she thought, was disposed to react to anything she said as though it were about to bring him out in spots.

"I'm not due for 'supper,' " he said irritably. "Not for another five hours. Right now I'm on eastern daylight time. Are you intent upon bludgeoning me into your time zone?"

Alice didn't mind. In fact it made her laugh. She had unconcernedly stuffed in the last of her French fries and her mouth was too full to allow for reply. A goods train lumbered heavily over the railway bridge as she munched. She was feeling unreasonably elated. She had found Jem's books. She was going to see Jem. What more could one ask for in this life?

The cardboard box lay between them on the backseat alongside the cellular telephone. Once again they spoke hardly at all for the duration of the journey. Angeletti, having used the telephone to rearrange his flight schedule, had seized the opportunity to catch up on sleep. This had had the effect, at least, of saving Alice from his cigar smoke. She took the opportunity to scrutinize his appearance and registered, to her satisfaction, that he had become pretty filthy from his encounter with the skip. His trousers were ingrained with plaster dust and so were his beautiful black shoes.

The driver, with the assistance of his AA road map, delivered them to a village adjacent to where she had assessed Jem's hospital to be. He stopped outside a small, rather pretty old inn which, miraculously, still had a night clerk at the reception desk. Angeletti went in to make sure. Then he came back.

"Okay," he said. "They have a room. Come, Mizz Pilling. *Andiamo*. We could both of us use a decent shower." Alice went rigid. He opened the back door and took up the telephone and the cardboard box. "Move your ass now, Mizz Pilling," he said. "We got business to transact in the morning."

Alice got out and followed him determinedly down the driveway, wondering how best to resolve the business of the "room." She cursed the fact that she had not thought to bring her handbag with her, wherein she had all those items necessary for asserting her independence. Checkbook, Visa card, driving license. But then Angeletti had so domineeringly manipulated her from her own living room.

"I want my own room," she said. Angeletti swallowed.

"Look. I'm sorry about this," he said. "The place is thick with tourists. The room they offered is vacant only because it's to be refurbished. That's why it's available. I twisted an arm or two to acquire it for us, Mizz Pilling. But maybe you would prefer it if I slept on the forest floor?" Alice, who would undoubtedly have preferred it, hardly felt in a position to admit to it.

"And if you would kindly stop calling me 'Mizz' Pilling," she said irritably. "It's been getting on my nerves all evening." Angeletti then emitted the first laugh she had heard him utter. It was brief, sardonic and menacing.

"Okay," he said. "Okay. Since we are about to pass the night together in this enchanting and intimate little hostelry, maybe I ought to know. Is it Miss or Mrs.?"

"It's Mrs.," Alice replied with unnecessary haste.

"Mrs. Pilling," he said. "Okay."

"Mrs. Riley, as it happens," Alice said. "I use my own name in my business capacity, that's all."

Angeletti paused on the path as if knocked back. His response, though delayed, was predictably offensive.

"Not 'Mrs. Riley' as in Mr. Matthew Riley of the pigeon house?" he said. "Or ought I to say 'of the Dovecote'?"

"If you don't mind!" Alice said angrily. "You are talking about my husband."

THE INN HAD a very nice reception hall. Its ambience was cozy. There was a barometer, a grandfather clock and a polished oak settle. Two Baluchi rugs lay on the floor, while a brass fender, brass fire irons, brass equestrian accessories and a Georgian brass coal scuttle adorned the fireplace. On the chimney breast there hung an oil painting of a hunting dog with a bird in its mouth. In the warm light that bathed the reception desk, Alice could see that Angeletti's thinning black hair had acquired an outer coating of dust, broken cobwebs and miscellaneous Koplinski filth.

"Any luggage, sir?" said the reception clerk.

"Just the carton," Angeletti said firmly. "Which I prefer to carry myself."

Mercifully, the room had twin beds, though it smelled of Rentokil and perishing rubber carpet underlay. On the walls it had a sort of fecal green damask wallpaper that, in the glow of the unshaded forty-watt bulb, appeared to match Angeletti's eyes. A jaundiced green carpet gave stickily underfoot and, through a small casement window, Alice looked out upon a concrete servants' yard with mop buckets and drains.

Angeletti, meanwhile, having put down the cardboard box and locked the door, was surveying his own reflection in the oval mirror of the wardrobe door.

"Santa Maria," he said a little bitterly, and he picked fastidiously at a cobweb adhering to one of the strands of hair that still adorned the upper reaches of his brow. "Behold the man of letters." Alice turned on him at once.

"What?" she said. "What did you call yourself?" She had not meant to sound quite so confrontational, but Angeletti's presence was not conducive to serenity. Angeletti reacted angrily. He took a small step backwards and bristled.

"I called myself a 'man of letters,'" he said. "Have I offended against one of your codes of etiquette here, or what?"

"Well no—," Alice said. "I—" But Angeletti had seemed to become increasingly disagreeable with their admission to the hotel.

"So what do you suggest I call myself?" he said. "You have some suitably understated and misleading British way of describing a person such as myself?"

"Oh no," Alice said. "I—"

"'I read a bit; I scribble a bit'?" Angeletti minced viciously. "I 'cough in ink'? You call that a 'profession,' Mrs. Riley? To cough in ink? Or a 'hobby'? Which is the more discreet? To earn one's living from a profession, or from a hobby?" Alice blinked. She wondered why he didn't swallow tranquilizers and get on with it. He spread his hands as he confronted her, spewing fire and smoke. She noticed then that Angeletti wore a wedding ring. It caused her to donate a moment's thought to Mrs. Angeletti. What did the woman do all day? Alice wondered. Was she required to consume her life in appeasing the wretched man?

"P-please," Alice said. "Don't shout. It's late. I only wondered if you'd ever worked in a summerhouse, that's all."

Angeletti's anger modified itself into a sort of touchy puzzlement. "Sure I've 'worked in a summer house,'" he said. "I have a small cabin in New Hampshire. I take a break there in the summer. So what?"

"Oh, but that's not a summerhouse," Alice said, with relief. "That's just a summer house."

"Go take a shower, Mrs. Riley," Angeletti said. "As you said. It's late."

The bathroom had no shower and the bathwater, which coughed and gurgled through pocky, nickel-plated taps, set up a horrendous, compromising knock that ran like morse code through the hotel plumbing. *Frappe-frappe.* It ran hot for about three inches and then it began to run cold. Alice washed her hair in soap and rinsed it as best she could. Since there was no towel in the bathroom, she dried herself on the bath mat and finished the job on the curtains. Then she got back into her clothes.

"There's no shower," she said to Angeletti. "But there's a bath. I've left my bathwater for you, because you may be glad of it. It is a bit scummy, I'm afraid."

"What?" said Angeletti. " 'Scummy'? Get rid of it, Mrs. Riley. Is there something the matter with you?"

"There is nothing the matter with me," Alice said. "There's something the matter with the plumbing. You can have your bath scummy or ice cold. It's all the same to me." Angeletti sent out death rays through his eyes.

"I'll take ice cold," he said. Alice returned to the bathroom. She pulled out the plug and sluiced the tub. Then she turned on the hot tap. To her immense satisfaction, the water ran as if drawn up from some underground refrigerator. After that she got into one of the beds. But was it safe to sleep?

"Try sleeping with one eye open," said Angeletti, who had managed to read her mind before taking off for the bathroom.

Angeletti made an uninhibited clatter in the bathroom, turning the taps on and off again and churning about like a tidal wave. Alice worried for the hotel's other guests. On top of this, he began, suddenly, to transmit various carpings and whinings through the bathroom door.

"Mrs. Riley?" he said. "There are no toilet items in here. Did you happen to remove them?"

"If you mean shampoo," Alice said, "there isn't any. You'll find there are no towels either. I used the bath mat, but you can have one of the bedspreads if you like." She got up and ripped the candlewick spread from off his bed. She pitched it, bunched into a ball, against the bathroom door. Then she got back into bed. Angeletti said nothing for a moment.

"So how come you were able to wash your hair?" he said.

"I used the soap," Alice said. She yawned and sank down on the pillows.

"Soap?" he said prissily. "I can't wash my hair with soap."

Alice sat up again, her patience sorely tried. "Use the soap and get on with it!" she said. "You've got practically no hair to bother about in any case." A deathly silence followed upon this utterance during which Alice began to hold her breath. When Angeletti spoke again, it surprised her to notice that his tone had changed. He was actually sounding slightly tentative.

"Mrs. Riley?" he said. "Do you mind if I ask you a question?"

"Fire away," Alice said.

"Do you have an opinion about hair replacement therapy?" Alice wondered if she might scream.

"It's really none of my business," she said. "Why don't you ask Mrs. Angeletti?"

"Now that's an interesting idea," he said. "The first or the second Mrs. Angeletti?"

"Oh, the second, I'd say," Alice said. And she lay down again on the pillows.

When Angeletti emerged from the bathroom, his loins were wrapped in the bedspread. His hair was wet and plastered darkly to his head and his almost hairless chest, covered in smooth, olive skin, rose powerfully above a flat, iron-hard abdomen. He ran a pocket comb through his hair in front of the glass. Alice sensed that he was feeling somehow aggrieved.

"You're really quite a long way from being completely bald," she said, wishing to make amends. "Your hair's receding, that's all. No, honestly. It makes your brow look higher. It's not altogether unattractive."

Angeletti turned and looked at her, cocky and sarcastic. " 'Not altogether unattractive,' " he said. "Maybe you'd like to tell me how I decode that, Mrs. Riley?" Alice found that irritation gave her speech.

"Decoded it means I think you're not altogether unattractive," she said. "Or you would be, if you weren't s-s-so in-c-c-credibly bad-tempered and vain." Then she turned her face to the wall and addressed herself to sleep. As she dozed, it was her impression that Angeletti had returned to his telephone.

When Alice rose next morning, she thought first of Flora and Matthew. Was Flora nestling with that virginal, Grünewald body in the crook of

Matthew's faithless arm? Were they breathing together in sleep after a night of gentle touchings? She saw the fine brown hair on Matthew's naked legs and the appealing angles of his toes. Then she thought of Jem. She had to think of Jem, though to do so caused her hands to tremble and her heart to pound violently against the cage of her ribs.

Had the letter been the last and most devastating of Jem's dazzling repertoire of "ventriloquism"? Was it all a gigantic hoax? Could Jem seriously no longer distinguish fact from fiction? Was the hospital in truth a hospital for the mentally ill? Was Jem completely off her tree? Or was it all true?

Jem had said nothing about wanting to see her. Alice was deeply grieved by this, but she tried hard to understand. Did she not wish Alice to see her in her condition of "rot and putrefaction"? In which case, what right had Alice to come at all? Had all Jem's buoyant brown curls been thinned to nothing by galloping illness? Had that magic bell, Jem's golden voice, been half consumed by voracious disease? Was Jem, at this moment, lying on a bed of sores, oozing putrid substances from the surface of that radiant, girlish skin? Jem had kept the bracelet, she said. She would be wearing it even after death. Was this the latest of Jem's many wacky, ghoulish postures? Was Jem now posing Donne-like in her shroud; staging her own death complete with "bracelet of bright hair about the bone"?

Angeletti, cocooned in eastern daylight time, slept on. He was sleeping on his stomach, like a Benjamin Spock baby, his face turned sideways, his bare right arm dangling to the floor. Alice moved uncertainly to the bathroom. She felt sick. Sick from anxiety and distress and too much driving amid the stink of Angeletti's cigar smoke. She rinsed her teeth with warm water and tried to comb her hair with her fingers. It was dull and tangled from the night's assault with soap. As she ran her fingers through it, she came to a decision. She would stay behind in the hotel room with the exercise books and make Angeletti go on alone. His could be merely a business call and nothing like so intrusive. Meanwhile she would write Jem a letter, brief and to the point. Angeletti could hand it to her and explain that she was in the neighborhood. Then he could summon her to the hospital as soon as Jem gave the go-ahead.

She picked the pocket of Angeletti's evening jacket, which yielded up pen and memo pad. On this she wrote her letter. Coffee, she then thought desperately. Black coffee would not come amiss. But could she possibly venture out and leave Angeletti alone with all Jem's manuscripts?

Angeletti was a mystery to her. A mystery and a powerful irritant. Yet perhaps having him there had, after all, been a help. It had awakened reserves of malice in her and had certainly sharpened her wits. These things had distracted her from grief over Jem and had helped to block out the treachery of Matthew and Flora. She saw in a moment what she had been doing all evening. She had been caustically bantering time away, like a prisoner condemned to long nights before the rope. She had behaved like people everywhere who have reason to fear the dawn.

She could of course take the book box with her, she thought, but Angeletti had stowed the thing under his bed. She crouched with care and reached for it. But at the first, faint swish of cardboard shifting against carpet nap, Angeletti's right hand came down and closed like a steel clamp around her outstretched wrist. Her heart leapt into her mouth.

"Ouch!" she said. "Don't do that!" Angeletti, like a predator roused from slumber, was instantly awake. He released her wrist immediately and sat up.

"I'm sorry, Mrs. Riley," he said. "Forgive me. I guess I thought you were a thief. God knows what I thought. It's been a rough night."

"Yes," Alice said. "I suppose so." The pain in her wrist was quite considerable. It caused her for an instant to recall the bird in the oil painting over the hotel fireplace. In order not to have Angeletti observe this, she tried discreetly to flex it behind her back.

"I hurt you," he said. "I'm sorry." He reached out and took possession of her arm and began to massage the bones of her wrist. "Did you have your breakfast yet?"

"No," Alice said. "I was just going to."

He smiled at her quite suddenly. It was the first smile he had allowed himself in something like fourteen hours. The effect of it was astonishing, with his beard growth showing so blue against his hangman's jaw.

"You're a nice woman, Mrs. Riley," he said. "Do you mind if I ask you a question?"

Alice withdrew her arm immediately and stood up. "What question?" she said, suspiciously, and she walked over to the window.

"Is your husband Catholic?" he said.

"Oh for heaven's sake!" Alice said irritably. "Can we please go and get our breakfast?"

When they entered the breakfast room, Angeletti was carrying the book box. They drank black coffee and ate tinned grapefruit, which was served in sundae glasses. This they followed with cardboard triangles of toasted Wonderloaf. Angeletti looked at his watch.

"Time to get moving," he said. "On your feet now, Mrs. Riley."

Alice felt her teeth tap-tapping against the glaze of her coffee cup. She wondered if Angeletti could hear it. "Angeletti," she said hoarsely. "I want you to go without me."

Angeletti stared at her hard. "Oh no you don't," he said. "Oh no. This is your friend, Mrs. Riley. We are in this together, you and I."

"You've read her letter," Alice said. "Sh-she doesn't really want to see me." She took her letter out of her pocket and passed it over to him. Her arm was vibrating so markedly as she did so, that it knocked his empty cup sideways into the saucer, making it clatter against the teaspoon. "P-please," she said. "Give her this. Then after that, if sh-she wants to see me—"

Angeletti took it and stood up. He took the back of her chair. "Mrs. Riley," he said. "You are coming with me."

Alice stood up. As she did so, the issue resolved itself, because the room began to spin and the floor rose up to meet her. For just a moment Angeletti wondered which to pick up first. The book box or the woman. Both of them were lying on the floor at his feet.

 WHEN THE TELEPHONE RANG in the hotel bedroom the sun was high overhead. Alice, who had been resting there since she had come round from her faint, had at some time during the morning fallen asleep. She started and groped clumsily for the receiver.

"Mrs. Riley?" said the voice. "This is Giovanni."

"Who?" Alice asked.

"Angeletti," said Angeletti. "I'm sorry it's been so long."

Alice sat bolt upright as her heart began to race. "What time is it?" she said.

"It's five after twelve," he said. "Listen. It's all over. Your friend is dead. I'm sorry."

Alice said nothing. She was unable to cry or speak. She saw her life suddenly as an endless, pointless, featureless plain stretching cruelly ahead in place of all that might have been and once was.

"Are you hearing me?" Angeletti said eventually. His voice jarred in her ear. "Mrs. Riley, are you still there?"

"I'm here," Alice said. "Thank you. I'll hang up now if that's all right."

"Look," Angeletti said. "Wait. You will have to forgive me. This whole business. It has been a little taxing for me."

"I'm sorry," Alice said woodenly. "I'll hang up now." But Angeletti seemed anxious to talk.

"Your friend had been administered a sedative drug," he said. "Literally just as I got here." Alice felt a spasm like retching seize her throat. "The sisters were kind enough to let me talk to her," he said.

"But you'll understand that I had to work fast. I'd like you to know that I read her your letter, Mrs. Riley. I gave it priority over the novel." Angeletti waited for her to speak, but she said nothing. An ice splinter was penetrating her heart. "The sedative was prior to anesthetic and rather effective in its soporific result," Angeletti said. He seemed determined to weigh her down with detail. "The doctors couldn't hold out any longer. They had to operate, Mrs. Riley." Alice still said nothing. She envisaged Angeletti's intrusion as a relentless, obscene jabberwocky of copyright and contract as Jem—having commended her soul to her Maker—lay sinking into sleep. It appalled her to consider that she had provoked it. "It's too bad," Angeletti was saying, "that our timing worked out that way."

"So if you'd believed me yesterday—," Alice began, but she couldn't go on. The thought was too poisonous for utterance. "I need to hang up now," she said. "Thank you for letting me know."

"Look," Angeletti said, with a tenacity to induce despair. "There's something that really puzzles me about that letter. The letter you gave me yesterday. There's a sister here who says she mailed a letter to you over four weeks ago. Did you never get that letter?"

"I only got one letter," Alice said. "The one that came yesterday. Is there really any point to all this?"

There was a longish silence.

"Hold on," Angeletti said, his voice neutral with the dawning of terrible knowledge. There was a pause. "Jesus, Mrs. Riley," he said with difficulty. "It's a mistake. I made such a stupid, obvious mistake. She's written the date as eight colon seven."

"That's the eighth of July," Alice said. "You told me August the seventh—"

"God forgive me," he said. "She never wrote you any earlier letter. I made a mistake. See, in the States we'd read that as August seventh. You people reverse the month and the day."

Alice assimilated this bitter little irony of Angeletti's fallibility with a pain that went beyond recrimination.

"You're saying I could have talked to her last night," she said weakly.

"I guess so," he said. "Had we been aware of the greater urgency."

It was his use of the plural pronoun that suddenly provoked her to accusation. " 'We'?" she said.

"I," he said. "Look. I can't begin to tell you how deeply sorry I am." Alice had every wish to be spared the depth of Angeletti's sorrow.

"I'd like to hang up now," she said.

"Wait!" Angeletti said desperately. "Please. Your friend's priest here will need to speak with you. There's a newborn child who requires your attention."

Alice was becoming frantic to be alone with her own grief. And she was suddenly about to cry.

"I don't care about the child," she said, and her emotion tumbled into the phone. "Can you please understand that, Angeletti? I don't care about the child. Or the book. Or the priest, or you, or me, or anything. I care about nothing. I cared about Jem, that's all. I never got to her in time, that's all." And she put down the phone. When it rang again she picked it up only in order to cut it off. Then it rang again.

"Leave me alone," she said. "Please."

Angeletti's anger assaulted her unexpectedly through the wires. "Do that again and you will be in trouble," he said. Alice was momentarily awed into silence. "Just you get yourself in gear now," he said. "Okay? You can't torment yourself in that flophouse for the rest of your life." Alice had no stomach to reply. She let the receiver fall slowly into her lap, though his voice went talking on, into the air. "I know you're there, goddamnit," she heard him say. "I know you're listening to me. Now there's a letter here for you. A sort of a will, I guess. Your friend Veronica McCrail has expressed her wish for you to become the baby's guardian."

Alice raised the receiver to her ear in agitation. "But that's not true," she said. "Her letter never said that."

"Her wish was for you to raise the child," he said. "I'd read it to you but the letter's with her priest. Listen. Father Mullholland is anxious to meet you, Mrs. Riley. I really think it inadvisable for you to keep him waiting. It's my impression that he's pushed for time right now." He paused effectively. "I need not remind you that it's his business on occasion to undertake emergency baptism," he said.

"*What?*" Alice said.

"Emergency baptism," he said. "I guess none of us likes to place an immortal soul in jeopardy." Alice became transfixed. "The child is female, incidentally," Angeletti said.

"What do you mean 'in jeopardy'?" she said. "Angeletti, she's not going to die, is she?"

Angeletti sounded equivocal in reply. "The baby seems pretty well okay," he said. "She's underweight, of course. She was delivered six weeks before full-term, Mrs. Riley. And in rather critical circumstances. It's my impression she's doing all right. She's on a respirator."

"I'll be there," Alice said. "I'll be there." She got up as she spoke and pushed her feet hastily into her shoes. "Forgive me, Angeletti. I'll telephone for a taxi right away."

"No need," Angeletti said. "I called it for you already. It's waiting for you outside."

 IN THE TAXI, in order to keep at bay her terror that Jem's baby would die, Alice fixed hard upon the baptism. Jem's priest was waiting for her and she would have to be ready with the baby's name. She recoiled a little from the business, about which she knew almost nothing. Would the baby have to be named after a saint, or was it possible to have her called Jem? Would Father Mullholland—the "adorable" priest—be sufficiently adorable to contemplate calling a child after a jam sandwich? Or would he not? Alice rather thought the latter. Then the baby would be called Veronica. Once she had established this, it gave her a tenuous kind of poise. It gave her sufficient composure to step purposefully from the taxi, where Angeletti was waiting.

Angeletti was standing in the hospital driveway like the centerpiece of a triptych. He was flanked by a nun and a priest, but he broke ranks when the taxi pulled up and came over to open her door. Then he paid the driver. The nun was dressed in those awkward, halfway civvies that made her look, Alice thought, as though she had taken the scissors to the hem of her habit. The priest, who wore glasses, was a head shorter than Angeletti, though he was similarly broad in the shoulder. He was thickset and had curly fair hair and a fleshy, deeply cleft chin. Angeletti led her, by the arm, back to the nun and the priest. Alice found herself warmly enveloped in a cloud of crisp convent linen.

"It's the little mother," said Sister Teresa. "Welcome, Mrs. Riley." There was something in the woman's determined radiance that caused Alice to react against her. She tensed, feeling that yesterday's sweat and dust were adhering to her clothes. And she found that Sister Teresa's resolutely sanguine goodwill was an affront to her feelings of bitterness, disappointment and loss. She was acutely and painfully aware that, somewhere in the building before her, her dearest friend lay dead on a slab, with an ugly scar across her abdomen where a doctor had extracted a child. She was painfully and morbidly conscious that Jem's perplexing month-old letter—written in the last five weeks of her life—had been in receipt of no reply.

"Mrs. Riley?" Angeletti said, once Sister Teresa had released her. "Meet Father Mullholland."

The priest shook her by the hand. "How do you do, Mrs. Riley," he said. Alice tried hard not to stare at him. Her impulse was to scrutinize his features for giveaway signs of Jem's devotion. What clues were there to those elements of his being that had so endeared him to Jem that they had qualified him for the role of more recent "dearest friend"? Nothing. Nothing beyond the priestly function about which she felt herself wholly inadequate to judge. She registered, rather irrelevantly, that he wore trousers under his cassock.

"I'm sorry that I've kept you all waiting like this," she said. "Forgive me. Mr. Angeletti has explained the urgency."

Sister Teresa turned to Angeletti and smiled her radiant smile. Alice could hardly believe it, but she took him by the hand. Then she addressed herself to Alice.

"You poor dear creature," she said. "You've been worried sick about the baby. I know it. But you can rest easier, Mrs. Riley. The little girl is quite safe now. The doctors anticipated all the difficulties. They were very well prepared. Indeed, we were all very well prepared for Veronica's precious baby." Alice considered that she had finished speaking, but then the nun went on. "I hope Mr. Angeletti did not alarm you with his telephone call," she said, "but we all felt we would like to have you here as soon as possible. The baptism was an emergency, as I'm sure he will have explained to you. It is a great pity that you could not have been with us, but never mind, Mrs. Riley. You are with us now." She smiled again at Angeletti and gave his hand a little squeeze. " 'Pamina,' " she said. "Not 'Pamela.' Pamina Mary. Beautiful names, for a beautiful little girl."

Alice turned her gaze upon Angeletti in outrage and disbelief.

"I'm sorry, Mrs. Riley," he said, sounding just a little cautious. "As

Sister says, there was an emergency. And I thought that since we had both of us missed the opera last night—and today being the Day of the Assumption— Look. You'll have to forgive me."

Alice continued to stare at him in disbelief. "You told me her immortal soul was in jeopardy," she said.

"Now those were not exactly my words," he said. "I guess you jumped to conclusions."

Alice lost her rag. "Bastard!" she said. She spoke so intensely that she found herself fighting back tears. "You absolute bastard, Angeletti! How could you do this to me?"

"Come on, Mrs. Riley," he said. "You're upset. You're in a state of stress. You'll feel a little better tomorrow."

"Quite right!" said Sister Teresa, seizing eagerly upon Angeletti's clichés in the absence of comprehension for Alice's indignation. "That is exactly right. You must try to relax a little now and not worry too much, Mrs. Riley. You will feel a little less wretched tomorrow. Your friend Mr. Angeletti has been a wonder and a marvel, coming as he did. So much in the nick of time. That was a comfort to dear Veronica, I know it. To have news of you and of her little book. And all just before she died." She smiled again at Angeletti. "Mr. Angeletti came to us like one of God's angels, Mrs. Riley. He has been a 'little angel,' as his name so aptly implies."

Alice felt her gall rise as she watched Angeletti play to his audience. In the context of this day-to-day, practicing Catholicism, where she felt herself more and more uncomfortably marginal, Angeletti was behaving as though he were in his own backyard. And so he was, of course. He stood there with his hand in the nun's, just as if he had been transported back to his parochial grade school. He was once again Sister's "best little reader" in all of the diocesan elementary school. Alice envisaged him, venomously, as an infant black marketeer in sacramental holy cards. And then, to crown it all, as she stood in her jaded garments, giving off an odor of yesterday's sweat, she noticed suddenly that Angeletti had shaved and that he was wearing a different shirt.

"Where did you get those clothes from?" she demanded. "And how is it that you've shaved?" Angeletti and Father Mullholland looked at each other. It was clear that they were striving to suppress any hint of improper eyebrow raising in the face of what they read as her unreasonable indignation.

"Say, cool it, Mrs. Riley," Angeletti said. "Father Mullholland was kind enough to lend me his razor, okay?"

Alice was aware that the priest was regarding her with interest. He spoke soothingly.

"As it has turned out, Mrs. Riley," he said. "Mr. Angeletti and I share a collar size. That is really all there is to it."

Alice turned her fury upon Angeletti. "God Almighty," she said. "If it isn't the Catholic Boys' Club, networking here at HQ. You sound like a pair of Freemasons!"

For a moment the three of them blinked at her with curiosity. Then Sister Teresa stepped forward, capably determined upon forgiveness and understanding. She enveloped Alice once more in the convent linen.

"My poor lamb," she said. "You will feel so much better after a good cup of tea and a long night's rest. Come along now, dear Mrs. Riley." Tears began to spill from Alice's eyes onto the cloth. Tears of exhaustion and disappointment and loss. Tears of sudden, enormous gratitude for the woman's seemingly unending and uncritical kindness.

"That's better now," Sister Teresa said. "There now. Veronica was a brave and exceptional young woman. You are grieving for her, Mrs. Riley. Of course. That is exactly what all of us would expect." She fumbled briefly among the folds of her habit, but gave up as Angeletti passed over his handkerchief. The nun took it and used it to mop Alice's eyes. Then she tucked it up Alice's sleeve. "Now I'll take you to your friend," she said. "Once you have had that cup of tea. You will be longing to see her, I am sure."

JEM'S BODY was covered with a sheet, which Sister Teresa drew down to the waist. Under it the body was clothed in a short-sleeved, back-fastening surgical gown from which the head emerged, ash-colored and skeletal. Jem's hair, which had grown thinly to the shoulders, was arranged in neatly combed, clod-colored curls about her neck. The orifices of her face had become so predominant that she appeared to Alice all dental arch and eye socket. Her arms, covered patchily in raw, mottled skin, were wide at the elbow and ended in large bony hands on which the skin hung slackish over the knuckles. The cuticles of Jem's fingernails were thickened and fissured while the nails were whitish and displaying dry, fluted grooves. Fixed to the wrist of her left arm was a narrow silver bracelet with a raised floral motif that Alice could dimly remember as having once occupied her mother's jewelry box. Jem's hipbones made two gaunt peaks under the white gown, between which Alice envisaged the surgical wound, and below that, under a sheet, were two further peaks formed by her feet.

"What did she die of?" Alice asked tonelessly.

"Ovarian cancer," the nun said. She placed a plastic stacking chair beside the bed. "I'll leave you alone," she said. "Take as long as you like, Mrs. Riley."

Alice sat down. She did not look at the body at first, once Sister Teresa had gone. She put her head in her hands. Small inhuman noises began to emanate from her throat, like those made by a cold, abandoned puppy. The noises went on and on. When Alice finally became aware that she had saturated her lap, she stopped to stare absently at the unattractive compound that Koplinski's plaster dust and her own tears had made of her skirt. Then she got up and approached the bed. She stared hard at Jem's face. Gradually, as she became accustomed to its gauntness and pallor, she was able to relate it, tentatively at first, to the face of that tall marvelous girl who had stood with such definition in the form-room doorway on that magical Wednesday afternoon, dragging a canvas toolbag. Alice stretched out her hand to stroke Jem's cheek, feeling only love and tenderness for the curious absence of elasticity under the skin. Then she bent her head and kissed the cheek where her hand had been. Two heavy tears rolled from her eyes and fell in runnels down the body's face. Alice took a handkerchief from her sleeve and wiped them off. As she was doing so, she realized that she was using Angeletti's handkerchief.

"Sorry, Jem," she said. "I'm sorry I'm such a sniveling weed. It's only because I haven't seen you for such ages and ages. Honestly." Her tears began to flow more copiously. "I'm not saying that you can't be dead or anything. I'll always like you the best, Jem. Even if you're dead. It's so amazing to see you again. I wanted to see you again more than anything in my whole life." She blew her nose hard on the handkerchief. Then she looked at Jem's face and she laughed. "Angeletti's noserag," she said. "First he's so revolting that he makes you snivel and then he lends you his snotrag. Did you notice that about him? How omnipotent and bossy he is. Like God. 'Therefore that He may raise, the Lord throws down.' All that sort of sado-God-the-Father crap. Oh crumbs, Jem. Sorry. I'm probably even insulting your religion." She laughed again between sniffs. "What I mean is, can you trust him, that's all. He sets himself up like the high priest of the Brotherhood. I'm sure that you will know just what I mean." Then she ran her hands slowly like a blind person down the length of Jem's body from her jawline to her feet. She sat down on the bed beside the body. "You're so tall, Jem," she said. "You always were. And you've got such huge feet. Whatever happened to those shoes you had that shocked my poor mother so much? 'State of the girl's shoes, Harry!' " Alice nudged the body gently, wishing to conspire with it against the adult world. "All of them—all the grown-ups—they all thought you were such a subversive. They must have known you were brilliant. You scared them, that's all." Alice kicked off her shoes and lifted the sheet. "I wish you would budge up a bit," she said. "But I don't suppose you can really, if you're dead. God, if I had just half your powers of intercession, I'd probably have you standing up and walking around by now, never mind budging up." She covered herself with the sheet and stretched her legs, struggling downwards with difficulty until she felt her feet against the body's feet.

"I didn't exactly come clean with you either, you know," she said. "Though even the skeleton in my cupboard looks a bit puny next to all of yours. I was called Alice after Alice Springs in Oz. Do you realize that? Not after Alice Liddell at all." She giggled at the body. "I wish we could have grown up together," she said. "Gosh that would've been lovely. I'd really love your opinion about men for a start. Frankly, I'm completely baffled by them. I somehow haven't thought about him for months and months, but all through last year there was Roland. I was really fond of Roland. I don't know why but he always made me stammer. We had an accident in his motor car. He never came to see me after that. So strange. When I came round there was Matthew Riley. Like a dream. Maybe all of life is a dream? Matthew pulled me out of the river. That was no small thing really. Somebody saving your life. Well. No offense of course. If you're alive, I mean. I was going to marry Matthew but now he wants Flora. I don't really mind as much as I ought to. Not yet. I minded far more about you. They told me about it yesterday. Flora and Matthew.

"God in heaven, Jem! Yesterday! That was the worst day of my life, if you can believe it—well, except for today. And for the day you left me. Flora and Matthew were only a part of yesterday. And for all I care they can spend the rest of their lives slurping that oil-globule soup together and chewing on gristle and Bisto." Alice paused and sighed. "I do really," she said. "I do care. I'm a bit too manic to take any of it in as yet—what with your letter and the heavy breather and Flora's relatives in plastic bags and Angeletti making me excavate for your exercise books before he'd believe a word I said. And now today. This business. This business of finding you dead and the local Roman collective all preempting me over your baby's name."

Alice sighed and lay back with her head beside Jem's. "Look. I'm a bit knocked back by the baby. I wasn't expecting it. I haven't even seen her. But don't you worry about it. I'll look after that baby somehow. Better than I looked after your stories, anyway. And frankly, I'm terribly honored. I have always honored you, Jem. I have honored you in everything." She kissed the body's cheek. "It's so lovely to be with you again. She was sweet to me, that nun. Letting us be together like this. If you try not to mind about being dead, I'll try not to mind either. Look at it this way, my dearest friend. You may be dead but so what? At least you made it. At least you sort of drank your beaker full of the warm south. You didn't just stay at home like some of us, letting your parents ponce up a house for you and do a rethink on pastel and cane interiors. And then there is the book. *My Last Duchess.* I know you say you don't care about it, but it's all dead glamorous, Jem. Even you would have to admit. You're a 'woman of letters.' Who needs a 'man of letters,' whether he's real or not?" She smiled at Jem's face and leaned up on one elbow. Then she gave the body's cheek another, final kiss. "Goodbye, Jem," she said. "God, my darling. You really did smell Naples and die." Alice then turned to get up off the bed. It was as she did so that she noticed Angeletti. He was standing in the doorway and watching her.

 ALICE LEAPT CLUMSILY from the bed, feeling her heart knocking against her ribs. She looked at him for a moment like a hunted animal, but, whatever Angeletti was thinking, he wasn't letting on.

"Pardon me," he said. "I startled you."

Alice groped along the floor with her right foot until the foot encountered its shoe. Then she did the same with her left foot.

"No," she said. "No. Not at all. I was only—I was only—" Alice broke off, being unable to find the words. I was only in bed, with a dead woman, she thought. And kissing a dead woman's cheek.

"That's okay," Angeletti said quickly. "I only just came."

Subtly, with her back to the bed, Alice tried pulling up the covering sheet, which she had rumpled as far as Jem's thighs. All the while she kept her face turned toward him.

"Come see the baby," he said. He took her arm and walked her through a brief, unintelligible maze of passageways for which he had evidently already acquired a reliable internal map. They came to a narrow corridor with glass panels that gave on to small, cell-like cubicles. Angeletti stopped alongside one of the panels of glass. When Alice stared through the panel, she saw, lying alone under a transparent Perspex barrel vault, a small, doll-sized form; an elongated parody of human bones and skin with plastic tubing taped to the face somewhere in the region of the nose. The naked vertebrae ran prominent down the center-back to the waist, from which point the form was encased in a vast, plastic-coated nappy. Below the nappy, Alice could see only the soles of two grotesquely wrinkled feet, topped by the prominent underpads of ten disproportionately long toes.

"Your daughter is beautiful," Angeletti said, in a voice to induce instant cringe. "She has very fine long toes." His sudden honeyed tone of paternal tenderness brought Alice almost to violence. She stared fixedly at the small, unprepossessing little creature who was not her daughter. Not yet. Alice did not know her; had not touched her; felt nothing for her except fear and the dull futile cruelty of the fact that Jem was gone and in Jem's place was this small mockery; this shrinkie-dink with Jem's long feet. The circumstances of that first meeting with Jem's daughter served only to overpower her with feelings of remoteness and inadequacy.

But it squared, she thought, bitterly, that Angeletti, whose coercion and domineering had had the effect, all through last evening, of keeping her from her dying friend, would now be able to master with such immediacy a package of wholly ersatz emotions. Like all bully-boys everywhere, he would be sentimental—to a degree. She turned woodenly from the window and began to walk away. As Angeletti fell into step beside her, she registered for the first time that he was carrying a half-dozen large, new, padded envelopes and a bright green plastic bag. Its color was such as she had come morbidly to associate with Flora's female relations, but Angeletti's bag said "Marks and Spencer" across it.

"You've been out shopping," she said. Angeletti once again took a hold of her arm.

"Come," he said. "Mrs. Riley, we need to talk." He led her away from the corridor toward an outer door and a courtyard. Beyond that lay a small garden and a chapel.

"If I could put the screws on you a little," he said as they walked. "I need to go quite soon. I have some urgent personal matters awaiting me back home." He was having more trouble with Schmutzburger, Alice envisaged. And with Mary-Lou and MacMahon. Perhaps they were all beating down his door trying to flog him stolen manuscripts. Alice was finding him very puzzling. Why and how was it that he had somehow co-opted whole events? Jem's book, Jem's dying, the baptism of Jem's baby. Jem was nothing to him. He had not heard of her before the previous night.

Angeletti had taken a memo pad and a fountain pen from the pocket of Father Mullholland's shirt. He wrote down four telephone numbers and handed them to her. At the top of the page he had written "Giovanni Angeletti," in looped American cursive. It approximated so much more closely to Jem's writing than any current calligraphic fashion in England, that even this detail somehow compounded Alice's resentment.

"You can call me at home at the top one," he said. "Don't lose it, okay? It's unlisted. The second is my office. Now it's just possible you may need the last two. Those are my parents' home in San Francisco and the cabin in New Hampshire."

"Thank you," Alice said. She stowed the paper in her pocket.

"I appreciate it may be difficult to call from here," he said. "Call collect if at any time you feel you'd like to." He made another of his illtimed shots at humor. "Preferably not before eight-thirty A.M.," he said, "since I detected that you didn't like to engage with my recorded message." Alice thanked him again. Angeletti went on. "Regrettably, I've had no opportunity to make photocopies of your friend's manuscripts," he said.

Alice looked at him. "I notice you're not denying they're 'her' manuscripts?" she said.

Angeletti behaved as if he hadn't heard. "If you feel able to entrust them to me," he said, "I can deal with the matter fairly rapidly. How about that? You still sleeping with one eye open?"

Alice hesitated a moment. "All right," she said. "You can take them."

"Thank you, Mrs. Riley," he said. "I really appreciate that. I really appreciate your trust."

"Oh," Alice said. "That's all right."

"Next item," he said. "I just had a word with Sister Teresa about you. She'd take it as a favor if you could stick around for a matter of weeks. She'd like to make a guest room available to you in the convent. Is that a possibility at all? Or is it a problem for you with regard to your 'business capacity'?" Alice glanced at him suspiciously. "But you'll want to discuss it with your husband," he said.

"It's not a problem," she said. "I ought to be selling houses, but that's all right."

Angeletti looked at her curiously. "You sell real estate?" he said.

"Why not?" she said.

"Nothing," he said. "Nothing at all. And how about Mr. Riley? He also sells real estate?"

"Yes," Alice said, daring the stammer to come back.

"I was in the stores for a few minutes just now," he said. "I took the liberty of buying you some things."

"Things?" she said.

"Clothes," he said. "It struck me you could use a change of clothes." He gave her the green plastic bag.

"Thanks," she said. She looked in the bag. In it were two white shirts, a plastic pack containing three pairs of sober white cotton knickers, a plain dark navy skirt and a navy cardigan.

"Gosh," Alice said. "Thanks, Angeletti." She registered that what Angeletti had acquired for her looked remarkably like a school uniform. "That's very kind of you," she said. "I'm sorry to say that I smell."

"We'll consider it the Odor of Sanctity," he said. "Don't worry about it, Mrs. Riley."

"I'll arrange to pay you back as soon as I can," she said.

"My treat," he said. "There's a little cash in there—just to see you through until you are reunited with your pocketbook."

"You're very kind," she said. "I will certainly pay you back."

"Now to the last item," he said. "Forgive me, Mrs. Riley, but I am unacquainted with your particular brand of spiritual allegiance."

"What?" Alice said, feeling the return of the irritable edge.

"Given your surname," Angeletti said insidiously, "I have hazarded with Father Mullholland that your husband is almost certainly Catholic."

Alice paused here, in her progress along the path, to gawp at him, first with indignation and then with terror.

"Mrs. Riley," he said, as he had said once before. "Is your husband Catholic?"

An icicle was again seizing her by the throat. Jem had left her the baby. And now the whole bunch of them—the adorable priest and all—they were all hotfoot to wrest Jem's baby from her. They would refuse to yield up the child to her until she produced for their scrutiny a card-carrying Catholic husband. Jem's baby had appeared to her, not fifteen minutes before, as a mere unlikable nothing; an affront to her grief for Jem. Now, suddenly now, she knew that she would fight to keep that baby. She would lie and cheat if necessary. And what's more she would not stammer. She would never stammer again. Not as long as she lived. And, damnit, Matthew *was* a Catholic, wasn't he? The only problem was, he wasn't her husband.

"Yes," Alice said, "Matthew is Catholic."

"And the marriage ceremony?" Angeletti said, snooping offensively. "That was in the Catholic Church?"

Alice wrestled valiantly to rouse within herself a capacity for deception. She hoped that Jem might be her inspiration.

"W—," she said. "The th-th-thing-thing. No, Angeletti. It wasn't." Angeletti, much to her surprise, seemed more amused by her embarrassment than troubled by her disclosure. He emitted the second laugh of their acquaintance. "But if you think," she said, "if you think I'm going to let that bunch of Holy Romans claw Jem's baby off me—"

"Now look," Angeletti said. "Please. There's nobody here wishes you any harm, Mrs. Riley. Relax. What do you take these guys for? You think they're all avid to disregard your friend's wishes?" Alice, still suspicious, was mollified for the moment.

"I'd like to offer you a piece of advice," Angeletti said. "Maybe you could stop behaving as though you were a captive Turk at the Siege of Vienna."

"I'm sorry," Alice said, feeling justly rebuked.

"That's okay," Angeletti said. "Try to bear it in mind. Your friend was Catholic, Mrs. Riley. This is a Catholic child. There is perfectly legitimate concern around here for your daughter's spiritual well-being."

"Yes," Alice said gloomily. She imagined, with more than a little misgiving, the series of excruciating little "talks" that she would have with Jem's priest—rather like the sex education class at school. She thought, suddenly, of Roland's father. They were not unalike, physically, Jem's priest and Peter Dent. Only Peter Dent was taller and markedly better-looking. As she wondered, grimly, whether Father Mullholland kept bees, she saw that they had reached the door of the chapel.

In the chapel, Alice watched Angeletti as he touched the compass points of his powerful upper body with his fingertips, which he had dipped in the holy water. Then he led her toward the nave.

"The thing is," Alice said, feeling unnerved—first with terror and now with gratitude—to the point of wishing to come clean, "Angeletti—?" But politeness arrested her midsentence, because Angeletti was in the act of genuflection. She wanted to tell him that Matthew Riley was not really her husband. When he had accomplished his gesturing, he took hold of Alice's arm. He was looking fixedly down the nave toward the altar as he walked, which was making opportunities for unburdening rather difficult. Angeletti stopped beside one of the pews and looked around. Alice did the same. She had never been in a Catholic church before and the smell of candlewax and incense intrigued her. So did the somewhat relentless pictures on the walls. Jesus was stumbling all over the road, dragging His cross and looking up to see His mother staring at Him dolefully. Alice's memory threw up fragments of nervous irreverence. Better He should have been a doctor. She turned again to Angeletti, her agitation quite evident.

"Angeletti?" she said. "There is something I need to explain."

"You're in church, Mrs. Riley," Angeletti said unexpectedly. "I would strongly recommend that you try unloading it onto the Deity." Alice looked at him in surprise.

"But I'd like to tell you something," she said. She felt Angeletti tense slightly. "Excuse me—"

"Come on and try it," he said. "On your right knee now, Mrs. Riley. Just imagine you are dropping a nice, respectful little curtsy to God." Alice, since she thought it expedient in the circumstances, dropped with alacrity a nice, respectful little curtsy to God. She wondered, as she did so, whether Angeletti was seriously unhinged. Perhaps he was some sort of maniac who would at any moment proclaim himself incarnated from the Book of Revelation?

"Angeletti?" Alice said. "I really do need to talk." But for Angeletti, it seemed, she had become his captive Turk at the Siege of Vienna. He handed her into the pew.

"Kneel, Mrs. Riley," he said. "I recommend it to you. Try the power of prayer." Alice knelt. She put her head in her hands. Then, to oblige Angeletti, she tried the power of prayer.

She could think of nothing to tell Angeletti's God, nor remotely how to address him. She moved her lips silently and respectfully for a moment, hoping that Angeletti would be appeased. Angeletti's God quite evidently spoke another language and had very different tastes in interior decorating. Might he like some Latin? She wondered for a moment whether she could legitimately recite from the *Aeneid*. But perhaps that was too pagan? Or was he really in favor of all that *laudamus te, glorificamus te, adoramus te,* et cetera? In the circumstances, it would sound like blatant and hypocritical crawling.

Alice spoke soundlessly, moving her lips and hearing the words in her head. " 'Elsie Marley's grown so fine,' " she said. " 'She won't get up to feed the swine, / But lies in bed till eight or nine.' " She marked time and waited for the voice of God to boom at her from the walls of the temple. When it did not, she tried praying some more. " 'Dr. Foster went to Gloucester / In a shower of rain,' " she said. She said it silently and respectfully, just as before. " 'He stepped in a puddle, / Right up to his middle, / And never went there again.' " When she had done enough praying, she got up from the floor. She turned toward Angeletti, but Angeletti wasn't there. He had gone to catch his airplane. He had important personal business to attend to when he got back home. There was Schmutzburger and Mary-Lou and, of course, MacMahon.

 THE FIRST THING Alice did once she left the chapel was contact Matthew Riley. It seemed to her a courtesy to let him know where she was. She did so from the visitors' pay phone, having first got change for one of Angeletti's bank notes, which were lying in an envelope in the bottom of the green plastic bag.

"Pet," Matthew said, as though nothing had come between them, "where have you been? I've been that worried about you." Alice could hear, coming from the CD player in the background, the fine, edgy precision of Domenico Scarlatti. From this she deduced that Flora was in the room.

"Back in a jiffy," Matthew said. "I'll just switch off that crap on the gramophone." It was a curious thing about Matthew, Alice considered, that, for all he was up to the eyeballs in recent computer terminology, he still called the CD player "the gramophone." She waited for him to get back.

"Is Flora not with you?" she said.

"Just missed her, pet," Matthew said with a tone of regret, as if the news would come as a big disappointment to Alice. "She's just popped round her nan's." From this Alice deduced, with a newborn, open-eyed clarity, that Flora was currently raking through the drawers of the superior heritage-style investment property, looking for bankbooks and insurance policies.

"Matt," she said, "I'm in Hampshire. I ought to have got in touch before, but it's been a rather difficult day. My friend Jem McCrail died this morning." She wiped her eyes quickly on Angeletti's handkerchief, to banish new tears.

"Oh aye," Matthew said. "Now don't you go upsetting yourself." Alice blinked as she heard Matthew's words—detached, as they now were, from his congenial physical presence. A woman most dear to her had died that day. A woman dearer than the moon and the stars. Dearer, certainly, than Matthew Riley—and she was not to "go upsetting herself"? Did the man have a part of his brain missing? Or what was the matter with him?

"There's a newborn baby," Alice said, sounding as businesslike as possible. "Jem has left me to care for her child."

"Blow me down!" Matthew said amiably. "Nev-er. A little bairn, did you say?" Alice suddenly realized that Matthew was eating an apple. She could hear the crunch, which made a sound as if she had reached him in the horse barn.

"The baby's premature," she said. "I'm staying over at the convent."

" 'Convent'?" Matthew said. "Never in a henhouse full of bloody nuns, bonny lass?"

"It's a Catholic hospital for the dying," Alice said.

"Sounds like a ball of fun," Matthew said. He had evidently made his way to the core of the apple by now and was wrestling with the cellulose and the pips. "What say I come round and get you?" Alice recoiled in astonishment.

"If you could possibly put my handbag in the post . . . ," she said.

"No worries," Matthew said. "I'll drop round. Three shakes of a lamb's tail. What's the address?"

Matthew Riley had felt a little ashamed, truth to tell, since he had allowed his intended to be bullied out into a cab the previous evening by a man ponced up like Count Dracula, who was clearly out for her blood. He owed Alice one, no doubt of it, but things went deeper than that. He had enjoyed two nights of passion with the *belle dame sans merci*. And, truth to tell, now that she was presently not with him in the house, he was suffering from cold feet. The familiar presence of his computer mags meant he could not quite reconstruct the magic of that bejeweled Parisian hideout and he had begun to think perhaps it had not been real. And Flora's assault on Alice had really been quite unnerving. Mother McCree, but the enchanted princess could really chew bent nails! And the opera had been a right piss-off. All those screeching women and the bloody rows of men around the altar. Just like bloody church.

And Flora had spent all the following day discussing the price of coffins. She had weighed up burial or cremation. Her mother and her grandmother, it seemed, had expressed a preference for burial but what of it? Hadn't the old biddies cremated themselves already? Flora had seemed to get quite worked up about the Protestant graveyard. Her father was buried in the graveyard, she said, and she didn't want the old bats near him. She had decided upon cremation.

Matthew had surprised himself, that afternoon, with the vehemence of his negative emotions. He was passionate about Flora, he knew that, but passion, he had begun to suspect, was a game for mugs. And the thought of returning to Paris gave him increasingly less joy. Flora's friends in Paris had been nothing but a bunch of faggots. And, besides that, they all spoke bloody French.

Alice's voice on the telephone now sounded reassuringly familiar. There was not much wrong with Alice, pretty little pet that she was. She cooked the supper far too late, but that was a minor failing. Her mother was just the same. And his father-in-law-to-be had always been really champion. The whole thing could turn out to be an almighty bloody embarrassment. He had his graduate studies to think of. Whatever could have got into him that day in the fairy's bower? Chucking his prospects away like that when he was sitting with his rump in the butter.

"Pet," he said with the conviction of those blessed with the facility for rewriting history. "Bygones be bygones and all that. I'm sorry ol' Flora upset you last night. All a bit over the top really." Alice was momentarily stumped for words. It was suddenly profoundly irrelevant to her—as though Matthew and Flora and the dream home and the coordinated bed linen and the file box with all her recipe cards existed in another world.

"That's all right," she said eventually. "I wish you both well, Matt. You and Flora. Now if you would send on my handbag—"

"Temper-temper," Matthew said teasingly, in a voice that all at once induced unambiguous aversion in Alice. "Hell hath no fury an' all that, bonny lass. Now listen carefully an' don't you go getting your little knickers in a twist. When it's between you and her, Flora's well and truly down the plughole as far as I'm concerned. Didn't I say I'd make an honest woman of you? Didn't I now?"

"L-look, Matthew—," Alice said. "Please—" But Matthew had become drunk on the idea of his own benevolence. After all, he was offering to take on board not only Alice, but the bairn as well. And giving up his mistress into the bargain.

"So what's the little lad's name?" he said. "Matthew after his da?" Alice swallowed hard.

"Matthew," she said firmly. "I have decided that I never want to see you again."

After Alice had cast off Matthew Riley, she sought out Sister Teresa, who took her to her room. The room was small and sparsely furnished with an iron bedstead, a small wooden table and a white-painted, plywood cupboard. A crucifix was fixed to the wall over the bed, and on the opposite wall hung a cheaply framed color print of Jesus pointing to his heart. It seemed to Alice that he was wearing his heart on the outside of his clothes. There was a sort of radiant glow around the organ, like the glow the children got in the Ready Brek commercials after eating a four-square breakfast. She wished she could have asked Jem about the picture. It disconcerted her a little to think she would have to sleep between an image of Jesus nailed to the wall and another of him practicing what looked like an eccentric form of indecent exposure.

Then she took a bath. She removed her smelly knickers and her filthy navy skirt and filthier white blouse and stepped into the tub. Once she was bathed and dried, Alice put on clean knickers. She put on the clean navy skirt and one of the clean white school shirts that Angeletti had bought her. Then, invited by the convent bell, she went to eat some food.

Father Mullholland only summoned her the next morning. She met him in a small office that lay off the hospital reception area. Alice thought he looked tired. But he was courteous and businesslike and came directly to the point. It was to be regretted, he said, that Veronica had not made him party to her wishes for the child before she died, since these had thrown all previous, provisional arrangements into some confusion. But it was nonetheless important, and indeed much to be welcomed, he said, that she had made her wishes known so clearly—albeit in a characteristically idiosyncratic document that made up in charm and persuasiveness what it lacked in legal validity.

"Validity?" Alice said.

"The document was secreted in her bedside locker," he said. "Where Sister Teresa found it. Need I say that it has not been witnessed?" Alice began to freeze inside as she damned Angeletti and his false reassurances. She wondered, had it been her sense of security in the child that had led her, the previous evening, into the high-minded act of casting off Matthew Riley more precipitously than might have been judicious? But the priest appeared to be regarding her with a perfectly benign intent. "I think you will understand only too well what I mean, Mrs. Riley," he said a little sadly, "if I observe that Veronica was rather chronically incapable of putting all her cards on the table."

"Yes," Alice said.

"How fortunate that you should have materialized like this," he said. "And I may say that Veronica always made it perfectly clear to me in the course of our friendship that she held you and your parents in the highest esteem. I think we can take it from there, Mrs. Riley. That is, if you feel yourself able to take on the responsibility."

"Yes," Alice said. "Oh yes of course."

"Well," he said. "I hope that you will feel comfortable here. I will of course arrange a longer meeting with you and your husband as soon as possible."

Alice, feeling herself dismissed, took her courage in both of her hands. "Excuse me," she said. "But there are things I would like to tell you." It embarrassed her slightly that she did not know how to address him. It was a problem she had experienced before, not only with God, but with Whitecross. "Mr. Angeletti has told you certain things. And some of them aren't true. I don't mean to say that he lies, but he doesn't really know me very well and I misled him, I'm afraid." The priest looked up at her, expecting her to go on.

"I am not an estate agent married to a Catholic," she said. "I am a student of classics at Oxford—or I was until I got ill last spring. And, you see, I'm not married at all." The priest continued to look at her rather neutrally. "I don't usually tell lies, but I told Mr. Angeletti I was married because I had to share a hotel room with him on the night before Jem died." She paused, waiting for an interjection, but it did not come. "Well, he *is* sort of large," she said. "And I knew he was very strong. I'd just seen him heave half a house off a builder's skip. That was how we found Jem's manuscripts." When the priest still did not speak, she blurted out rather defensively, "Well, I had had a whole lot of calls that afternoon. Obscene calls from a pervert. And I had just had to identify dead bodies in the coroner's court. Flora's mother and grandmother. I think that you know about Flora?" It was a relief to her when he finally spoke.

"And you thought that if you lied about your marital situation, it would protect you from molestation?" he said.

"Well yes," Alice said, feeling suddenly very young and silly. "Yes, I suppose so." The priest's facial expression wavered only slightly.

"Then you evidently considered Mr. Angeletti to be a man of honor," he said. She thought he looked faintly amused.

"Well," Alice said, and she surprised herself. "I suppose so." The priest's eyes were returning to some papers on the desk. She assessed that he was rather busy with sorting out the headache into which Jem's clandestine inclinations had led him. "Well—," she said again. "That's all really. That was what I wanted to tell you."

The priest got up. "Thank you for being so frank with me," he said. "Now, with your permission, I would like to talk to you tomorrow about Veronica's funeral. Good day to you, Mrs. Riley."

Alice had already got up from her chair. "So the thing is," she said firmly. "I am *not* Mrs. Riley."

And then there was Jem's funeral. It was so extraordinary and so unexpected in the scale of its poignant grandeur, that Alice saw the sages standing in the holy fire. There was a choir, whose polished excellence Alice was in no position to question, throughout the sequence of the mass. And Jem's priest prayed that Jem, who in baptism had died with Christ, would share in His resurrection and that her mortal body would be raised and made in glory like His own, and that she would be welcomed into that Kingdom where—through, and in, and with, the power of Christ the Lord—she would see God. The curious, insistent prepositions hung like dewdrops in the mazes of Alice's brain, recalling for her that winding sheet and that ravishing power through which dazzling paradox the soul of man was made chaste.

She walked away from the graveside, feeling her grief by no means gone, but milled from rag and bone by the psalm and the *miserere* and the absolution, and by the tender, almost domestic intimacy by which the music had presumed to make its reference to the Holy Spirit. And all through the Benediction, the tall, hand-held cross in the graveyard had risen darkly against the clouded sky.

THE TIME that Alice spent at the hospital and the convent was agreeably quiet and structured. While her life outside had taken on too much complexity, there inside the walls she was able to fix her mind on the simple round of the day. It did not trouble her that, after four weeks, she had still not heard from the office of Giovanni B. Angeletti. The baby had become so much a priority with her that she was more amused than angry to reflect that, for the second time, she had lost Jem's manuscripts. Jem had not cared about the stories and why, therefore, should she? They were only pen and paper. Jem had cared about the baby. She had cared enough and trusted Alice enough to make a confident ecumenical leap in the name of human friendship. This was the shining reality that had finally released Alice's heart from half a decade of grief.

From the first, the nurses had required Alice to take on the care of the baby between the hours of seven in the morning and ten o'clock at night. In order to accomplish the necessary routine tasks she had become a regular occupant of the intensive care unit. During these times her interaction with the women who made up the nursing staff gave her very great pleasure. It underlined for her how much she liked the company of her own sex. And to watch Jem's baby evolving rapidly from that small, wizened parody toward smooth-skinned cherub was a source of indescribable satisfaction.

Sister Teresa, throughout her stay, was invariably kind and reassuring. She strove to make Alice feel indispensable by allotting to her a multitude of minor tasks that helped make up the daily running of the hospital. Alice carried bed linen to the laundry. She folded night-dresses and counted tea cloths. She mended worn patches in hospital sheets and found herself surprised by the pleasure she took when—thanks to Miss Cummings's protracted indoctrination in the needle-work room—the regularity and finesse of her stitching became a focus for the nuns' hyperbole. Her renown in this respect led her into replacing the pocket fabric and the linings of Father Mullholland's black winter coat. In a world where the run-and-fell seam had fallen into disuse, these things gave her back the flavor of the form room. And, because she went to bed so very much earlier, Alice found that she rose equivalently early, which gave a morning hour to be con-sumed in reading library books, or in undertaking dawn walks.

For almost a week after the funeral, she saw very little of Jem's priest, but one afternoon, on her way to the library, she met him in a news-agent's shop and accompanied him to a small café. There she discov-ered not only that he had an impressive appetite for German apple cake smothered in dollops of whipped cream, but also that his father, like her own, was a successful building contractor. She found that these discoveries made him all at once more accessible.

"But I must not be out too long," Alice said, enjoying the innocent treat. She brushed cake crumbs from the corner of her mouth. In the context of her recent plain life, the occasion stood out like a birthday party. "I must get back and see to the baby."

"On the contrary," said the priest. "The sisters worry that you are quite incurably industrious. You may regard this hour with me, Mrs. Riley, as a lesson in the profligate waste of time."

"But I am not Mrs. Riley," Alice said.

"Then I will call you Alice," he said. "If I may."

She had begun to like him enormously. She tried to envisage him talking with Jem in that engaging Irish way, every word so carefully measured, in contrast to the kinetic energy of Jem's bright verbiage.

"But I have such hours in my day somehow," she said. "I am in serious danger of taking up drawn thread work." Father Mullholland laughed. He glanced rather ironically at her library books. These comprised a single doctrinal work along with a selection of what Roland had called "the Old Worthies."

"So you have signed up at the library," he said. "In order to improve yourself."

Self-consciousness made Alice satirical.

"I have been reading a book about the Eucharist," she said. "And I have learned from it that it is extremely inadvisable to celebrate the Mass at sea—that's for fear of having the chalice overturn in choppy weather."

Father Mullholland took this rather gracefully, she thought. "You are making fun of my religion," he said. "But as a person tempted by drawn thread work, Mrs. Riley, the church's laudable attention to detail will surely not have passed you by."

"But I am not Mrs. Riley," she said.

"Alice," he said. "Of course."

She swallowed and paused and spoke rather awkwardly. "I think that I sh-should become a C-thacolic," she said.

"Why?" said Father Mullholland.

"Well," Alice said. "Because it would be a c-convenience to me in bringing up Jem's child."

"And why else?" said Father Mullholland.

"Well, because I like it here," she said. "At the hospital and at the convent, I like the simp-limp-plimp—" She stopped and swallowed and started again. "I like the order and the peace here. I find it comfortable."

"Why else?" he said.

"Gosh," Alice said. "Why else? Well, perhaps because Jem always made it sound alluring. Are you saying that-that it's a club that won't have me?" She began to feel both embarrassed and piqued. "I always thought that C-catholics liked c-converts," she said. Father Mullholland filled her teacup from the pot.

"You would like some more hot water in that tea," he said in the tone of a concerned hostess. "It has taken on the color of brown ale." He summoned the waitress to bring more hot water and handed over the jug while Alice watched him. She felt considerably put down.

"In fact," she said, "I was taught that c-c-cru-s-saders made people k-kiss the c-cross. Bloodstained knife to the throat and all that."

Father Mullholland didn't get needled. "The church is our mother," he said. "Will you—since you are now also a mother—undertake never to make any mistakes?"

Oh, Alice thought, admiringly, but that's clever. To wrap one's debating society skills in that winning, rural accent. No wonder Jem was charmed by it.

"Are you saying that my reasons are rubbishy?" she said, feeling defensive. "Like convenience. And safety. And wanting the badge and the membership card?"

"Now you are being rather hard on yourself," he said. "What about belief, Alice?"

Belief, Alice thought with shock. But belief was absolutely impossible, of course! Belief was completely out of the question.

"I think that my g-gullibility could be a great help," she said. "Jem will have explained all that to you—about how gullible I am. If you could tell me what to believe, you see, then I will go away and believe it." Father Mullholland seemed very much amused by this. She watched him laugh with pleasure.

"Now I see that you are subversive," he said. "It is not any wonder to me that you were Veronica's dearest friend."

Not believing made Alice so irritable at first that she strove hard to give him offense, even though he was more than generous with his time. On one occasion, for instance, it was the statue outside the chapel. There was a curious wooden canopy over the figure of Christ. A rustic log roof topped a sort of three-sided chalet inside which Jesus hung. He was nailed to the back wall. The figure of Christ, which was about half life size, was painted a pale russet beige. There was a jam-colored trickle of blood painted on it that ran down from the left side of his chest to the bottom of his ribs. Jesus's feet were nailed to the post on which the chalet was perched. One day when she went past it on her way to see Father Mullholland, Alice observed that one of the female patients—no longer quite in possession of her wits—was dancing around the statue and throwing up flowers into the air. Alice stopped, unobserved, and watched the patient, transfixed. After a while the woman stopped dancing and began to slot flower stems into the spaces between Christ's toes. Alice went on her way. It gave her a feeling of eavesdropping to have witnessed the strange little scene. It made her feel ashamed.

"I'm very sorry I'm late," she said to him. "But I've been admiring your Donatello."

"I beg your pardon?" said Father Mullholland.

"Your statue," Alice said. "Really. It makes Christ look like one of those little charity models where you put your money into a slot in the head. You know. Those little old figures of crippled boys on calipers. Do you suppose those are collector's items by now?" When he did not reply she went on. "I expect your statue could go under the hammer any day. Like Jem's sister's gnomes. Gosh, but don't Catholics love kitsch?"

"Well," said Father Mullholland mildly. "It is not a very beautiful statue."

" 'Beautiful'?" Alice said. She heard herself sounding like Iona Morgan. "So where does it say in the Bible that Jesus was crucified in a very large nesting box?"

"My dear Alice," he said. "You must try not to be so angry with yourself."

"I'm not angry," Alice said.

"The wish to believe is in itself a gift of grace," he said.

Alice tried to fix her mind on this assertion. She did not feel in any way endowed with grace. She felt irritable and covetous. She wanted access to the Holy Spirit. She wanted that wooing, brooding *Spiritus Sanctus* that the choir at Jem's funeral had seemed to evoke and embrace with such a tender and familiar devotion. She looked at Father Mullholland through narrowed eyes.

"There is a picture in my room," she said crossly, "of Jesus exposing his heart." Father Mullholland talked, with a provoking lack of touchiness, about the sacred heart as a symbol of Christ's charity and interior life.

"But this heart," Alice said. "Well, *this* heart, it isn't 'interior.' That's exactly what I'm saying. It's very much 'exterior.' It glows on the outside of his clothes. Really, it's very nasty. It looks a bit like Woolworth's jewelry." She thought that she had succeeded in shocking him, because he did not speak for quite a while. But then, when he did, it was every bit as nicely as before.

"These things have no sanctity in themselves," he said. "If the picture is a hindrance to you, then I suggest that you try not to look at it."

"But don't you hate it?" she said.

"Alice," he said. "The church is not a society for aesthetes and clever undergraduates like yourself. It is a very broad-based institution. Forgive me for observing that the church is 'catholic.' " It was nice of him, she thought, to call her a "clever undergraduate," when she was really a bit of a dropout with a kitchen file box and a festoon blind collecting dust in Surrey and a pot of small white pills that she had neglected to bring with her to the hospital. And she had the baby. That was marvelous, but it was surely the end of Homer. She tried to remember which galling male it was who had observed that the pram in the hall was the enemy of promise.

"I'm sorry," she said. "I oughtn't to be so offensive. I suppose that what I'm trying to say is that religion is about spirituality. And—well—to worship bits of the body of God—doesn't that place the emphasis on something inappropriately physical? Well, doesn't it? I mean a heart is a muscle after all; a lump of flesh. It's a thing that one sees oozing blood in a butcher's shop. Or in biology textbooks."

"You are really very squeamish about the Flesh," he said.

"What?" Alice said.

"The Flesh," he said. "Why do you balk so at the Flesh?" The remark surprised her, coming as it did from a celibate priest. "Our Lord is the Word made Flesh," he said. "The Word made Man. Not the Word disguised as a Man. That is the whole crux."

Alice found that the idea crashed suddenly into her rather rarefied modes of thought as a jarring, powerful reality, every bit as compelling as it was repulsive. It threw at her disturbing images of the Five Wounds and the Passion, of the nails and thorns and the stripped garments bedded with blood and skin. Things that had been only words to her in the past. And she saw in her mind the jam-colored blood that trickled from the ugly statue and it made her feel like retching.

"Gosh," she said. "I really find that a very disturbing idea."

"Religion is often very disturbing," Father Mullholland said. "Disturbing and adventurous. That is to say, it is anything but 'convenient' and 'safe.' Though the 'badge of membership' can be a gratifying source of comfort and support." And he smiled at her as though she had arrived at something. Alice said absolutely nothing. "But you will either believe, or you will not believe," he said. "And I really think it is quite likely that you will. One day—you might be walking in the park, or frying eggs, or taking the train to meet a friend—you will pause in your head and think 'yes,' 'now I see it,' 'now it all makes perfect sense to me.' " Alice still said nothing.

"Tell me about your life at Oxford," he said. So she told him about Homer and Hesiod and about David and Maya Morgan and the children and the filthy, congenial house, and about crazy Iona and the typewriter, and about dear, kind Roland who had taught her to drive, but who had finally, sensibly, given up on her after her touchiness about Pyecroft and the cricket fixture and her squeamishness about the flesh. And she told him about Matthew Riley, and about the curious feeling of longing and deprivation she had experienced when she had gone into her attic bed-sitting room and had found her essay half finished upon the desk, but how she had not been able to linger, because Angeletti had been grinding his teeth in the kitchen with a rent in his gabardine coat.

"Well," said Father Mullholland, just as though there were no obstacles in the way. "It is perfectly obvious that you must return to Oxford in October in time for the new term. From what you have told me about Dr. and Mrs. Morgan, I hardly think that an additional young child will present too much of a problem. And I am quite certain that some adequate form of child care will be procurable. That is, for a young woman such as yourself who is not wholly devoid of means." Alice blinked at him but words failed her. "Now, it may be that you would like me to write some letters on your behalf to the various authorities in question."

"Well," said Alice, "yes, please."

"Good," he said. "Then we will consider it settled." Father Mullholland got up and went to the cupboard. He produced from it, with a certain comforting show of camaraderie, a Sony Walkman and a cassette of the Schubert Mass in E-flat Major. "You may like the loan of it," he said.

"Well, yes please," Alice said. "Thank you. I've got a little Walkman just like that in Oxford."

"But yours is not with you," he said. "You may have mine while I am away."

"What?" Alice said. Because it transpired that, just when she really wanted him, he had arranged to be away on holiday.

ANGELETTI APPEARED, quite unexpectedly and with maximum inconvenience. He came on the very morning of the day in early October when she was due to return with Pamina to Surrey en route to her digs in Oxford. Her parents were returning from Spain the following day and, since she had told them nothing either about Matthew or the baby, she was anxious to get there ahead of them.

Angeletti looked most extraordinary. He was standing in the doorway of the convent porch, taller than the doorway itself. His hangman's face was half hidden under a white panama hat and he was dressed top to toe in a white linen suit of stunningly elegant cut. Under the jacket he had on a silk polo neck the color of cinnamon sticks and in his left hand he was holding an absurd explosion of small pink rosebuds. Angeletti, but for his olive skin, was as ludicrously pink and white as the pair of coconut-ice brides.

"Mrs. Riley?" he said. Alice was wearing the Marks and Spencer school uniform. He took off his hat and stepped into the porch. When he took her hand and bent to kiss her cheek, he gave off a dandified odor of designer soap and aftershave. Then he gave her the flowers. She thanked him and got down to business.

"So where are Jem's books?" she said. Angeletti was constrained from making a reply because Sister Teresa had just then come bustling into the hall.

"Dear Giovanni," she said. "Come in. Come in." Alice did not know at what point in their acquaintance Sister Teresa had got into Christian names, but it was evident to her that Angeletti inspired no lessening of palpitations in that lady's breast. She had clearly been forewarned of his advent and she swept forward to greet him as if he were a favorite nephew. Angeletti entered the hall where she pointed him hospitably to the settle. "You will make yourself *entirely* at home now," she said. "While Mrs. Riley gets her bits and bobs together."

"Bits and bobs?" Alice said, and she tried not to think that the invitation to Angeletti sounded just a shade Boccaccio. The nun was drawing forth a small hard chair for herself. She and Angeletti smiled at each other, evidently wreathed in mutual affection.

"Sister means your pocketbook," he said. "I came by to take you out, Mrs. Riley. Sister felt you might like a break." Sister Teresa brought her hands together purposefully.

"Mr. Angeletti has plans for a picnic," she said. "And the weather is so very suitable—a real Indian summer."

Alice looked from one to the other. Picnics would not be Angeletti's genre, she reflected cynically. For all his physical strength, Angeletti was too much a city slicker; too much a man to snap his fingers at a bellboy. He was a man in possession of a mobile telephone. A man too easily put out of countenance by a hotel bathroom without shampoo. Sister Teresa, on the other hand, would picnic to the manner born. She would spread groundsheets with the best of them and issue sandwiches filled with egg and cress. Her spirits would remain undampened by rain clouds gathering overhead. No, Alice thought. Angeletti had somehow got this delightful, competent and trusting woman to collude with him over the morning's engagement. Once again Sister's best little grade school reader, her most avid and scheming little peddler of Holy Childhood stamps, had been operating for some devious purpose of his own. She glanced at him in his white linen. Angels are bright still, she thought, though the brightest fell. And did the brightest angel relinquish all his brightness with the fall? She would have to ask Father Mullholland.

"Excuse me," Alice said. "I'll go and see to the flowers." She heard Sister Teresa's voice as she made her way up the stairs.

"But Mrs. Riley must show you the baby," she said. "Little Pamina Mary. Oh but you must go at once and admire your baby!"

Before the picnic could proceed, Angeletti took from his hired car a Pentax camera with a flash attachment and a telescopic lens. He also took an abundance of soft-soaping gifts. To the nuns he gave large boxes of handmade chocolates and useless, expensive lace hand-kerchiefs. To the baby he gave a cobweb-fine lace shawl, a quilted rush basket containing an assortment of smocked silk and lawn romper suits and a small silk cap with beaded quilting of the sort worn by infants in Holbein paintings. In addition he gave her a book, bound in white leather and cloyingly illustrated in the post-Murillo style, enti-tled *A Catholic Child's Missal and Prayerbook*. He also gave her a silver fork and spoon.

Angeletti seemed entirely to lose his head over the baby and be-haved with her like an irritating and highly partisan parent. He took a great number of photographs. Then he tutored Sister Teresa in the management of his camera and, having settled the infant in the cradle of his forearm, he got the nun to take his photograph. The others meanwhile plied him with coffee and biscuits, displaying a solicitude that might have been more appropriate, Alice thought, had it been employed on a visiting bishop.

"She's tired," Alice said tetchily, and she immediately felt small-minded. For six weeks now she had existed in a community of women without any such feelings of ownership and encroachment. She had been perfectly happy for Pamina to pass from hand to hand like an infant with ten mothers. Now, suddenly, she felt not only that the baby was her own exclusive property, but that Angeletti was trying to supplant her. How dare he choose the baby's clothes and have himself pictured with her? How dare Sister Teresa, in chatting with him, refer, however innocuously, to the child as "your" baby? He had admittedly been present at the moment of her birth, but only as Alice's messenger. And why, right now, had someone else so suddenly swooped down and carried off Pamina to her cot as if Alice were a mere bystander?

Alice walked with Angeletti toward the site of his hired car in a state of sullen confusion.

"What's going on here, Angeletti?" she said. "Why did they take my baby away? I mean why are they suddenly shunting me out with you like this?" Angeletti kept on walking.

" 'They'?" he said.

"Them," she said. "You. Everybody . . ." She paused. "You walk in here like a GI handing out Hershey bars and suddenly everyone is singing choruses to you. What have you done, Angeletti?"

"Mrs. Riley," Angeletti said. "It's a nice day. We are going to eat lunch in the forest, okay?"

"And when I get back?" she said. Angeletti's laugh—the third she had now been witness to—was, as always, brief, unpleasant and sardonic.

"You think those Romans are conspiring to abduct your child?" he said. Alice bit her lip in some embarrassment.

"Well, it's only because of you," she said. "I haven't thought like that for over a month. Not since you said they might not let me have her . . ."

Angeletti looked at her a little quizzically. "I said that?" he said. Alice stared at him with loathing.

"You implied it," she said. "So just you swear to me now that there's no sort of funny business going on." Angeletti disdained to reply. He kept on walking. "What I mean is," she said with feeling, "I'll bet you wouldn't swear to it on that cruddy little propaganda book you've just seen fit to give my daughter."

Angeletti appeared to find her vehemence entertaining. "You're very gracious with me today," he said. "I'm delighted to see that life in a convent has left you so unbowed." Then he opened the passenger door and held it while she hesitated. "Oh come on," he said. "Get in. We have business together. Are you planning to turn down a working lunch?"

On the backseat, alongside his telephone, there was a sort of *The Wind in the Willows* picnic basket and a carrier bag from Saks.

"I don't mean to sound so ungracious," she said, capitulating. "But why do you behave like this, Angeletti? You tell me absolutely nothing. You carry away my friend's books. You turn up out of the blue—all kitted out like the Great Gatsby and behaving like Toad of Toad Hall—"

"Oh my," said Angeletti. He turned from the wheel for a moment and smiled at her, coconut ice, in his milk white clothes. Then he turned back to the road.

"So why?" Alice said. "Or are you chronically incapable of putting your cards on the table?" She paused. "You walk in here. You start manipulating everyone. This time it's with gifts. Well, I'm sorry to say so, but it's true. Even if your gifts are beautiful. Even if they hoodwink Sister Teresa. She's in love with you, I hope you realize."

"Sister Teresa," Angeletti said resolutely, "is a woman consecrated to God."

"She seems equally consecrated to chocolates and lace-trimmed snotrags," Alice said irritably. "But since they come from you they probably classify as holy relics." Angeletti concentrated on changing gear—a thing that evidently gave him trouble. Her outburst, on reflection, had left Alice feeling cheap.

"I didn't mean that," she said. "I love and admire Sister Teresa. I love all of them. They've all been marvelous to me. It's only you, Angeletti."

Angeletti changed the subject. "So how's life with a baby?" he said.

"Oh, life with a baby is wonderful," she said. "Why are you keeping me from her?" Angeletti ignored her. He leaned his left arm over the back of the seat as he drove and reached for the carrier bag from Saks, which he dropped into her lap. Inside it was a dress made of pale sea green silk.

"So what's this?" she said.

"A dress," he said.

"Well I can see it's a dress," she said.

"I have plans to prolong your deprivation, Mrs. Riley," he said. "I have tickets for the opera this evening."

Alice contained anger only with difficulty. "I don't remember your asking me," she said. "I don't remember saying that I'd go." She seethed in silence for a moment. "And I'll bet it's *Carmen*," she said.

"What's wrong with *Carmen*?" he said. "You don't like a strong, difficult heroine?"

Alice closed her eyes. She would be required to mark time all day in the forest, pandering to Angeletti's preening ego and, all the while, itching to be with her baby. And then, on top of that, she would have to sit through bloody *Carmen*.

"I'm not going," she said with finality. "I'm sorry, but I'm not going to the opera with you."

Angeletti drove her into the forest in silence and parked the car. Then they got out and sat down. He took a contract from the inside pocket of his jacket and gave it to her. Alice looked it over. She gleaned from it that Aaron Schmutzburger, who had evidently drawn it up, did not after all have an *m* in his name. He was called Aaron Schutzburger. The document pertained to *My Last Duchess* and it was full of percentages and words like "hereinafter." The book had been attributed to Veronica Bernadette McCrail and the contract made provision for the author's issue, in the person of Pamina Mary McCrail, to be in receipt of any royalties, etc. It then protracted itself into a string of jabberwocky about film rights and serialization, and, finally, awaited her signature. When she had read it she looked up.

"Thank you," she said. She felt compromised by her previous suspicions. "I'm really sorry if I seemed a bit paranoid."

"Now look," he said. "If you'd feel more comfortable seeking legal advice before you sign that, you go ahead, Mrs. Riley."

"Oh no," Alice said. "No really . . ."

Angeletti took a fountain pen from his pocket. He unscrewed the cap and handed it to her. "Both copies," he said. "If you wouldn't mind."

Alice hesitated. Then she signed. "Alice Pilling," as in her business capacity. First one copy, then another. Then she gave him back the contracts together with his fountain pen.

"I guess we ought to drink on that," he said. He fetched a bottle from the car and two glasses and other miscellaneous items. Then he opened the bottle and filled the glasses and gave her one of them. "We're going to do well with that little book," he said. "You excited? I'm excited, Mrs. Riley." He gestured briefly with the glass and drank. Then he placed before her a small, rather exuberantly decorated cake box containing a single, very small spiced pastry. After that he gave her Jem's page proofs, bound between plain paper covers. He handed her, along with the proofs, a rather ornate-looking book jacket, heavy on chiaroscuro and gold paint.

"I'd like to have you read these while I take a nap," he said. "Excuse me, but I just got in this morning. As far as I'm concerned it's five A.M." He set a button on his wristwatch and stretched himself horizontal on the floor of the forest with the panama hat over his eyes. Then he fell asleep.

Alice approached the page proofs in a state of high excitement. It was delightful to see *My Last Duchess* printed like that, with Jem's name on the title page, and on the following page, opposite the publication date and the catalog number, it startled her to see her own name. The dedication said, "for Alice." That was all. And reading it confirmed for her that the story was enchanting. It was like hearing again the pointed cadence of Jem's own voice.

Alice poured some more to drink from Angeletti's bottle. She had almost finished the reading and Angeletti was still asleep. It had taken her nearly three hours. She had begun, with the reading, to flow with gratitude for Angeletti. For his extraordinary effectiveness, for his efforts on Jem's behalf. That was until she came to the end. Angeletti had changed the end. In it, Alice read how the Highland brain surgeon, while homing in for the rescue, had got his head cut off by falling sheet metal from the back of a small white van. She stared in disbelief at the camped-up words on the page. *"This is no sight for my dear young wife to witness," Umberto said, and he steered the Ferrari deftly round the cascade of gleaming sheet metal under which the Scotsman lay beheaded. . . .*

Alice read that when Gabriella died—which she did much later that evening—it was with a greater sadistic delicacy than Jem's Umberto had ever dreamed of. Having taken care to place a dish of poisoned figs beside his suitably rococo marriage bed, Umberto had then got her to put on her wedding clothes before making highly explicit and passionate love to her. Then she had eaten one of the figs. The effect had been instantly fatal. She had died the moment the venom touched her lips. Umberto had thus had no need to scar that skin whiter than snow and smooth as monumental alabaster.

Gabriella died so charmingly at the hands of the Demon Padrone that she never knew the mutilated *Scozzese* on the *autostrada* was none other than her own dear Angus, come all the way from Aberdeenshire in response to the recorded telephone message that she had left for him the previous day.

When the *carabiniere* turned up at the *palazzo* to question him, Umberto was in his embroidered silk bathrobe, tippling at a glass of grappa and admiring a new portrait of his wife. Before the police officer could respectfully state his business, Umberto had offered him a glass. *"It has been sent to me by my brother the Cardinal from his vineyards in Liguria,"* Angeletti's Umberto observed. *"I think you will agree it is very fine."* Umberto was touched with urbane amusement once the officer had stated his business. *"My wife? My beautiful young wife? Pitched over a cliff?"* he said. *"Good sir, my dear wife is sound asleep in her marriage bed where, within this hour, I have come upon her with my passion. You may verify what I say with the greatest of pleasure, but I beg you do not wake her, for I am an exacting lover and I left her very tired."*

Alice read, with increasing indignation, that the *carabiniere* had taken a peek—hesitant, of course, and suitably deferential—through the heavily draped door of the Padrone's bedchamber, from which he had seen, against a backdrop of faded silk tapestries, that a hauntingly beautiful girl lay peacefully asleep between the silk sheets of her marriage bed. The *carabiniere* had then crossed himself and bowed his head before backing quietly away. *"È bella come la madre di Dio,"* he had murmured, and he had taken his leave at once.

The Padrone had given it out next day that his wife was confined prematurely in childbirth in the sixth month of pregnancy. When the news of Gabriella's death reached the villagers, she was much lamented by great numbers of black-clad crones and her funeral was really quite something—though Umberto had already begun to negotiate for the acquisition of a suitably patrician fourth wife, since he needed a son and heir for the *palazzo*. A thing that the divine Gabriella had seemed so unable to provide.

Alice slammed down the book and got up. Her first response was to look for the contracts that she had been all too easily duped into signing. Having failed to find them, she was trembling so hard with anger and panic that she could not wait for the alarm to bleep on Angeletti's watch. She bashed him awake on his iron thigh and rounded on him at once.

"Where are those contracts?" she said. Angeletti took the hat from his face. He blinked and looked at her. Then he raised himself onto his elbows. "You've completely messed up Jem's story!" she said. "How dare you do this, Angeletti? How could you do this to her?"

Angeletti slowly drew forth a cigar and a lighter from his pocket. "D'you mind if I smoke?" he said.

"Do what you like," Alice said. "But don't think you can mess about with my friend's story like that." It seemed to her that Angeletti was quite deliberately taking as long as he possibly could over unwrapping and lighting his cigar. It was like watching somebody starting a fire with a magnifying glass.

"So what's the trouble?" he said eventually.

"You've changed the end," Alice said.

"Sure," he said complacently. "The end was lousy." Alice watched him inhale and release a cloud of smoke. "Had the author been living," Angeletti said, "I'd naturally have gotten her to make the change herself." Alice sat, staring at him from a well of bitterness, saying nothing. "Alice," Angeletti said coaxingly. "Your friend's story is perfectly enchanting."

"Don't you 'Alice' me," she said.

"Alice," he said. "Listen. I love this story. You know that. It has a most delicious sense of the absurd. I adore that precarious balance of sophistication and naïveté. God knows but this was truly some remarkable child who could convey all that kooky, High Renaissance intrigue and still get away with the Ferrari and the telephone answering machine. Her detail is all so extraordinary. Do you happen to know, did she read Lampedusa at all?"

Alice said nothing for a bit. "You changed the end," she said.

"Oh come on," Angeletti said. "The Highland brain surgeon is a disaster."

"And Umberto is a murderer," Alice said.

"So what?" Angeletti said. "He's a thoroughly delightful character. And he's sexy. Now the brain surgeon is just monumentally boring. That's half the point, isn't it? If you'd thought about it for half a minute, you couldn't possibly want that Gabriella should marry him."

"Well, at least she'd be alive," Alice said.

Angeletti laughed. "Alive and married to Mr. John Knox? You disappoint me, Mrs. Riley. And I thought you'd like it the way I amended it—with the dead girl in the bed."

Alice, though she averted her eyes, was mortified to know that Angeletti's hawk's eyes were picking up on the signs of her embarrassment. She was infuriated to feel that she was blushing. She was equally infuriated to realize that Angeletti was right. Angus was monumentally boring. He was prissy about Gabriella's modeling. He didn't like foreign parts. And hadn't Jem's letter itself expressed a hint of serious disappointment that Umberto had not materialized for her?

"All right," she said grudgingly. "I agree with you."

"Good," Angeletti said, and he filled her glass. "That's nice. I mean that we can agree about something." Alice drank.

"What is this stuff, anyway?" she said.

"Grappa," Angeletti said.

For Alice, Angeletti's lunch was a wholly new experience in gastronomy. It knocked Minette McCrail's *charcuterie* into a cocked hat. Angeletti's picnic basket contained the dried eggs of grey mullet and the salted eggs of tuna fish. It contained dark red slices of Parma ham, which he served to her with fresh, purple figs. It contained a whole glazed salmon with a garnish of mayonnaise made green with pounded basil leaves. Angeletti's picnic basket contained a cold breast of veal stuffed with raw artichoke hearts and sweetbreads. It contained the seasoned corpses of miniature inkfish that had been impaled upon sharpened green twigs.

"Gosh!" Alice said. Angeletti, for all that she was ravenous, appeared to operate upon the principle that food should titillate rather than satiate, because, once he had filled her plate rather modestly, the store of food seemed to have disappeared. It must have gone back into the basket, she supposed, but she had not seen him reload it. Perhaps it had vanished through the forest floor. Or perhaps she had been a bit too boozy to notice. She had no idea what the wine was that she was drinking. She only knew that Angeletti had been filling her glass rather often. And the wine's lightness was such that, really, even on top of the grappa one could quaff it with the ease of downing lemonade.

Angeletti crisscrossed the delicacy of his crucified inkfish with one or two brutal wisecracks with regard to Aaron Schutzburger's ongoing rout of poor Iona Morgan. It was perfectly apparent to Alice, even through the mellow haze of wine, that Angeletti thrived on blood sports. Any prospect of litigation, ritual asset stripping and public humiliation quite evidently turned him on.

"You're a real swine, Angeletti," she said, giggling lazily. "She's just a loony, unwashed schoolgirl." She was lying indolently on her belly on the ground. "She's a very brainy girl, Iona Morgan. You should commininishion-commish-commission her to write you something. You really should."

Angeletti seemed entertained by her benevolence. "That little lady cheated on you and she took me for a ride," he said. "She cost me a considerable sum of money—"

"Oh Angeletti!" Alice said. She paused because she felt the wine's cold bubbles burst delicately in her nose. "Excuse me, but it's perfectly obvious to me that you don't mind squandering all your money." The usual tidal rush of Angeletti's spleen seemed remarkably sluggish that afternoon in the face of her repeated provocation.

" 'Squandering'?" he said mildly. "You call it 'squandering' for me to buy a few small gifts for my author's daughter and for the people who helped save her life?"

"Well," Alice said. "If you're going to put it like that—"

"You call it 'squandering,' " Angeletti said, "for me to take a beautiful and deserving young woman to the opera?"

"Well," Alice said, and she smiled at him radiantly, "if you're going to put it like that—"

Angeletti smiled back at her. "I have a little present for you," he said.

Alice watched him get up. "Is it the prettiest little ring?" she said, and she blinked at the phrase, as though she had heard it somewhere before. "Angeletti? Would you call this 'dense mixed woodland'?"

"No," Angeletti said firmly. "I would say that it was rather sparse woodland. Excuse me." And he returned to the car.

In the parcel, which he handed to her, there was—along with a calligrapher's pen and a bottle of green Indian ink—an old handwriting practice book, which Alice opened at once. The sentence inscribed at the top of the first page jumped at her with a bizarre familiarity.

" ' 'Tis better to Die than to Lie,' " she read out loud, and she burst out laughing. "Good God, Angeletti!" she said in a rush of unsuppressed delight. "I don't believe it. You've rifled the stockroom of the Convent of the Ascension. Oh how can I ever thank you?"

"Watch yourself, Mrs. Riley," Angeletti said. "You're mellowing."

"But wherever did you get it?" she said.

Angeletti gestured modestly. "Those things were printed in great numbers," he said. "Getting ahold of a copy was really not at all difficult."

"Well, thank you," Alice said. "I'm vastly touched that you went to all that trouble."

"There's a catch," he said.

"What catch?" she said.

Angeletti filled her glass. "I took a look at that bunch of stuff you left with me. The schoolgirl stories and so on."

"And?" Alice said.

"It bores me," Angeletti said. "I admit your friend wrote with an enviable flair. That Miss Davidene Delight, for example. She surely has to be the hottest little female pedagogue I've met with in a long while. She is certainly by far the best dressed. One peek at those 'exquisite rosettes' and it's tantamount to ripping off her panties."

"Perhaps you're a pervert, Angeletti?" Alice said. "Has that ever occurred to you?"

"I took the liberty," Angeletti said, "of handing on some copies to an editor. In London, that is. I figured the British are maybe fixated on that sepia-tinted bun-monitor scenario. Now I guess you're angry with me."

"What did he say?" Alice said expectantly.

"She," Angeletti said. "She liked them. She liked them a lot, as a matter of fact. With your permission, she'd like to publish three of the stories together in one little volume. Now, I suggested to her that you write an introduction." Alice stared down at the earth, fixing on the blades of grass as evidence of external reality. They appeared to be dilating. "Two thousand words or so," Angeletti said. "Is that an agreeable prospect?"

Alice looked up. "Oh yes," she said. "Oh yes. Really. I can't think of anything that I'd rather do." Angeletti, she observed, was once again looking at her in that way that made her feel slightly uncomfortable. She turned quickly to examining the label on the bottle of green Indian ink.

"The ink was a mere flight of fancy," he said. "You may prefer to use an IBM compatible."

 DOUBTLESS through the advantageous ratio of Angeletti's wine to his food, Alice had fallen asleep in the coarse, dry grass of the forest. When she awoke, blinking through a haze of dappled sunlight, she was feeling acutely hungry. Angeletti was talking on his telephone. He was reclining with his face half turned from her and shaded under his hat. He was exchanging affectionate wisecracks with a woman whom he was calling "Nance." It was apparent to Alice that he was colluding with this female person over the unexpected ease with which he had got Alice's cooperation over the changes in the book.

"Sugar and spice," he said. "No problem at all. Mrs. Riley decided to put away her meat-ax." Alice took no offense. She was feeling remarkably mellow and this in spite of her encroaching hunger. She had had a truly marvelous day. It had been extremely good, in retrospect, to have escaped from the baby and the hospital. And Angeletti, for all his half-menacing dottiness—or, more accurately, because of it—had proved the very soul of excellent company.

She had felt a kind of sustained thrill, as though she were somehow playing hooky from the nunnery. Perhaps not unlike the feeling she had had during that first little tea with Father Mullholland, only this had been writ so much larger and wilder and altogether more dangerous. It came to her as a pleasant discovery that she was not after all incapable of enjoying the company of men—because the only male company she had otherwise enjoyed was that of David Morgan, who was as sexless to her as a rumpled teddy bear.

"I'm in Hampshire," Angeletti was saying. There was a pause

followed by laughter. "Hamp shy-er, England," he said. "Not New Hampshire. Listen, bimbo, just how fast do you imagine I can work?"

The remark bounced at Alice with the force of complete surprise. It had not crossed her mind until that moment that Angeletti had been making a play for her and she inspected her feelings to discover whether or not she felt affronted. Not a bit of it. It made her feel very high. She found it delectably amusing and she promptly began to gloat. It was all so outrageously blatant, once she thought about it. All day he had been drowning her in booze and buying her favors with expensive treats. Ha! And he the married man; the conspicuously practicing Catholic, doling out missals to babies and schmarming the sisterhood with handmade sweets. Mr. Angeletti, the "man of honor." And all the while he was plotting a little lechery on the side. Alice gorged on inward laughter. Because here he was, effectively laying bets with a person who was clearly his working partner in New York. He was rating his chances of maneuvering Mrs. Riley into a dirty weekend in his "cabin" in New Hampshire. And all no doubt while the second Mrs. Angeletti stayed home wiping little noses and diligently trimming the bassinet. Ha! She reflected, for a moment, upon the fate of the first Mrs. Angeletti, because he surely hadn't divorced her. Perhaps he had fed her from a dish of poisoned figs after making explicit and passionate love to her. It was suddenly crystal clear to Alice that Angeletti was sexy.

She recalled, now, that through some fortunate miracle she had actually not yet disclosed to Angeletti the fact that she wasn't married. God only knew, she had told him almost everything else in the course of the afternoon. She had got very high and voluble. She had bombarded Angeletti with a constant barrage of anecdote, which had caused him to respond with well-aimed shots of dry, laconic wit. And these, which ought to have wounded her, had somehow not done so at all. Perhaps she had been too drunk to take offense? It surprised her now, on waking, to remember how often he had made her ache with laughter.

She had, for example, regaled him with a most reprehensible account of Mr. Fergusson's dying. She had told him, with a quite unprecedented and graphic relish, how Flora's father had swelled and curdled and breathed his last before her eyes in The Fisherman's Grotto. And how—with his soul sent all unhousel'd to account—he had then recurred in her restless, childhood dreams as the leering Giant Mollusc of the Protestant graveyard.

"So your mother is an infamous poisoner," Angeletti said. "The Lucrezia Borgia of the pigeon belt." Yet this quite unfounded calumny had caused a cascade of disloyal merriment against her female parent.

"*And* she kept Jem's letter from me," Alice said, confiding darkly. "That's why I got it so late. The secretary must have boobed in giving it to me, you see. My mother wanted me not to have it, Angeletti. It's perfectly obvious. She always hated Jem. And she thinks all Catholics are fanatics. I will have to fight her tooth and nail, Angeletti. May God give me strength. I've never really quarreled with her before." Then she had paused while Angeletti filled her glass. "She has behaved very badly toward me," Alice said. "Just like Sister Teresa's mother."

"Pardon me?" Angeletti said.

"Oh, not *your* Sister Teresa," Alice said. "Jem's Sister Teresa." And she had then told him, in another irreverent crescendo, about the orange and the epileptic nun and how Jem's mother had leapt over the convent wall for Gordon McCrail, the exquisite man of letters, with his summerhouse and his cordless telephone and his concern for the health of Mr. Ezra Pound and his deep and moving compassion for the common garden snail. Angeletti had evidently enjoyed it all enormously, especially the bit about Ezra Pound.

"I observe," he said, aiming deftly below the belt, "that Mr. Matthew Riley has all the while been playing second fiddle to this excellent gentleman of the mind."

Alice now, as she eavesdropped Angeletti's phone call, felt no shame at all in doing so. Because to be with Angeletti seemed in itself an invitation to employ any strategy to hand. It was like constantly having to skirt minefields and avoid trapdoors in the floor. One employed what means one could muster.

"What's a 'meat-ax,' Angeletti?" she said audibly. And it delighted her to see him twitch.

They drove to Angeletti's hotel in Piccadilly before they left on foot for the opera house. Alice put on the sea green silk in the ladies' room of the bar while Angeletti went up to his bedroom to change into his evening dress and run a razor over his jaw. She paused awhile before the glass, treading the spongy, cloud grey carpeting beneath her feet. She felt very good in the dress, even though she wore it with her flat, laced-up shoes. There was something remarkable about the way it had been cut, which gave it a subtle, almost schoolmarmish sexiness. High-necked and long-sleeved, it caressed her hips suggestively before falling in nice, soft pleats almost to her ankles.

Alice's excitement was underlined by the sharp edge of hunger, because Angeletti, in spite of her hints, had not proposed that they have supper along the way. She began, now, to hanker after Mars bars. She saw in the glass that behind her on the wall were fixed two vending machines, but neither of them, sadly, was in business to dispense junk food. One provided a selection of scents and the other provided tampons.

When Alice met Angeletti in the vestibule, she noticed with some amusement that he was wearing a voluminous old-fashioned dress shirt, goffered and starched in the manner once undertaken by Mrs. Tiggywinkle and her kind.

"You're a very natty dresser," she said. "Mr. Alphabetti-Spaghetti. I really like your shirt."

Angeletti offered his arm. "My shirt?" he said. "You like a man in a boiled shirt?"

Alice burst out laughing, for no other reason than that she had never heard the term before.

"But really," she said, a bit primly, to temper her unguarded admiration. "I really see no reason for us to be all glammed up like this." When Angeletti smiled at her, she could smell the toothpaste on his breath.

"I guess that's the Protestant in you," he said. "You may rest assured, Mrs. Riley, you look like Minnie Mouse around the feet."

 ALICE WAS ENCHANTED by *The Magic Flute*, just as she had been that very first time when Jem had played it to her in the cubicles off Mrs. Fergusson's music room. She knew that it made sense the way a dream makes sense, deeply at the center of her being. And here, in the dark, toward the end of Act Two, when the young prince stood robed before the altar in the Temple of Wisdom, though she knew that he was beautiful and honorable and brave and that he had just passed unflinching through the waterfall and the fire—and that he was eminently competent to construct an emergency shelter for her in the tundra— she also knew more clearly than ever that she did not want him or any of his kind, because he lacked subtlety and guile. Not like Sarastro.

Sarastro was the *mächtiger böser Dämon*, the big smell at the top. Sarastro was the operator; the con man; the abductor; the devious high priest. Sarastro had stage-managed the entire event. The others had all been putty in his hands. He had made food appear in the forest and the talisman belonged to him. He had wrested it from the Queen of the Night. She knew that there was no way he would ever behave as if he were running the Citizens Advice Bureau. Why should he? Alice had never been in love before and the knowledge now weighed on her heavily. It awed her and brought to ground, painfully, all the agreeable airborne ebullience of the day.

Afterwards she walked with Angeletti in silence through a maze of small streets. He stopped when they came upon a late-closing delicatessen and he bought a paper cone of black olives. He also bought a tin of *amaretti* and a bottle of red wine, which the shop assistant uncorked. Then Alice accompanied him to his room.

Angeletti put down the biscuits, the olives and the bottle of red wine on the cabinet beside the bed. Then he took off his jacket, his shoes and his tie. He reclined on the bed with his feet on the covers and took up the cone of black olives. Alice watched him drop the fruit into his mouth and chew at the flesh. Then he spat the stone into his hand.

"Take your clothes off," he said. Alice began with her shoes and her stockings. Then she started on the buttons of the sea green silk. She placed her garments, carefully folded, on the floor beside her feet. She accomplished these things quickly, making efficiency a cover for her awkwardness and contriving for herself the illusion that the process was really not very much different from taking one's clothes off in the doctor's surgery. Matthew Riley had never required ritual undressing of her. When she looked up, Angeletti was still chewing on black olives.

"Are you in a hurry?" he said.

"No," Alice said. "If you must know, I'm embarrassed."

"Your embarrassment is delightful," Angeletti said. "And all too patently obvious. Carry on." His speech was slurring rudely as his tongue worked at the fruit. Alice kept on until she stood awkwardly exposed, with the no-man's-land of the hotel carpet stretching between them. Angeletti put down the cone of olives.

"Take a walk to the glass," he said. He gestured to the mirror on the opposite wall. "Go practice a little narcissism."

Alice walked to the glass. She practiced a little narcissism. She looked at her hair and at the tilt of her head and at her neck and shoulders. Then at her breasts and her navel and at the triangle of pubic hair at the parting of her thighs. Reflected in the glass behind her, she could see that Angeletti had taken up the tin of *amaretti* and had removed a pair of small, prettily wrapped biscuits. She watched him twist off the tissue papers and crumple them in one of his hands. He put down the tin and the wrappings on the bedside cabinet and got up. She watched him crush the biscuits in his teeth as he approached her. When he bent and kissed her nipples, he did so through the fine, abrasive gravel of crushed apricot kernels and sugar, which goose-pimpled her arms and made her wince. Then he kissed her on the mouth and quickly released her.

"Turn around," he said. "Take a look over your shoulder." Alice, as she craned to follow the journey of her spine, was surprised and pleased by the depth and symmetry of the three equidistant dimples that nestled above the groove of her buttocks. When she looked up, she saw that Angeletti was back on the bed, eating his biscuits. Alice registered that his black silk socks had picked up some of the carpet nap on the soles. She turned and approached the bedside table, assuming that the curve of her pretty rear end would have won her the right, at last, to eat. As she reached out her hand to the tin, Angeletti took it up and passed it into his right hand so that it lay out of reach on the far side of his body.

"Angeletti!" she said, a bit frantically. "Can't you see that I'm starving to death?" She knelt on the bed and reached for the tin, realizing too late the compromising effect of stretching herself naked like that across Angeletti's chest. It disconcerted her to feel the proximity of his breathing under the delicate, starched fluting of the shirt.

"Okay, Alice," he said. "You win. Hold on." He took out a pair of biscuits and unwrapped them. Then he held them out to her on his palm. When she reached for them, he closed his fingers. "With your mouth," he said.

Alice stopped in her tracks and stared at him. "What?" she said.

"With your mouth," he said. "Take them with your mouth, Alice." Alice hesitated. Then she bent forward to take the biscuits with her mouth. It was once her mouth had closed around the coating of kernel and sugar that she felt the vibrations of Angeletti's soundless laughter.

"I have you eating out of my hand," he said. Alice did something then that she had never done before to any living thing, though she knew full well that Iona Morgan had. She sank her incisors viciously into the flesh of Angeletti's palm.

"Stop it!" he said so ferociously that she immediately complied. And then he was looming over her and flaying himself clumsily out of his clothes.

◆

Angeletti was like a holy maniac in bed. An unlovely crusader, grooving on a brutal cause. Alice found it an affront to all her tender expectation. It was grimly evident, after all, that Angeletti detested her. Or, at best, that she had become a featureless irrelevance. The desert underhoof; the infidel terrain. Anyway, it was making her feel sick. She began to count out numbers in her head. It was only when she had got to seventy-eight that the additional, persistent discomfort in her shoulder blade impinged upon her consciousness. It came to her what was causing it. She was lying on one of the jeweled button studs of Angeletti's exquisite boiled shirt. Emotion crowded in on her in the form of poignant regret. She lost count in the number sequence and struggled unsuccessfully against a girlish flow of tears.

Angeletti paused and looked at her once the tears had spilled from her eyes. He addressed her, she thought, in the tone of a kindly, reassuring lifeguard who has happened upon a small, wayward boat.

"Hello in there," he said. "Are you all right? You look like you could be suffering a little from motion sickness." Alice said nothing. His tone was an obscenity to her. Angeletti wiped her eyes on the corner of the sheet. "Come on," he said. "You're soaking the pillow. What's the matter? You don't like me?" Alice said nothing. He wiped her eyes on the sheet again and followed this by planting a run of small, soft kisses on her mouth. "My dear Miss Elizabeth Barrett," he said. "Are you tormented by a crippling malaise? Are you currently burdened with a poetical surfeit of delicacy?" Alice said nothing. He wiped her eyes again on the sheet.

"I hate you, Angeletti," she said. Angeletti merely behaved as though she had uttered a small endearment. He planted another sequence of light kisses on her face.

"Bedroom etiquette, rule one," he said. "My name is Giovanni. I would really be most gratified if you would use it, Alice."

"I hate you, Angeletti," Alice said. She wondered for a moment why it was, exactly, that she had never been able to use his name. Even while she liked him, she had merely toyed inwardly with the idea of calling him "the Don." Was she afraid that the floodgates would open? Would they release an emotion too powerful for her to keep in check? Was it the power within the name itself—that stunning, operatic name? Might it have been easier had his name been David or Henry or

Charles? Angeletti was holding her chin between his forefinger and thumb.

" 'Joe-vanni,' " he said coaxingly. "Come on now. After the first time it's not going to be so difficult."

"Giovanni," Alice said woodenly, and she waited for the ghost voice of the Commendatore to boom at her from the walls. Angeletti's face was promptly suffused with pleasure.

"And again?" he said.

"Giovanni," Alice said.

"Oh my," Angeletti said. "Oh glory be." And he kissed her and wooed her and talked out at her, then, such a curious, gentle, primeval cadabra that it drew her toward some violent unknown whirlpool and made her hum and shake.

"I'm drowning," she said, panicking wildly.

"No, no," Angeletti said. "You're okay. Take it easy now. You're not drowning."

Alice found that the pleasure of it was rare and strange and high. It made her give herself up; trade herself unguardedly for its exquisite, indescribable finesse. And she knew that over her shoulder were the waterfall and the fire.

"Do you mind if I smoke?" Angeletti said afterwards. Alice looked at him rather bitterly for what had recently taken place between them. It had required from her a huge and galling capitulation. Yet, from the ease of Angeletti's manner, it was perfectly apparent that he was resolved to behave as though nothing momentous had happened. All he had done was to get up and stumble to the bathroom where she had heard him clatter up the loo seat and pee with the door open. Then he had idled about the room for a moment, gathering his cigars and his lighter. She had watched him scratch inelegantly at the back of his naked thigh as he returned to the bed. He was behaving, in short, as though the act that had occurred between them had given him the right to display his nakedness, not for erotic purpose, but rather as if he were in the men's locker room at the gym where he went to lift weights.

"What's the matter?" Angeletti said. "You're perfectly all right, Alice. I didn't let you drown." He reached out amiably to pat her thigh. "Drowning is merely analogous to sexual climax," he said. "Though I believe that to drown for real isn't half as much fun." "Fun." How did he dare to call it "fun"? "Welcome to the climax, Alice," he said. "It's not a thing to be so afraid of."

Alice stared grimly into the bedclothes. "I think what happened to me was everything to be afraid of," she said.

Angeletti laughed. "I guess you're absolutely right," he said. "As you very often are. You have a most inconveniently sharp and penetrating mind."

"For a woman," Alice said.

"Ouch!" Angeletti said, faking a wince. "You really are very angry with me."

"Oh go ahead and smoke!" Alice said irritably. "You don't have to soft-soap me with compliments."

"No," he said. "I don't have to soft-soap you with compliments."

"Nor do you have to ask me about your filthy, stinking cigars," she said. "I've just exhibited for your entertainment that I am incapable of minding anything that you do."

"Hey now, but that's abject," Angeletti said. "That's unworthy of you."

She shot him a look just in time to see the Adam's apple rise and fall again in his throat as he swallowed. She found it quite alarming in its power to attract and she quickly looked away.

"As if you didn't know they make me feel violently sick," she said.

Angeletti looked amused by her vehemence. " 'Violently' sick?" he said. "Oh my! I can see that I had better reform myself, or I could be in trouble." He handed her the box. Alice took it but she looked at him no less caustically as she did so.

"I suppose you're telling me I can do what I like with these?" she said.

"Be my guest," he said. So she got up naked from the bed and carried the cigars into the bathroom where she broke them irritably into small pieces and dropped them into the lavatory bowl. After that she planted herself on the seat and issued forth, with relief, the longest pee of her life. Then she returned to the bedroom.

"So what have you done with my cigars?" he said.

"I've thrown them down the bog and I've peed on them," she said. Angeletti appeared to be delighted. He laughed with pleasure.

"I'll tell you one thing," he said. "It sure as hell won't be me who picks those things out of the john."

"Nor me neither," Alice said. " 'Sure as hell,' you pig-swill bastard."

"I beg your pardon?" Angeletti said.

"I called you a bastard," she said.

Angeletti held out his hand to her. "Oh, come here, my sweetheart, my wrangling queen," he said. "You still want to know what a meat-ax is?"

Alice stayed where she was. It was almost exactly the spot where she had taken off her clothes.

"Come where?" she said. Angeletti laughed. He pointed hospitably to the crook of his arm. Alice stood still, trembling slightly, with the expanse of carpet between them. "You scare me to death," she said.

"Oh come now," he said. "You're not scared of me. You're the woman who wrapped me in barbed wire, remember? You damn near threw me down a hole in the floor."

"Oh rubbish," Alice said. "You entertain yourself with lies. You're a filthy great bully, Giovanni, and you know it." She considered, with shame, that his bullying did not make her love him less. Perhaps it even made her love him more. But she didn't like it and she didn't understand it. "I don't think I know anything anymore," she said.

Angeletti looked her over carefully, a bit painfully, from head to foot. He began to enunciate slowly.

" 'I do not know what it is about you that closes and opens,' " he said; " 'nobody, not even the rain, has such small hands.' "

She was thrown by the unexpected lyricism of the words. "That's very lovely, Giovanni," she said. "Did you write that?"

"Not me," he said. "Just an American poet. You may pay it no attention." Alice looked down, a little bitterly, at her hands.

"Your prettiness is about more than I can bear right now," Angeletti said.

Alice's glance was both bruised and suspicious. "I want you to tell me that you're sorry," she said.

Angeletti stared at her for a moment. "For what?" he said.

She made no reply. She began to pace the floor, running a hand nervously through her hair. She reached the chest and began to fidget with some of his things. Keys, nail clippers, a small pile of letters. Somebody's page proofs with penciled markings, bound with two elastic bands. A box with new running shoes. The characters jumped at her eyes. Adidas. Then she turned to him.

"You've always abused me from the moment you walked into my life," she said. " 'Grab your coat,' 'jump in the cab,' 'curtsy to God'—" She wanted to add, "With your mouth. Take them with your mouth, Alice," but she couldn't. The words stuck in her throat. "You've always manipulated me," she said.

"Alice," he said sincerely. "That time we met. I appreciate I wasn't all that nice to you. Believe me. I had things on my mind."

"You christened my baby," she said bitterly.

Angeletti looked suddenly as if he might erupt, but he did not. "Baptism, so help me, is not my job," he said.

"You know what I mean," she said. A hideous doubt, as yet unacknowledged and unexpressed, overcame her. "You could have called me," she said. "How do I know you didn't keep me from my friend . . ."

Angeletti wiped a hand over his mouth. "I beg you, Alice," he said. "Don't pursue this. It's damaging. You delegated to me and then you passed out. God knows—about the whole business—I told you I was sorry. I couldn't be more sorry if I walked the earth for you from end to end in a hair shirt. What do you want from me? You want my head on a plate?"

"Yes," Alice said unreasonably. "I want your head on a plate." Or did she? She half wanted his head, severed by sheet metal and bleeding on the *autostrada*. But then again, she half did not. And one glimpse of the Highland brain surgeon striding toward her with his brogues and bedside manner and she wanted his head back on again. Oh be my Green Knight, Giovanni; be my Magic Man. Take your head on and off like a top hat full of rabbits. Let it roll, grinning among bitten macaroons—bitten *amaretti*—my Mr. Apollinax. My angel. Mr. Angeletti has come upon us like one of God's angels, Mrs. Riley. I would like to have your head and to keep it, Giovanni, but how? In a pot like Isabella? Like the head of Clordio-Cloudio? Like a necromantic? The dead girl in the bed? I thought you'd like that, Mrs. Riley. Oh, not *your* head, Giovanni! Let's make it the brain surgeon's head.

"All right," Alice said sulkily. "I'm sorry. All those things. They weren't your fault. I know that." She paused. "But about tonight. I mean about what you did to me. Well, I still think you should say you're sorry." Angeletti was maintaining his usual disconcerting eye contact. It obliged her to look away.

"You're having a tantrum because you got fucked," he said.

Alice began edgily to pick up her clothes. She stepped into her pants. It angered her intensely that all her garments were those that he had bought for her.

"I guess this sounds a little unmentionable to a person of your refinement and sensitivity," Angeletti said dryly as he watched her, "but during the act of sex it is inevitable that a person will get fucked." Alice mumbled furiously into the buttons of her dress, wanting him both to hear and not to hear. "Pardon me?" he said.

"I said, 'Jug Jug,' " she said. "It's T. S. Eliot on the subject of violation." Sylvan. As in the change of Philomel by the barbarous king so rudely forced. "Just another American poet," she said. "You may pay it no attention."

Angeletti's face gave no sign of emotion in response, though he paused and swallowed before he spoke.

"You're a clever girl, Alice, and you've been well educated," he said. "I guess your parents gave it a great deal of their money and their concern. Were it not for your willfully placing your body supine under Mr. Matthew Riley, I might have met you at Oxford University. Not messing with pigeons in burgundy. I beg you now, for your own sake and mine, stop demeaning yourself like this."

Alice pulled with venom at the ratchet of her zip. She loathed him for having bought her stockings and a suspender belt, but the Marks and Spencer school uniform was currently in the boot of his hired car, along with her tights. And to mess with a suspender belt right then was unthinkable. Like working in a club for bent businessmen. She put her shoes on over her naked feet.

"You behaved like a roughneck," she said. "You practically raped me." She picked up her handbag and she slung it over her shoulder. Then she headed for the door. He waited until her hand had made contact with the latch.

"Will you answer me a question before you go?" he said. "Just one word. Yes or no." Alice paused and let her hand fall.

"All right," she said.

"Are you hurt?" he said.

"That's got nothing to do with it," she said.

"Yes or no," he said. "Answer me yes or no."

"All right," she said. "No."

"And did some ghoulish, hooded monster spit on your face? Pee in your mouth? Jam broken bottle glass up your female orifice?"

"No," Alice said. "That's three questions."

"Thank you," Angeletti said. "You got fucked, Alice. Now I care for you with all my heart and I'm sorry if I bruised your pride and your tender soul, because I prefer to believe that I cherish those things. So maybe I was a little emphatic. You came to my bed with your libido wrapped in chain mail. What did you seriously expect from me?"

"I expected nothing," Alice said. "I don't know what I expected. I told you I don't know anything anymore."

"You expected that I would offer myself gift wrapped for a mechanical aid," he said. "You expected that I would collude with you so you could work out in your head on your dead friend's ninth-grade father fixations." Alice felt her indignation rise and fall again as it gave way to a kind of dying inside. Angeletti continued, relentless, but then she knew already that he was temperamentally disposed toward blood sports. "The Divine Miss Davidene Delight," he said. "In her dress of sea green silk." Alice looked down at her clothes.

"You dressed me up like this on purpose," she said. "I hate you more than I can say."

Angeletti was lying immobile on the bed, his long brown hands under his head. It was a while before he spoke.

"That was a nice thing you did with me," he said. "Don't think I don't know how difficult it was for you, Alice. Don't think I don't appreciate it, because I do." Alice felt herself shaking. I am dying, she thought, dying. And the sea shall be my element. "Congratulations," Angeletti was saying. "You came, Mrs. Riley—just like a gorgeous little birthday treat."

Alice held on to her sanity by fixing hard upon Giovanni's little birthday treat. Two scoops of vanilla ice cream on a bath bun washed down with a Cherry Coke. Then she added hot fudge sauce.

"Believe me, I'm distressed that you should hate me so much," he said. "I really had no idea you felt so badly."

"I love you," Alice said bleakly. Angeletti did not move. He remained as he was, with his hands under his head. Alice stood, similarly immobile, at the door. She had her back against the wall and she was staring down into the carpet. It was the same, uniform, cloud grey carpet as covered the floor in the ladies' room of the bar where she had first put on the dress. In fact it covered the floors of the entire hotel. She recalled, now, how she had stood admiring herself before the glass as though she were about to embark upon a bright little adventure. Alice in Wonderland. She had already been on the edge of hunger then and that was five hours ago. Right now, she thought suddenly, I will commit murder for part shares in a Cadbury's Flake. Where is my meat-ax and why does that bastard not feed me?

Then, with a creeping horror, she remembered something else. Something so much worse than hunger that she slid slowly down the wall until she was squatting on her haunches. That machine on the wall of the ladies' room that hadn't been vending chocolate bars. She had had no need of a tampon in something like ten weeks. Or could it simply be that if a person took up residence in a nunnery, then that person would, by grace of God, stop ovulating? For the second time in one evening Alice found herself grimly beginning to count out numbers in her head.

"Giovanni," she said eventually, and she heard her voice sound cautiously as if against the wall of a tomb, "can I please tell you something absolutely dreadful?"

AT FOUR O'CLOCK in the morning Giovanni put down the typescript he had been reading by lamplight while Alice slept. He got up to clean out the toilet bowl. Piece by piece he extracted his broken cigars and laid them on the absorbent wad of the *New York Times Book Review*. He parceled them up and put them into the plastic disposal bin. Then he washed his hands. He was dressed in dark green exercise pants and a voluminous dark green hooded sweatshirt. When his watch said four-fifteen, he pulled on his sports socks and his brand-new running shoes and he stepped out in search of a baker. He found one, eventually, plying his nocturnal trade in the narrower mazes of Soho. After that he returned and woke Alice, whom he had previously coaxed to sleep at one o'clock in the morning.

"Time to wake up now, my sweetheart," he said, and he gave her the bread. He watched her bolt it in lumps.

"You're eating for two," he said.

"Not for certain," she said. "I mean, I can't be certain, can I?"

Giovanni smiled. He helped her back into the sea green silk and bent to lace her shoes. He put his jacket of the previous evening around her shoulders. "Put it on," he said. "Button it. It's cold outside."

She accompanied him down in the lift and watched, blinking, as he settled the bill. Then she walked out with him to the car. "Who's Nance?" she asked suddenly.

"She's my assistant," Giovanni answered. "Why do you ask?"

Alice shook her head dismissively. "No reason. What did you do while I was asleep?" she said.

"I read," he said. "I cleaned out the toilet bowl."

"Oh, but you shouldn't have," Alice said. "I would've done that."

"For sure," Giovanni said. "A pregnant woman on her knees before my toilet bowl at four o'clock in the morning. Now I could grow accustomed to that kind of homage."

Alice watched him throw his luggage into the back. Then they got into the car.

"What will you do when you've dropped me?" she said.

"Exercise my new running shoes," he said. "Cover a few miles. I'll come by for you after mass. I'll drive back with you to your parents."

"Aren't you sleepy?" she said.

"Nope," Giovanni said. "For me it's around midnight." He laughed a little at her yawnings. "Do we ever get to inhabit the same time zone?" he said. She leaned her head against his shoulder as he drove. Sleep combined with the novelty of Giovanni's new tenderness had left her feeling like a well-nurtured and trusting child.

"You're funny," she said cozily.

"How's that?" he said. " 'Funny'?"

Alice shrugged contentedly. "You're being nice to me," she said. "I expect it's because you think I'm pregnant." She entertained herself along these lines in the darkness. "I expect it brings out the gentleman in you," she said. "The prospect of one yukky little glob of mucus and cells—all gummed together with dear Mr. Riley's emissions."

Giovanni kept his eyes on the road. "I really don't need that kind of talk," he said. "Not from you."

Alice sat up and looked at him. "Well I hope you're going to sign me up for the right-to-life crusade," she said. "Just before you fly out of Heathrow on Monday morning."

Giovanni took a while to respond. "You took your head off my shoulder," he said. "Put it back."

Alice tried, for a while, to engage in sober contemplation. To be pregnant would be an unambiguous disaster. Jem's baby was one thing, but Matthew Riley's as well? And to follow within seven months? It was impossible. And whatever would become of Homer? Yet it seemed such a waste to lose her last precious time with Giovanni in fixing on such things. Especially now that they had at last arrived at a point of quietude. She returned her head to his shoulder. Wrapped in Giovanni's jacket, she escaped instead into a blissful, assuaging fantasy. She would give up the pigeon house, give up everything; would have the new baby and Jem's baby too, and she would live in the English countryside and be Giovanni's English mistress; Giovanni's country girl. Giovanni was rich. Giovanni would love her and keep her and plant roses around the door. She saw the sole of his Adidas running shoe on the edge of the spade as he pushed down, with his prodigious strength, into the wholesome earth. He would visit her whenever his business brought him to London. He would get children upon her in great numbers. Apple-cheeked children in smocks and velvet knickerbockers with hands outstretched to catch falling apples, who would all be the best of friends. Dominic and Arabella and Ganymede and Amanda-Jane. And two fingers to the tawdry bridegroom whom she had been obliged to share with Flora. Thumbs down to him. Thumbs down to you, Matthew Riley, liar and cheat. And, as for Giovanni, to be his mistress would not be a problem. He was a Catholic, was he not? Catholics didn't get that fussed about a little bit of fornication. It was people like Miss Aldridge and Oliver Cromwell who bothered their heads about things like that.

"Giovanni," Alice said, in a voice like ash in a graveyard. "I wish that you would tell me about the second Mrs. Angeletti."

Giovanni was silent for a very long time. Alice thought that he would not reply at all.

"Now I have a little story to tell," he said. "And it's not so elevating here and there. I expect that you will listen until I'm through."

"Yes," Alice said. "I'll listen."

"Good," Giovanni said. "Then I'll begin. That night I got your message. That message on the answering machine. Yours was not the only message I got that night. The other was from the police."

"The police?" Alice said.

"Shut your mouth and listen," Giovanni said. "That is what you have undertaken to do."

"Sorry," Alice said.

"My wife's car collided with a truck," he said. "The second Mrs. Angeletti is dead."

"Dead?" Alice said. It came over her, with a kind of creeping horror, that Giovanni had been all dressed up for the opera that night. She wondered, again, whether Giovanni was seriously mad.

"Mary-Lou was absconding to join her lover," he said. "She had left me a while back, as a matter of fact—for a man who was big in pornography."

"In what?" Alice said.

"Pornography," Giovanni said. "Do you suffer from hearing loss?"

"No," Alice said.

"Good," Giovanni said. "Then I'll go on. Now understand me, Alice. This is a truly wholesome character we're dealing with here. This is a man who keeps a twelve-foot-high bronze statue on his lawn of himself screwing a goat." He paused. "A case of bronzing one's first sexual experience. I guess it's somewhat analogous to bronzing a child's first shoe. He got raided doing prepubertal castration scenarios with abducted Hispanics."

"You're not serious, I hope," Alice said.

"Once MacMahon was jailed," Giovanni said, "Mary-Lou came back to me. I guess she was always afraid of the dark and she never liked to play on her own. She discovered a consuming passion for meeting my every whim. She decided I liked to get my shirts ironed on both sides. All that kind of stuff."

Alice was suddenly struck by the notion that Mary-Lou had expended her efforts upon Giovanni's pretty boiled shirt. Mary-Lou would have laundered it and starched it and goffered the frills. And Giovanni had then unseamed her on it. She had lain in his arms on a shirt made lovely by the hand of the porn king's dead mistress.

"And by 'both sides' I don't mean front and back," Giovanni said. "I mean inside and outside. The woman stood around in my kitchen all day long, struggling to make *gnocchi* by hand and mixing up batches of peanut butter cookies. Now it's true I adore peanut butter cookies and, besides, Mary-Lou was so monumentally incompetent that the performance was in itself gratifying."

Alice winced. She could not help feeling rather sorry for Mary-Lou as she envisaged Giovanni provoked by the odor of blood. She saw him, like Petrucchio, ordering away the dishes of homemade *gnocchi* and sending the trays of peanut butter cookies crashing to the ground.

"Mostly I tolerated it because Mary-Lou was pregnant," he said. "God knows she really wanted that little baby and, God knows, so did I. I guess she was just nesting, poor girl." Then he said nothing for a while. He drove on in silence, staring ahead at the road.

"And then?" Alice said.

"MacMahon got sprung from jail," Giovanni said. "About two months before I came to London. Now, I knew she'd make a run for it—just as soon as he'd succeeded in bribing his way out of the country. As a matter of fact I could deduce it from the number of cookie sheets that were currently dropping out of her hands."

Alice heard the baking trays crash like cymbals as he spoke. She tried to recall wherever before she had heard such an everyday tale of ordinary folk.

"I needed to come to London," he said. "I'd meant to come in July and I'd already delayed over a month." Giovanni paused. Then he added, "And you will appreciate, Alice, that I could not in any case keep a watch on my wife twenty-four hours a day."

"No," Alice said.

"Quite apart from it gets unimaginably boring," he said, "to cohabit with a not very bright pregnant woman with ants in her pants who is dropping cups of butter and cornstarch all over your kitchen floor."

It came to Alice with shame, at that point, that she was beginning to enjoy the story of Mary-Lou every bit as much as she had ever enjoyed some of Jem's domestic anecdotes. Perhaps the unreality of the day was playing tricks on her, but it seemed to her not dissimilar to the story of Maddie and the suicidal cellist. Or the snail expert who had bled in Holy Week.

"I've always wondered," she found herself saying unguardedly, "how Americans measure butter in a cup."

"Pardon me?" Giovanni said.

"No, nothing," Alice said.

"So I hired two guys to watch her," Giovanni said. "Professionals, as I thought."

Alice turned to him wide-eyed. "But you don't mean spies?" she said. "What I mean is—well—you don't get spies to watch your wife."

"Are you reading me?" Giovanni said. "My wife was thirty weeks pregnant. She was in a delicate state of mind. You expected that I should sit back and allow her to liaise with criminals in some godforsaken hole? I had the child to think of."

Alice conceded the point. It was after all not unreasonable, in the circumstances, for him to insure against her absconding with his baby.

"I'm sorry," she said. "Forgive me."

"To cut a long story short," Giovanni said. "She got wise to them. When she noticed she was being followed, she panicked and hit the gas. The car smashed into a truck. Mary-Lou went prematurely into labor. She was crushed screaming behind the wheel until men with crowbars hacked off the doors."

Alice had subsided into a state of nauseous horror. She was grateful for the dark and the hypnotic uniformity of the stretch of road ahead.

"I have to say it," Giovanni said. "For a woman who couldn't rip off her own Band-Aid, she must have suffered the most unendurable pain."

Alice sat bleakly confronting what Giovanni had just told her. She was suddenly terribly cold. She drew the evening jacket around her and endeavored to control her shivering.

"I got to see the bodies after I left you," he said. "Mary-Lou's was just the most indescribable mess. The baby's was miraculously unblemished." Something then occurred to Alice to which she could hardly give voice.

"You delayed your flight for me," she said. "You were booked to leave at six o'clock that morning."

"Don't worry about it," Giovanni said grimly. "Nobody ever got impatient waiting around in the morgue." Alice said nothing. She considered morbidly how she had made him go in her place and watch Jem die; how she had despised him for his humanity toward Jem's unprepossessing and undersized baby. It left her too deeply appalled even to apologize.

"As a matter of fact you did me a favor that night," he said. "I couldn't make a flight back home till morning and frankly I could see no point in passing up *The Magic Flute*. But it's not much to be recommended as an escape from the rack, I guess. Instead you allowed me the privilege of watching you rip your hands open on old boards."

"Some privilege," Alice said.

"For sure," he said. "It was a privilege and now I'll tell you why. You were doing it to support your dying friend. I'd been giving you a hard time, Alice, but it made no difference to you. And then you yelled at me. I took a good look at you and I said to myself, 'Keep looking, Giovanni. Keep looking at that woman. She's yelling at you. So what? She's got shoes on her feet like Minnie Mouse and she behaves like she never got screwed. She has furthermore attempted to wrap you in barbed wire and she has destroyed your clothes. She has caused you to miss the opera and she has damn near thrown you down a hole in the floor. So what? All around the rest of your life lies the shark pool. And here, under this precarious circle of golden lamplight, is your guardian angel. You go easy on this woman, Giovanni, because this is the most beautiful, most loyal, most precious woman you are ever going to meet.' I said to myself, 'Giovanni, fight dirty for this woman if necessary, but bind her to your body and your soul. È bella come la madre di Dio.' "

"Oh Giovanni," Alice said. "Oh Giovanni."

Throughout the remainder of the journey, Alice wove in and out of sleep.

"As to an annulment," she heard Giovanni say, "I guess it won't give the Vatican too much of a problem."

"What?" Alice said.

"Your marriage to Mr. Riley," Giovanni said. "Given that it was never consummated."

"What?" Alice said again. She wondered whether he had been proposing marriage to her in her sleep and whether, in that event, she had accepted him. She sat bolt upright at once, feeling the necessary propriety of adjusting her deportment in the face of so significant an offer.

"It is perfectly apparent to me," Giovanni said, "that Mr. Riley never brought you to climax. That constitutes an unconsummated marriage."

Alice began to revel in Giovanni's dottiness. It delighted her to reflect that while she would quibble with Father Mullholland about absolutely everything from the Woman of Syrophoenicia to the Holy Handkerchief, Giovanni blithely called himself a Catholic and believed whatever he liked.

"You are as mad as a hatter," she said, and it came to her in a glorious rush that Giovanni was very much like Jem. He had wrested the talisman from her, that was all. Sarastro had finally outwitted the star-crowned queen. Or he had won more than a round or two, she had to concede. "I really love you, Giovanni," she said. "Pray forgive me for having disliked you so much in the past."

"Now, it is my impression," Giovanni continued relentlessly, "that your adorable Father Mullholland is bent upon talking doctrine to you until the conversion of China. I would like it for him to receive you as soon as possible."

"Oh yes," Alice said, and she raised an eyebrow in the dark.

"I'm sure that you will appreciate it's essential for the children," he said. "And I have to admit that it will give great pleasure to my mother."

Alice tried not to laugh. "The 'children'? And your 'mother'?" she said. And she thought about Giovanni's mother, dead in childbirth. And she thought again about Mary-Lou and the cookie sheets and the porn king with the bronze statue and the shirts being ironed on both sides and her whole soul filled with joy at the absurdity of it. Gullibility is the sin of stupidity, she thought. And what is the matter with me? I pick nits all day with Jem's priest and yet I swallow, hook, line and sinker, a meshwork of wacky absurdity. A tissue of macabre and ridiculous fabrication. Infected stigmata. A porn king buggering a goat.

"With your permission, it is my intention to adopt Pamina just as soon as we are married," Giovanni said. "I am, of course, more than ready to assume paternity for the unborn child. That goes without saying."

"Giovanni?" Alice said. "Tell me now about the first Mrs. Angeletti. Did she also 'die in childbirth'? And was she 'confined in the sixth month of pregnancy'?"

"She drowned," Giovanni said.

"She drowned?" Alice said.

"She drowned on her wedding night," Giovanni said.

Alice, caught all unawares, heard her laughter disgorge inelegantly, like a snort. She was deeply admiring of Giovanni's effrontery. That he should call himself a "man of letters" and then not even bother to fabricate something less purple. No wonder he did not balk at *Carmen*.

"On her *wedding* night?" Alice said gleefully. "I expect it was from a surfeit of sexual climax."

"She drowned in a hotel swimming pool," Giovanni said curtly. "She walked in her sleep, Alice. I didn't know that before I married her."

"Oh what a pity," Alice said. "Had you not slept with her before?"

"No I hadn't," Giovanni said. "She was very young. We were both very young." Alice tried to envisage a very young Giovanni with his very young, virgin bride. His lank black hair falling unthinned into his hooded, predator's eyes. Would she have wanted him like that? She decided no. The receding hairline had the effect of counterbalancing the jaw. And if it was true that people mellowed with age, well, Giovanni at twenty must have been all distilled assassin.

"Was she 'promised' to you at birth?" Alice said.

"We met in college," Giovanni said. "You are behaving very badly, Alice. Do you suffer from retrospective jealousy?"

Alice saw then that the sky was streaked with the first sweet signs of day and that Giovanni was approaching the convent gates. She could not remember ever having felt so completely, so divinely happy. Not since the day that she and Jem McCrail had shuffled into Miss Trotter's office, wedged like pincushions in the resolute shorts. And now Giovanni had asked her to marry him. She would go and tell Miss Trotter. She would climb in through the window of the assembly hall and confront Miss Trotter on the platform. "The fact is," she would say, all shimmering in her silks and fine array, "the fact is that Giovanni and I have become completely inseparable." *Mann und Weib und Weib und Mann reichen an die Gottheit an.* Oh, the bliss of it! Then Giovanni turned in through the gates and stopped the car.

"Dear Giovanni," Alice said. "Dearest Giovanni, you're brilliant. And thank you so much for being a man." Giovanni did not turn to her, but stared out pensively into the foreground, somewhere beyond the windscreen. For a moment Alice paused to regard his profile. He was a grey, brooding silhouette in the delicate monochrome light. It did not surprise her to see, now, that Giovanni was awesomely beautiful. She kissed him at the angle of his jaw, below the ear. "I love you," she said. And she laughed a bit, through elation. "Please don't crush me under a truck," she said. "Or heave me into a hotel swimming pool." The color was high in her cheeks as she opened the door and got out. She closed the door quietly and leaned in through the window. "Don't feed me from a dish of poisoned figs after a day out on the *autostrada*. So long, Giovanni. I'll see you after mass."

WHEN THE CLOCK on the wall of Sister Teresa's office said ten past twelve, Alice knew for certain that Giovanni would not come. He would simply, sensibly, have rescheduled his flight and headed out directly for Heathrow. It was a thing for which his experience with her had given him much practice. And what could she expect?

In the bright light of noon, she examined her conduct in the car the previous dawn. She had as good as accused Giovanni of murdering both of his wives. Why ever had she done that? Why had she behaved so badly? He had asked her to marry him and had confided to her the most scarring and terrible secrets of his heart and she had laughed in his face and abused him for it. Had she really been quite awake, or had she been sleepwalking like the first Mrs. Angeletti? And now Giovanni was gone. She would head out alone with Pamina and confront her parents in Surrey.

All that remained for her was to take leave of Father Mullholland. She picked up the baby in Giovanni's basket and set her face toward the priest's house.

Father Mullholland took the basket from her and ushered her into his sitting room.

"Your baby is looking very fine," he said.

"Yes," Alice said. She had selected the most exquisite of Giovanni's smocked garments to celebrate the baby's departure from regulation hospital nightgowns and she had tied the Holbein hat under the baby's chin. Father Mullholland drew up his large wing armchair for her until it faced the window and he placed the baby's basket beside the chair. Once she had sat down, he approached a sort of old linen press in which he kept supplies of alcohol and glasses. He opened it and took out two tumblers and an unopened bottle of malt whiskey, which he proceeded to uncap.

"Now you are surely not going to insist on drinking sherry?" he said. "Not on a day like this."

"Yes I am," Alice said. "If I don't shock you too much." She did not, in fact, want to drink anything at all, but she knew that he probably did and she was unwilling to be the cause of his deprivation. He traded the glass for a smaller one, after a little persuasion, and poured sherry into it and gave it to her. Then he poured whiskey for himself, which he drank neat, without any ice. He seated himself on the cushioned window ledge with his back toward the garden.

The garden was flowerless and darkly shaded with rather too many large trees. Ivy crept up the tree trunks and had begun to decorate the stone sill around the low bay window where he sat. Alice had always liked his garden. It was like a pleasant, Victorian graveyard that had been left in peace to harbor mosses and squirrels. And today, over and above these charms, his house was smelling curiously spicy as though somebody were baking a cake. She could hear that the daily woman was moving in the kitchen, making a soft clatter as she sorted cooking pans.

"Your Mrs. Murphy is turning out German apple cake for you," Alice said.

"It is a well-known fact," said Father Mullholland, "that the clergy live in the lap of luxury."

"Yes," Alice said, and she tried, not very successfully, to smile at the jape, because she was grieving for Giovanni and because, sitting there, it weighed on her how much she was going to miss Jem's priest. In her friendship with him, as with so many things, Jem had handed her a kind of baton. She looked around the room, shoring up its features.

"Did Jem ever come here?" she said. "I mean, did she sit here, in this room?"

"Oh yes," he said. "But that was before she got too ill of course."

"And did she sit in this chair?" Alice said.

"Oh yes," he said again. "Quite often." After that they said nothing. She sat and watched him as he took swigs at the whiskey.

"But you have come to talk to me," he said. Alice colored a little.

"Not really," she said. "I came to say goodbye to you, that's all." She paused so long that he spoke again.

"Yesterday you went to the opera with our mutual friend Giovanni," he said. He said it in a voice so neutral that it put her on her guard.

"But *is* Giovanni your friend?" she said.

He seemed to think rather carefully before he answered, but when he did, it was with certainty.

"Yes," he said. "I have known him no longer than you have, of course. But yes. Giovanni is my friend." He looked as if he were amusing himself with a sudden afterthought. "I have observed in that short time that he might make one a rather formidable enemy."

"Yes," Alice said. "I suppose so."

"I spent a week with him in America," Father Mullholland said, making idle small talk into the silence. "He was kind enough to invite me and I must say that he proved to be a very delightful host."

"Your holiday," Alice said with feeling. "You spent it with Giovanni. And that was exactly when I wanted you most."

"But it seems that you managed very ably without me," said the priest.

"All right," Alice said, reluctantly. "I was all right." She couldn't but accept the reasonableness of his assertion.

"Are you at war with Giovanni?" he said. Alice considered this. Was she at war with Giovanni? Probably. It seemed that simply to coexist with Giovanni implied a state of precarious truce.

"I might as well tell you that I have a problem about Giovanni," she said. "I only discovered it last night. You see, I'm in love with him. But it's all right. I'll be all right. I'm quite safe now because he's decided to abandon me."

"Has he?" said Father Mullholland. "And why should he have done that?"

"Because I accused him of murdering his wives," she said. "Which was hardly diplomatic in the circumstances."

"No," said Father Mullholland. "I suppose it was not—though he has admittedly managed to lose two of them and he is only thirty-five. You would have been completely justified in telling him it looked like carelessness."

"Well, it was unforgivable of me," Alice said. "But something must have made me say it. Don't you see? Do I sense that Giovanni is the sort of man who would hound a woman to death? And then he would endow a convent full of nuns to say masses for her soul. Look, I wish you wouldn't smile at me like that. He did ask me to marry him last night. And I do know for a fact that he's making handouts to the convent."

Father Mullholland seemed entertained by the imputation, though in general he took her seriously.

"Oh come now," he said. "As I understand it, Giovanni is deeply and sincerely in love with you and I advise you to apologize to him at once."

Alice narrowed her eyes as enlightenment came upon her. "He's been tattling to you," she said. "And furthermore you know exactly where he is."

"Yes indeed," said Father Mullholland. "He is in my kitchen where he has been busy all the morning. He is preparing a nice little leave-taking tea for his nuns."

Alice found her indignation rising. "Well," she said. "I see that the Catholic Boys' Club has been in session again. Please don't mind me, will you? Please carry on. Five minutes after you meet each other you're exchanging razors and shirts."

He looked at her a little skeptically. "You are a perfectly ridiculous girl," he said. "To be always making so much fuss about a razor and a shirt."

"Has it occurred to you that I'm jealous?" Alice said. "Because I'm your friend too, aren't I? So when are you going to lend me your razor and your shirt?" It struck Alice all of a sudden that she was flirting with him and it made her blush. She hurriedly picked up the baby, who had begun to stir in her basket. She took a feeding bottle from a holder under the shawl and she turned in readiness to rise and go to Giovanni. After her initial indignation, she was suffused with relief to learn both that Giovanni loved her and that he was, after all, within reach.

"Excuse me—" she said.

"If I may detain you a little longer," said Father Mullholland, unbearably. "I would like to talk to you about Giovanni." Alice conceded with enormous difficulty, because to know that Giovanni was in the kitchen was making it impossible for her to sit still.

"It concerns me," said Father Mullholland, as if blithely unaware of her problem, "that Giovanni may be a little—how shall I say this?—a little dangerously impetuous with regard to your good self."

Alice laughed at his diplomacy. "Oh," she said. " 'Impetuous'? Well, I must say that's very politic, Father. You may as well call him a psychopathic bully. And manipulating—" She stopped and laughed. "Oh well," she said. "He might hear me."

"If he bullies and manipulates you," Father Mullholland said firmly, "then you have a clear duty to teach him otherwise."

Alice opened her mouth. She was all incredulity. "Well, I hope you're joking," she said. "Or perhaps you haven't noticed that Giovanni is about three times my size? On top of that, he lifts weights. But I don't suppose you've ever had cause to observe the power of dear Giovanni's right arm."

Father Mullholland seemed to brush this aside as if it were a minor irrelevance. "Giovanni is the only child of rather simple, wealthy and indulgent parents," he said. "It is hardly surprising that he plays the Grand Turk."

"And what about me?" Alice said. "I'm also the only child of rather simple, wealthy and indulgent parents."

Father Mullholland finished his whiskey and put the glass down on the floor. "Then you are fortunate in being so much the moderate and reasonable person that you are," he said. "It is probably your sex which has helped to save you."

Alice pulled a face; doubtful, contentious. She didn't debate the point with him. She merely reminded herself that this was the same person who had so kindly put himself out writing letters on her behalf to reinstate her at Oxford. She resented deeply at that moment that his beautiful, seductive religion had made God carnate as a man. Not hermaphrodite, like Tiresias, biologically equipped to enter into the range of human experience across gender, but as a man. A celibate man who was nice to women. Like Father Mullholland. *Et homo factus est.* The Flesh. Male Flesh. You are rather squeamish about the Flesh, Alice.

"It may be that I have no brief for speaking to you like this," he said.

"In which case I hope you will tell me so. But you really ought to recognize your responsibilities with regard to Giovanni."

Alice allowed her pique to vent itself in sarcasm. "Oh that's right," she said. "But of course. Make me responsible for Giovanni. And then you can sit back and say, 'Oh, but how she failed him, poor little thing. And dear impetuous Giovanni is so *special*. What a pity she wasn't adequate to wheedle away his lunacies with a few more feminine wiles.'"

Father Mullholland watched her without blinking. "You think it is none of my business," he said.

"No," Alice said. "Please—" She shrank, like an awkward schoolgirl, into the chair and strove to avoid eye contact. She stared down at the baby, who was clamped to the teat of the feeding bottle.

The priest continued, undaunted. "Giovanni is very determined to be your husband," he said. "Now I may as well tell you that I believe he would make you a very suitable husband. He loves you and he has a great deal to give—"

"I don't believe this," Alice said. "But I expect they still have marriage brokers in certain parts of Ireland." He ignored her.

"—and I don't mean money, of course, though it is true that Giovanni is very comfortable—"

"And fixing for male supplicants has always been part of the priestly function, after all," Alice said, though he seemed not even to hear her.

"—he is enormously able and generous and passionate," Father Mullholland was saying. "Passionate about all those things for which you yourself have such enthusiasm, Alice. Books and music and paintings . . ." He paused. Alice wanted suddenly to weep with the truth of it. "Passion and love don't come to us so often that we can afford to quibble them away," he said. "I am speaking about human love, of course."

She wanted to tell him that he moved her with his good sense but she could not. "*And* he's Catholic," she said, bitchily. "Only think. A proper Catholic father for Veronica's baby. Good old Sarastro. He strides in and takes the center stage. He can take on Pamina and everything will be just fine and tickety-boo."

"Why yes," he said calmly. "It is true that I think Giovanni would make a very good parent for Veronica's child. Just as you do, Alice.

Why are you so angry with me? If it is because you are certain that you do *not* want to marry Giovanni, then forgive me."

Alice was completely thrown by his directness. "Do I get to name the day?" she said. "Or has that been fixed as well? And as to my bottom drawer—I've got all the stuff, don't worry. Cartloads of it. I'm also a dab hand with a needle, as you know, so to hem sheets in a hurry is really not a problem for me."

"When you have quite finished talking nonsense," he said, "my point is precisely this. Giovanni is not your husband. Not yet. Nor ought he to be for a considerable time if you, at least, are capable of exercising your sense. You have your degree to complete and it may have struck you that Giovanni has only recently emerged from a personal experience which has disturbed him very greatly. So have you. Isn't it possible that right now you may easily help to drown each other?" Alice noticed that, as her hand shook, the baby momentarily lost her grip on the teat and nuzzled efficiently until she found it again. "I beg you to consider for a moment what Giovanni's second marriage has really been like for him, Alice."

Alice tried hard to think seriously about Mary-Lou and the bronze goat and MacMahon, but she could not. It was all so far beyond her own experience that she blinked and gave up.

"I can't," she said. "It all sounds to me like a tasteless and over-blown melodrama. And how Giovanni could ever have got himself embroiled with a woman like that is completely beyond my understanding."

"Because he is impetuous and rich and he expects that people will capitulate to him, which they nearly always do. Because he stamps his foot and flexes his right arm and reaches out for whatever he wants."

"Yes," Alice said, and she remembered vividly the occasions on which Giovanni had stamped his foot and reached out and flexed his right arm.

"He is also, I think, rather susceptible to glamour."

"Glamour," Alice said woodenly, and she cast an eye involuntarily over her navy skirt and her white blouse.

"The woman's face appeared on magazine covers," said Father Mullholland. "You have probably seen her at the newsstand." Alice tried to drink this in. Mary-Lou, embalmed on magazine covers, and she in her sensible laced shoes. "Yet, for all that, I think you will agree that Giovanni is a person of considerable stature and distinction."

"Oh yes," Alice said. "More so than anyone. Well. Except for you, I suppose."

"Thank you, Alice," he said. "But I will continue if I may." Alice began to think that he would never stop. Giovanni would be out through the back door and on to his plane bound for JFK before the priest had stopped talking. "Now, Giovanni loves you because you are steadfast and honorable and because, in the first instance, you stood your ground with him so splendidly in the matter of Veronica's manuscripts."

"Oh, good Lord!" Alice said. "But really. I'm by nature so weedy and pliable. I'm the original shrinking violet. And haven't you noticed how I stammer?"

"No," said Father Mullholland, and he laughed at her. Alice became quite urgent in her need to force home the point.

"Well I do," she said. "Maybe I don't when I'm with you, that's all. Or with Giovanni. Anyway, it's only when I'm with Giovanni that I discover such a talent for self-assertion. It's only because he needles me so much. I mean, if people didn't stand up to him he'd be always having them for breakfast."

Father Mullholland said nothing. He sat and smiled at her. When he finally spoke, it was as if rather casually.

"And am I right in thinking that Giovanni is very fond of children?" he said. In the use of that sly plural, Alice understood at once that the priest had been adequately briefed on the possible effect of Mr. Riley's emissions. It made her indignant, almost beyond bearing, that Giovanni had taken that liberty with her confidence. Damn and blast the man. He had had no right to go co-opting her body and preempting any decision she might wish to make by tattling like that to her friend. Not when her friend was a Catholic priest. She was quite sure he had done it on purpose.

"Oh well," she said. "So Giovanni has told you. I must say, he hasn't wasted any time. And to think how much he enjoys withholding information from me."

"I think," said the priest slowly, "that Giovanni's marriage has perhaps left him out of practice for dealing with a woman of integrity. Now if you allow Giovanni to take your integrity from you—as he will

surely try to do in the process of his obsession with possessing you—
then where will that leave you, my dear? And where will it leave
Giovanni? He will be like a spoilt child who has been given the
rainbow in a bottle."

Alice could suddenly not bear it any longer. Her impatience re-
vealed itself as irritability. She put away the feeding bottle and began
to gather the baby's things. She almost stamped her foot.

"So why didn't he come for me?" she said crossly. "Why did he
stand me up like that?"

Father Mullholland watched her carefully as he spoke. "He is not
very happy about the things you said to him. But neither is he happy
about his own conduct toward you last night."

"Conduct?" Alice said.

"Because his late wife behaved reprehensibly," said the priest, "that
is no reason for him to go venting his anger and hurt upon a blameless
young woman in a hotel room."

Alice found that she had got beyond embarrassment. She resigned
herself to the fact that Giovanni had told him everything. The Ma-
sonic handshake had extended into the bedroom. She wondered
whether to feel betrayed by it. Curiosity caused her to speculate
about what exactly Giovanni could have said. I fucked her like a
maniac, Father, until I made her cry. And after that she was sugar
and spice. Vanilla and hot fudge sauce. I do not know what it is
about her that closes and opens. I only know, in retrospect, that I
was a little overemphatic.

"I don't think Giovanni did anything wrong," she said curtly, wishing not to pursue it. She saw him weighing her words.

"That may well be what you think," he said. "But it is not what
Giovanni thinks. Giovanni has been brought up to revere a woman's
body as the temple of the Blessed Virgin Mary."

Alice gulped. "You're not serious?" she said. "You're not serious?"

"Holy shit!" she heard Giovanni say loudly. The expletive had followed
upon the crash of earthenware that had come from the region of the
kitchen. This was followed by the sound of cupboard doors banging
open and shut in quick succession.

"I think," Alice said, "that Giovanni is being a little dangerously impetuous in your kitchen." Then, though her chair was turned against his entrance, she heard Giovanni burst in through the door.

"Michael!" he said irritably. "Does your kitchen not support such an item as a floor cloth?"

Father Mullholland gazed at him serenely. "What is the matter?" he said.

"The matter," Giovanni said, "is that I just dropped all my nougat. Your whole goddamn kitchen is awash with egg whites and crap."

"Leave it," said Father Mullholland. "Let it be. There is a person here, Giovanni, who has been waiting to see you all the morning."

Giovanni was silent for something like five seconds.

"Alice is here?" he said edgily. "Where?" Alice shrank with a kind of terror into the chair.

"Here," said Father Mullholland. "She has her back to you, that is all."

When Giovanni came into her line of vision, Alice saw that he was no longer wearing his exercise suit. He was wearing a beautiful rose pink shirt, with finely tailored pocket lapels, which was open at the neck. Over his black trousers he had pinned, in lieu of a cook's apron, an Irish linen glass cloth with a red stripe running through the middle. His sleeves were folded back to the elbow and his fine, long hands, which he held delicately upwards, were coated with what looked and smelled like ground almonds.

Giovanni's dressiness once again amused her and delighted her, lifting her into a state of sudden exhilaration. Did he change his clothes in telephone boxes, she wondered, like Mr. Clark Kent? She hoped that he would kiss her, but he did not. He showed no sign of affection toward her and merely stood there on his tall legs with a demeanor balanced halfway between confrontation and sulkiness.

"I thought you had abandoned me," she said.

Giovanni ignored her. His eyes came to rest upon the baby at her shoulder and he assumed an expression of tenderness. He stepped forward as Alice watched and extended the back of his hand. He brushed Pamina's cheek delicately, leaving it touched with slight evidence of ground almond.

"Giovanni," Alice said, in gentle reproach. "It's half past two and you said that you would come for me after mass."

Giovanni made as if to look rather casually at his watch, but found that his wrist was bare. "I took my watch off to cook," he said. "I guess the time ran away with me."

"That's not true," Alice said. "I have been waiting for you since dawn."

Father Mullholland rose. "But I think," he said appeasingly, "we might go and see what Giovanni has made."

"Watch your feet," Giovanni said irritably as they followed him into the kitchen. "My nougat is all over the floor." His nice little leave-taking tea, on the other hand, was all over the priest's kitchen table. Alice saw at once that what Giovanni had created for "his nuns" was certainly no mere tea. It was nothing short of an orgasm in confectionery. She wondered, with a degree of ambivalence, whether she ought to envy the nuns their explosion in sugar when she had got the rack of crucified inkfish.

"Gosh," Alice said, and she stared in wonder at the table, because, standing taller than the rest, darkened with flaked, bitter chocolate and reeking of cognac, stood a vast, elaborately layered, cylindrical cake. Around it stood a variety of prettier, lighter cakes—so light in fact that they looked more like soufflés. Giovanni had made them, Father Mullholland proceeded to explain, with frothed egg whites and sugared cream cheese. In front of these stood an extraordinary jeweled miscellany of pastries and sweetmeats upon which Alice feasted her eyes like a child in Santa's grotto. There were meringues spread with whipped cream and spiced chestnut puree. There were small, layered flaky things, bursting exuberantly with almonds and candied peel. There were apricots glazed with sugar and cubes of what looked like dense chocolate fridge-cake with fine mine seams of marzipan running through their centers. And splashed onto the floor at her feet, lying among a dispersed scatter of broken earthenware and ground almonds, lay the frothed-up whites of something like sixteen eggs in a daunting pool of honey.

"Gosh!" Alice said again, and she burst out laughing. "Giovanni! What can I say? I'm really very sorry about your nougat." Giovanni continued to ignore her. He was busy at the workboard where he was committing scraps of pastry to a plastic dustbin, along with about four dozen eggshells.

"Giovanni's parents are pastry cooks," Father Mullholland offered amicably into the tension. "Has he ever told you that, Alice? They own a number of justifiably profitable bakeries which supply all of San Francisco." Giovanni had begun to scuffle aggressively at the sink. He was gathering dishes and cutlery onto the old wooden draining board by a system of dauntingly rational classification and he was frowning with displeasure as he did so.

"I don't know why you pamper that girl with reality," he said. "She prefers to believe that I depend on what I harvest from stolen manuscripts."

Something occurred to Alice at that moment, which warmed her heart and made her feel more tenderly toward Giovanni than she had ever felt so far. It was not his publishing house that made him rich! No, of course not! The publishing house would all be floating on the proceeds of Italian sweetmeats. Because what sort of funny little publishing house would take a risk on a book like Jem's? No! Giovanni was the pampered child and grandchild of adoring Italian pastry cooks. They had been diligent enough and skilled enough and lucky enough to have made an absolute pile. And the publishing house was Giovanni's shiny toy. Mr. and Mrs. Angeletti would have taken their clever, expensively educated son into whatever was the equivalent of Hamley's toy shop and watched his terrifying, snot-green hawk's eyes light with pleasure. And that, she thought, would go for the summer house as well. The 'cabin' in New Hampshire. With the proceeds of Angeletti *pasticceria*, Giovanni would have bought himself the summer house—not any old summer house any old place, but the Golden Pond scenario. Alice's love for him grew and surged in the wake of this delicious speculation. Giovanni had acquired a summer house among descendants of the *Mayflower*. A *summerhouse* in which to read manuscripts and scribble a bit. Giovanni "coughed in ink." Was that his "profession"? Or was it his "hobby"?

"Dear Giovanni," she said. "Dear Giovanni, don't be grumpy. I think your cakes are completely beautiful. I think you are the most extraordinary man."

She reached out then for a cube of Giovanni's fridge-cake, since there was so much of it, after all, and since it looked so wonderfully tempting. And since, anyway, she had not yet had any lunch.

"Don't touch that!" Giovanni said viciously, with eyes in the back of his head. "Not one crumb of that is for you, my girl. Touch that and you don't get lunch!"

"I'm sorry," Alice said. "I'm a bit hungry, that's all. I haven't really eaten since yesterday's lunch."

Giovanni addressed Father Mullholland in a fit of petulance. "The woman's appetite is gross beyond imagining," he said. "I guess it's in the nature of her condition." Father Mullholland fetched her a bread-board and a knife. He placed a loaf on the board and got her some butter. "Don't stuff her with bread," Giovanni said. "I'm taking you both out for lunch."

"Will you let her alone?" said Father Mullholland mildly. "And not behave so much like a tinpot dictator, Giovanni?" He turned then to Alice. "You would like some cheese with that, Alice," he said.

Alice nodded on a mouthful of dry bread. "Yes I would, please," she said. Father Mullholland fetched a cheese dish from his cupboard.

"Giovanni's father taught him to make pastry and his mother taught him to read," he said, engaging her attention with agreeable small talk. "Both of them excellent teachers, wouldn't you say?"

"Oh yes," Alice said. "Oh yes. And Giovanni so remarkably preco-cious, of course—with his reading, at any rate. Bit like Saint Nicholas really. I think he leapt, reading, from his mother's womb, don't you? She died while giving birth to him, you see." Father Mullholland studied her curiously. Then he looked, with some amusement, at Giovanni.

"Take the child from her, Michael!" Giovanni said, sounding like a playground bully. "Give her a floor cloth, will you? Get her to wash the floor!"

"Your mother, Giovanni?" Father Mullholland said, mildly.

"Do it!" Giovanni said. "Give her a cloth! That's unless you want eggs and crap all over the hem of your cassock!"

Father Mullholland and Alice looked at each other and smiled. Giovanni caught the end of the smile, which provoked him to further annoyance.

"Or failing a cloth," he said, rising wonderfully, "get her to lick the floor!" And he rammed a mountain of silverware into the sink with a clatter like that of pounding scrap metal. Alice and the priest colluded enjoyably in laughter.

"Okay," Giovanni said in fury, and his voice got louder and louder.

"Okay. Laugh. It's funny. So maybe I told her something like that. I produced it as a mere hypothesis. And let's remember my wife died that day. She died in childbirth, didn't she? She died screaming." Both of them had stopped to stare at him and their laughter had abruptly ceased. "And all the while," Giovanni said, "I had this"—he indicated Alice with his forefinger—"this two-bit suffragette person gorging on the contents of my skull. God forgive me, Michael, but maybe you can't appreciate what she's like." He tore off the glass cloth from around his waist and he threw it over the nougat. "My wife got killed that day!" he yelled. "I hounded her to her death, didn't I?—Her and the unborn child. You think I felt especially good that night? You think I felt ready to open my heart for real to little Mrs. Cromwell here? Little Mrs. John Knox with her house in a cuckoo clock and her mind in a plain-sided strongbox?"

Giovanni bent to scoop the spillage. He paused, staring hard at the floor. He was concentrating so intensely on the glass cloth that Alice, who was watching him, did not register at first that Father Mullholland had taken the baby from her. Then she bent down and took the cloth.

"There is something else you ought to tell her, Giovanni," Father Mullholland said quietly. Then he left the room with the baby.

Alice scooped up nougat and took the cloth to the sink and rinsed it. She bent beside where he was squatting on his haunches and she scooped again.

"It was only a joke, Giovanni," she said. "Please. I'm sorry. I'm deeply sorry about everything that I've said or done to hurt you." And she waited in trepidation to hear what he had to disclose.

"Okay," Giovanni said. "Alice. I oughtn't to have yelled at you like that. I hope you can overlook it. I was planning on not telling you this. Not yet. But I guess you have a right to know."

"What?" Alice said. "Know what?"

"I'm infertile," Giovanni said.

"What?" Alice said, and she let the glass cloth drop out of her hand. "What did you say, Giovanni?"

"I'm infertile," Giovanni said, in a voice like ash in a graveyard. Alice stared at him and blinked.

"So Mary-Lou's child?" she said. "Giovanni? That was not your child? Well, I'll try not to say that I'm glad." And she smiled at him with a smile like benediction.

"Alice, what I am saying to you," Giovanni said emphatically, "is that I cannot father your children."

"So what?" Alice said, in some puzzlement. "So what, Giovanni? Who cares?"

Giovanni stretched out his arm and brushed her cheek with the back of his hand. He looked at her with the kind of tenderness with which she had seen him look at the baby.

"I do," he said. "Maybe right now I care a little less than I did."

 THE LEAVE-TAKING TEA marked the departure of Alice and the baby with a certain stylish aplomb. Giovanni was undoubtedly the star, of course, the *padrone*, the big smell at the top. His spirits had lifted considerably since lunch and his confectionery certainly hit the mark. He cut a dashing figure in his pale pink wool jacket, which he wore thrown unbuttoned over the morning's rose pink shirt. And Alice knew, because Father Mullholland had whispered it to her during the course of the proceedings, that in the pocket of the pink jacket Giovanni had not one air ticket, but two.

"It is not for me to say that one of them is for you," Father Mullholland said, and he adopted a manner of darkly teasing conspiracy with her. "But I saw him check his pocket this afternoon just before we left the restaurant."

Alice gawped at him, incredulous. "But I didn't see him," she said.

"Excuse me," he said politely. "But that is because you did not accompany him to the men's lavatory." Alice began to laugh. "Now, as you will know," he said, "it is no longer necessary for a person such as yourself to have a visa before entering the United States. It seems that the immigration authorities have recently amended their regulations for the purpose of pleasing Giovanni."

"Devious bastard!" Alice said.

"Look to your passport," Father Mullholland said. "We are not meaning to do Giovanni down here, you and I, but we are in solidarity with Homer and Hesiod." Giovanni had been far too busy uncorking champagne to notice the exchange. He dandled the baby and embarked just then upon a somewhat audacious speech in which he explained to his audience of rapidly mellowing nuns that dear Mrs. Riley, who was not in fact Mrs. Riley, was to become the third Mrs. Angeletti instead. He gave account of this felicitous development by reference to the power of prayer. Giovanni then wound up the proceedings by producing a group ticket to a West End theater, making provision for over fifty nuns to attend a revived performance of *The King and I*. After that, he embarked with Alice on the short drive back into Surrey.

"But what an appalling show-off you are," Alice said. They were at last decisively on the road. "Do you have no sense of restraint, Giovanni? What I mean is, fifty nuns in a theater at a musical about a harem? I hope you are truly ashamed."

"We have things to be grateful for," Giovanni said. "Plus it happens Sister Teresa is an admirer of Yul Brynner."

"And how do you know that?" Alice said. "Does she confide to you all her secret lusts?"

Giovanni appeared unamused, deadpan. "She told me so one time," he said. "There is a significant difference, my girl, between admiration and lust."

Alice digested the put-down with glee. "She's an 'admirer' of yours and all," she said. "And I wonder what it is that you and Yul Brynner could have in common." Giovanni's grip on the steering wheel tensed so markedly, she thought, that she fell then to contemplating what it might possibly feel like to be Giovanni—to be thirty-five and infertile and to be losing one's hair and to care so terribly about these things, when they seemed to Alice so profoundly unimportant.

"Giovanni," she said. "Did you ever believe me about Matthew?"

Giovanni laughed. "I guess only until I got you in the chapel," he said. "Until just before I left. You're a natural Catholic, Alice. You're impelled toward the confessional."

"But you wouldn't let me confess," Alice said. "And when I turned round you weren't there. I hope you realize that was a terrible thing you did."

"I wanted you to miss me," Giovanni said baldly. "Plus I wanted to make you sweat."

Alice lapsed into a moment's impotent sarcasm. "And all that 'Mrs. Riley, is your husband Catholic?' " she said. "I hope you're proud."

"Oh come on, I needed to know," Giovanni said. "Had Mr. Riley married you in the Catholic Church? It was important to me, Alice. Look at it my way. You think things weren't bad enough for me without you telling me you were married? You damn near destroyed me, you know that? That night in the flophouse."

"That was no flophouse," Alice said. "That was an 'inn of character.' It had a Jacobean settle in the vestibule."

Giovanni ignored the correction. "You lied to me," he said. "Don't you ever do that again."

"You left me on my knees," Alice said. "Groveling in a church. I thought that what you were saying to me was I needed a Catholic husband. I thought you were saying they wouldn't let me have the baby. You put the fear of God into me." She saw him turn and look at her, carefully, from head to foot. She could tell, in the look, that Father Mullholland was right and that Giovanni loved her deeply. Then he turned back to the road.

"Is that so terrible, Alice?" he said. "To fear God?"

Two things happened after that, and everything fell into place. The first occurred as they passed the sign giving promise of Farnham and Aldershot.

"Roland saved my life," Alice said. She said it clearly and out loud. "It wasn't Matthew at all." And then she told Giovanni about Roland for the very first time. She told him because it was all at once so apparent. That Roland had been about to make love to her and that, rather than have him do that, she had driven his beautiful old Citroën into the river at great risk to both their lives. Giovanni said nothing. He listened to her and he drove.

"Roland had an ice ax in the car," she said. She talked as if transfixed. "He was about to take a party of schoolboys to Snowdonia. He knew all about survival. He'd been playing soldiers for most of his life. Roland could get people out of burning aircraft, Giovanni. He came to see me in hospital and he tried to shake my hand. He had lacerations on his forearm. He held out his hand to me, Giovanni. He held it out and I couldn't take it. It was like trying to run in a dream, Giovanni. I couldn't make the limb move."

"It sort of figures," Giovanni said.

"Roland is a kind of prince," Alice said. "He's handsome and honorable and brave. I behaved very badly to him."

"And Matthew?" Giovanni said.

"Matthew was driving the van," she said. "When I came round, Matthew was there and Roland was gone. The circumstances made it so easy for him. My parents loved him and Roland was gone. He fell into picking up the credit. That's not so unthinkable really. No worse than Papageno—and don't we all have a soft spot for him?" The likable birdman. The prince and the snake. It all made sense just as Jem had said. Deeply at the center of one's being. Papageno, the eternal wheelbarrow, glad to be of use. Standing with such apparent stability, wherever the last man has pushed him. He wins friends. He loses friends. Easy come, easy go. In the end the loss is his. He can never make it into the holy place. The portals of the temples are closed against him. For a little while he inhabits the spaces because he climbs in at the window. And he carries those enchanting bells that are easy on the listener's ear.

"I will have to apologize," she said. "I will have to go and see Roland." And her eyes were fixed on Giovanni's left hand as he struggled a little with the manual gears of an English car.

It was nothing dramatic that happened to Alice next. No tongues of fire descended. She was not blinded or struck unconscious, or lifted by antigravitational force to a place distant from the passenger seat of Giovanni's hired car. It was more like realizing with mild surprise, after years of attention to grammatical exercises, that one can understand a foreign language when one hears it alive on a stranger's tongue. It was more like the point of intuition in a mathematical puzzle, when the fact of congruency rises toward one like a gift of grace from the web of intersecting lines.

" 'I believe,' " she said, but she said it only inside her head. And to hear her mind say it made her feel like dancing; like tracing out a pattern with her feet, slow and rocking and graceful, as if to that part in the Schubert *Credo* marked out like a pastoral canon. And she registered, again, with the mildest surprise, that she was still focused on Giovanni's hand and that Giovanni was still changing gear.

"You're not very good at that, are you?" she said, and she smiled at him and she put her hand, for a moment, over his on the gear lever. And then, because it had only just struck her, she said, "You've taken off your wedding ring, Giovanni. Or did you do that a long time ago?" And that was all.

"I think," she said some minutes later, "that I began to believe with Jem's funeral."

"And you imagine," Giovanni said crassly, "that a funeral like that didn't cost me?" But Alice had ceased to care. He no longer had the power to outrage her. It no longer seemed terribly important to her, against the weight of her new understanding, that Giovanni, whom she loved so passionately, had played such games with her; that he had played hooky from his dead wife in the morgue for her and had forked out the cost of a first-rate choir to sing the rite and the liturgy for a woman whom he had met only once and that at the hour of death; that he had fed her sadistic food in the forest and had got her heady on sparkling wine and had dressed her up in the guise of a schoolmarm and had rudely forced her in a hotel bedroom where she was playing Mrs. Knox with her mind in a box.

"I want you to be nice to my parents," Alice said. "Please, Giovanni. Especially to my father. This isn't going to be easy for either of them."

"My darling!" said Mrs. Pilling. "This is really very well timed. But where on earth have you been?"

"In Hampshire," Alice said. The two women embraced each other and Alice noticed that her parents were still so recently returned that their luggage stood out in the drive.

"But you're looking so pale," said her mother. "You funny little things—you and Matt. All the islands and the costas to choose from and you bury yourselves in Hampshire." Mrs. Pilling glanced, without much interest, at Giovanni who, she noticed, was carrying a baby. She was sporting a most becoming golden tan, which set off the blond highlights in her hair. She wore high-heeled sandals and her lip gloss smelled of ripe peaches. Alice felt sure that Giovanni would appreciate her.

"And where *is* Matt?" said Mrs. Pilling.

"This is Giovanni," Alice said.

Mrs. Pilling held out her hand. "What a dear little baby," she said politely. "Is she yours, Mr.—er—?"

"Angeletti," Giovanni said, taking her hand. "How are you, Mrs. Pilling?"

"She's my baby, Mum," Alice said, jumping in more through nervous excitement than through precocious intent. "Jem left her to me. But she's really just as much Giovanni's. He was there when she got born." Mrs. Pilling looked somewhat nonplussed.

"The baby is the child of Veronica McCrail," Giovanni said, intervening with a cautioning sobriety. "She's the child of your daughter's deceased schoolfriend."

"Deceased?" said Mrs. Pilling.

"Jem died," Alice said. And then, wishing not to dwell upon a matter that might provoke in her mother certain symptoms of guilt, she fixed her mind instead on the excitement of all that had happened. She was pleased to see her mother again and unable not to communicate the giddiness of her last two days.

"Giovanni has been her fairy godmother," she said. She looked delightedly at the baby, who made her finger ends twitch. "He bought her that beautiful hat," she said. "Giovanni is rather good at hats."

Mrs. Pilling regarded her in some confusion. "Where is Matt?" she said.

"In Paris?" Alice hazarded. "But that's all rather complicated." She saw that the baby looked irresistible there in the grip of Giovanni's prodigious arm and she longed to snatch her up. "I'll tell you all about it," she said. "But isn't she just the loveliest little baby? You must say that she's beautiful."

Giovanni cleared his throat. "Mrs. Pilling," he said. "Your daughter is in point of fact the legal guardian of this child. The mother died seven weeks ago, leaving a will to that effect."

Mrs. Pilling, suddenly enlightened, looked protectively at Alice. "But my darling!" she said. "What does Matthew think? Oh wait and have your own, my lovey. Go on now, sweetheart. You and Matt. That way you'll know what you're getting."

"Oh Mum," Alice said. Her mother's remark, in front of Giovanni, touched her vicariously with shame. Mrs. Pilling was evidently distressed.

"I mean *surely*?" she said. "Why you? There must be an aunt or a grandmother or somebody. I do remember Miss Trotter telling me that the girl had a father somewhere. Italy. That was it. There's an Italian father."

Alice gulped down a sense of hurt that her mother had known these things, but she wanted the hurt not to surface.

"Giovanni's Italian," she said hopefully. "Well, his family is, anyway."

"Alice," Giovanni said firmly, "you are screwing up." He looked again at Mrs. Pilling. "My role in this matter," he said, "was, in the first instance, as Mizz McCrail's publisher. She wrote a little book a while back, which gave your daughter cause to liaise with me."

"Someone stole Jem's novel," Alice said. "And then they flogged it to Giovanni."

"Will you shut your mouth?" Giovanni said. "I am talking to your mother."

"Who is the baby's father?" Mrs. Pilling said sharply, and she looked at Giovanni with such undisguised suspicion that Alice couldn't help but laugh.

"Some Roman bike mechanic," she said. "Jem picked him up on the Appian Way. He's completely untraceable, that's the point. He was a very casual, one-night stand."

"That girl!" said Mrs. Pilling. "That wretched, troublemaking girl! Excuse me, Mr.—er—"

"Angeletti," Giovanni said.

"Ah—" said Mrs. Pilling.

"Mum," Alice said. "Can we come in, please? I really need to change the baby and do you mind if Giovanni smokes?"

Alice terribly wanted her parents to admire and love Giovanni just as she did, yet they were inexplicably short on rapture. All through dinner—and with Pamina belly-down across his lap—Giovanni had been the very soul of charm and grace. Yet it was perfectly clear that her father did not care for him and that her mother wished him dead. Mrs. Pilling had even gone so far as to serve him mussels—a thing she had done to no man since the demise of Flora's father. But Giovanni did not die. He ate the mussels with every sign of satisfaction, and afterwards moved through into the sitting room where he conversed with Alice's father and drank cognac and smoked cigars.

"Darling," said Mrs. Pilling rather urgently to Alice. They were in the kitchen together making coffee. "Oughtn't you to think again about this baby? Now, of course you and Matthew would love to have a child, but there's really no hurry, my lovey. Good heavens, you're only just twenty. You're not even married yet." She placed her hand coaxingly on her daughter's neat blond head, offering protection and love. "Your father and I," she said, "we waited four years for you, my precious."

Alice summoned her courage. "And I waited four years for Jem," she said. "And you kept her letter from me. And she died before I could see her."

Mrs. Pilling winced. "Oh, my lovey," she said. "I didn't know. I only meant to keep it until you were a little bit stronger—"

"You treated me as if I were crippled," Alice said. "The constant special treatment. The constant special voice. Look, Mum. I'm all right. I'm saying that I waited, too. That's all. I waited for Jem and now she's dead. You never understood. You never began to try. And now you're trying not to understand all over again. I love the baby. I love Giovanni. And for all I know Matt is probably back in Paris after all. Wherever he is, I don't care. I don't want him anymore and nor does he want me. It was perfectly obvious to me that he was in love with Flora."

Her mother, in the face of this outburst, looked momentarily numb. Then, in her confusion, she turned on her daughter.

"*Flora?*" she said in contempt and disbelief. "And no need to ask what you were doing to drive him there, of course."

"I was doing nothing," Alice said. "They fell in love."

" 'Nothing'?" her mother said. "And you call this business 'nothing'? This carry-on with Mr. Whatshisname—"

"Giovanni," Alice said. " 'Joe-vanni.' It might help ease things a bit if you could bring yourself to use his name."

"All right, Alice," her mother said. "This Gee-o-varni. For a start, the wretched man is old enough to be your father."

"No he isn't," Alice said irritably. "He's only thirty-five. He looks a bit older because his hair's receding. Anyway, he can't be anyone's father. He's infertile, if you want to know." The moment the quip had dropped from her, Alice knew it for a glaring strategic blunder, but having uttered it she couldn't take it back. Mrs. Pilling, oddly enough, seemed to ignore it.

"Give him another five years, Alice, and he'll be as bald as a coot," she said. Alice was aware that they had descended into pointless and unconstructive sniping.

"But that's silly," she said. "Really, Mum. That's silly. You don't love people because they've got hair. You'd see that for yourself if this wasn't about me. Anyway, I think he's divinely beautiful."

"Then you really have lost your mind," Mrs. Pilling said. "He looks like the public executioner in that telly thing you used to watch with Flora."

Alice helped stack the tray. She tried to put her arm around her mother. "Oh Mum," she said. "Please . . ." But her mother seemed very much against her. And Alice knew then, for real, that there were times when your parents turned around and they were wearing different faces.

"I'm going to marry him," she said. "But first I'm going back to Oxford. That's another thing you never tried to understand." Her mother ignored this last; instead she raised the weapon that Alice had so conveniently deposited at her feet.

"Have you tried to ask yourself what he wants you for?" she said. "Given that the man is impotent?"

"Infertile," Alice said. "There is a difference, you know."

"Try giving up that baby," Mrs. Pilling said. "See how long he sticks around."

"YOU WILL APPRECIATE," Roland was saying, "that the lines *OA* and *AB* not only have magnitude. They have direction."

Iona, who sat beside him at her parents' kitchen table, watched his well-made right hand move over the page as he marked each of the two lines with a small arrowhead. She noted both the shapeliness of his pristine fingernails and that the lower joint of his fourth finger was slightly thicker than the rest and did not bend quite as readily as the others.

"Does your finger hurt you?" she said.

Roland had his mind on the task in hand. "Only slightly when the weather changes," he said dismissively. "I took a catch rather awkwardly in the summer. Tell me what you notice about the arrows here, Iona."

Iona blinked at the arrows. "Parallel lines?" she said idiotically, because she had allowed her mind to wander.

Roland controlled impatience. "What can possibly be parallel with what?" he said.

Iona shrugged. "Nothing," she said. Fuck, she thought, but he's so fucking lovely to look at. She lost herself for a moment in the delicate curve of Roland's right nostril. Fucking jock, she thought. You couldn't even bum a fucking smoke off him. She began to envisage him stripped to his underpants. Or perhaps he wore only his jockstrap under his trousers. Sod it. If only he'd just fancy her a bit. How come a fucking weed like Alice could provoke a great fucking bulge in his crotch and all she, Iona, could do for him was provoke words like "equidistant" and "magnitude"? It was having blond hair that did it. Blokes went fucking crazy for anything with blond hair. Especially jocks. It was the only color they could see. She could dye her hair purple for him tomorrow and he wouldn't fucking notice.

"Exactly," Roland said. "We're talking about a journey here, not so? Concentrate please, Iona. We'll give it another five minutes, all right?"

"All right," Iona said. "It's direction, I suppose."

"Good," he said. "Now if you would care to mark in the shortest route from O to the destination . . ."

Iona looked at the page. "It's from where that zero thingy is, straight up," she said.

" 'Straight up'?" Roland said. "You can be more precise than that." He began to wonder if he'd been off his head when he'd turned down the job in North Yorkshire. He'd been a week back into the term here in Oxfordshire, on something like half the salary he might have been earning up there, and with bloody Braithwaite looming as incompetent as ever. And now, for his sins, here he was at the Morgans' kitchen table, keeping company with unwashed supper plates and coaching Iona. Still. She was a bright kid and she'd clearly been through hell. Her father in America sounded like a certifiable case of arrested development and he had evidently done nothing to help her at all— other than dump her back on her poor old mother and stepfather once the heat was on. Roland was pretty open-eyed about the odds where it came to rehabilitating Iona educationally, but David had been quite insistent that he try. And Maya, God help her, had spent the four days since Iona's return looking red-rimmed around the eyes. In three one-hour sessions with her, Roland had discovered that Iona knew almost nothing. Frankly, he could have got a couple of boys from his first-form maths class to deputize for him, were it not for the outside possibility that the poor, scrambled girlie would introduce his boys to a syringe. She had no idea what a denominator was. She could not accomplish the simplest algebraic equation. She could not so much as label the axes on a graph.

"Come on, Iona," he said. "Mark it in. Use the ruler. A decent straight line will help both of us to tidy your mind." Iona hesitated to raise her hand from where she held it clenched in her lap. She was ashamed of her fingernails in front of him. Or rather the lack of them. While she had always been a nail biter, all that carry-on with Schutzburger over the book, plus her ignominious flight back home, had meant that she had now bitten her nails so far into the quick that the flesh of the nailbeds was swollen and red. It bulged hideously over the almost extinct nails and was here and there ruptured and bleeding.

"It's *OB*," she said.

"Terrific," Roland said. "Now draw it for me and mark in the arrows." He smiled encouragement at her and offered her his pencil. Iona took it. She picked up the ruler and joined *O* and *B*. Then she drew in the arrows. Roland watched her.

"That's excellent," he said, but his eyes were fixed on her nailbeds. "God in heaven, child," he said, wincing slightly. "You want to have the doctor look at those fingernails, you know. That a severe case of self-mutilation? Or has your Mr. Angeletti had recourse to hot irons?"

Alice had become more than eager to reenter the Morgans' house. After the debacle at her parents' home, it seemed to her that the Morgans' warm and cluttered kitchen would be waiting to welcome her like a pair of wide-open arms. She stepped from the car upon arrival, leaving Giovanni to park and take up the baby. Then, having reassured herself that Paul Koplinski's skip was still alive and well, she had tried the Morgans' front-door bell and had found it to be defunct. She had waited impatiently for Giovanni to join her on the path and had once again led him down the Morgans' unlit and obstructed side passage with intent to enter her landlord's house by the kitchen door. She itched to see dear David again and, having observed the basement light on through the drawn curtains, she had anticipated that she would find him drinking black coffee at his kitchen table and working out his overdraft repayments in the margins of *Marxism Today*. What she actually found surprised and startled her, but her sense of shock was nothing compared to that of poor Iona.

Nothing could have been more unfortunate for Iona than to have Alice enter through the kitchen door at that moment in the company of Giovanni B. Angeletti; the very man she had fled America to avoid; the man who, having once lunched her in a restaurant on Broadway, had more or less ever since been after her blood. She stared in horror for a second or two at the contours of his black felt hat. Then she burst into a flood of tears and ran in panic from the room. The other three listened, suspended for a moment, until they heard the slamming of an upstairs door. Then Roland rose politely from his chair.

"Alice," Roland said graciously. She ran to him. Tears leapt to her eyes as she embraced him and her chest heaved in one huge unbearable sob that made a sound like a saw going through wood.

"There now, sweetie," Roland said. "Come on now, poppet." And she wiped her eyes on her sleeve and tried to compose herself for speech. Giovanni had taken off his hat. He watched them intently, from his position near the door.

"R-roland," Alice said. "Y-you. I. I f-f-f-f-"

Roland wrapped his arms more tightly around her and gave off a small, affectionate laugh. "Stop, take a deep breath and start all over again," he said.

Alice stopped, took a deep breath and started all over again. "I b-b-behaved very b-badly," she said. "I've only just-j-just-just—I've only j-j-j-" She stopped. "I drove your car into the river, Roland. And in return you saved my life."

"Oh good Lord," Roland said. "No need to mention it, Alice." He held her in his arms for a moment longer and, much as he yearned to hope that she had come back to him, he knew almost immediately that she had not. She was in the company of a man. A tall, dark, rather strange-looking man who wore a pale pink jacket and carried a baby in a basket. A man who stood watching Alice with a curious, hawk-like, brooding certainty like the King of Hades with an undisputed claim; a high priest to whom there clung an aura of slightly dangerous but undeniable authority. Roland's grief for himself was momentarily all smothered in anxiety for his little Alice as he hoped that she would be all right. But she had the look of a woman who had newly sucked on pomegranates and there was evidently nothing that he could do about it now. It passed ruefully through his mind that Whitecross's pretty sister would possibly not quite do after all, though he had twice gone boating with her in the summer and the family had pressed him to join them for Christmas in Tuscany. He tried hard to wish that Alice had not come, but he could not.

"Th-thank you," Alice said. And her tears flowed, persistent. "I'm

s-s-so so terribly s-s-sorry, Roland. I'll n-n-n. I'll never forget
you. I—"

Roland moved firmly toward Giovanni with Alice still under his
wing. He held out his hand. "How do you do?" he said. "Roland Dent."

Giovanni took his hand. "Giovanni Angeletti," he said. "How
are you?"

Roland, taking note of the name, smiled ironically and thought of
hot irons. "Ah," he said. "Ah yes."

"Giovanni f-f-found Jem for me," Alice said. "But she was dead."

"Oh poppet," Roland said. "Oh, believe me, I'm so sorry."

"This-this is her baby," Alice said. "I'm g-go-going to billet her
here among f-filthy Marx-arxists. David s-s-s. David said I could,
but I s-s-s. I think it might b-be awkward."

Roland smiled a bit. "David 'cares about everybody's family,' " he
said. "I should give it a try, Alice."

"Y-yes," Alice said. "B-but there's another th-thing. I'm going to-to-
to to t-take instruction. W-will he mind?"

Roland smiled again. "Leanings," he said. "There you are, my
poppet. What did I tell you?"

"Y-yes," Alice said. And she understood at last that what Roland
had called "leanings" had been the gift of grace.

"Excuse me," Roland said. "But I must fly." He collected his jacket
from the back of a chair and picked up his textbook from the table.
"David and Maya are due back from the cinema shortly," he said. "If
you would look to Iona, Alice. It's my impression that she's a wee bit
wobbly at present."

"Y-yes," Alice said. "I will."

He gave her a small embrace in parting and touched Giovanni
briefly on the arm.

"So good to see you both," he said. "Good night." And he was
gone. Alice stood with her back to Giovanni, staring fixedly into the
Morgans' sink. She heard Pamina stir faintly in the basket behind her
and settle again.

"Tell me about the stuttering," Giovanni said finally. "I never heard
you do that before."

"Oh," Alice said. "It was always bad with Roland." She turned around to face him. "I used to have speech therapy when I was a child. With Dr. Neumann. I think he was my first love."

"That man," Giovanni said, in a voice something sober with awe and reproach. "That man who just left. You gave up that man for Matthew Riley?"

Alice reflected upon this in shame. "I had suffered a severe blow to the head at the time," she said. She brooded on it for a while. "Life is very dreadful, Giovanni," she said. "Life can make one very squeamish. I can't even so much as replace Roland's car. He's got no money and I'm very comfortable. Yet to do so would be an affront. That car was his pride and joy, Giovanni. That car—it was the last car André Citroën designed before he died. It was exhibited at the Motor Show in 1955—the same year that Roland's darling parents got married. Peter Dent gave up his intended, you see. She became a nun. Then he married Roland's mother."

"Roland's father was affianced to a Catholic?" Giovanni said.

"Oh good Lord, no," Alice said. "He didn't go as far as all that." And she left him and went upstairs to Iona.

Iona had not slit her wrists with a Swiss army knife. Nor had she damaged the wallpaper. But when Alice entered the bedroom, she saw that Iona was gouging out lumps of flesh from her left forearm with a pair of sharp-pointed hairdressing scissors and that the wounds were giving forth alarming gouts of blood. Iona was gibbering wretchedly that nobody loved her, and Thomas and Sophie, barefooted in their nightwear, were standing side by side watching her, wide-eyed, from a distance of some four feet. William, mercifully, remained asleep.

When Maya and David returned, the doctor was on the point of leaving. He had treated and bound up Iona's wounds and had given her an antitetanus jab and a sedative, which had sunk her in sleep. Alice had repaired to the adjoining room, where she was reading to Thomas from the stories of King Arthur. Sophie, meanwhile, had tiptoed downstairs and had found Giovanni in the living room with the baby. He was sitting in an armchair reading *Marxism Today*. Behind him on the window, facing outward onto the street, was a smallish notice whose ciphers read:

ꓤƎHƆⱯƎꓕ Ɐ ꓘИⱯHꓕ ,SIHꓕ ꓷⱯƎꓤ ИⱯƆ ꓵOY ꟻI

"Hello," Sophie said. "I'm Sophie."

"Hello, Sophie," Giovanni said. "I'm Giovanni. Oughtn't you to be in bed?"

"No," Sophie said, and she settled herself, uninvited, beside the basket near his feet. She sucked contentedly at her thumb and began to talk sweetly to the baby.

"Can't you even suck your little thumb yet, little baby?" she said, and she guided the baby's tiny thumb tenderly into its receptive, mammalian mouth.

"Don't do that," Giovanni said.

"Why?" Sophie said.

"It'll distort her teeth," Giovanni said.

Sophie left the baby's thumb where it was. She smiled pleasantly at Giovanni and giggled.

"You're silly," she said. "Your baby hasn't even got any teeth." She did not stir when her parents came in. Neither did Giovanni. "This is Giovanni," she said, with an air of sanguine propriety. "And this is his little baby. I showed her how to suck her thumb." She took her own thumb out of her mouth. "Alice came back," she said serenely. "And Iona made holes in her arm." The doctor appeared in the doorway in time to catch the last of Sophie's intelligence. Maya had gone deathly white with shock.

"She's all right, Mrs. Morgan," said the doctor. "I've given her a sedative."

Giovanni kept his eyes on Maya Morgan's face as she questioned the doctor in her soft, anxious West Coast voice. He did not see in her that sanctimonious string-haired flower person who always brought Roland out in spots. He saw the slight, sweet-faced, rather ineptly dressed woman whom David Morgan cherished; a woman whose pale, delicate beauty, worn by sensitivity to every emotional vibration, was in danger of slipping away altogether. He wanted to shore it up; spare it from ruin. Something about her voice and her aspect reminded him of childhood and made him tender. The words *dimitte nobis debita nostra* etched themselves on his mind and almost reached his tongue. Then he dwelt gratefully on the blessed fact of Alice, who had been given to him over a pile of debris in his hour of greatest need. He resolved always to honor and revere her body as the temple of the blessed Mary, ever virgin, and to go out first thing in the morning and buy exquisite rosettes for her shoes. When Maya left the room with the doctor, he addressed himself to David.

"I'm Giovanni Angeletti," he said. He saw that David strove politely not to groan. "Your daughter misled me about her age," he said. "I guess we can take it as understood that I have received my pound of flesh."

"That's more than reasonable of you," David said, and he sighed and sounded tired. "Christ knows. The silly bloody child."

"Your wife is from California," Giovanni said.

"Yes," David said. "Yes she is."

 THOUGH ALICE longed to have Giovanni share the attic bed with her that night, it became clear to her that he would not. Though she yearned to have him take her nipples in his mouth through an abrasive gravel of Italian biscuit crumbs, Giovanni sat determinedly in the Morgans' living room, long after Maya and David and the children had at last gone to bed. He had exchanged his number of *Marxism Today* for a biography of Mozart. That was all. And there he sat, as immovable as Mr. Jackson in the house of Mrs. Tittlemouse. Tiddly widdly pouff pouff puff. And I, Alice thought, with my cupboards full of thistledown. She came up and stood behind him and looked at his text over his shoulder.

"Mozart is very Catholic," she said. "In the operas, I mean." Giovanni kept on reading. "He's very Catholic about marriage," she said.

"Go to bed," Giovanni said. "Take the child and go to bed, Alice."

"*And* he's very sexy," she added hopefully. Giovanni kept on reading. "Especially in *Don Giovanni*. All that '*Andiam, andiam.*' Well. That's if it means the same thing in Italian." She thought that she detected a faint, responsive twitch in Giovanni's right shoulder, but still he kept on reading. "Does it?" she said.

"Go to bed, Alice," he said. "It's late."

"And you?" she said.

"I'm not sleepy," Giovanni said.

Alice retired and brushed her teeth, defeated by eastern daylight time. She placed the baby in the basket beside the bed. For a while she lay awake, staring at the ceiling. She envisaged her parents in their house in Surrey, grieving together over the departure of Matthew Riley and over the sorry fate of their precious only daughter, who had so perplexingly fled the dreamhome with intent to cleave to the hangman in a children's television cartoon. The balding and impotent Mr. Alphabetti-Spaghetti. She understood now that they would never see how gilded were the masts of his tall ship.

Alice slept fitfully through that night and churned in the bed somewhat. Toward morning she had a dream. She was in the convent bedroom, but one of its walls was not there. In its stead was a sheet of plate glass, like a shop window—or perhaps like that hostile, impenetrable expanse of glass through which she had first viewed Pamina's long toes. She stared through the pane rather anxiously to find that it overlooked the school playing field. At the far end, if she trained her eyes, Alice could see that Jem was telling a story to two little girls who sat near her on the grass.

Though the two girls had their backs to her, Alice understood that they were Claire and Flora. Jem was not the emaciated woman whom Alice had embraced in the hospital bed, but the tall, flamboyant schoolgirl with rich brown curls and large feet in unpolished shoes. They were all in a state of childhood. Except Alice. Only Alice was trapped, high in the present, behind the prison of the plate-glass window. Jem, she could see, was striking attitudes as the story proceeded. She was tossing her head and spreading her hands. It shamed Alice, in the dream, to recognize that there was something in Jem's manner too fanciful for adult tastes; something rather too blatantly attention seeking. Perhaps almost a bit like Iona Morgan. It was perfectly apparent to her that Jem was unhappy. Alice yearned to join her. To touch her. To love her. She felt profoundly that she was failing Jem; had always failed her. She did not believe that Jem was shutting her out. Did not. Nor was Jem consciously playing her off against the others. No. And then she heard Jem's voice, clear as a bell across the passing time.

"Umberto needs her to give him an heir for the *palazzo*," Jem said. "Because both his other wives have died childless in 'mysterious circumstances.' " She turned and looked straight up at the plate-glass window, but she did not seem to see Alice there and she turned back slowly to the others. And then it was all quite different. The scene had cut and the figure was no longer Jem at all. And the person who had moved into close-up was standing within the glass. She was between Alice and the picture of Jesus exposing his heart. A person capable of moving through locked doors and fastened casements. She was wearing blue mascara and her lip gloss smelled of ripe peaches. "Try giving up that baby," she said. "See how long he sticks around."

When Alice woke up she was badly needing to pee. Her heart was pounding with anxiety. She looked for Jesus on the wall, through the first glimmer of day, but the picture was not there. And the bed was different and Pamina was no longer in the basket beside the bed. And there was a letter to her lying in the basket addressed in Giovanni's hand. Alice grabbed it and leapt up. She ran like a hare on unshod feet to the living room with the letter crushed in her hand. There, to her immense relief, she saw that Giovanni had fallen asleep in his clothes. He had moved from the chair to the sofa, that was all, and Pamina, wrapped in her shawl, was lying asleep on his chest. Her body was moving gently with its rhythmic rise and fall, her almost nonexistent nose bedded comfortably in the fabric of Giovanni's rose pink shirt. The biography of Mozart was on the floor beside them and so was the empty bottle from the baby's two o'clock feed.

Alice breathed relief. She hovered for a moment to watch them. Giovanni, she was touched to realize, had let her sleep through the night. He had got up in the small hours and had taken the baby from the attic. He had warmed her bottle in the Morgans' kitchen and had fed it to her and kept her company in sleep.

Alice went to the bathroom. Then she went downstairs to the kitchen, where she sat down at the table to drink a mug of instant coffee and to open Giovanni's letter.

Dear Mrs. Angeletti [said the letter],
   Forgive my surly inattention to your supplicant ass this night. At the risk of incurring your fine wrath yet again, I do not mean to do it with you until such time as I have weeded the wormwood from my soul.

Alice gasped in panic. She caught coffee in her larynx and sputtered it over the page. Beneath this communication, after a gap, Giovanni had written:

You are adorably right about Mozart and marriage, but then, as I have observed to you before, you have a sharp and penetrating mind. That is, for a woman.

Under this, after another gap, he had written:

Do not let me sleep after seven. I have a plane to catch.

Alice got up and went vengefully to the sofa where he slept. She could not wait until seven but bashed him awake at once. Giovanni opened his eyes and blinked a little at the crumpled letter, which she brandished at him in her fist.

"You devious bastard. You swine, Giovanni," she said. "How can you do this to me?" Giovanni sat up slowly, inching up with care. "You're trying to make me miss you," she said. "You're trying to make me sweat."

"Take the baby from me and sit down," he said. "Here. Try not wake her." Alice took the baby from him. Then she sat down. She watched Giovanni push his feet into his shoes and reach for his pink wool jacket. He looked at his watch and got up. "I guess I have time to shave," he said.

"I'll come with you," Alice said. "Don't do this to me, Giovanni. Please. I don't care about my degree. Not anymore. And what if I *am* pregnant? I can't be pregnant without you."

"Trust me," Giovanni said. "I'll see to it you have all the backup you need. I won't let you down."

Alice watched him with increasing resentment as he gave his attention to undoing the buttons of his shirt. "I wish that you would go to hell," she said.

"Now that," Giovanni said dryly, "is precisely what I am striving to avoid. And I expect to have your support, Alice. For God's sake help me to deserve you. Don't be a pain in the ass."

"Look," she said. "I know you've got a ticket for me in your jacket pocket."

Giovanni smiled at her tenderly. "Congratulations," he said. "How did you know that?"

"Because I'm not gullible, that's why," Alice said. "Not anymore."

Giovanni brushed her cheek with the back of his hand. "You get better all the time," he said. "Do you know that?" He took out the ticket. She watched him slowly tear it in half and then in quarters. After that he put the pieces into his trouser pocket. "Go make me some coffee," he said. "I need the bathroom."

Alice returned to the kitchen. She took her handbag from the coat peg and groped in it for her Kleenex. She put the bag down on the table beside her mug of cold coffee and got the baby's bottle from the fridge. Then, having steeped it a moment in hot water, she sat down and put the teat into the baby's mouth. Tears fell onto the baby's shawl and she smudged them away with her hand. Then she smoothed Giovanni's crumpled letter and read it again. At the bottom of the letter Giovanni had written his name, larger and more flamboyantly than all the rest, in his looped American cursive. Alice noted now, as she had done once before, that his writing was really quite a lot like Jem's.

Her hand began to shake as her eyes fixed on the letters. G-I-O-V-A-N-N-I. For a moment she froze. Then she drew Jem's letter from her handbag and studied both of them. The one she had received in Surrey and the one Sister Teresa had found in the bedside locker after Jem had died. She scanned the pages for all the letters *i* and *a*. Alphabetti-Spaghetti. She checked Giovanni's letter against the posthumous letter that had given her the baby. Then she checked both of these against the only one that Jem had actually written.

Giovanni's effort was terribly good, of course. Marvelously well done. But then Giovanni was extremely competent and he knew how to make things happen. Nobody else would have been able to tell the difference. Certainly Father Mullholland hadn't noticed and even she, who knew Jem's handwriting better than anyone, had noticed nothing until that moment. There was something just faintly different, not only about the letters *i* and *a*, but also about the final *r* in "Veronica McCrail"—as though Giovanni, having accomplished his task with such brilliant virtuosity almost to the end, had allowed himself to relax. He had looped the letter, albeit minutely, in the region of its top left.

Alice cradled the baby and stared down stunned into the pages. The sisters had given Giovanni access to Jem in the hour before her death. He had been with her in the minutes before she had been taken to the operating theater. After that, Giovanni would have been alone with Jem's bedside locker, which had contained her writing pad and her fountain pen, still filled, as ever, with brown ink. Burnt Sienna. He had also had the genuine letter on his person to assist him in the venture—the one that had provoked Alice's first and only telephone call to Giovanni's office in New York.

Giovanni must have concocted the second letter while Jem was under anesthetic, during the difficult and critical birth of the baby. He had aped not only her calligraphy, but had made a more than creditable effort at aping her style. It certainly made up in charm what it lacked in legal validity. But then Giovanni was a man of letters, was he not? And he was Jem's editor. First he had changed the end of her story. And then he had changed the end of *her* story. And now he was intent upon restoring his soul. Whatever could he have in mind? To "go with speed to some forlorn and naked hermitage"? Or what? And who, if anyone, had been his confessor? Obviously not Father Mullholland. It was quite certain that Father Mullholland did not know. It was also quite certain that Giovanni was slightly mad.

Everything fell into place for her. It was all so perfectly obvious. It accounted for why Jem's letter had made no mention of her intentions for the baby. It accounted for what Alice had read as Father Mullholland's faint sense of betrayal that Jem, even to the last, should have been so incapable of putting all her cards on the table. Alice's heart went out to him now. Jem had been very precious and special to him. She had always understood that. Jem had also, quite obviously, flirted with him. Nonetheless, he had scrupulously helped her through the appalling and protracted act of dying and had duly gone about the business of making provisional adoption arrangements for her child. That Jem, in the last resort, had seemed to behave so skittishly toward him must have struck him as both unworthy and distasteful.

He was no fool, Jem's charming priest. Alice respected his intellect enormously. It was perfectly understandable that he hadn't quite sussed Giovanni. He had vested interests in Giovanni. Giovanni was a new and delightful friend. A man of honor and high standing. A man who, by additional and extraordinary good luck, had presented himself as an ideal Catholic father for Veronica's precious baby. His words of the previous day struck home to Alice now with a new, ironic force. "If you allow Giovanni to take your integrity from you, where will that leave you?"

Alice put down the bottle and lifted the baby to her shoulder. She held Pamina so much more tightly in her embrace than was necessary that the baby's habitual burp induced a splat of white milk curd, which soured the shoulder of her nightgown. Pamina was *her* baby. Her baby for whom she would live and die if necessary. And cheat and perjure herself? And Giovanni was the man she loved.

When Alice looked up from the table, she saw that Giovanni was standing in the doorway. He had taken off his shirt in order to shave and he was leaning his sinewy right arm against the doorjamb. His beautiful, almost hairless chest was rising smooth and brown from the black trousers. He was staring down at Alice's arrangement of letters. Then he looked at her. Tears sprang to her eyes as she looked back at him but she did not sob and her eyes did not release them. The tears shone suspended in the corners of her eyes. Then she dabbed them away with her index finger. She was overcome by his extraordinary beauty and power as he stood there framed in the doorway. And she wondered, had his brightness tarnished with his fall, but it seemed to her he was bright as ever. Bright, terrible and stunning, like the iron Angel of the Annunciation.

"She never gave me the baby," Alice said. Her voice was clear and composed. "Jem didn't give me the baby."

"I gave you the baby," Giovanni said.